BOOK OF SHADOWS Vol. II

THE
SUICIDE
LAKE

A Novel

MICHAEL PENNING

THE SUICIDE LAKE
First edition. October, 2020
ISBN: 978-1-7771812-2-2 (paperback)
ISBN: 978-1-7771812-6-0 (hardcover)

www.michaelpenning.com

For my wife,
the bravest woman in my life.

Chapter 1

Abigail Jacobs had only moments to spare before the man across the room shot the boy. How many seconds remained before he pulled the trigger? Ten? Five? Even fewer?

"Lower your pistol, Mr. Tunstall," she said. "I assure you it will do no good."

Robert Tunstall didn't lower the pistol. Instead, he cocked the hammer and squeezed the trigger.

Abigail shouted and lunged for the flintlock, even as the eight-inch iron barrel erupted with a blinding flash and a deafening roar.

The lead bullet rocketed through the boy's forehead like a stone hurled through smoke. The peculiar child remained unscathed as he glared at Tunstall from the center of the fire-lit parlor.

"He... he's a ghost!" Tunstall exclaimed with a note of unhinged panic.

Dressed in threadbare wool breeches and a shabby hemp tunic, the boy couldn't have been more than eight or nine. But what arrested Tunstall's attention—what filled his stomach with dread—were the boy's eyes. They were dull and lifeless and made Tunstall think of battlefields and funeral parlors when he saw them.

"Oh, Mr. Tunstall…" Abigail sighed. "I had sincerely hoped you wouldn't provoke it."

"Provoke it?" Tunstall's brown eyes were round and huge with fright as he waved his discharged pistol. "Provoke it to what?"

"Violence."

In a flash, the boy grabbed Tunstall by his exposed forearm. A freezing bolt of pain shot up to his shoulder and he let out a shriek. He sank to one knee and dropped the flintlock to the floor with a clatter. Another scream rose in his throat, but died when the apparition hauled him from his feet and hurled him across the room. Tunstall slammed into the parlor wall, shattering the gilded frame of an oil landscape and destroying a chestnut side-table as he crashed back down to the floor.

The boy's spirit swung around, his small eyes simmering with black malevolence. A low, animal snarl rumbled in his chest and evanescent wisps of mist trailed after him as he floated across the parlor.

Abigail dashed to Tunstall while he groaned and rolled to his knees. "Stay behind me!"

The boy stretched out his skinny arms and reached for her, intent on snaring her in his freezing grip.

"Get away from it!" Tunstall clutched at Abigail's sleeve to drag her away.

Abigail shrugged him off. With no time left to spare, she swung her fist and thrust a small iron amulet at the spirit. The boy slid to an abrupt halt at the sudden appearance of the rune-shaped charm. His mouth twisted and dropped open to an impossible size, like a snake unhinging its jaw to consume a larger prey. An ear-piercing wail burst from his gaping maw, carried on a blast of hot wind that smelled of a moldy grave. The floorboards trembled with the ferocity of the ghost's fury. Cracks appeared in the plaster walls.

Abigail remained firm, wielding the talisman and repelling the shrieking spirit. She felt a rush of exhilaration as the boy's figure came apart before her eyes, his ghostly body dissolving into swirling tendrils of white mist. The vaporous mass hung in the air for a moment, coiling and writhing like a serpent ready to strike. Abigail punched the talisman at it and the churning mist recoiled as if wounded before it surged across the parlor and shot up the darkened staircase.

An eerie silence descended. Nothing moved.

Abigail became conscious of the pounding of the blood in her veins as she hung the iron charm around her neck and let it dangle around the collar of her Spencer jacket. Her breathing came fast and hard in the uneasy stillness, and she could feel her muscles vibrating with an exquisite rush of adrenaline.

"How…? How can it be possible?" The bristling, salt-and-pepper tufts of Tunstall's sideburns puffed in and out on his cheeks and a line of sweat trickled from beneath his mass of waxed hair. His shirttail had come loose from his pantaloons and his sleeves were bunched to his elbows, exposing a skeletal handprint the ghost had left emblazoned like a tattoo on his forearm.

Abigail willed herself to maintain her patience. A man's first encounter with the undead was always harrowing, but most of her clients didn't have a loaded flintlock on hand when it happened. The pistol had appeared in Tunstall's hand so unexpectedly that Abigail cursed herself for having let it come to this. If she didn't find some way of getting the man to regain his wits, the consequences could be catastrophic for them both.

"The boy is here because we summoned him, Mr. Tunstall." Abigail's voice was smooth as honey. "You must believe me when I say there is nothing to be afraid of. This is why you engaged my services as a paranaturalist."

"But he—he couldn't be real! It can't be possible!"

"Please be silent," Abigail snapped. Her cool blue eyes remained fixed on the staircase where the sinister mist had retreated. She had bought them some time before the ghost returned, but not much. "'Tis possible because your house is haunted, just as you suspected. Have you ever heard of Venable's Home for Wayward Children, Mr. Tunstall?"

Tunstall's legs wobbled as he staggered to a wingback and sunk into the chair's plush cushion to examine his injured forearm. "Venable's? No, I... I can't say that I have."

Abigail frowned. "That is unfortunate, considering you have been living in it these past seven months. Sixty years ago, this house was an orphanage owned and operated by Mr. Phineas Venable and his wife Winifred. When Phineas died of cholera, Winifred found herself the legal caregiver for a house full of willful orphans. Apparently, the saintly burden was too much for her to bear. On a bitter January night, Winifred set fire to the orphanage with all the children locked inside. This house—*your* house—was built on the foundation of the ruined orphanage."

"How dreadful." Tunstall looked around the parlor as if something horrible was about to spring from the shadows at any moment. "Exactly how many children perished here?"

"Seventeen."

"Seventeen! There are seventeen of those... those *monsters* haunting my home? Dear God!"

There was a dull thump and a low moan from somewhere upstairs.

Abigail swung around. "Is there someone else in the house?"

The color drained from Tunstall's face. "I instructed my wife to remain in our bedchamber..."

Abigail's heart lurched. "I gave you explicit instructions to ensure the house was empty!"

"Well, I didn't bloody well expect to be raising the dead!"

"What exactly *did* you expect, Mr. Tunstall?"

"I don't know! Perhaps some kind of séance?"

Abigail snatched the pistol from the floor, turned her back on Tunstall, and hurried to a low chestnut table at the center of the room. There, something large and round lay concealed within a burlap sack. Abigail cast the sack aside and uncovered an unlit jack-o'-lantern.

Tunstall gave it a dumb look. "A pumpkin?"

Abigail threw him an irritated glance as she withdrew the melted stub of a tallow candle and went to the fireplace to light the wick. "A trap for the ghosts of the children haunting your home. Their last earthly memory was of the scorching pain and blinding light of flames. They are quite literally *afraid* of the light of the afterlife and so they remain here.

With this, I intend to show them there is nothing to be frightened of."

The orange glow of the flames rising on the hearth turned Abigail's blond hair to molten amber as she placed the candle at the bottom of the hollow pumpkin and waited for the grinning visage of the jack-o'-lantern to come to life. "We must get your wife with us immediately. Without my protection, she is all too vulnerable."

Tunstall hustled after her as she marched across the room toward the staircase. "Vulnerable to what?"

"Possession."

"Possession! What do you—"

Tunstall's voice failed him as he skidded to a halt and gazed up the stairs into the gloom.

Eleanor Tunstall stood on the second floor landing.

She was draped in a shapeless cotton nightgown and appeared as little more than a silhouette looming in the darkness. Her hair was loose and her head hung to one side at an awkward angle, like a marionette with cut strings.

Tunstall peered up at his wife's shadowy form. "Eleanor!" He beckoned her with a wave of his hand. "Eleanor, please come down here."

The shape didn't move.

A sickening feeling took root in Abigail's gut. She was already too late.

"Eleanor, darling…"

Eleanor's jaw dropped open and remained hanging wide as a voice slithered out from within. It wasn't Eleanor's voice; it was that of a very young girl intoning the singsong cadence of a nursery rhyme.

"What are little boys made of? What are little boys made of? Snakes and snails and puppy dogs' tails; such are little boys made of..."

Abigail stepped back from the foot of the stairs and laid a hand on Tunstall's arm. "We must protect the jack-o'-lantern at all costs. The candlewick is charmed; only I may extinguish it. But if the phantoms can somehow destroy the pumpkin..."

Abigail didn't tell him that if the pumpkin were destroyed, the ghosts of the dead children would tear them both limb from limb.

"What are little girls made of? What are little girls made of?" the chilling voice inside Eleanor chanted on. *"Sugar and spice and all things nice; such are little girls made of..."*

The thing that was Eleanor Tunstall hurtled down the staircase without warning. Her bare feet thundered on the wooden planks and she let loose a bloodcurdling scream as she lunged for her husband's throat. Her fingernails dug deep into Tunstall's flesh as they both toppled to the floor.

Abigail grabbed at the talisman slung around her neck, but Eleanor whirled on her and whipped out a clawed hand, ripping away the charm and sending it spinning into a dark corner. With Tunstall pinned beneath her, the possessed woman hissed and stuck her tongue out at Abigail like a grotesque parody of a child. In a flash, she sprang to her feet and launched herself, catching Abigail around the knees and sending them both pitching to the floor. Eleanor's mouth hung loose and wide as she clung to Abigail's ankles. A thick line of drool dripped from her lower lip while the child's voice inside her giggled and howled.

Abigail lost her grip on Tunstall's pistol as she fought to

scramble away. Wild with fright, Tunstall wobbled to his feet and went for it. His eyes boggled and rolled in his head as he raised the barrel and cocked the hammer.

"No!" Abigail cried. "You'll kill your wife!"

But Tunstall was too terrified to hear.

Abigail swung around and punched Eleanor just as the pistol roared.

Tunstall's shot missed his reeling wife by inches and slammed into the parlor table, blasting off one of its thick wooden corners with a spray of chips and splinters.

For one sickening moment, Abigail saw the jack-o'-lantern teeter onto its side and roll toward the shattered edge of the table. She dove across the floor without thinking. Her hand shot out just in time to get beneath the pumpkin and cushion its impact. Still illuminated by the charmed candle within, it bounced off her palm and tumbled away.

Eleanor pounced, slobbering and giggling and clawing at Abigail all at once. Abigail struggled to get free as she stretched for the jack-o'-lantern, straining to reach it. Her outstretched fingertips brushed against its waxy surface, but it remained maddeningly out of reach.

Somewhere behind her, Tunstall was reloading his pistol. His next shot wouldn't miss; he would murder his own wife.

Abigail summoned all of her strength to tear her leg from Eleanor's grip. She pistoned it back and caught Eleanor hard in the face with a kick that connected with a loud *crack!* The howling, laughing thing inside Eleanor barely reacted as the woman's jaw dislocated from her skull.

Still, there was just enough of a flinch to give Abigail the time she needed.

She ripped herself free of Eleanor's grasp and lunged across the floor to scoop up the grinning jack-o'-lantern. "Look! The light is harmless! You've nothing to fear!"

Eleanor came to an instant halt and looked at the flickering light as if she was spellbound.

"Come to it," Abigail said. "Follow the light. Let it guide you from this house and its terrible memories…"

Eleanor didn't move.

Abigail's heart sank and went cold. It would not work. She had made a terrible, terrible mistake.

But just then, a thick white mist poured from Eleanor's sightless eyes. Released from the ghost's influence, the woman collapsed in a heap and Tunstall rushed to her.

Abigail ignored the man's sobs as the mist slithered through the air toward the pumpkin perched on her palm. The candle within flared unnaturally as the mist crawled through the jack-o'-lantern's eyes and mouth. A brilliant orange flame leaped from the pumpkin's lid.

Abigail winced and shielded her eyes.

Then it was over.

When Abigail opened her eyes, she found herself surrounded by a gathering of ghostly children of all ages and sizes. "Come… This light will not harm you."

One by one, each child turned to mist and went into the jack-o'-lantern with a blinding burst of flame. When the last of the children had vanished, Abigail rose to her feet. She reached into the jack-o'-lantern and murmured a strange, sibilant word before snuffing the candle with her fingertips. She then turned to where Robert Tunstall sat, cradling his unconscious wife in his arms.

"Now regarding my fee, Mr. Tunstall…"

Chapter 2

Joseph Lowell was daydreaming again, staring out the window from his desk while Abigail lectured. Of the dozen boys she taught at Boston's St. George's Academy, ten-year-old Joseph's mind was the most prone to wandering. Where it was at this moment was anyone's guess. Perhaps his attention had been caught by the angle of the sun glinting off the late-September splendor of the maples beyond the window. Abigail thought better of that; Joseph was more likely imagining himself battling pirates somewhere on the southern coasts. Abigail often thought a child's imagination to be a wonderful thing—as long as they were kept from knowing that the scariest things they could imagine actually existed.

Abigail left her spot at the head of the classroom and continued her lesson while meandering among the rows of desks. "The ninth circle of Hell is where the traitorous were frozen in a lake of ice named Cocytus. Dante tells us that this lowest and final circle is composed of four concentric rounds of traitors, each more grievous than the last. The outermost ring is reserved for traitors to kindred, who are encased in ice up to their chins."

Abigail's sudden proximity to Joseph's side brought the boy's attention back from wherever it had escaped to. It was a trick Abigail often used with daydreaming boys and one she employed almost on a weekly basis with Joseph. She saw no use in embarrassing the child in front of his friends. She lingered at his shoulder, pretending to gaze out the window while Joseph now sat straight as a ramrod next to her.

"The next two rings are composed of traitors to community and guests respectively," she went on. "The fourth and final ring is reserved for traitors to benefactors. These poor souls are entirely encased in ice, their bodies twisted into inconceivable positions."

Satisfied that Joseph's thoughts wouldn't be leaving her again soon, Abigail turned and strolled from his side. "Satan himself resides at the very center of these rings, frozen up to his waist where the lake of ice is at its thickest."

The shrill ring of a chime beyond the classroom door signaled the end of the school day. Abigail wished her students a good evening as they filed from the room. Their gleeful echoes receded down the corridor. She was straightening the contents of her desktop when she noticed a presence at her door. She looked over to find Robert Tunstall leaning against the doorframe.

"Dante's poetry would seem to be a rather unusual study for boys their age, would it not?" the headmaster remarked. Dressed in clean, fall-front breeches and his usual cutaway coat, Tunstall looked far more composed than when Abigail had left him caring for his traumatized wife just three nights prior.

"On the contrary," Abigail returned. "One is never too young to begin a study of classics such as *Inferno*. One never knows when such knowledge might prove useful. Wouldn't you agree, Mr. Tunstall?"

Tunstall took her meaning. "Ah, yes. Regarding our, ah... *incident* the other night. Mrs. Tunstall and I would appreciate your absolute discretion regarding the details of what transpired."

"Naturally. I would expect the same. In my experience, people would be more likely to deem you insane than to accept the truth of your story. It would be a shame to have the fine reputation of St. George's Academy sullied with such an unfortunate matter as your commitment to a sanatorium."

Tunstall gave a nod. "I believe we have an understanding." He paused a moment to cast a furtive glance over his shoulder. Satisfied that they were alone, he lowered his voice. "Ms. Jacobs, might I enquire how you came to be such an expert in your rather, shall we say... *unique* field?"

"You may not."

"But... but you're a schoolteacher, for God's sake!"

"A schoolteacher only by day, as you've come to discover." Abigail gave him an icy look as she pulled on her overcoat. "Will that be all, Mr. Tunstall? I would like to be on my way. I've a recipe for a harvest chowder that I've been eager to try."

"Actually, Ms. Jacobs, there is one more thing. You have a visitor waiting to see you in my office."

"A visitor?" Abigail's spirits sank. The last thing she wanted was an impromptu meeting with one of her students' overbearing fathers. At twenty-seven, Abigail was remarkably beautiful. Her face was the shape of a heart, with fine cheeks that stood high above a narrow chin. Her complexion was soft as morning snow and her eyes were as large and blue and luminous as stained glass. She had full lips that seemed perpetually pursed and her tiny nose dipped slightly downward like the petal of a daisy. She wore her honey-blond hair tied back in an elegant chignon, exposing her long and slender neck. Abigail's beauty wasn't lost on her and she often wondered if it wasn't what inspired the frequent visits of her students' fathers.

"Who is it?" she asked.

"She says her name is Emily Emmons."

Abigail started at the name. "Emily?"

"She is an acquaintance of yours?"

Without answering, Abigail brushed past Tunstall and marched down the corridor to the headmaster's small office. She threw the door open and found a slender brunette about her own age rising from a worn leather chair in front of Tunstall's desk.

Emily Emmons gave Abigail a warm smile. "Hello, sister."

Abigail stepped into the office and shut the door in Tunstall's face as he appeared behind her. "Emily, what are you doing here?"

"I'm sorry for such an unexpected visit, but it couldn't be helped. I fear something terrible has happened."

"What is it?" Abigail asked with a prick of alarm. "Is it one of the boys?"

"No. It's about Duncan."

Chapter 3

Emily Emmons stood admiring the curious collection of books and paintings that Abigail kept on display in her parlor. It had been a short walk from St. George's Academy in Boston's wealthy West End to Abigail's snug row house in nearby Beacon Hill. On any other evening, Emily might have savored the changing colors of the leaves, the earthy scents of autumn, the crisp touch of the evening air rolling off the Charles River. But her purpose in Boston had tied her stomach into knots. Despite the urgency of her business, she had spent most of the walk avoiding the subject, speaking instead of her two young sons who she had left in the care of their grandfather while she made the journey from Salem to Boston.

The last pink and purple colors of the autumn sunset were giving the sky over to the shadows. Abigail had laid a fire and the dry wood crackled with a heartening glow as Emily glanced over Abigail's collection. Astonished by the lifelike rendering of a snowy owl that hung above a bookcase, she inspected the artist's signature. Despite the rare quality of the work, it was by some unknown artist named John J. Audubon.

"Many of those items are gifts from past clients," Abigail said as she laid a pewter tray laden with apple tarts next to a matching teapot on her parlor table. "I'm often willing to forego my usual fee in favor of an unusual piece that strikes my fancy." She sat in a plush chair across the room and gazed at her sister. "Now... perhaps you had better start from the beginning."

"I suppose I don't really know where the beginning is anymore," said Emily. "You and I have hardly spoken since you left Salem." Plucking a book from a shelf, she examined the title: *Sense and Sensibility*. She wasn't surprised that she had never heard of it; the author was simply *A Lady*. There was an inscription beneath the cover: *Dearest Abigail, With eternal gratitude. Jane.*

"Start with what has happened since I saw you last."

"Eight years ago?" Emily returned the book to the shelf and took her seat while Abigail poured her tea.

"Has it been so long?" Abigail wondered aloud. "Yes, I suppose it has."

Emily sipped her tea, an exotic blend that mingled sweet hints of vanilla with an infusion of cinnamon and some unusual spices that she couldn't quite identify. "Well, you recall that map-making has always been one of Duncan's passions."

"Of course. Along with geology, astronomy, entomology, and any other number of scholastic pursuits. Your husband was precocious even when we were children." Instead of pouring a tea for herself, Abigail went to a sideboard and poured herself two fingers of whiskey from a crystal decanter. "Go on."

Emily tried not to stare at the glass in Abigail's hand as she returned to her seat. "A little over a year ago, Duncan decided to pursue an earnest study of cartography. Nine months later, he was hired by the Witherbee & Rand Logging Company to survey the areas surrounding Tahawus, the company's largest lumber camp in the mountains of northern New York. 'Tis a dreadful land; remote and wild and infested with savages. But the timber is plentiful and they are compensating Duncan well for his work." A tremor crept into Emily's voice. "But I fear something terrible is going on out there, Abby."

"What is it?"

For a moment, Emily couldn't answer. She just sat, staring into her tea while her slender thumb plucked at the delicate cup handle.

"Emily?" Abigail pressed. "What has happened?"

Emily looked up. "Over the past month, three men have committed suicide."

"Three in one month?"

Emily gave a somber nod. "Each ventured into the forest alone and took his own life for no apparent reason." She shook her head. "Something evil is at work in those woods."

Abigail's expression grew skeptical. "Emily, we mustn't jump to conclusions. The paranatural must always be our last assumption when all other *natural* possibilities have been eliminated. As dreadful as these deaths may be, there could be any number of rational explanations. You described it as a harsh and inhospitable land; 'tis entirely possible these men simply couldn't withstand the strain of their isolation."

"No, there's more to it," Emily insisted. "There was something horrible about the way each man died, some circumstances that don't even seem possible."

"Such as?"

Emily frowned and sighed. "Duncan spared me the details in his letters. But I am convinced this is a matter for someone with your, ah... expertise."

"You mean a witch?"

"No!" Emily nearly spilled her tea. "Abby! That isn't really what you call yourself, is it?"

Abigail shrugged as she drained the last of her whiskey and rose to pour herself another. "If we are being precise, I am a necromancer. I engage in arcane rituals to conjure and commune with the dead. Four hundred years ago, I would have been tortured and burned alive. Little more than a century ago, our own countrymen would have hanged me. You may call me a paranaturalist if it makes you more comfortable, but the ancient art of witchcraft is at the heart of all that I do."

Emily struggled to hide her discomfort. "At any rate, I'm worried about Duncan. At first, he was thrilled at the opportunity they had afforded him. Duncan has always longed for grand adventures. But lately, his letters have become brooding and melancholy. Sometimes he even seems frightened—and it's not like him to be afraid, not after what happened to the three of us as children." She drained the last of her tea and laid her empty cup on the table. "I know Duncan would never ask for your help personally, not after..." She left her thought hanging in the air.

"After what?"

"We both know how he felt about you, Abby."

Abigail stiffened. "Emily, I—"

"'Tis quite alright, Abby. We needn't speak more about it. What matters now is that our family needs your help. Something is driving good men to kill themselves in those mountains, and my husband is up there with them. You're the only one who can help him."

"Forgive me, Emily, but I don't see how."

"By doing what you've been doing all these many years: hunting down this evil and putting an end to it!"

There was a long silence while Abigail thought it over. The shadows were growing longer in the failing twilight and the fire needed tending, but she made no effort to see to it.

"I'm truly sorry, Emily, but it is quite impossible," she said at last. "I've my classes at St. George's to tend and there are more than enough hauntings here in Boston to keep me occupied. All Hallows' Eve is approaching and—"

"And you would rather risk your life saving strangers than help your own family? You've risked your life countless times for far less! For something as trivial as a drawing or a book of poetry!" Emily waved a hand around the parlor. "Why then, are you resisting now? Is it because of Duncan? I've made my peace with what happened between you both years ago. Haven't you?"

Again, Abigail fell silent and her face remained unreadable.

Emily's eyes drifted over the fresh apple tarts sitting on the tray and she realized she had lost her appetite. "Abby, ever since Father took you in as a child, I have never seen you as anything but my sister. Not my adopted sister, but my *true* sister. After what happened to us that All Hallows' Eve..."

Her words trailed away and a moment passed before she found them again. "I've never held it against you that you hardly respond to my letters, or that you didn't come home to pay your respects to Father when Aunt Clara died, or that you've never even met your own nephews. I don't know what made you leave us behind, but ever since we were children, I've asked for nothing from you but your love. I'm asking you now for your help, Abby—I'm *begging* you for it. Please, we're all the family you have. Don't turn your back on us."

Emily felt tears springing to her eyes. She wished Abigail would comfort her.

But Abigail didn't.

"There's something evil about those woods. I can feel it." Emily's whisper cracked. "You must believe that I wouldn't be here if I wasn't certain that Duncan's life was in danger. I'm so very afraid of losing him, Abby. I'm so very, very afraid..."

Abigail's heart seemed to soften as Emily gave way to sobs. "Alright, Emily. I will help you. But we must do one thing first."

Chapter 4

The old house at the end of the lane echoed with children's laughter. Abigail stood by the kitchen window and watched as her two young nephews chased each other across the yellow meadow behind the barn. Their gleeful shrieks floated on the warm autumn breezes. Emily had brought a chair outside from the kitchen to enjoy the mellow September sunshine.

Part of Abigail envied her step-sister as she watched Emily with her sons. Late at night, when her muscles ached and her flesh was bruised and her mind was numb from the strain of holding the lives of others in her hands, Abigail sometimes dreamt of nothing more than a life of safety and comfort.

But a husband and children of her own were just fantasy. None of it was possible now. How could she involve a man in a life such as hers? How would she tell her children that she spent her nights fighting monsters while they slept?

"'Tis a lonely life you've chosen for yourself, isn't it?"

As if reading her thoughts, a deep voice behind her gave Abigail a start. She turned to find Jonas Hobbes watching her from the kitchen door. For a moment, she had the strangest sensation of being transported back eight years. She was nineteen again and her adoptive father had stood in that very spot on the day she had announced she was leaving Salem for Boston.

She hadn't seen him since.

The years since had been good to Jonas. His breeches stretched a little tighter around his waist, but otherwise he was still the same tall and brawny man who had come to Abigail's rescue on that terrible All Hallows' Eve twenty years ago. He had let his beard grow long since she had last seen him. It was now full and dark except for some gray streaks at his chin and temples. A widow's peak had appeared above the deepening lines of his forehead, but he still kept his hair long and tied in a ponytail behind his neck. There were crows-feet around his eyes now; otherwise they were just as dark and languid as Abigail remembered.

She gave him a thin smile before returning to the window. "I didn't choose this life. It was thrust upon me when my parents were taken from me."

And yet, there was some truth to Jonas' remark. Abigail had to admit her life *was* lonely, sometimes unbearably so. Given the path she had chosen as a ghost-hunting witch, relationships were cumbersome. She had long ago found a way to cope with the loneliness. She just couldn't bring herself to tell Jonas of the taverns by the docks she often frequented or of the sailors she sometimes met there. It wasn't that she was ashamed of her promiscuity, only that the revelation would break the kind man's heart.

"And this is how you honor your parents?" Jonas moved across the kitchen to fill a kettle and stoke the fire in the stove. "Risking your life at every turn?"

"I don't require your approval for the life I lead," Abigail shot back with a rising edge in her voice. "And I needn't be reminded that my mother sacrificed herself so that I might live to become what I am today. She died saving me and that is exactly how I honor her memory: by saving others."

"'Tis an insult to her memory, is what it is," Jonas muttered.

Another angry retort sprang to Abigail's tongue, but she bit it back before it could escape. "I didn't come here for an argument, Jonas."

Jonas flinched at the pronouncement of his name and Abigail knew she had stung him. Ever since he had taken her in as a seven-year-old, he had never expected her to call him *Father*. She had been old enough to remember her own father when he died. Still, after all he had done for her over the years, it smarted to know she hadn't warmed to him enough to see him as anything more than *Jonas*.

"Then what did you come here for?" he grumbled.

Abigail's eyes wandered back out the window to the boys playing outside. "I decided it was time that I met my nephews."

"Why now? After all these years?"

"Because I know fully that I may not return from this journey. If that should be the case, I wanted to meet them finally and…"

"And what?"

"And to say goodbye to you."

"Oh, now don't talk like that, Abby." Jonas' tone softened. "What is it that has you so spooked? Why go at all, for that matter? 'Tis an awfully long journey just to set your sister's mind at ease."

"Because if I don't do anything, those two boys could be left without a father. If there is even the slightest chance that Duncan's life is in danger..." Abigail shook her head. "This family has seen enough loss and I may be the only one who can stop it from happening again."

"That's 'naught but nonsense and you know it," Jonas huffed. "If Emily is so afraid for Duncan's safety, then he should come home and be with his wife where he belongs."

"Oh? Is that what you would have done?" Abigail heard the words escape her lips and instantly regretted them. Twenty years ago, Jonas' own ambitions had nearly cost Emily her life. He had lived a life of atonement ever since, giving up his career as the first mate on a prosperous merchant ship for a menial job in a chandlery shop so that he would never be away from his daughter again.

"There are always other jobs," Jonas humphed.

The stricken look on his face made Abigail feel low and miserable. Small wonder she seldom wrote and never visited. No matter how hard she tried, somehow it always seemed to come to this. She knew Jonas deserved better, but for some reason, she couldn't seem to help herself. And why not? Why couldn't she just be grateful for his years of kindness? Where did this bitterness and resentment come from?

"What of your classes at St. George's?" Jonas asked as he dragged a chair from the kitchen table and plucked an apple from a wicker basket.

"Mr. Tunstall will see to them in my absence," Abigail replied, relieved at the abrupt change of subject. "I considered it a fair exchange for some recent services I provided."

Jonas sighed and took a bite of the apple. "The journey northwest will take you a week at the least. It'll be as dangerous as all hell now that President Madison's declared war on the Brits. Those damned Indians have gone and allied with the wrong side. I've heard they've been slaughtering Americans up and down Mohawk Valley."

"Chauncey Beck has planned a route that will keep us away from the Hudson. It will add a day or two to our travel, but we should be well out of harm's way until we reach Tahawus."

Jonas swallowed and wiped a trickle of juice from his beard. "Beck, you say? That old walrus might still know how to steer a coach, but he won't do you much good as an escort if you find yourself in trouble."

"I haven't required an escort for many years." A hint of a wry smile played at Abigail's lips.

Jonas nodded once. "No, I suppose you haven't." A moment passed before he spoke again, making no effort to hide his worry. "You *will* stay out of trouble, won't you?"

"Of course." Abigail crossed the room to stand behind him and lay her hands on his broad shoulders. "I apologize for what I said. You've been nothing but kind to me and all I do is hurt you. I don't know why I say such things."

"I do." Jonas reached across his chest and covered one of Abigail's hands with his own. "Emily and I have always tried to be a family to you, but we're not *your* family. We will forever be a reminder of all you lost long ago. Childhood, love, companionship, children of your own: all taken from you in a single night of blood and horror. You can't get them back... and you have forever carried that rage around with you."

A silence fell between them.

"Perhaps you are right," Abigail said at last. Outside, the sounds of her nephews' laughter floated across the meadow. "Perhaps I will always carry it."

Chapter 5

The weather-beaten sign read *Welcome to Tahawus*, but Chauncey Beck had been nowhere less inviting in his life. The forest was so dense and black, even the pale afternoon light seemed afraid to enter. The old coachman shifted his bulk on his bench and shivered as he steered the horses across yet another treacherous log bridge. Below the small coach, a flood of whitewater rushed through a deep chasm riven through the solid bedrock of the mountainside.

Eight days had passed since Chauncey and Abigail had left Salem. The coachman's clever route had avoided the usual post and military roads that had become so vulnerable to Native ambushes now that America was at war with Britain. Instead, he had kept east of the Hudson River as they traveled north, sticking to a meandering network of trails leftover from the busier days of the fur trade.

Civilization seemed like a distant memory with each passing day. They traveled long through the daylight hours and spent the nights at lonesome trading outposts where the beds were hard and the meals meager. Mostly, they passed the miles in silence. Abigail remained inside the coach, studying the strange book that never left her hands. Chauncey had no desire to know what forbidden knowledge lay within its ancient pages and had been glad to settle into the welcome solitude of the box seat on which he had spent most of his adult life.

Now, with the evergreens closing around him and the steep flanks of the mountains looming like fortresses on all sides, Chauncey's old bones told him he was getting too old for such adventures. The slivers of sky he glimpsed between the treetops were as gray as dull bayonets. Despite the heavy layers of his shoulder capes, he could feel the mountain air growing colder and more damp the higher they climbed.

Chauncey swore this would be the last time he drove Abigail anywhere. *Let her find someone else to take her on her damned ghost-hunts.* But even as the idea crossed his mind, he knew he was lying to himself. He would never stop escorting Abigail, not as long as she held *the recipe.*

Six years ago, Chauncey's career as a coachman had been over. Stricken with a crippling arthritis in both hands, he had hardly been able to dress himself, let alone grip the reins of a pair of coach-horses for hours on end. There were days when his knuckles had been so sore and swollen, he felt like someone had taken a hammer to each of them. His nights at the pub became longer and more frequent as he turned to drink to numb the pain. Coaching was the only livelihood he had ever known. Having just turned sixty-two, he questioned how he would survive. The future looked bleak and short.

And then Abigail Jacobs had appeared at his door.

Chauncey had recognized her immediately as the spitting

image of her mother, whose family he had served so many years before. Abigail was looking for transportation to some obscure cemetery in southern Maine, and she insisted only Chauncey would do. When she learned of his disability, she returned that same afternoon with some kind of dried tea that smelled as foul as a rancid beaver pelt.

Within days of drinking it, the pain had left Chauncey's hands. He had been working for Abigail ever since.

There were times when Chauncey wondered if Abigail had bewitched him that day when she had brought him that foul-smelling potion. Sure, she paid him well for his services, doubling and sometimes tripling his usual rate. The only thing she asked in return was his utter silence regarding whatever he might witness in her company.

But Chauncey didn't think money alone could sway him. It had to be more than mere coin. No one in his right mind would venture this far into the godforsaken wilderness in the middle of a war, dodging bloodthirsty Natives and risking certain death—or worse—in some haunted forest. No, there had to be something enchanted about that tea. But what? Chauncey couldn't figure it out. The only thing he knew for certain was that Abigail had bought his undying loyalty with it. As long as she held the recipe, he would follow her to the ends of the earth.

Soon, another sign came into view: *No Trespassing. Property of Witherbee & Rand Logging Co.* Chauncey thought it comical that the company found it necessary to warn against intruders this far into the vast, feral wilderness. He couldn't believe *anyone* could survive out here, let alone a thriving logging camp. Except for the two signs he had encountered, there was nothing here but forest and rock and beasts that had hunted each other since the dawn of time.

And yet, minutes later, the first traces of the village itself materialized among the trees. Timber shacks and storage sheds gave way to the larger barracks that housed the lumberjacks. More buildings sprung up as the road continued to widen. Chauncey was soon rumbling over the muddy pits and ruts of the outpost's Main Street.

The size of the village was surprising. This wasn't the roughshod, backwater logging camp Chauncey had imagined. The Main Street ran straight for perhaps two hundred yards and was flanked on both sides by a hodgepodge of timber buildings. Another muddy lane bisected the street at its midpoint and provided the village with its only intersection. Ahead, the road ended at a small, whitewashed chapel. Its steeple rose high into the air before a wall of dense forest.

Chauncey felt the weight of the villagers' eyes upon him. He straightened his spine, hauled on the reins, and brought the horses to a halt before what the coachman took to be the community mess hall. There, a man in a brown waistcoat stood waiting on the low porch.

"Mr. Emmons?" Chauncey asked.

The man nodded. "At your service."

Duncan Emmons was not particularly tall and his wiry frame seemed built for armchairs and reading rooms. His shock of yellow hair—straight and coarse as straw—had grown long and fell down his neck and over his bright blue eyes. Beneath his waistcoat, he wore a thick wool shirt tucked into his gray breeches. A week's worth of fair-haired stubble lined his angular jaw and cheeks.

Duncan stood by while Chauncey heaved himself from his bench, descended with a grunt, and opened the coach door for Abigail. Chauncey could have sworn he heard the breath catch in Duncan's throat at the sight of her—not that the coachman could blame him. Even wrapped in her heavy travel pelisse and with her elegant hair tucked into a modest bonnet, Abigail was a breathtaking sight.

"Hello, Abigail," Duncan said with a quaint bow. "Welcome to the Adirondack."

Abigail paid no attention to the ankle-deep mud clinging to her leather boots as she wrapped herself tighter in her shawl and cast a glance around. "The Adirondack?"

"'Tis what the Indians call these mountains." Duncan motioned to the tall peaks that rose above them on all sides, their summits lost in the low-hanging clouds. "In the Mohican dialect, it's a derogatory term for their hated enemies, the Algonquin. *Adirondack* means bark-eater. The two tribes have been—" Duncan stopped abruptly when he saw the amused smile playing at Abigail's lips. "What is it?"

"Oh, Duncan…" Abigail nearly laughed. "You haven't changed a bit; always so eager to enlighten others with your learning."

Duncan smiled sheepishly and shrugged as he brushed the straw-like hair from his eyes.

Chauncey Beck was good at reading people, at recognizing the stories that went unsaid between them. While busying himself with Abigail's trunks, he kept an eye on the pair as they continued their conversation. There was more to their story than he was privy to. Chauncey just couldn't figure what it was. Is it possible that Emmons and Abigail were once lovers? He found it hard to believe. What was it, then? The mystery was almost enough to make the coachman wish he would stay around long enough to find out. He let out another involuntary grunt as he struggled to heave the second of Abigail's trunks from the roof of the coach.

"Can I persuade you to stay the night, Mr. Beck?" Duncan offered as he came to Chauncey's aid and transferred the trunk to the porch of the mess hall. "You'll have a hard go of it, getting back down to the valley before dark."

"Quite sure, Mr. Emmons," Chauncey replied a little too hastily. He and Abigail had already agreed that he was to return to the tiny outpost of North Hudson where he would wait in relative safety until he returned to retrieve her in ten days time. He had no desire to spend any longer in Tahawus than was absolutely necessary.

"I'm afraid Chauncey would rather take his chances with flesh and blood Indians than spend the night in a town where three men have killed themselves inside of a month," Abigail chided.

A sudden change came over Duncan. "Four," he said in a voice that barely rose above a whisper.

"I beg your pardon?"

"There have now been four suicides. Another man took his life yesterday."

Abigail's eyes gleamed. "Have you interred his body yet?"

Duncan shook his head.

"Excellent. I must examine it immediately."

"Right now? Why?"

"If this is indeed some kind of haunting, 'tis imperative that we determine the nature of the entity we are dealing with. This man's body could provide us with some vital clues."

"I'm afraid that won't be possible," Duncan said.

"Why not?"

"Because there isn't enough left of him to examine."

Chapter 6

A pattern of dark stains remained where the dead man's blood had seeped into the forest floor. Abigail hitched up the hem of her coat, crouched, and pressed two fingers to the earth. She came away with a rusty smudge on her fingertips. "You are absolutely certain this couldn't have been an accident?"

"Not a chance," Duncan replied. "Not Chester Prue."

They stood at the edge of a wide gash of freshly cleared forest about a ten-minute walk from the village. A constellation of jagged pine stumps sprouted from the ground like fat, round tusks. Knee-high mounds of wood chips surrounded each stump. The air was thick with the scent of chopped timber and wet pine needles. The afternoon was growing late and a front of angry clouds rolling over the mountain peaks promised both an early twilight and a stormy night.

"Am I to understand the man just stood here and allowed the tree to fall on him?" Abigail asked.

"According to the man Chester was with, that's precisely what he did."

"He couldn't have simply made a mistake?"

Duncan shook his head and motioned to an area about sixty yards away where the land disappeared down a steep hill. "The men fell the trees so that they come down parallel to that ridgeline. Once the logs are bucked and rounded, they're rolled down the hill to the lake at the bottom of that ravine. They chop the trees in two-man teams, alternating their strikes and angling their blows so that the tree falls in the desired direction."

Duncan moved to stand by a massive stump easily three feet in diameter. "Yesterday, Chester was partnered with Augie McMullen. According to Augie, they had this tree about to topple when Chester stopped swinging. Augie figured he needed a rest and kept on with the final blows. When he looked up, Chester was standing directly in the fall line. Augie says Chester just stood there, staring up at this huge pine as it tilted toward him." Duncan shook his head. "Chester had been logging for a decade. He knew exactly which way the tree would come down. Augie remembers shouting for him to get out of the way. Then his memory becomes somewhat unreliable."

"How so?"

"Augie's never been the most articulate of men. He has a hard time finding words for what happened next, but he swears he saw Chester look straight at him. He says there was a kind of awful terror in Chester's face, as if he wanted to move but was somehow being held in place. Then the tree came crashing down on him."

Abigail looked up from the massive stump to the empty space in the sky where the tree would have towered. "How much would such a tree weigh?"

"A hundred-foot white pine? At least four-thousand pounds." Duncan joined Abigail on the periphery of the gruesome pattern of stains. "When they finally got the branches stripped enough to roll the trunk off of him, we found..." He shuddered and swallowed hard. "We tried to move his body, but there wasn't enough bone left intact to keep it together. We had to use shovels to get Prue's remains into a crate."

"Where are they now?"

"We're keeping them in one of the storage sheds until Father Carnes decides on the internment."

Abigail understood the situation at once. "If Mr. Prue committed suicide, they would deny him a Christian burial."

"Precisely."

"Did Prue have a family here?"

"No." Duncan cocked an eyebrow. "You're looking for a motive, aren't you? Well, you can believe Chester wasn't some lonely logger who couldn't cope with the isolation. Something *compelled* him to kill himself. What else would drive a man to such an end?"

Abigail chose not to respond as she went to examine the giant tree stump. The circumstances of Chester Prue's death were strange, but none of this fit the profile of any haunting she had ever seen. She had encountered many spirits over the years, but she had never come across an entity powerful enough to drive a man to suicide. Not to mention the fact that spirits from beyond the Veil desired *living* bodies to possess.

From the corner of her eye, Abigail spied Duncan biting

his lip as he stood watching her. There was something else on his mind. Abigail hoped he wouldn't take this opportunity to drag up the past; now wasn't the time.

"Abigail," he said. "When Emily's letter arrived two days ago, I… I didn't quite know how to feel about you being here. I know it's been years, but I… I just wanted to tell you I'm glad that you've come. We've a lot of frightened people here."

Duncan gave her a wan smile and Abigail relaxed, glad to further delay a conversation that was likely inevitable. She noticed for the first time that Duncan had grown to become quite handsome. He had been barely out of his teens when she last saw him. Now in his late-twenties, he had shed his boyish awkwardness the way a fawn grows into a lean buck. His bright blue eyes still shone with youthful exuberance, but his face had lost its pallor. The months he had spent in the wilderness had hardened him and he now bore the weathered glow of the high mountain elements. Abigail thought the rugged look suited him, as if his outward appearance reflected the adventurous soul that lay beneath.

"Duncan, I—" Whatever Abigail was going to say was interrupted by the sharp bark of a dog from somewhere down in the ravine. Seconds later, a large black mutt crested the ridgeline, followed by two men.

"Damn," Duncan swore under his breath at the sight of them.

Abigail followed his gaze. "What's wrong?"

"I thought I'd have more time to tell you."

"Tell me what? Who is that?"

Duncan's expression grew anxious as he looked her in the

eye. "Abigail, I need you to follow my lead for the moment. No matter how odd it may seem, I need you to play along with whatever I say. Will you do that?"

"Yes, of course."

"Who's the stranger, Emmons?" asked the first man as he drew near. His voice was as deep and cool as a mountain lake. He was a lumberjack; tall and solidly built, with hair as dark and thick as a bear hide. The black scruff of a long beard covered his face and his eyes were dark and penetrating. He wore a flannel neckerchief tied loosely around his throat, a woolen shirt rolled up to his elbows, buckskin breeches, and Native-style leggings. A leather bag, hunting knife, and flintlock pistol were fastened to a rawhide belt looped around his trim waist. He carried a heavy timber axe hefted over a broad shoulder and Abigail could make out the gray shapes of woodsman tattoos emblazoned on his thick forearms.

The second man was a curious sight. He was a Native of average height; lean, bandy-legged, and much older than the lumberjack. The leathery skin of his face was stretched taut across his prominent cheekbones. He shaved his head to the scalp except for a long, black topknot tied with a leather thong adorned with three eagle feathers. He wore buckskin breeches, leggings, leather moccasins, and an old, red British soldier's coat. Abigail could see the scorched hole above the breast pocket where a rifle shot must have killed the coat's previous owner during the War of Independence. The man had thick steel bracelets fastened around the sleeves at each of his biceps. A necklace of beads and bear claws dangled from his neck. A blue sash wrapped around his waist secured his tomahawk, and a bulky leather satchel was slung across his chest. He carried a long Baker rifle folded in his arms.

"Glenn Colvin, I'd like you to meet Abigail Jacobs." Duncan made a sweeping gesture toward Abigail as he introduced her to the lumberjack. "Ms. Jacobs is the new schoolteacher sent by the company."

Abigail shot Duncan a sharp look, but his pleading glance forced her to bite her tongue. "Glenn is our camp foreman," he explained.

"A schoolteacher," Colvin mused. Lowering his axe to the ground, he leaned his palm on the butt of its oak handle. "I wasn't aware Witherbee & Rand had appointed us one. You would think I would have known."

Colvin's face hardened and Abigail noticed his eyes weren't black at all, but deep molten amber. Unlike many men she encountered, she detected nothing lewd in his gaze as he looked her over. He was simply accustomed to scrutinizing everything, and everyone, in turn. It was a trait Abigail could respect.

Duncan shrugged at Colvin's suspicion. "You know how unreliable our communications with the company have been, what with the entire northeast at war."

Colvin pursed his lips as he ran a palm over his thick beard. "Aye, I suppose they have been." He paused again before offering Abigail his hand. "Pleased to make your acquaintance, Ms. Jacobs."

"Likewise, Mr. Colvin."

"Though I haven't a clue what incentive could have drawn you out here, I'm sure the children of our little slice of heaven can only benefit from your services."

Colvin's calm languidness told Abigail he was accustomed

to leading with easy self-assurance. She suspected he was the type of man others followed out of respect, not fear—although he was likely deserving of both.

"This handsome fellow is our Indian guide, Josiah Benedict." Colvin motioned to the man at his side. The Native nodded but said nothing, his face a mask of passivity. "You needn't be alarmed, Ms. Jacobs. Josiah's a Penobscot, not a Mohawk."

Colvin's eyes went to the black dog, sniffing and pawing at the dark stains on the ground. "Timber, *here*." He pointed to a spot at his side. The dog responded and sat by Colvin's boot, where it remained staring up at Abigail with narrow, suspicious eyes. The lumberjack ran an affectionate hand over the animal's furry head and nodded at the bloodstains. "Helluva place to bring a lady, wouldn't you say, Emmons?"

"I… Yes, well…" Put on the spot, Duncan froze.

"Mr. Emmons was simply indulging my request, Mr. Colvin," Abigail broke in smoothly.

Colvin's eyes fell on her and Abigail was struck by the ability of his gaze to be both intense and engaging at once.

"Your request?" he asked mildly.

"Indeed. You see, upon his engagement of my services, Mr. Witherbee apprised me of the tragedies that have lately befallen your village. At first I paid them no mind, but when I heard of this most recent incident, I… well…" She shuddered visibly. "I must admit to being somewhat spooked by the thought of so many suicides. Mr. Emmons merely desired to ease my fearful imagination by proving that yesterday's casualty was nothing more than an unfortunate accident."

Duncan stared at her in disbelief, stunned by the ease with which the lies came to her.

A moment passed as Colvin eyed her, chewing it over in his mind. "Yes, of course. A most unfortunate accident."

An awkward silence settled on the clearing until Colvin cocked an eye toward the darkening sky. "Rain's moving in again. Looks like the autumn storms are coming. Hope you're not afraid of foul weather, Ms. Jacobs. Out here in the Adirondack, we've got three seasons: rain, snow, and mosquitos." He gave her a grin and a wink before turning once more to Duncan. "It's gonna' be a wet one tonight. I'll have someone give Ms. Jacobs a proper tour of the camp in the morning. Until then, be sure the lady has a hot meal before she retires for the evening."

Duncan nodded and after wishing Abigail a good evening, Colvin and his Native companion disappeared up the trail, with Timber bounding ahead of them.

Abigail waited for them to move out of earshot before turning on Duncan, her eyes smoldering. "Perhaps now would be an appropriate time to explain what is going on?"

"I have told no one why you're really here."

"I beg your pardon?"

"I just couldn't. Most of the villagers are fresh immigrants, Scots and Irish mostly. Many still cling to their Old World faiths and superstitions. Some are devout to the point of fanaticism. If they knew you were…" His voice trailed off.

"Knew I was what? A witch?"

Duncan's face grew somber. "They never would have let you come here. *I* would never have let you come here. There's no telling what they would do if they found out about your, uh... methods." He motioned to where the two men had disappeared down the path. "Colvin's a fine man; level-headed and fair. We could trust him, but I wouldn't think of burdening him with keeping such a secret from the rest of the village. And so, until you discover what evil is at work here, you've no choice but to play the part of a schoolteacher sent by Witherbee & Rand."

Abigail couldn't believe what she was hearing. "You expect me to rescue these people from an entity that has driven four men to suicide, despite the fact that they could very well hang me if they knew what I was doing?"

Duncan frowned. "This is why I gave Emily explicit instructions not to involve you in what is going on out here. I told her it would be too dangerous for you. But now that you are here..." He pinched his shoulders together and gave a mirthless smile. "Come on, I'll show you to your cabin. You'll need your rest; you'll be teaching your first lesson tomorrow."

Chapter 7

It was after midnight when Abigail snuck from her cabin. Rain came down hard upon her and turned the wooded path into a sloppy morass as she stole through the inky blackness of the sleeping village. Bundled in an oilcloth cloak she had packed for the mountains, she carried an unlit hurricane lamp swinging from her hand as she skirted the puddles and darted past the darkened windows of the slumbering cabins. The green scent of pinesap and wet earth filled the chilly night air.

The trail widened and the timber cabins crowded closer together as Abigail approached the village center. Once she reached the only intersection, she ducked beneath the overhanging roof of a squat building on the corner. She receded against the wall and waited to be sure no one was around. The downpour hammered the tin roof as she lingered there a moment. She hadn't seen a single light during the dash from her cabin. Shrouded in darkness, the village had every appearance of a ghost town.

But that didn't mean she was safe. Despite the storm, the loggers would have posted a nightly sentry to guard against

Native raids. After what she had learned about the villagers' religious fervor, she couldn't chance being discovered— especially not with what she had planned.

Abigail felt a growing sense that she was about to make a foolish mistake as she huddled in the darkness, straining to discern any signs of movement through the heavy sheets of rain. There would be no way of explaining herself if they caught her inside the shed with Chester Prue's remains. In all likelihood, the villagers would accuse her of attempting to defile Prue's corpse.

And then what? Would they search her cabin once they had seized her? What would they do if she refused to open her trunk, the black one with the unsettling markings? Worse yet, what if they somehow discovered the strange collection of arcane artifacts that lay inside? There would be no explaining them either. Once the true purpose of her presence in Tahawus was laid bare, would the villagers be content to simply run her out of town? Given Duncan's grim warning, Abigail surmised she would be lucky to escape so easily. Out here in the lawless wilderness, far from any shred of educated civility, a hanging for witchcraft wasn't entirely out of the question. There certainly wasn't anyone around to prevent it.

Abigail's thoughts went to Glenn Colvin; the brawny camp foreman she had met earlier that afternoon. Duncan had called him a good man, but could she count on Colvin to defend her from a lynch mob? The more Abigail thought about it, the more she became convinced that she was indeed taking a substantial risk—perhaps *too* great.

And yet, dangerous or not, examining Chester Prue's body was essential to her investigation. The village pastor, Father

Carnes, might decide to burn the corpse in the morning. Besides, the shed in which Prue's remains were being stored was on the outskirts of town, past the chapel at the north end of Main Street. It wasn't near the cabins or bunkhouses. Under the cover of the rain, sneaking in shouldn't be difficult at all. This could be her only chance to find answers. She had to act quickly, and she had to act now.

Abigail wrapped herself tighter in her cloak and took one last look around before darting from her shelter. Through the driving rain, the chapel's whitewashed steeple rose like a finger-bone into the night. Abigail's leather boots splashed through the mud as she stole in its direction, moving through the rain-soaked gloom. Out on the open width of Main Street, she was far too exposed. Even in the heavy downpour, her cloaked shape was visible to anyone who might be watching.

Abigail quickened her pace, closing the distance to the chapel until she pressed herself flat against the clapboard siding, careful to avoid the streams of rain pouring from the steeply pitched roof. The steel ring of the unlit hurricane lantern felt cold in her grip as she listened, expecting the strident cry of a sentry to peal through the darkness at any moment.

She only heard the steady patter of the rain.

The village remained still and silent.

Abigail's breath streamed from her hood and bloomed white in the night air as she rounded the back corner of the chapel and peered into the murky darkness beyond. The path she was looking for eluded her for a moment, but she finally spied it. It appeared as little more than a vague shadow in the dense forest.

Abigail left the chapel behind and raced for the cover of the tree line, where she plunged into absolute darkness. She went still and waited for the dreadful sensation of blindness to pass. The pause did no good. Under the heavy cover of the evergreens, an utterly black oblivion had replaced the driving rain. It crossed Abigail's mind that it might force her to light her lantern, but she quickly dismissed the idea; the glow would give her away instantly. As much as she hated to admit it, she would have no choice but to turn back if she couldn't go on without a light.

Abigail strained her eyes as best she could. A minute passed and still the darkness yielded nothing. She was losing hope when, to her great relief, she discovered she could make out the vague outline of shapes looming black-on-black in the gloom ahead. She picked her way along the lightless path as she crept toward the hulking silhouettes, dragging her toes across the forest floor to avoid tripping over the exposed roots and rocks.

Part of her wondered what she would do if the shed doors were locked. She had stashed her set of lock-picking tools in her pocket in anticipation of such a possibility, but she would need light to use them. But as she approached the crude structures, Abigail quickly realized she had a more immediate problem to contend with: she had no idea which of the three sheds housed the remains of Chester Prue. With the threat of discovery hanging over her head, she wouldn't have time to search them all.

Abigail's outstretched hands probed the darkness as she crept to the first shed, located a knothole in a timber plank, and tried to peer into the yawning blackness. Nothing was visible. She would have to find a better way of determining the right shed and she would have to do it quickly. The risk of being caught was growing greater with each wasted second.

The solution to her dilemma presented itself when she moved to the next hut. Emanating from within was the sour, unmistakable odor of decaying meat. With renewed determination, Abigail ran her hand over the barn door, combing it for the latch. Her hopes fell when her palm closed on the cold, unyielding iron of a large padlock. Whoever had deposited Prue's corpse here wasn't taking any chances with hungry scavengers.

Abigail probed the lock with her fingers and determined it was a common warded variety. It would be the work of a minute for her to pick it. Her set of tools was among the best that could be found, a gift from Niall O'Leary, Boston's most notorious thief. But in this darkness, Abigail wasn't certain how effectively she could manipulate the picks. Did she have enough time? Even now, the sentry could be making his rounds past the chapel, heading her way.

A persistent voice inside Abigail's head told her it was already too late; she should turn back. And yet, she still thrust her hand into her pocket, reaching for the lock picks.

Setting the hurricane lantern on the ground far enough from her feet that she wouldn't inadvertently kick it over, Abigail cupped the tiny tools in one palm and probed them with her fingers until she found the right one for the job: a thin steel rod bent at a ninety-degree angle at one end. She located the keyhole on the lock's faceplate and inserted the bent end of the pick, scraping it around the interior of the hole to turn the wards. Her wet hands made the thin tool slick and tricky. Suddenly, the pick snagged on something inside the lock and almost tumbled between her fingertips. Abigail's stomach lurched as she imagined losing the pick in the darkness. She would never find it again and her one chance to examine Prue's remains would disappear with it.

Abigail heaved a deep breath and forced herself to concentrate. Her hands trembled from the cold now. The pick struck against something solid after several more seconds of prodding. There was a brief resistance before the ward gave way and the padlock come loose in her hand.

Abigail returned the pick to her pocket, retrieved the lantern from the darkness with one hand, and gathered a handful of wet pine needles with the other. With a groan of rusty hinges, she eased the door open and slipped into the blackness.

Chapter 8

The nauseating stench of decomposition permeated the darkness. Abigail had spent more time in moldy crypts and mausoleums than she cared to remember. Still, the reek inside the shed was almost unbearable. She kept the handful of pine needles clamped to her nose as she inched her way deeper into the darkness. The pungent scent of pinesap helped to mask the awful smell, but only slightly.

Once she had secured the door behind her, Abigail no longer had a choice. If she wanted to locate and examine Prue's body, she would have to light her lantern. This wasn't unexpected; she had brought the light along knowing she needed to use it eventually. But even here, within the seemingly safe confines of the shed, sparking the wick wasn't without risk. If the gaps between the planks were wide enough, or the knotholes large enough, her light would stream through the walls like a beacon in the darkness. This was one part of her plan over which she had no control. The risk of discovery was great, but it was also unavoidable.

Abigail uncovered her nose and let the pine needles drop

from her palm, brushing away those that still clung to her fingertips. The cloying reek was suffocating in its intensity, hinting at the gruesome human remains that lay somewhere in the blackness. Abigail fumbled with the lantern and managed to spring the glass chimney without shattering it. She then drew a tinderbox from her pocket, struck the flint, and lit the oil-soaked wick.

A bright flame flared to life and flooded the shed with light. Abigail winced and squeezed her eyes against the sudden brilliance. A heartbeat passed before she quickly twisted the lamp's regulator down as far as she could. The flame sputtered inside the chimney and threatened to gutter before stabilizing and suffusing the shed with a dull orange glow.

Abigail let out her bated breath, held the lantern high, and got her first look at her surroundings.

The space was larger than she had guessed, about twenty feet wide and perhaps fifty feet deep. Dusty crates of supplies were piled high against the walls. The lantern's short radius lost the furthest stacks in the shadows. Most of them were packed with flammable whale oil. Abigail now understood why they erected this shed on the outskirts of the village. If it were any closer and somehow caught fire, the entire community would be engulfed in a hellish inferno.

A large area had been cleared in the center of the space. Here sat another crate. It was rectangular and larger than the others, its lid sealed tight at each of the four corners. Two shovels rested against the nearest wall, their rusty blades plastered with pine needles and dried blood. Abigail had found what she had come for: the makeshift coffin of the unfortunate Chester Prue.

Abigail set the lantern on a tall stack of crates and went to work at prying open the coffin lid, using a shovel for leverage. Despite her best efforts to remain silent, the nails gave a shrill screech as they pulled free. Abigail cringed at the noise. She was fairly confident the rain would drown out what few sounds she made, but she couldn't be certain. Anyone could pass within earshot at any moment.

Abigail laid the lid aside, careful not to bend the nails. She then retrieved the lantern and played the dim light over the open space.

What she saw there shocked her to no end.

Inside the crude coffin was a pulpy mass of mangled flesh and fractured bones. Except for Chester Prue's blood-soaked clothes, what remained of the man was barely recognizable as human. The entire area from his pelvis to sternum had been crushed, the bones pulverized into hundreds of pieces that sat beneath the skin like sticks in a bloody sack. Without a solid skeleton to hold it together, the corpse had come apart like a scarecrow losing its stuffing. Prue's right arm was detached entirely from his crushed shoulder socket and now lay splayed across his crumpled chest. The lower vertebrae of the spine were obliterated. Above the waist, the torso had been nearly divided from the lower half of the body and was held together by skin alone. A large portion of ropy viscera bulged from a long tear in the flesh below the man's gut.

Worst of all was Prue's head. The skull had been smashed flat and oozing heaps of gray matter were visible between shards of shattered cranium. The waxy skin of Prue's ruined face sagged like some hideous mask waiting to be worn on All

Hallows' Eve.

Never in all of her adventures had Abigail seen such catastrophic damage inflicted on a human body. A scorching rush of bile leaped into her throat and she recoiled involuntarily. The rancid stench emanating from the crate poisoned the air. Abigail felt a wild impulse to flee, to escape to where she could gulp deeply of the fresh night. She closed her eyes and steeled her nerves, waiting for the nausea to pass before returning to the makeshift casket and setting about her grisly task.

She began with the dismembered right arm. Abigail's hands tremored as she removed the limb from its place and turned it over, searching for the blackened fingernails that were one of the telltale signs of spirit possession. There was the usual dirt and grime, but nothing different from what was expected of a lumberjack.

Abigail replaced the bloody limb where she had found it and looked for the left arm. It was nowhere to be seen. A prickle of revulsion rippled across her skin when she realized it was pinned somewhere beneath the mutilated torso. She would have to reach in and search for it.

Abigail drew a deep breath as she rounded the crate to the other side. With her air held in her lungs, she plunged her hands into the reeking mess. The dead man's clammy flesh was spongy and yielding beneath her fingers as she reached into the bottom of the crate. *Just five more minutes*, she told herself as her throat constricted against another fiery rush of bile. *Five more minutes and you'll have the answers you need.*

Her palms located a hand, and she raised it up into the feeble light to give the fingernails the same thorough inspection. Again, there was nothing unusual.

Abigail felt a swift prick of doubt as she let the limp arm drop back into the crate and wiped her bloody hands on a rag she found atop another crate. Perhaps she had been right all along; perhaps this wasn't a haunting.

Prue's head was the last to be examined.

Abigail moved to the upper end of the crate and positioned herself over the man's shattered skull. Clumps of thick, salt-and-pepper hair hung from the shredded flaps of scalp. She looked at the grisly remnants of Prue's face and hesitated as she contemplated how to proceed. Ordinarily, she would begin with an inspection of the eyes, searching for the early onset of cataracts. But both of Prue's eyeballs had ruptured under the crushing weight of the fallen tree. They had now disappeared somewhere into the viscous mix of blood and brain. Without a skull to give them shape, the empty sockets below his brow were oblong and drooping.

Abigail proceeded to the next step in her process: Prue's mouth. She held her breath once more and stooped low, leaning very close to get a look at the slack lips. Her face was now mere inches from the stinking mass of twisted body parts and the charnel smell of blood and viscera assaulted her mercilessly. Abigail fought an irresistible urge to gag as she examined the area around Prue's lips, looking for signs of bruising. In the dim light of the lantern, it seemed an impossible task. The flesh was too severely spoiled and was already turning color with decay. Still, all the damage was sustained at the time of Prue's death, not before. Yet another significant mark of possession was absent.

Abigail let her breath out and pursed her lips as she stood

up. Only one more test remained now. She took a moment to stretch her neck and prepare herself. What would come next would be the most unpleasant of all.

She reached down and inserted her two index fingers into Prue's wilting mouth. She worked slowly and gingerly as she eased her thumbs in and parted the lips. The sensation against her skin was moist and spongy, not unlike poking the insides of a pig's carcass. Abigail became conscious of her heart pounding in her chest and she willed herself to calm down. When the gap between the dead man's lips was wide enough, she leaned in to take a closer look inside the mouth.

The only solid things present inside the hollow cavity were the hard, yellow bits of what she understood to be Prue's crushed teeth. Abigail plucked one from his mouth and deposited it in her pocket for a later examination. She peered closer, angling to see the gray lump of the man's tongue. There was no trace of the discoloration she was looking for.

A strange apprehension came over Abigail as she withdrew her fingers, wiped them on the rag, and stepped back. Prue's corpse didn't bear a single sign of spirit possession.

Instead of feeling satisfied, an uneasy sensation continued to gnaw at Abigail's gut. All the evidence presented by Prue's remains confirmed her suspicions that his death was nothing more than a terrible suicide. But with the horrific heap of flesh and bone before her, Abigail believe any man would deliberately choose such a fate. Somehow, it just didn't seem possible.

Abigail couldn't shake the nagging sensation that she had missed something. She wondered about Prue's missing eyes. Perhaps they would have revealed the vital clue she was looking for? Perhaps they—

A sudden sound came from outside the shed.

Chapter 9

Abigail froze and listened. Was that a footstep? A long moment passed in silence. Then she heard it again: the unmistakable crack of a twig echoing through the forest.

Someone was coming.

Abigail's blood went cold as a stark awareness of her vulnerability washed over her. How could she be so careless? She had been so engrossed in her examination of Prue's corpse she had forgotten where she was and the danger she was in.

Now she was trapped.

Abigail remained still, her heart racing, hoping against hope that whoever was out there would continue along the path. Instead, the steady crunch of footfalls on the wet forest floor only grew louder as they approached the shed.

Abigail's eyes darted around the closed space. There seemed nowhere to hide. Discovery was unavoidable.

Abigail grabbed the coffin lid and replaced it atop the crate, hoping that whoever came through the door wouldn't notice that it was no longer nailed shut. She snatched the lantern and crept into the shadows at the far end of the shed. There, she discovered a narrow space between the back wall and a tall stack of crates. Within moments, she had opened enough of a gap to squeeze herself between the wooden boxes and the wall.

She quickly doused the lantern.

Darkness rushed over Abigail as she stood motionless in her cramped hiding space. How long had her efforts taken her? Thirty seconds? More? How much had the stranger heard?

Flattened against the wall, Abigail quieted her breathing as she listened for the crunch of footsteps.

Nothing.

Nearly a minute passed in silence.

The footsteps had stopped.

Abigail could only imagine what was happening beyond the shed door. First, the stranger would notice the padlock hanging open from the latch. He might even see the fresh footprints she had left in the mud. Would he suspect someone hiding inside? Or would he assume that whoever had brought Prue's body here had forgotten to lock the door?

The shed door swung open.

Abigail stiffened, her pulse thudding in her throat.

The bright glare of a lantern banished the darkness. The thump of a heavy boot followed the creak of rusty hinges. The stranger was a man. More footsteps resounded as he strode across the floor to Prue's coffin.

Then silence.

Abigail held her breath. Her mind cast about for any clues she might have left behind in her rush to hide. The bloody rag? The pine needles strewn across the floor? The muddy footprints? All seemed incidental, easily attributed to the men

She scurried across the floorboards, pressed her hands to the door, and pushed hard. It swung open easily. A cool splash of rain spattered over her as her apprehension deepened. Why had the man left the shed unlocked? She was a stranger in town, trespassing on company property where the remains of a dead lumberjack were being held. Why was she being allowed to leave?

Abigail shivered, and she threw the hood of her cloak over her head to repel the rain streaming through the boughs as she scanned the darkness of the forest one last time. Her intuition told her she was alone.

The man had vanished into the night.

An unsettling dread took root in Abigail's stomach as she returned to the shed and pressed the coffin nails back into their holes, sealing the lid shut. The anxious feeling only grew more insistent as she fled through the downpour back to her cabin. She had been in Tahawus less than a day and she had already made a costly mistake.

Someone knew her secret. And whoever it was now had her at a terrible disadvantage.

Chapter 10

A knock at the cabin door brought Abigail out of sleep. She shot up in her bed as the memory of the previous night's events leaped into focus: the storage shed; Prue's body; the lantern light falling across her; the heavy tread of the man's footsteps walking away, letting her go.

Another knock.

A slow sense of foreboding came over her. Had the villagers waited for daylight before coming for her? Were they here to seize her, after all?

Part of Abigail welcomed the prospect of a confrontation as she cast her blankets aside and slid her feet into her woolen slippers. She couldn't tolerate waiting and wondering who the mysterious man in the shed had been and what he might do with the secret they now shared. The awful sense of vulnerability made her feel violated. It was better to get it over with now.

Abigail threw a heavy shawl over her flannel nightgown and went to where her rain-soaked cloak hung from a peg behind the door. The lock picks were in the pocket. She quickly sorted them, selecting the most useful and tucking them deep into her knee-high stockings. There was every chance the men outside would put her in irons. If they left her alone for even a couple of minutes, she could free herself.

But then what? How would she get out of town and down the mountain?

There wasn't time to think about it now. Abigail let the hem of her shift fall back to her ankles, drew a deep breath, and pulled the door open.

Instead of armed men, she discovered a young woman smiling at her in the yellow morning sunlight.

"Ms. Jacobs? My name is Evelyn MacIntyre." A heavy Scottish brogue colored the woman's voice. "Mr. Colvin has asked me to show ye' around this morning. Would ye' care for some breakfast?"

"How very kind of you, Mrs. MacIntyre," Abigail said, doing her best to hide her relief as she accepted the breakfast basket the woman offered. "Won't you please come inside?"

Abigail stood aside and noted the round bump of Evelyn's pregnant belly as the young woman entered the cabin. Evelyn MacIntyre was shorter than Abigail and maybe five years younger, in her early twenties. She had thick red hair that was tied in a neat bun behind her head. Her bright green eyes were flecked with copper and a dusting of freckles sprinkled her pert nose and milk-white cheeks. She wore a dun-colored gown stretched tight over her bulging belly and a woolen cape draped over her shoulders.

"Here, please be seated." Abigail motioned to the hard bed. "I'm afraid I've nothing more comfortable to offer."

"Nor are ye' likely to find any." Evelyn sat and flashed a

smile that revealed her small, pearly teeth. "A woman grows accustomed to her share of privation out here in the rough country."

"Yes, I suppose it will take some time to adapt." Abigail glanced around the spartan room. Located at the end of a meandering trail about a five-minute walk from the center of the village, her cabin was built of rounded logs chinked together with plaster mortar. It comprised one square room of perhaps fifteen by fifteen feet. Her wooden cot was pushed into the back corner, padded only by a thin straw mattress. Next to it stood a crude nightstand on which Abigail had found the hurricane lantern she had used on the previous night's excursion. She had arranged her two travelling trunks against the wall opposite the bed, beneath the drab curtains of the cabin's only window. Next to them was a rickety table. A pot-bellied stove stood in the other back corner. The cramped space smelled of musty wood-smoke and dampness.

Abigail took a seat on the lid of the larger of her trunks and balanced the breakfast basket in her lap. Tucked into a clean cloth was a small loaf of freshly baked rye bread, a hunk of cheese, and an apple.

Evelyn took notice of Abigail's pleased reaction. "Couldn'a help but notice ye' missing from the mess hall this morning, and I thought you'd be hungry. Did ye' sleep well, Ms. Jacobs?"

"Like the dead," Abigail lied. In her experience, the dead often didn't rest well at all.

"I see you've got yourself a leak to contend with." Evelyn nodded at a washbasin that sat nearly overflowing on the floor.

Abigail bit into the apple. "It would seem so, yes. Last night was quite a storm.

"That? That was barely a Scotch mist." Evelyn chuckled. "Out here, you'll know we're fit for a drowning when even the midday sky darkens blacker than the Earl of Hell's waistcoat." She gave Abigail another of her dazzling smiles. "If you'd like, I'll have my husband see to your leak when he returns this afternoon."

"If it's not too much trouble, that would be much appreciated," Abigail said as she finished the last of the apple. The breakfast should have been delightful, but she had little appetite—not with the memory of the previous night still weighing on her.

"Very glad of it." Evelyn rose to her feet. "Now if ye' be ready, I'll leave ye' a few moments of privacy to dress for your tour."

Abigail's gaze strayed to the bump of the woman's pregnant belly. "Oh no, I couldn't possibly trouble you to—"

"Tsk, 'tis no trouble at all." Evelyn waved off Abigail's objection as she went to the door. "To be sure, there's no one else to do it. The men have all gone to work and the other women have chores enough to attend to." She ran a caressing hand over her round belly. "But never ye' worry, Ms. Jacobs. This little one's not due for another month and seems fit to sleep 'till then. Hardly kicks at all. In the meantime, I've very little to keep myself occupied. It would be me pleasure to welcome our new schoolteacher to the village."

Abigail gave her a grateful smile as Evelyn exited and closed the front door. She wondered what the young woman might have thought had she noticed the rain-soaked cloak hanging from the peg.

A few moments later, Abigail emerged from the cabin into the crisp mountain air. The sky had cleared, and the cerulean was now unmarred. The greenery sparkled and danced with the gleam of glistening dewdrops. A gossamer morning mist hung within the lush forest, biding its time before the sunlight chased it away.

"Now ye' look like a proper woods-woman." Evelyn grinned, admiring Abigail's rugged, linsey-woolsey bib dress and her leather Wellington-style boots. She noted Abigail's hesitation at her doorstep. "You'll find we haven't much use for locks around here. We're the smallest of communities and thievery's never a worry when no one has 'aught to steal."

Evelyn turned and led the way toward the village. The puddles from the previous night's downpour had already soaked into the earth, leaving behind a black, boot-sucking sludge. It seemed to Abigail that the forest was exhaling a pleasant fragrance of oak moss and fir. Despite the sunlight streaming through the boughs, the fresh air was cool on her skin; a welcome change from the cramped stuffiness of her cabin. For the first time since her arrival, she noticed how majestic her surroundings were. All around her, the rocky peaks of the mountains rose to the sky like ancient sentinels guarding the threshold of heaven.

"That one's the village namesake." Evelyn pointed out a massive peak towering over them to the northeast. "As far as Mr. Emmons can tell from his surveys, 'tis the highest mount of them all. Our Indian, Josiah, says *Tahawus* means Cloudsplitter in the native tongue."

"It certainly is impressive," Abigail said, admiring the bald summit that rose high above the limits of where even the most tenacious trees could grow.

"Aye, it is, isn't it?" Evelyn's green eyes twinkled as if she had raised the mountain from the earth herself.

"Have you been in America long?" Abigail asked.

"Just a tad over a year now."

"From what part of Scotland did you come?"

Something like a shadow flickered across Evelyn's face, but it passed so quickly Abigail paid it no attention. "Dornoch, in the Highlands. A two-day's ride from Inverness."

"I'm familiar with the area."

"Do ye' say so?" Evelyn cocked a surprised eye. "Relatives?"

Abigail shook her head. "Whiskey."

Evelyn stopped in her tracks and stared at Abigail with a look of such astonishment that Abigail worried she might have offended her. Then Evelyn burst out laughing, her round belly shaking and her freckled cheeks flushing pink. "Oh, I believe I'm going to like ye' Ms. Jacobs! And I thank ye' for the laugh! The Lord knows there's been little cause for them these past few weeks."

"You are alluding to the recent suicides?"

The mirth faded from Evelyn's voice. "Aye. But we don't speak of 'em for fear of bad luck."

A somber look fell over the young woman's face and Abigail sensed this would be all she would say on the matter.

Evelyn continued to point out various sites as they drew nearer to the town center. The layout of the village resembled the veins of a maple leaf: a network of increasingly narrower paths forked-off from the wider stem of Main Street. Scattered across this area were the community's storage sheds, family cabins, and communal "doghouses" where the unmarried lumberjacks slept.

"Is it customary for women and children to accompany their men to lumber camps?" Abigail asked.

"Not at all. As far as I know, we've got claim to being the first of our kind in that regard. Most camps are small—about eight to ten men—and the shelters are temporary so as to be torn down and moved to new cutting lands. They founded Tahawus as just such a camp almost six years ago. But this far into the mountains, the timber is so plentiful Witherbee & Rand decided it was less expensive to establish a permanent village, rather than transport the men to and from the region every season."

"How many loggers are at work here?"

"We're down to fifty-one men now. All told, we've about seventy-five people living in Tahawus, if ye' count the women and children."

Once they reached the intersection at Main Street, Evelyn stopped and jerked a thumb over her shoulder at the company office on the corner. "Here's where you'll collect your pay." She then pointed south down the street toward another squat building where a sign advertised *Bingham's General Store and Post Office*. "And there's where you'll spend it. Bingham's tea is atrocious, but he keeps his coffee as fresh as he can. His deliveries aren't what they used to be, what with the war and all."

"Is the company not at all concerned about the possibility of an invasion?"

Evelyn chuckled. "Brit or Indian?"

"Both.

"All the way up here, there's little chance of either. Truth be told, Ms. Jacobs, this war is the best thing that's ever happened to Witherbee & Rand. With all the battleships being built, the demand for good timber has never been higher and the company doesn't much care which side they sell to."

Abigail nodded her understanding. Another of her lingering questions had just been answered: what had been Witherbee & Rand's response to the recent suicides? With the profits from their logging operations making them rich, it was unlikely they had paid much attention to the unfortunate fates of a few lumberjacks.

"Over there is the mess hall." Evelyn indicated a flat building across the street. "We all have our tasks 'round here. Some women clean, others take care of the cooking. We serve meals every day at six and six. For now, the mess hall is where you'll be teaching the children. They'll be meeting ye' there at one this afternoon, but after today you're free to set the learning hours as ye' see fit, so as long as the little ones are home for dinner."

"I wouldn't dream of keeping them any longer. How many children will attend?"

"Eight, soon to be nine." Evelyn smiled and patted her belly. "I must say, Ms. Jacobs, we're all sure and mighty excited that you're here. To think! A real and honest to goodness schoolteacher here in Tahawus!"

They continued on, strolling up Main Street toward where the chapel stood near the forest's edge. Evelyn talked animatedly as they went, pointing out establishments like the blacksmith and the barbershop and sharing colorful anecdotes about life in a logging town.

And then she drew to an unexpected halt. The grin vanished from her lips.

A coil of black smoke was rising above the treetops in the distance.

Abigail followed Evelyn's gaze skyward. "What is it, Mrs. MacIntyre?"

"Mr. Prue," Evelyn replied with a grim frown. "Father Carnes announced his decision after breakfast this morning. He wouldn't commit Prue's remains to rest in consecrated ground, but he would at least cremate them to spare Prue from scavengers." Evelyn bowed her head, closed her eyes, and mouthed a silent prayer. When finished, she crossed herself and turned to Abigail. "Ms. Jacobs, if ye' don't mind me asking... what brought ye' all the way out here to this hard land?"

Abigail's eyes lingered a moment longer on the oily column of smoke that was now marring the clear blue sky. "I can't rightly say that I know. I suppose it was the mystery of the place."

Chapter 11

"Are you trying to get yourself burned at the stake?" Duncan exclaimed. "Have you any idea what could have happened if they caught you in that shed?"

Duncan stood with Abigail on the shore of a long lake nestled between two towering peaks. It was almost midday and the forested shoulders of the mountains lay blanketed beneath a quilt of greens, yellows, and reds. The rocky pattern of the lake bottom was clearly visible beneath the glassy surface of the water, the slope of the land growing ever more steep until it fell away into nothingness.

Abigail allowed a soft chuckle at Duncan's fretfulness. "Duncan, in the history of the New World, there has not been a single instance of a person being burned alive for witchcraft. *Hanging* has been our traditional means of execution. Being from Salem, you of all people should know that."

"I don't find that amusing, Abigail. You know very well what I mean."

"I do," Abigail said coolly, irritated at Duncan's tone. "And

I am well aware of the danger I chanced last night. But as long as I am hindered in my investigation by this ruse of playing a schoolteacher, such risks may continue to be necessary. I need not remind you that this charade was *your* idea."

Chastened, Duncan went quiet and looked away. Half a mile to their right, a long section of shoreline was clear of trees and brush. Hundreds of timber logs were stacked high on the water's edge. A series of slanted braces and struts hewn from thick timber kept the enormous stockpiles from spilling into the lake. A gang of loggers was busy lashing and securing the stacks of timber with ropes. Further back, a steep hill rose like a fortress rampart above the worksite.

Abigail followed Duncan's gaze and looked on as a massive log came rumbling down the incline. It collided with the uppermost logs of the nearest stack with a concussive impact that echoed throughout the valley.

"That area's called the stacking ramp," Duncan explained. "It may be October, but we're still early in the cutting season. The real work will be done in the winter when the sap hardens and the trees are easier to chop. By then, this lake will freeze over and all of those logs will be allowed to spill out onto the ice. In the spring, the flood of meltwater will carry them to the lumber mills downriver. As it is, the water levels are too low and the logs would just get hung-up on the riverbanks."

Abigail nodded. There was a school of minnows swerving and dancing in the shallows past the reeds.

"Last night... what did you find?" Duncan asked at last.

Abigail hesitated; this would not be easy. "There was

nothing paranatural about Chester Prue's death. He chose a terrible fate, to be sure, but it was a simple case of suicide, nonetheless."

Duncan stared at her. "Nothing more? That's not possible. How can you be so certain?"

"What remained of his corpse displayed no blackening of the fingernails, no bruising of the flesh around the mouth, no —"

"Wait, slow down. What is this about his fingernails?"

"Have you ever seen the effects of lightning on the human body?"

"No, I can't say I have."

"They can be quite illuminating, if you'll pardon my pun. I've an acquaintance at Harvard, a doctor who specializes in the study of pathology—"

"A former client, no doubt?"

Abigail cracked a smile. "Indeed. He was kind enough to admit me to a private review of the remains of a Cambridge man who had recently been killed by a lightning strike. The passing of the bolt through his body had blackened the victim's fingernails. His tongue was scorched as well. In many places, his veins had broken from the intensity of the electrical current and were plainly visible beneath his skin, appearing as what the doctor referred to as *lightning flowers*. The unfortunate man's inner ears had also ruptured and sudden cataracts beset his eyes."

Duncan peered at her. "What has this to do with Chester Prue?"

"When a spirit inhabits a human body, the resulting effects are often similar to those of a lightning strike. 'Tis a natural consequence of our worldly flesh being incapable of hosting the spirit's otherworldly energy."

"And Prue's body displayed none of these symptoms?"

Abigail shook her head.

"What about the bruising around the mouth that you mentioned?"

"Another consequence of the spirit occupying the body. Should it enter or exit through the mouth, it often damages the surrounding flesh as if frostbitten."

"This, too, was absent from Prue?"

"As far as I could discern, yes. Albeit, his flesh was already spoiled with decomposition."

"So it's possible that you missed something."

Abigail hesitated, mindful of her own lingering doubts in the moments before she had been interrupted in the shed. "Is it possible? Yes, but not likely. Duncan, I'm afraid we must accept the fact that Chester Prue was not possessed at the time of his death—at least not by any entity I have ever encountered."

Duncan bit his lip and ran a hand through his shock of yellow hair. "Then what if it wasn't possession? What if it was some other sort of spectral attack?"

"I beg your pardon?"

"Augie McMullen swore he saw Prue looking straight at him, as if pleading for help. Perhaps Prue was being held in place against his will by some invisible force."

Abigail thought it over. "I suppose it's a possibility. Unfortunately, we now have no way of knowing."

"How so?"

"When a man is touched by a spirit, the ghost's freezing

grip leaves a distinct impression on the flesh. This mark may fade to nothing over time, but it remains there like an invisible brand. It can always be revealed with the correct incantation."

"And you know such an incantation?"

Abigail's eyes gleamed as she tugged her sleeves up to her elbows and held her arms out. Dozens of mysterious scars crisscrossed the otherwise flawless white of her wrists and forearms. She closed her eyes and murmured a sequence of strange words that seemed to be composed entirely of vowels and sibilants.

To Duncan's amazement, an array of skeletal handprints materialized on the surface of Abigail's skin. They appeared as livid stains, the outlines of finger bones distinctly visible like macabre tattoos.

"Abigail!" he exclaimed with alarm.

Abigail opened her eyes and ceased her chant. The ghastly handprints vanished.

Duncan glanced around, anxious to see if anyone had witnessed what had just happened. "You mustn't do such things out in the open! As long as you're here investigating these suicides, you must refrain from any such spells, from anything that may be used against you to prove you are a... a —"

"A witch?" A stinging retort sprang to Abigail's tongue, but she bit it back as she pulled her sleeves down to her wrists. "At any rate, with Chester Prue, such an incantation wouldn't have been necessary; any phantom handprints would have been fresh and visible. However, given the state in which I found Prue's body, 'tis possible that decay could have camouflaged such marks. Of course, now that his corpse has been cremated, we have no way of knowing for certain."

Duncan shook his head and pried a rock free from the soft ground with the toe of his boot. "There was nothing else of note?"

Abigail opened her mouth, ready to tell him about the mysterious man who had caught her and let her go. Instead, she shook her head and remained silent. She didn't know why, but she suddenly thought it would be wiser if she kept the information to herself. Perhaps it was because she was growing weary of Duncan's constant haranguing about the need to be cautious around the villagers. Or maybe—just maybe—she wasn't certain who she could trust yet.

High overhead, a formation of geese passed across the clear blue sky, squawking as they retreated to the warmer climates of the south.

"Why are you so convinced Chester Prue could not simply have committed suicide?" Abigail asked.

"It's not just Prue. It's the other three men as well, the ones who killed themselves before Prue."

"What can you tell me of them?"

Duncan sat on a large boulder by the water's edge and looked out at the lake shimmering in the pale light of the October sun. "Jed Hawes was the first. He was a scout sent to explore the high interior of the northern range. When he went a week overdue, we knew something had gone wrong. Colvin and Josiah went looking for him. Two days later, they found Hawes dead on a sheer cliff overlooking a lake on the shoulder of the Cloudsplitter. He had shot himself in the belly with his own pistol."

"Could he have gotten lost and given up hope for rescue?"

"Not Hawes. He was an old-timer, a former military scout with three decades of experience tracking in the harshest environments. And besides, if a man wants to end his life with a pistol, he shoots himself in the head, not the belly. A wound like that takes days of unspeakable agony before it is fatal."

Duncan reached for a flat stone and sent it skipping across the water. The ripples spread out across the surface in five neat, concentric circles. "The second man was named Jean Beaulieu, a Frenchman lumberjack down here from Lower Canada. He was felling pines when he took his axe and walked off into the woods by himself. When his partner went after him, he found Beaulieu had hacked off his own left arm below the elbow. He was sitting cross-legged in the forest, feasting on the severed limb. They tried to save him, but Beaulieu died of blood loss before they could get him back to the village."

Duncan lowered his head and wavered for a moment, as if reliving a memory he had fought hard to suppress. "The third to die was Cyrus Gill. I was with him when it happened. We were charting the land about ten miles to the northeast and Cy was serving as my assistant. On the fourth night of our expedition, I awoke to a brilliant glow from somewhere beyond the tent. I rushed outside and found Cy engulfed in flames. He had soaked himself in lantern oil and set himself ablaze."

Duncan's lips tightened and his gaze went down to the ripples lapping at the shoreline. "Cy was a family man. His wife and daughter are still here in Tahawus. I expect you'll meet the girl in your lesson this afternoon. Her name is Hannah."

Duncan raised himself from the boulder and turned his back on the lake. His bright blue eyes sparkled in the sunlight. "So you see, Abby, it's not possible that these men willingly inflicted such horrific violence upon themselves. There has to be some other explanation. Perhaps now you can appreciate why I cannot accept their suicides as being anything but the work of some unnatural evil—and why I cannot understand why you are so intent on proving this is not a haunting."

It wasn't lost on Abigail that this was the first time Duncan had called her by her old nickname since she had arrived. She wondered how long it would be before he evoked other mementos of their past as well. "'Tis not a matter of my intentions," she answered delicately. "'Tis a matter of *facts*. A vengeful spirit cannot simply *will* itself into existence. It is born of the soul of someone who has died a violent death. Such was the case when we were both haunted by the spirit of my great-grandmother twenty years ago. They unleashed her vengeful spirit the moment they hanged her during the Salem witch trials. And unless you can tell me otherwise, such an incidence of violence has never been recorded in the history of this village."

Duncan's face was a battlefield of defiance and defeat. For the first time, Abigail saw that the carefree wonder of the boy she had known had been overrun by the fears and duties of manhood.

He let out an exasperated sigh and brushed past her on his way up the trail.

"Duncan." Abigail waited for him to stop and turn. "The first two victims, the ones who killed themselves before Mr. Gill. Are their bodies accessible for exhumation?"

Duncan shook his head. "They buried Jed Hawes somewhere near North Camp. The others were left in shallow graves where they died."

"Who was the last person to be in contact with them?"

"Glenn Colvin."

Chapter 12

Father Elias Carnes still reeked of smoke. The acrid smell clung to the wool of his black cassock as he shrugged it off and hung it behind the door of the chapel's vestry. Later, he would hang it outside to air. The priest's hands were black with soot and he was careful not to further soil his linen shirt as he rolled the cuffs up to his elbows and plunged his hands into his washbowl. The cold water went a murky gray as he washed his palms and fingers clean.

A glance at the chipped mirror on the wall revealed a face that looked drawn and tired beyond Carnes' thirty-three years. White specks of ash sprinkled across his thick, coal-black hair. His beard—long and dense and cut square across the bottom—was now bristling and streaked with grit. Pale green eyes that were usually as striking as stars on a cloudless night were now leaden and encircled with shadowy rings.

Carnes wrung his hands dry and did his best to straighten himself before leaving the vestry and entering the sanctuary of his small chapel. It was still early afternoon, but having spent the morning assisting in the cremation of Chester Prue,

Carnes felt the evening couldn't come soon enough. Even as he knelt before the unassuming altar, he could still smell the stench of Prue's burning corpse. When he closed his eyes, he saw Prue's flesh sizzling and dripping from his fractured bones like rendered fat. Bowing his head, Carnes whispered a silent prayer that he could forget all that he had seen, all that he himself had decreed. With a quiet *amen*, Carnes then stood and turned, hoping the silent peace of the sanctuary might ease his burden.

The chapel was small—perhaps fifty feet long and thirty feet wide—but was large enough to accommodate nine rows of pinewood pews divided by a single aisle. White pine paneling imbued the sanctuary with a light and airy ambiance. Three tall, rectangular windows were set into each of the side walls, ensuring the congregation was always bathed in sunlight: brilliant and yellow from the east in the morning; warm and rich from the west at sunset. Dust motes coasted through the air, materializing and vanishing over and over as they traveled from sunbeam to sunbeam.

Carnes himself had taken part in the construction of the Georgian-style building on his arrival in Tahawus three years ago. The humble country chapel was a far cry from New York's St. Peter's, where he had been an altar boy. But grandiosity wasn't what had drawn Carnes to the priesthood. He had an impoverished childhood in New York's Sixth Ward to thank for his calling. After surviving the squalor of his early years, Carnes had been eager to leave the urban slum behind and escape as far into the wilderness as was possible.

Tahawus was just the place the young priest had imagined.

Carnes moved to the foremost pew where he sat and craned

his head to one side, stretching the aching muscles of his neck and shoulders. Moving Prue's crude coffin from the storage shed to the cremation site hadn't been easy, but Carnes would never have asked Colvin and Josiah to carry out the unpleasant chore on their own. The cremation was *his* decision. Once they had arrived, Carnes himself had insisted on being the one to douse the crate in whale oil and set it ablaze.

Carnes inhaled and tried yet again to shake himself of the memory. Sometimes when the breeze was right, he could still smell the rough-hewn oak of the chapel's framing beams lingering beneath traces of stale incense and musty mountain air. But today, the stillness of mind Carnes craved eluded him. Prue's cremation had been too draining, both physically and emotionally, and he now felt weary and perplexed.

A sound came from somewhere behind him, a shuffling from the rear of the church that roused Carnes from his reflection. He swiveled in the pew to find Evelyn MacIntyre framed in the sunlight of the open door.

"Am I disturbing ye', Father?" she asked. The sunshine at her back wreathed her red hair with a fiery radiance.

"Not at all, Evelyn." Carnes rose to his feet and smoothed his linen shirt. "What brings you here this fine afternoon? The Lord knows we haven't enjoyed many sunny days of late."

"Will ye' hear my confession?" Evelyn asked as she entered and closed the door behind her.

As draining as the morning had been, Carnes still found himself curious. Most of the confessions he heard from the village women involved lustful thoughts directed toward the more handsome of the lumberjacks. Those same bachelors sometimes came to him to confess having snuck into the woods to pleasure themselves. Such was life in an isolated logging town.

But Evelyn MacIntyre was different. Although she had been a dutiful parishioner since arriving in Tahawus with her husband nearly a year ago, never in that time had she attended confession. What could have arisen so abruptly that she now felt the need to unburden herself? Carnes was intrigued despite his fatigue and even welcomed the distraction Evelyn presented. Perhaps hearing her confession would help dull the memory of the grim task from which he had just returned.

"Of course, Evelyn. Please, be seated." Carnes motioned to the empty pew and stood ready to offer his hand to the pregnant woman as she eased onto the bench. Once she was comfortable, he took a seat next to her while she crossed herself and began her confession.

"In the name of the Father, the Son, and the Holy Spirit. My last confession was..." Evelyn hesitated for a moment. "My last confession was nearly three years ago."

Carnes gave her a curious look, but said nothing.

"It has been three years since I committed the sins I am about to confess," Evelyn went on, "and I've only begun to feel contrite."

There was something different about Evelyn this afternoon, a strange solemnity that Carnes had never seen in her before. "Very well," he said. "Do you open your heart to me and welcome me into your soul as your confessor that I may give you absolution?"

"I do, Father."

"Then please continue. Tell me how you have sinned."

Evelyn wavered a moment, as if she had suddenly forgotten her lines in a stage play and was struggling to find the words. "As ye' know, before coming to America, Heath and I lived as farmers in the Old Country. What ye' don't know are the circumstances by which we came to leave our homeland behind."

Carnes gazed at her and listened intently.

"Our land in the parish of Dornoch was owned by Lady Stafford, the Countess of Sutherland. Generations of MacIntyre clansmen had worked the soil before the homestead fell to Heath and I to keep the tradition. The house wasn't much—little more than a hut of thatch and mud, to be sure—but it was to be our own. We were so excited, Father; glad at the prospect of home and family. We were disposed to work hard and pay our due to Lady Stafford as was fair… but the Countess had other plans for the land. Wool fetched a far better price at market than potatoes, and what had forever been the MacIntyre glen was to be sold to sheep farmers from the south."

Evelyn's green eyes traveled up to the altar and remained fixed on the wooden crucifix hanging there. "It was late in the summer of 1808 when the Countess' factor came with his men to evict us from our farm. His name was Patrick Sellar, a cruel and hateful man the likes of which I'll never see again lest I go to Hades and meet the devil himself. Even as I sit here in the Lord's own house, I can find no contrition in my heart for the ill will I've wished the man."

Carnes nodded without judgment. "Please, go on."

"By Sellar's decree, our entire clan was to vacate the land

immediately—nearly forty families all told. We were chosen because we were Catholic and we were to be among the first to be removed to the Countess' properties on the nor'east coast. There, we'd be given a croft of land from which we'd continue to pay our taxes."

Evelyn paused and Carnes noticed a trembling in the breath she took. "As I'm sure you'll understand, Father, our clansmen were fairly at daggers drawing. But when Heath stood firm and refused to give up our farm, Sellar had the roof of our house pulled down and the rooftree set ablaze to prevent us from resurrecting it. He then had the clan's grazing fields razed to starve our cattle. Even now, I can smell the stench of the fires; hear the terrible bellows of the affrighted beasts, the screams of the children, the wails of the elders scrambling to save their meager valuables. Driven out like dogs, we'd no choice but to leave."

A lock of red curls fell over Evelyn's face as she bowed her head and closed her eyes, struggling against the emotions stirring within. A gentle breeze passing through the bell tower high above sent a creak through the ceiling beams.

When she was ready, Evelyn opened her eyes and continued. "The journey from Dornoch to the seacoast was long and difficult—long enough to be the undoing of my ailing mother. We buried her in a rocky grave in the shadow of Dunrobin Castle. When we arrived in Caithness, we found the crofts were rotten and useless for anything but kelping. The Sutherlands continued to profit from our toil, but the work was intolerably hard. Within six months, Heath's father fell ill with fever and we were left to work the kelp alone. No longer able to pay our tribute to our landlords, Heath sought an audience to plead our case before the taxman."

Evelyn's fingers now worried at the folds of her skirt. "Sellar came for us while Heath was gone. I'll not tell you what the vile man did to me on that black day, Father. Indeed, I've vowed never to speak of it again. But I will tell you that when Heath returned, I'd been left homeless to the rain and his father was dead. Such was my misery that I'd a mind to fling myself from the cliffs. It was that very day we decided to make the journey to America... it was also then that I turned from God."

"Under such circumstances, it would be understandable that you should question your faith," Carnes said in a reassuring tone. "Many are the afflictions of the righteous, but the Lord delivereth him out of them all."

"Oh, but I didn't just question my faith, Father. I lost it altogether. On the eve before we were to set sail and leave Scotland forever, I went to the village church to pray for our safe voyage. But I couldn't enter, Father. Even with the tears streaming from my eyes, I couldn't bring myself to cross the threshold." Evelyn's gaze fell to the floorboards and her voice grew soft and quaking. "I know not how the rock came into my hand, but there I found it. My fist closed upon it and I brought it up, ready to shatter the chapel's window, ready to fling another and another and another. But something stayed my hand. Instead, I took the rock and scratched my name into the glass. Heaven forgive me, Father, but I wanted nothing more than to leave my name behind for all to see! A reminder of the poor soul their Lord had forsaken!"

Evelyn sighed. Tears welled in her eyes when she looked Carnes in the face. "I remained wrathful for a very long time.

Chapter 13

Glenn Colvin was sharpening his axe when Abigail found him outside his cabin. The shrill squeal of the grinding wheel scraping against the hardened steel blade echoed through the forest. The afternoon was growing late and sunlight streamed at long slants through the boughs. Shadows were already gathering in the furthest reaches of the woods. The smell of sizzling grease wafted through the village from where the women were preparing dinner in the mess hall.

Colvin's big dog, Timber, sat up and let out a low growl at Abigail's approach. The black fur of his neck bristled, and she knew the dog sensed something different about her. Animals were keenly sensitive to the powers she wielded.

The lumberjack caught Timber's reaction from the corner of his eye and looked up. "Ms. Jacobs," he said with a cool mildness that suggested he had known she was there all along. He rose tall and tested the sharpness of the axe blade with his thumb. "I see you've brought the sunshine with you from Boston. Can't recall when we last had a day such as this."

He flashed her an easy grin, his white teeth gleaming from

beneath his beard. His straight black hair was slick with perspiration, and his flannel shirt was unbuttoned to his navel, revealing his barrel chest and the hard muscles of his stomach. A pair of suspenders kept his breeches from slipping below his trim waist.

The proper thing for a lady to do was to avoid looking at a man so exposed. But Colvin didn't seem to care. He had rolled his sleeves to his elbows and Abigail could see the details of the crude tattoos on his forearms. His left bore the likeness of a howling wolf, a compass rose, and a timber axe. Emblazoned on his right was a long eagle's feather and a circular symbol that Abigail guessed might be Native.

She didn't judge Colvin for having the tattoos as other women might; she had lain with too many sailors to be critical of the custom. Besides, Colvin was young to be a foreman—likely in his early thirties. There must be something remarkable about him to have attained a position of such authority in a lumber camp this large.

"Did Evelyn give you a proper welcome this morning?" Colvin turned the head of the axe over and went to work honing the other side of the blade.

"Very much so." Abigail had to shout over the screech of the grinding stone. The noise was aggravating, and she wondered if it occurred to Colvin that he was being rude.

"Evelyn's a delightful woman, isn't she?" Colvin asked as he continued sharpening.

"Indeed."

"And your first lesson with the children?"

"Very pleasant." Abigail had done little more than learn her pupils' names and discover their knowledge of the alphabet to be nonexistent.

"Glad to hear it," said Colvin. "I hope you'll find the work rewarding, seeing as how you aren't getting paid for it."

"I beg your pardon?"

Colvin removed the blade from the wheel and the irritating grinding came to a halt. "We can't pay you—at least, not yet. Our clerk has no record of your employment with the company. He assures me it's probable your papers will arrive with the next supply wagon."

A spark of alarm went off in Abigail. "When will that be?"

"Hard to say. Four days, maybe six if there's Mohawk trouble in the valley."

Four days.

Somehow, Abigail would have to complete her investigation and get out of Tahawus before the men from Witherbee & Rand arrived. Colvin already seemed suspicious by nature and he didn't know how she would explain herself when the supply wagon arrived with no evidence that she belonged in the village.

"Don't trouble yourself about it," Colvin assured her while testing the blade again. "I'll see that Bingham extends you credit for your needs until this is all straightened out. If you aren't our new schoolteacher, why else would you be here, eh?"

Something about Colvin's last remark made Abigail wary. Did he already suspect her? "Indeed," she agreed. "It's not as if a woman such as myself would venture out here for a holiday."

"No, I suppose not." Satisfied with the sharpness of his axe, Colvin set it aside and slicked his hair straight back from his forehead before helping himself to a seat on an overturned log. He reclined against the timber wall of his cabin and folded one arm over the other across his chest.

"Truthfully, Mr. Colvin, there is a more pressing reason to see you," Abigail said. She watched as Timber sauntered over, curled up next to Colvin's boot, and gazed up at her with deep, amber eyes that very much resembled those of his master.

"Is that so?"

"It concerns a child I met in today's lesson, a young girl named Hannah Gill."

Colvin's face darkened slightly, but he said nothing as he waited for Abigail to go on.

"I understand the girl's father was one of the men who recently committed suicide," she said. "Is that correct?"

"Aye, it is."

"Might I trouble you for some details regarding his demise?"

A look of mistrust crept into Colvin's otherwise passive expression. "Exactly what is your interest here, Ms. Jacobs?"

Abigail had anticipated this question and had her answer ready. "As you may already know, Mr. Colvin, new work being conducted in what Johann Christian Reil has called *psychiatry* has revealed that childhood trauma may have a direct impact on future diseases of the mind."

Predictably, Colvin chuckled to himself and shook his head. "Well now, that is one long sentence you just put together, Ms. Jacobs. Care to simplify it for me?"

"I'm concerned that the death of Hannah's father may compromise her ability to form meaningful relationships with others later in life." The lie came easily to Abigail; She was aware that the same could be said about her. "The more I know about the circumstances of her father's death, the more I may help Hannah cope with his loss."

Colvin uncrossed his arms, reached into the breast pocket of his shirt, and withdrew a single boiled egg. He cracked it against the log on which he sat and started peeling away the shell. "Fair enough. If you think it'll do the poor girl some good, I'll tell you anything you want to know."

Abigail found something amusing about the sight of this brawny mountain man plucking at bits of brown eggshell and stacking them in a neat pile on the ground next to his boot. "Have you any reason to believe Mr. Gill was an unhappy man?" she asked.

"None." Colvin popped the egg into his mouth and devoured half of it with one bite. "Cy had been here since Tahawus was but a nameless, two-shack camp. His wife and daughter were among the first to join us once we'd built the family cabins. Cy kept a mean tweedledee on his fiddle at our monthly dances. He had his hard days just like the rest of us, but otherwise he took to the wilderness as if he'd been born in a burrow." The egg disappeared with a second bite. Colvin gathered the bits of shell from the dirt and deposited them back in his pocket. "Attracts bears," he explained with a wink.

"Bears?"

"Aye. Black ones. Big bastards. The scent of food brings 'em to the village. We've a strict rule against leaving scraps lying about. I hate to shoot the poor beasts simply on account of one of us being too lazy to clean up after himself." Colvin grinned at her as he swallowed.

"Mr. Colvin, why do you think Mr. Gill ended his own life?"

Colvin hunched forward and propped his elbows on his knees. His unyielding gaze seemed to be purposely engaging her defenses. "Out here, there's something we lumberjacks call cabin fever. Have you heard of it?"

"I believe it's madness inspired by prolonged isolation. Am I correct?"

"You are."

"Is that what you believe drove Mr. Gill to set himself ablaze?"

Colvin shrugged. "Life out here will get under your skin if you let it."

"What about the other two men? What can you tell me about them?" This was the trickiest part of Abigail's game. She hoped Colvin wouldn't notice he was being baited.

"You are a curious fox, aren't you, Ms. Jacobs?" Colvin goaded while smoothing Timber's thick coat. The dog rolled onto his side and let out a long and contented sigh at his master's touch.

"I ask only because I may have an alternate explanation for what motivated them to commit suicide," Abigail explained.

Colvin's hand froze in mid-stroke and he cocked an eyebrow. "Is that so? Do tell."

"Are you familiar with ergotism, Mr. Colvin?"

"No, I'm not."

"'Tis a type of poisoning related to the ingestion of contaminated grains. In the Middle Ages, they often referred to it as holy fire or Saint Anthony's fire. Besides some rather horrid physical effects, ergotism can also provoke symptoms such as hallucinations, melancholia, and mania."

"You think four of my men killed themselves because they ate bad grains?"

"I believe it's a scientific possibility worth considering. This morning, Mrs. MacIntyre kindly brought me a loaf of rye bread for breakfast. As it happens, rye is the most common carrier of the ergot fungus. I've also learned that the skirmishes between the Americans and the Indians in the valley have prevented Mr. Bingham from maintaining fresh stocks in the general store. 'Tis possible that his current supply of rye has been tainted from poor storage or shipping conditions."

Colvin's eyes narrowed slightly. "Just what sort of teacher are you, Ms. Jacobs?"

"A very well-educated one. Now, under the circumstances, 'tis entirely possible that your men killed themselves while suffering from the melancholy or mania associated with ergot poisoning."

Colvin ran a hand over the length of his beard. "An interesting theory. How would we test it?"

"As I said, ergotism often manifests physical effects as well as mental. Understandably, we have no way of knowing if Mr. Gill or Mr. Prue presented such symptoms, their corpses having already been destroyed. But Mr. Colvin, I understand you were present for the internments of both Mr. Hawes and Mr. Beaulieu. Tell me, was there anything unusual about their bodies?"

"One man had shot himself in the gut and the other ate half of his own arm. Would that be considered unusual?"

"I mean, aside from their self-inflicted injuries. Were there any strange marks on their flesh? A discoloration of the veins that may have looked like a flower blossoming?"

"Not that I can remember."

"What about any abnormal bruising around their mouths?"

"No."

"Any problems with their eyes?"

"What kind of problems?"

"A sort of cloudy film?"

Colvin shook his head.

That settled it. The gruesome circumstances of each man's suicide were extraordinary, but there hadn't been a single indication of spirit possession among them. Abigail would break the news to Duncan after dinner. Part of her felt liberated by the revelation. While the rash of deaths still remained a mystery, she was at least satisfied that nothing paranatural had driven the men to kill themselves. Tomorrow, she would start working on the problem of getting out of the village before the supply wagon arrived.

"Ms. Jacobs, if my men were under the influence of this poisoning you're speaking of, wouldn't we all be suffering from the same effects?" Colvin asked.

"That would be a fair assumption to make, Mr. Colvin. But based on what you have told me about the lack of physical symptoms presented by the dead men, I would have to conclude that Mr. Bingham's rye is safe after all."

Abigail saw no reason to waste Bingham's supply needlessly. She still had at least one more morning before she figured out a way to leave Tahawus.

And she very much enjoyed a good rye bread.

Chapter 14

Evelyn MacIntyre dreamed that someone was calling her name. The voice seemed to float to her from across a vast ocean. While she slumbered, Evelyn took pleasure in the notion that it was the voice of her homeland calling her back to its craggy shores. It was safe to return; her mother wasn't dead and Heath's father wasn't dead. Both waited for her in the grassy hills of the MacIntyre glen.

Slowly, the lovely voice evolved.

The echo of her name became more vivid, more present, as if Evelyn was rising up from deep waters toward someone standing on a sandy shore above. The voice became so distinct; it transcended her sleep and roused her to wakefulness.

Evelyn sat up in bed.

The small cabin was black around her—too black. An instant passed in confusion before she realized there was no moon. The clouds had closed in and there would be rain again tonight. The fire had gone low in the woodstove and a lonesome breeze whistled through the windowpane.

Evelyn blinked her eyes to clear her head. Her big and burly husband lay slumbering without a care next to her. Heath MacIntyre's face was turned away from her. Only his broad shoulders and the red mop of his head were visible above the quilted blanket. Evelyn watched him as he slept, letting the low rumble of his breathing comfort her in the suffocating darkness.

Without thinking, Evelyn's gaze drifted across the room to where the shape of a baby's cradle stood in the gloom. Heath had spent a week's worth of nights crafting it by the dim light of a lantern behind their cabin. The sturdy oak would last their family for generations to come. Evelyn imagined the cradle becoming a family heirloom, the only one they now possessed.

With a sigh, Evelyn lay back on her pillow and slid a hand under the blanket. Her palm brushed lightly over her swollen and tender breasts as she brought it to rest on her belly. Should she and Heath be blessed enough to have a boy, they would name the child Eadan in memory of Heath's father. The child would continue the MacIntyre name in their new home of America. The thought comforted Evelyn as she kept her palm where it was and waited for a kick.

None came.

Evelyn...

She froze.

This time, it wasn't a dream. Someone had spoken her name.

A cold prickle of fear stole over Evelyn as she lay there on her back. The voice was hushed and ephemeral, as if the wind itself were whispering to her.

And yet, she had heard it as clearly as she heard Heath's slumbering breaths rising from the pillow next to her.

Evelyn...

Evelyn's heart lurched and constricted. She knew that voice! She hadn't heard it for many, many years, but she knew it nonetheless.

It was the voice of an old, old woman.

It was that of her mother.

An icy tingle crawled across Evelyn's flesh. It wasn't possible! Evelyn herself had wrapped her mother's body in its winding sheet. She had seen the milky whites of her mother's dead eyes and shuddered at the hideous grin spread across the face of her mother's stiffening corpse. She had sunk to the ground and sobbed at her mother's lifeless feet.

Hear me, Evelyn...

The voice came to her once more, calling to her from somewhere beyond the timber walls of the cabin.

Somewhere out in the forest.

"Mother?" Even as the whisper escaped Evelyn's lips, she couldn't believe she had uttered it. She kept telling herself it wasn't possible, but the sound of her mother's voice was too real, too warm and inviting. How she missed that voice! How she missed the comfort it evoked, the sweet memories of youth and safety it rekindled. Tears sprung to Evelyn's eyes. She had thought she would never again hear that kind and soothing voice.

Come to me, Evelyn...

Careful not to wake her husband, Evelyn slipped from beneath the blanket and stood next to the bed. For a brief instant, she became conscious of what she was doing. Why had she risen? What was it about the voice that had drawn her to her feet? *This isn't possible*, she reminded herself. It had to be a trick; whatever was calling her name wasn't her mother. Her mother was dead, buried in a miserable grave far, far away.

Ancient stories sprang into Evelyn's mind; stories she had heard as a child in the Old World. She recalled dreadful tales of the *caioneag*, a weeping spirit whose wails in the night portended catastrophe and death. What if her mother's voice suddenly twisted into a ghastly wail? What if the *caioneag* had come for her?

What if it had come for her baby?

Evelyn crossed herself and whispered a prayer. She could feel her heart thudding in her chest. Sweat sprang to her palms.

Don't be afraid, my child...

Her mother's voice again. Soothing. Comforting.

The words banished Evelyn's fears as if she were once more a young girl. She wanted it to be true, she wanted it to be possible. She knew she should wake Heath, but she didn't make a move. She looked at the candle on the nightstand, but didn't light it. She didn't know why, but she remained there in the darkness, ears pricked, listening for the call, listening for the gentle whisper of her mother's voice.

Come...

Evelyn didn't pause to throw a shawl over her chemise as she moved toward the door. She heard Heath stir in his sleep as the hinges creaked open. Had she woken him? Evelyn no longer cared. She didn't feel the chill of the breeze against her bare skin as she slipped from the cabin into the night.

Her mother's voice had come from somewhere out here, calling to her, compelling her to follow it to its source… to follow it into the forest.

Here, Evelyn…

Evelyn no longer questioned what she was doing as she turned and strode past the cabin, seeking the sweet, sweet sound of her mother calling to her. A gust of wind blew fallen leaves against her face, but she paid them no mind. She paused behind the cabin. Heath's tools were there, laid out on his workbench. What were they doing there? Heath would never have left them exposed to the elements. The steel would rust in the rain…

Bring it to me, Evelyn…

Evelyn's hand closed on the hacksaw.

Aye. Now come…

Her mother's call was insistent and magnetic as it drew Evelyn ever deeper into the blackness of the forest. Evelyn couldn't resist going to it, even as the snarls of underbrush bit and tore at her legs. The hacksaw was weightless in her hand as she moved between the trees.

It was raining now, a fine drizzle that landed softly and saturated all that it fell upon. When had the rain started? How long had she been pursuing the voice through the trees? It was cold, but Evelyn didn't feel the rising hardness of her nipples as they brushed against her wet chemise. She no longer felt anything, no longer heard anything but the lovely call of her mother beckoning her further from her home, leading her deeper and deeper into the forest.

Suddenly, she stopped.

She had arrived.

Evelyn stood in an empty hollow. Her breath blossomed in the cold as the rain fell upon her. A limitless blackness stretched away from her in all directions. How had she ever found her way out here? She didn't know why, but she was certain this was the place. This is where she had been meant to come.

This is where her mother was.

"Why have ye' brought me here?" Evelyn asked aloud. The sound of her own voice echoing in the silence seemed distant, detached, surreal. Maybe she had never woken up. Could she still be sleeping? It all *seemed* like a dream.

But the rain... the rain was so real, so cold.

I've come to save you, my daughter...

"Save me from what?"

Your baby...

Evelyn stiffened. "What about my baby?"

'Tis going to kill you...

"No. That's not true." Evelyn's mind recoiled, but she couldn't silence her mother's voice.

'Tis already dead inside you, Evelyn. You don't feel it kick because it's dead...

"No! Don't ye' say that!"

'Tis gonna kill you too, deary. 'Tis gonna split you wide open when it comes out and you're going to bleed and bleed and bleed...

"Don't say that!" But secretly, Evelyn knew her mother spoke the truth. Her baby never kicked. It hadn't kicked in weeks.

Her baby was dead. And soon, Evelyn would be too.

Listen to your mother, child. When the time comes, it's gonna split you so wide, nobody's gonna be able to sew you back up. It's gonna take you hours to die... and oh, how you'll suffer, deary. Such unspeakable suffering...

"Please stop, Mother. Please, please, please..."

You'll suffer if you don't save yourself, child...

"How?" Evelyn moaned.

You have to cut it out of you before it's too late.

"No!" Evelyn cried, even as she came to realize that she had to do it. Her baby was dead; there was only one way to save herself.

Cut it out, Evelyn! Save yourself!

Evelyn closed her eyes and took a deep breath. Rain dripped from her fingertips as she lowered her hand and lifted her sodden chemise.

In one swift motion, she ran the hacksaw across her belly.

That's it! Cut it out! Cut it out! Save yourself!

Over and over, Evelyn sawed at her flesh, barely flinching as the steel teeth dug further and further into her womb. Blood washed down her legs and felt warm and welcome in the cold, cold rain. Evelyn didn't scream, didn't cry. There was no pain, only the loving embrace of her mother's voice.

Save yourself! Save yourself!

Chapter 15

The man's anguished wails carried across the morning stillness and ripped through the village. Abigail rushed toward their source, the cries growing ever louder as she sped past the cabins and shacks and plunged into the thick forest beyond.

Dawn had come. It was gray and dreary, as if the previous day's sunshine had been nothing but an uninvited guest. The overnight drizzle had just ended and a heavy mist now dampened Abigail's coat as she dashed through the woods. Ahead, she could spy the dark shapes of men materializing from the gloom as the echoes of a dog's furious barking ricocheted off the trees. Seconds later, she arrived at a small hollow where Glenn Colvin and Josiah Benedict were grappling with a giant, distraught lumberjack. Colvin's dog snarled and nipped at the big man's kicking feet.

Dressed only in breeches and a soiled undershirt, the lumberjack's broad face twisted with grief as he thrashed and struggled. His long red hair was a bedraggled mess and his thick goatee was scruffy and askew. His steely eyes were bloodshot, and streams of tears ran across his florid cheeks.

Gobs of spittle fell from his lips and flecked his hairy chin as he sobbed and howled incoherently.

Beyond the struggling men, the motionless form of a body lay concealed beneath a canvas sheet on the forest floor. A wicker basket sat on the ground nearby. Blood soaked the surrounding leaves, as if they had all fallen from the same crimson tree. Abigail could smell the coppery stink of it hanging thick in the crisp morning air.

"Leave her be, Heath!" Colvin grimaced as he fought to restrain the grief-stricken man. "Give Ned some time to find out what happened!"

Duncan Emmons hovered on the periphery of the hollow. His expression was grim as he observed a slight man with a bushy moustache and wire spectacles who was crouched beside the inert shape on the ground. The man's hand shook as he lifted the bloodstained sheet and peered beneath.

Abigail went to Duncan's side. "Another suicide?" she whispered.

Duncan nodded, his breath quavering as he drew it in and let it out. "Evelyn MacIntyre."

Abigail couldn't contain a gasp. "What happened?"

Duncan inclined his head toward the crazed man, still struggling to free himself from Colvin and Josiah. "Heath awoke before sunrise and she was gone. He picked up a trail outside his cabin. It led him here, where he... he found her."

The man with the spectacles lowered the canvas sheet and stood up.

"Ned Fitch," Duncan explained. "He's the closest we have to a physician out here. Spent a few years as an infantry medic."

Duncan turned as Fitch came toward them. Abigail could see the physician's pointed face had drained of all color.

"What happened to her, Ned?" Duncan asked.

Fitch gave a morose shake of his head and glanced back over his shoulder. "She did it herself, as far as I can tell."

"Did what?"

Fitch cast a sidelong look at Abigail and hesitated.

"It's alright, Ned," Duncan said. "This is Abigail Jacobs, the schoolteacher. Ms. Jacobs worked as a nurse in Boston. You can speak freely in front of her."

Abigail winced. She hoped this wouldn't be yet another lie that haunted her.

"Ned? What did Evelyn do to herself?" Duncan prodded.

"She... she cut her baby out."

Abigail's stomach filled with ice at the realization of what lay within the basket on the ground.

There was a sudden shout as Heath MacIntyre broke loose from Josiah's grip. Colvin lunged for him, but Heath swung around and caught him with a blow to the jaw that sent the foreman sprawling through the underbrush.

Timber sprang with an angry snarl and clamped his jaws around Heath's forearm, drawing blood. The lumberjack shook the dog off just as Josiah tackled him to the ground. Heath roared, but in a flash, Josiah had his knife drawn and pressed to the big man's throat. And yet, even as the sharp blade pricked Heath's skin, it seemed as if the weapon wouldn't stop him. Heath was too wild with grief, too inconsolable to care for his own life.

"Josiah!" Colvin's bottom lip was split and a trail of blood dribbled through his beard as he dragged himself to his feet.

"Let him go, Josiah."

Colvin stood waiting while Josiah lowered the knife from Heath's throat. The Native's black eyes narrowed dangerously as the lumberjack picked himself from the dirt.

"Go to her if you want, Heath," Colvin said as the big man started toward him. "We're not going to stop you. But I'm begging you to go home. You've seen enough here. You don't need to see anymore."

Heath slowed and drew to a halt within striking distance of Colvin. Abigail tensed as the massive lumberjack stood towering over the foreman.

But then, Heath just seemed to crumble. He sank to his knees, hung his head, and wept, his broad shoulders quaking with his sobs.

Colvin laid a hand on Heath's bulky arm. "You've done all you can here, Heath. You can't do anything more for her. Let us take care of her now. We'll bring her back to you."

Colvin made a motion and Josiah lent a hand in hauling the big man to his feet. For an instant, Colvin glanced in Abigail's direction and his eyes caught hers. Then he turned and led Heath from the hollow. The sound of the lumberjack's hoarse moans echoed through the trees and faded away into the distance.

Duncan exchanged a few more words with Ned Fitch before returning to Abigail's side. Minutes passed as they stood together in silence, each consumed with thoughts every bit as dark and cheerless as their surroundings. Soon, another man arrived with a long plank that he and Fitch would use as a litter to transport Evelyn's corpse.

Duncan was the first to speak. "Tell me honestly, Abby.

Have you ever seen anything like this?"

Abigail didn't need to think about it. She shook her head.

"Do you still believe there is nothing paranatural about this?"

An image flew into Abigail's mind. She saw Evelyn as she had been just yesterday: bright and joyful in the autumn sunlight; grinning easily and glowing with the bliss of expectant motherhood. What had changed overnight? What could have driven the woman to such a ghastly fate?

"No," Abigail replied at last. "You were right, Duncan. Something terrible is going on here. I just don't know what it is."

"I believe I might," Duncan whispered while the two other men lifted Evelyn's corpse and conveyed it to the litter. "Meet me at the company office in one hour. I've discovered something I think you'll find extremely interesting."

Chapter 16

Maps had fascinated Duncan Emmons for as long as he could remember. His grandfather had been a prominent sea captain and privateer during the War of Independence. In retirement, the old man had established a quaint Museum of Natural History in his home port of Salem. It was there, surrounded by his grandfather's collected curiosities of the world, that Duncan had experienced his first dreams of adventure. As a young boy, nothing symbolized the spirit of adventure like a map. Nothing else could so clearly delineate the frontiers between the known world and the mysterious; the mundane from the wondrous; safety from peril.

Now Abigail sipped a cup of coffee and watched as her childhood friend went to his own collection of maps. There were dozens of them, each chart rolled and tucked into a special rack against the back wall of the company office. By comparison, the rest of the stuffy room was a clutter of Witherbee & Rand's files and records. The space smelled of musty parchment and book bindings. A pale slant of colorless sunlight through the only window showed it was not yet midday. They had less than an hour before the company clerk returned from the errand Duncan had sent him on.

"Here it is," Duncan said.

As he turned from the rack to the battered length of the worktable, it surprised Abigail to see he held not a map, but an old company ledger he had hidden within the rack.

"I've been thinking about what you said about vengeful spirits being born of violent deaths," Duncan said. His eyes shone with excitement as he clutched the ledger. "As it turns out, Jed Hawes wasn't the first man to die in the northern range."

Abigail paused her sip of coffee. "I beg your pardon?"

"Nearly fifty years ago, a band of Mohawk warriors brought two Black Robes to the hunting grounds of these mountains."

"Black Robes? Do you mean Jesuits? Missionaries?"

Duncan gave an eager nod. "Their names were Edmund and Sebastian Legendre. They were brothers who came to the Mohawk to spread the word of the Christian God. On the third night of their hunt, the warriors brought the brothers to the edge of a lake high in the mountains. There, the Mohawk turned on the missionaries and lashed the brothers to two sturdy trees."

"Why did the Mohawk betray them?"

Duncan's tone grew ever more animated as he warmed to the tale. "It was a test of the Christian God. If the brothers could survive seven moons on the shore of that desolate lake, the Mohawk would see it as proof that the white man's God was as powerful as the missionaries claimed."

"What became of them?"

"Both were dead when the Mohawk returned. But somehow, the younger brother, Sebastian, had freed himself. Only instead of escaping, he had murdered his elder brother before taking his own life."

"How?"

"He had crushed Edmund's skull with a heavy rock. He then skewered both of his own eyes with his crucifix. When the Mohawk examined his tracks and realized what he had done, they saw the land as cursed and never returned."

Abigail eyed him skeptically while she considered his story. "How exactly did you happen to come by this information?"

Duncan grinned, his expression now lit and impassioned. "I had begun to despair that you were right about the suicides until I came upon an obscure reference buried in one of Witherbee & Rand's earliest prospecting records." Duncan laid the ledger upon the worktable and flipped it open to a bookmarked page. "It's all here. Decades ago, a company scout named Tad Seymour recalled the sad fate of a pair of Jesuit missionaries in the company of a band of Mohawk warriors. Don't you see, Abby? Jed Hawes killed himself on the shore of the very lake where the Legendre brothers died! This is the revelation we've been waiting for! Perhaps it is *their* spirits who are responsible for our suicides!"

Abigail went quiet as she reviewed the entry in the ledger. Something about Duncan's account struck her as suspicious. It seemed too neat and tidy—and this case was anything but clean-cut.

And yet, Duncan wouldn't have invented it to further his own conviction that the suicides resulted from a haunting. Abigail could see for herself that someone had carefully recorded all the details. The ledger itself was authentic. Still, if the old tale was true, there remained the troubling fact that none of the suicides displayed any evidence of paranatural influence. If the spirit of either Legendre brother drove the victims to take their own lives, how were they doing it? And more importantly, how could they be stopped?

"This lake," Abigail said at last. "Show me where it is."

Duncan spun to the rack of maps, separated a long roll from the others, and brought it to the worktable, pinning the corners with stones to keep them from curling. "There," he said, stabbing a finger at a spot.

Abigail leaned over the table and was struck by how stark this map was. Unlike Duncan's other works, which were flawless in their precision and rendered with an exacting attention to detail, this chart bore only some rudimentary indications of landmarks.

"I've yet to survey the land that far to the north personally," Duncan explained with chagrin. "That's why Hawes was sent ahead. He was to scout the terrain before I charted it. What you see here is merely a crude approximation based on what Glenn Colvin could describe upon his discovery of Hawes' body. I'm afraid this map isn't nearly to scale. The cliff where they found Hawes is over ten miles from here, a gruelling journey through tough forest up the sheer side of the Cloudsplitter."

Abigail stood up and sipped her coffee. "Perhaps there is something else linking the suicides to each other, something we aren't seeing."

"Such as?"

Abigail raised her cup again and realized it was empty. "It

could be anything," she said as she went for the pot on the stove. "Even the slightest commonality could be significant, something as trivial as, say, the water they drank."

"We all take our water from the same river." Duncan traced his finger along a long, meandering line that snaked its way across the entire length of the map from top to bottom, shrinking and widening as it passed through chasms and opened into small lakes along the way.

The name inscribed on the chart surprised Abigail. "The Hudson?"

Duncan nodded. "From what I've been able to discern, this same river eventually flows all the way to New York, where it drains into the Atlantic." He allowed himself a smile; faint, but proud. "This discovery has been among my most significant. The headwater of the mighty Hudson must be somewhere up there to the north, among the tallest of the peaks. Eventually, I hope to discover it."

Abigail smiled. For his sake, she hoped he did, too. "What of the victims' nationalities?"

"Hawes was born American; Beaulieu a Frenchman; Gill was Irish; Prue also American; and Evelyn, Scottish."

"Two Americans. There isn't enough commonality there. Religion?"

"As far as I know, all were Catholic."

Abigail looked up. "All?"

"As is most of the village, Abby. It's what draws so many immigrants out here; they feel safe among other Catholics. I'm afraid any link between the suicides in that regard cannot even be considered coincidence."

Abigail frowned. He was right. She was grasping at straws.

"There is one commonality between the victims that we haven't yet considered," Duncan suggested.

"What is it?"

"Colvin and Josiah."

"How so?"

"They are the only ones to have had contact with each of the victims' bodies."

Abigail went quiet and sank into a chair as she considered the implications. Could Duncan be on to something? Could they link either of those two men to the suicides? And if so, how? "What else do you know about those lands to the north?" she asked.

"Very little. Josiah calls the area *anachaju*."

"What does that mean?"

"It's Mohican for *empty*."

This struck Abigail as odd. "Josiah is from the Penobscot tribe. Why would he use the Mohican word?"

Duncan shrugged. "Who can say what goes on in his head? Josiah doesn't speak much to anyone but Colvin."

Abigail returned her attention to the crude map laid out on the table. "Empty..." she mused.

"Here there be monsters," Duncan murmured, quoting the old sailor's adage for what lay beyond the limits of the known world. His gaze fell upon Abigail's face and saw the fatigue of her sleepless nights gathered there. "We're running out of time. We must act quickly; we've only seven days until Chauncey returns for you."

Abigail let out a weary sigh as she sat and rested the back of her head against the wall. "We've only two days."

Duncan's eyes snapped up. "I beg your pardon?"

"In two days, a supply wagon will arrive from Witherbee & Rand. When there's no record of my employment with the company, Glenn Colvin will have even more reason to suspect I'm not what I seem."

"We needn't worry about that, Abby. We can always stall for time until—"

"There's something else, Duncan. Something I haven't told you."

A look of apprehension slid over Duncan's face. "What is it?"

"The night when I snuck into the shed to examine Prue's body... somebody saw me."

Duncan stared at her in disbelief. "What do you mean by *somebody?*"

Abigail told him everything: her certainty that the stranger had been a man; that he had seen her but had let her go; that the man hadn't revealed himself or exposed her secret in more than a day.

When she finished, there was something about the way Duncan was looking at her—a scornful condescension in his glare—that was worse than anything he could have said. A spark of anger smoldered within her. "I don't require your protection, Duncan," she said, her voice low and icy. "I never have."

"This isn't a matter of protection, Abby. It's a matter of being—"

"Cautious? You say that, Duncan, but it isn't true. This isn't about being cautious."

"Then what else could it possibly be about?"

"'Tis about you trying to turn me away from the dark path

I have chosen, just as you always have."

"Abby, that's not true."

"Yes it is, Duncan. Don't you see? Ever since I arrived here, you've been searching for ways to keep me from having anything to do with witchcraft." Abigail could feel her heart racing now, her blood throbbing in her temples. Now that she had started down this path, she found she couldn't stop. Why should she? It would all come out eventually, anyway. A dam had broken somewhere inside her and, all at once, eight years of resentment came rushing out like a flood.

"You have always wondered why I wouldn't marry you, Duncan. Why I went so far as to leave Salem after you proposed. Ever since that night long ago, when you discovered the dark secrets of my family history, you have been trying to convince me to renounce my calling. You can't stand what I've become and you would like nothing better than for me to give it up so that we might be together. You believe you're protecting me from myself, but it is *you* who needs protecting, Duncan! As long as you are by my side, you are in danger for your life because of what I do—because of what I *am*. 'Tis why I had to leave Salem! I had to leave you behind so that you might marry Emily, as you should have all along! With me gone, you had a chance at a normal life, a life of children and safety and comfort. You've taken that chance and you've done well for it. You've a wife who loves you in ways that I never could and you've two beautiful boys such as I could never give you. You should cherish the life you have chosen… and you should leave me to live my own."

Duncan's gaze dropped to the map on the table. He said nothing.

In the long silence that followed, Abigail noticed the steady ticking of a clock on a shelf. She wanted nothing more than to smash it. She knew she had wounded Duncan deeply.

After what seemed like an eternity, he looked up. "Abigail, I —"

A scream erupted from somewhere outside.

Chapter 17

Hannah Gill lay motionless on the muddy street. A stream of women and children were already rushing to the girl as Abigail and Duncan hurried from the company office.

"Make way!" Duncan cried. "Stand back!"

The knot of bystanders loosened enough for Abigail to kneel by Hannah. The five-year-old was unconscious, pale, barely breathing.

"Duncan! Bring hot water!" Abigail shouted. Duncan spun and dashed back to the company office as Abigail whirled to the nearest onlookers. "You! Find this girl's mother! You two! Go to my cabin! Fetch the black trunk you find there!"

The women exchanged looks.

"Go now!" Abigail thundered before returning her attention to Hannah.

The flesh around the unconscious girl's eyes was swelling, as were her lips and throat. Her skin was as white as porcelain. And yet, even as Abigail watched, a web of pale, red bumps was spreading up from Hannah's chest and across her throat. The girl's breaths came in wheezing fits as if she were suffocating. Abigail would have to work quickly before the girl's throat constricted and cut off her air. Where the hell was Duncan?

"She's dying!" A voice cried from the crowd.

Abigail ignored the cry; she wouldn't let this little girl die. She knew she could save her—she *knew* it. She gathered a handful of stones from the ground and lay them along Hannah's body.

"What are you doing?" Another woman shouted.

Abigail paid her no attention as she laid more stones, not stopping until she had formed a straight line from Hannah's forehead to her waist. A hand grabbed for Abigail's shoulder, but she shrugged it off. Years of hard-won instinct had taken control of her actions. She lay her hands on Hannah's body, closed her eyes, and chanted.

At that moment, Duncan broke through the crowd, breathing hard, a tin kettle in his hand. His expression fell at the sight of Abigail. "Abby, no!"

It was too late.

An intoxicating power tingled Abigail's flesh, coursing through her veins, heightening her senses. She was helpless to stop it. Instead, she opened herself to it, giving herself over, submitting to its energy and feeling it wrap around her. In it, she found love and invincibility.

A shocked gasp escaped the crowd.

The stones on Hannah's body were glowing an otherworldly green.

Abigail continued her chant, oblivious to the horrified stares of the surrounding women. The words she spoke were soft and sibilant, like a melody sung in some unearthly language. As if possessed of a life of their own, the stones aligned on Hannah's body slid away and slipped back to the ground at the girl's side. More stones flew aside as if whisked away by an invisible hand. Within moments, only a single glowing stone remained perched above Hannah's left hip.

Abigail ceased her chant and opened her eyes. Heedless of the stunned hush that had settled over the crowd, she tore open the buttons of Hannah's tunic to expose her bare skin. There, a small red welt lay directly beneath where the last stone had been.

Abigail felt a momentary relief as her eyes fell upon the mark and recognized it for what it was. She could cure this; she could save the girl.

But there wasn't much time left. Even now, Hannah's breathing was going from hoarse to faint. Soon, it would stop altogether. There was a shout and the gathering around Abigail parted. Her head snapped up to find the two women returning with her trunk.

"Quickly! Bring it to me!"

The women hurried to obey, laboring and fumbling with the weight of the coffer in their haste. Imported from the Orient over a century ago, the trunk was black as night, its exotic wood carved to depict a timeless battle among pagan deities. Although two intricate wrought-iron straps bound it at each end, the chest presented no visible lock. Instead, inlaid into its flat lid was a square iron plate comprising over a dozen smaller, overlapping square panels—a Chinese puzzle lock.

Abigail went to work at the puzzle, sliding each panel up and down and side to side in a memorized sequence. Seconds later, she solved the problem and slid the final panel aside to reveal a five-dial combination lock. Instead of numbers, each tiny dial was engraved with strange characters that very few could identify as symbols from ancient Chinese cosmology. Abigail aligned the characters into the proper order, sprung the lock, and swung open the lid.

Inside the trunk was an eclectic assortment of arcane objects, vials, and books. Abigail combed through them until she uncovered what she was looking for. She snatched the small vial, spun, and found Duncan in her way.

"Don't, Abby," he whispered. "It's not too late. We can still explain this."

"Would you have me let this girl die?" Abigail hissed. "Will you explain *that* to her mother?" She grabbed the kettle from Duncan's grip and emptied a mixture of foul-smelling herbs from the vial. She then lifted the girl's head and dribbled the pungent liquid into Hannah's slack mouth.

"Stop her!" A woman cried. There was a rustling of movement and Abigail braced herself, ready to fight them off if necessary. Her potion would work—she *knew* it would. She just needed a few more seconds…

But her time had run out.

Hannah had stopped breathing.

There was a moment of stasis—of clear, silent shock. Abigail's stomach went hollow with disbelief. Her heart hammered against her ribcage, and her chest constricted. What had she done wrong?

"She's killed her!" A voice shrieked.

Pandemonium erupted.

Abigail felt their rough hands upon her, seizing her,

dragging her to her feet. There was a riot of angry cries and miserable wails and fingernails tearing at her. Somewhere in the tumult, Abigail could hear Duncan shouting to be heard. She had a vague sense that she should defend herself, but she was too stunned. How could her potion have failed?

Then—very suddenly—Hannah's eyes flew wide.

Another gasp rippled across the crowd as the girl rolled onto her hands and knees and opened her mouth. A rush of bile spewed out like a broken spigot, pooling in the dirt beneath her face and spreading out to her planted hands. When it ended, Hannah collapsed to her side and blinked in confusion at the people gathered around her.

"We… we were just playing…" she said in a voice that was soft and meek.

The women closed around her like a swarm.

"Hannah!" The girl's mother broke through the crowd, panting as she raced to her daughter. She was middle-aged with strawberry-blond hair and tears streaming from her eyes as she swept Hannah into her arms.

The hands clamped on Abigail's shoulders released and she exhaled with relief until her gaze found the severe man standing over her open trunk. He was clad in a black cassock, his beard cut straight across the bottom, his eyes the palest shade of green.

Father Carnes.

Every one of Abigail's arcane books, objects, and talismans lay exposed in the black trunk at the priest's feet. She felt a terrible sinking in her gut as he lowered his cold green eyes and gazed at her. No matter what Duncan might think, there would be no explaining her way out of this.

Chapter 18

The only times Abigail visited churches was to steal holy water. She now felt like an animal trapped in a cage as she marched down the aisle that divided the nave of Tahawus's small chapel, her boot-heels echoing off the walls.

Father Carnes shut the chapel door and followed close behind. Tucked beneath his arm was an ancient, crimson-bound book he had seized from Abigail's trunk. "A bee sting?" he demanded with veiled skepticism.

Abigail halted before the altar at the head of the aisle. "Indeed. I suspect Hannah was playing in the woods when she was stung."

"The watchtower," Carnes muttered.

"I beg your pardon?"

"The children were likely playing in the old watchtower. It's a derelict hut on a bluff overlooking the lake. The camp settlers put it there to guard against Indians, but they haven't manned it in years. Ever since the children discovered it, we can't keep them away from it." Carnes leveled his pale green eyes on Abigail. "You would have me believe a common bee precipitated such dire effects on the girl?"

"The insect's venom provoked an adverse reaction that threatened her life," Abigail explained. "Such reactions are uncommon, to say the least, but they can be quite fatal. Fortunately for her, I am familiar with a treatment."

Carnes' brow furrowed. "Witchcraft."

"No, science. *That…*" Abigail pointed to the crimson book in Carnes' hands. "That is witchcraft."

Abigail took a momentary pleasure in the stunned look Carnes gave her. Of all the strange and terrible items in her collection, the book the priest held was her most treasured possession. The crimson leather of its binding glistened like blood even in the cold light of day. Exquisite filigree graced its surface and a five-pointed pentacle stood embossed at its center. Two iron latches affixed to the book covers kept the brittle pages locked away from prying eyes.

Carnes turned the book over in his hands to examine the black pentacle emblazoned on its cover. "What exactly is this volume, Ms. Jacobs?"

"'Tis my Book of Shadows."

"I beg your pardon?"

"'Tis my grimoire, my spell book. Contained within its pages is an extensive compendium on the occult, witchcraft, and the paranatural—an enduring chronicle of magic and horrors passed on through the ages from witch to witch. It is old—*very* old. I can only imagine how many hands it passed through before it found its way to me."

Carnes arched an eyebrow as he studied the book. "So you freely admit to being a witch?"

"A necromancer, actually. But *witch* rolls off the tongue so much more easily."

"I see." Carnes raised his eyes from the book and motioned to the nearest pew. "Please be seated, Ms. Jacobs."

Abigail didn't move. Her instincts told her to be wary, to be ready to resort to violence if necessary. Carnes might be young for a priest, but his words commanded the following of practically the entire village. If he condemned her publicly, there was no telling what his congregation would do to her.

And yet, Carnes' calm demeanor gave Abigail nothing by which to glean his motivations. Until he gave her a reason to think otherwise, the wisest course of action seemed to be cooperation. She gathered her skirt, lowered herself onto the bench, and glanced around, trying to piece together a plan of escape. She found very few options. The church felt oppressive, the only light being the gray of the sunlight through the large windows.

"Might I ask how were you able to cure the child?" Carnes' tone was relaxed as he stood before her and examined the latches that sealed her Book of Shadows. Abigail kept a watchful eye on him. Her muscles vibrated in anticipation of the thrashing she would give him if he dared to pry the latches open.

"Once I had diagnosed her ailment, I was able to apply my knowledge of herb lore to prepare a suitable remedy," she replied.

Carnes glanced up. "Herb lore?"

Abigail gave an impertinent smirk. "Science."

"Witchcraft... Science... Men of my faith often fail to see the difference."

"Science manipulates the natural world; witchcraft

manipulates the *paranatural* world. I have no intention of denying I am a witch, Mr. Carnes. A simple divination spell allowed me to locate the nature and location of Hannah's injury. What you witnessed was the invisible hand of a Familiar working at my command."

"A Familiar?"

"A spirit from beyond the Veil that I have bound to my service."

"Ah, I see…" Carnes said in a mocking tone. "And if I remember my fairy tales correctly, witches were believed to bear marks from where they suckled such creatures. Am I correct?"

Abigail returned Carnes' steady gaze as she leaned forward on the bench and extended her wrists and palms, revealing the crisscrossing scars that marred the milky white of her skin.

"Blood offerings." Abigail's blue eyes twinkled with amusement at the apprehension that bloomed on the priest's bearded face. "Make no mistake, Mr. Carnes. Witchcraft *did* play a part in saving that little girl's life. I am here, far from my home, to save *all* of your lives. You are free to judge me as you see fit, but I will no longer hide what I am."

Carnes still clutched the ancient book in his hands as he stared at her. "You say you are here to save us. From what, exactly?"

"From whatever is driving your people to kill themselves."

Carnes' eyes narrowed and remained on her for a long time. "This paranatural world you speak of. Can you explain it to me?"

Abigail's instincts went on the defensive, even as she

wondered if she had misjudged the priest. There was something disarming about him, a genuine earnestness that seemed to belie his reserved demeanor. Could Carnes be open-minded enough to believe her? Even so, could he be trusted?

"Mr. Carnes, what if I were to tell you there exist colors we cannot perceive because of the limitations of the human eye?" Abigail ventured. "Sounds we cannot hear because of the failings of the mortal ear? Would you say such things do not exist simply because we cannot experience them?"

Carnes remained silent, his face neutral as he waited for more.

"We can say the same about the world that surrounds us," Abigail went on. "All around us, there is another realm, an invisible world of spirits and monsters. It exists simultaneously to ours, separated by an unseen Veil but occupying the same time and space. Its inhabitants move unseen around us, and yet we cannot experience this world because of the failings of human perception. Witchcraft allows us to pierce through the Veil, to make the invisible visible and interact with the paranatural for good or for evil."

Carnes gave her a dubious look. "Spirits? Monsters? I don't believe in such things."

"Unfortunately, their existence does not require your belief, Mr. Carnes."

There was a soft pattering at the windows as the rain started again. Carnes pursed his lips beneath his beard, the creases of his forehead coming together in contemplation above his dark eyebrows. "Let us assume you are being truthful. How is it these entities can enter our world?"

"The Veil is a window between the two realms. Sometimes creatures can slip through... and sometimes they are *invited*."

"You mean conjured."

Abigail nodded once.

Carnes drew a deep breath and exhaled as he turned to the altar. "I don't know how I am to trust the truth of any of this. The Book of John tells us the only wisdom that witchcraft can offer is earthly, unspiritual, demonic. Only the wisdom of God can be believed, not that of deceiving spirits."

"I'm sorry you feel that way, Mr. Carnes." Abigail's patience finally reached its limit. There was a razor's edge to her voice as she stood from the bench. "I find this conversation is growing tiresome. If you intend to exile me, then kindly stop wasting my time and do it now. I should warn you, however, that if you intend to inflict some harsher judgment, I will do everything in my considerable power to defend myself."

Carnes held up a hand. "Calm yourself, Ms. Jacobs. You're no less welcome here now than on the day you arrived."

"I beg your pardon?"

"I have no intention of condemning you." A mirthless smile crossed the priest's face.

"May I ask why not?"

"Because evidently I need your help—*we* need your help." Carnes gave a weary sigh as he took a seat on the pew. "Yesterday morning, Evelyn MacIntyre came to confession for the first time since her arrival in Tahawus. We sat together in this very pew. She told me she was happy here, that she felt as if God had blessed her in her new home. But now, only a day later, she is dead by her own hand."

Carnes paused and bowed his head. "Five of my flock are

now dead, Ms. Jacobs. Despite everything that I hold to be true, I cannot help but believe that some evil hand is at work in this village. If there is any truth to what you say—if you can somehow shed some light on whatever malevolent darkness afflicts us—then we are in no position to refuse. Indeed, we would be in your debt."

Abigail gave him a mistrustful look. "What of the rest of your congregation? What will they make of your decision to harbor a professed witch among your parishioners?"

Carnes gave her a sage smile. "They will understand if I ask them to, Ms. Jacobs. From what I hear, Ned Fitch is already under the impression that you were once a nurse. Gossip sometimes has its value in a village such as this. You saved Hannah Gill's life, and while it may take some time, I'm confident I can reassure the villagers of your, shall we say... *scientific* intentions. However, while my flock may come to welcome your enlightened wisdom, they would never accept your true methods. While you are here, you must promise me you will abstain from practicing sorcery of any kind."

A moment passed as Abigail considered this unexpected turn of events. She still wasn't convinced she could trust the priest, but she didn't see any other alternative—not if she wanted to stop the suicides.

"You have my promise," she said at last.

Carnes turned Abigail's Book of Shadows over in his lap and gazed down at the pentacle emblazoned on the crimson leather. "In the meantime, I will safeguard this as a guarantee that you keep your vow."

Abigail's eyes narrowed and her voice went low and deadly serious. "I'm afraid that is quite out of the question."

"And I'm afraid it is the price of my trust in you, Ms. Jacobs. You must understand the position into which I am being placed by defending you. Given the display you put on today, it will be hard enough to persuade my congregation that you cured Hannah Gill through the use of modern medicine alone. While your knowledge of the occult may prove valuable in defeating this evil, there are limits to what I am willing to accept in the process. As long as you are among my people—as long as I am expected to defend you against their accusations—you shall not be in possession of a book such as this." Carnes gazed at her, his cool green eyes meeting hers and absorbing her glare. "Are we agreed?"

Abigail's blood simmered with outrage, but she saw there was no flexibility in the priest's gaze. "We are agreed." She was barely able to get the words past her lips. "But know this: if any harm should come to that book, the hurt I will bring upon you will be tenfold."

Chapter 19

Heath MacIntyre uncovered the stones with his bare hands. It took hours of toiling alone deep in the woods, prying the rocks from the forest floor as the rain trickled in icy streams through the boughs. Twilight was looming by the time he had amassed all that he needed to bury his dead wife.

The darkening sky hung low and oppressive like a heavy curtain as Heath stopped to catch his breath. His hair dangled over his face in long, wet strands and rain dribbled from his thick goatee. His sodden clothes lay plastered against his massive frame. Raindrops ran in rivulets across the alabaster skin of Evelyn's corpse, where it lay in a thicket to Heath's left. He had cleansed her himself. It was a womanly duty but he wouldn't tolerate anyone else assuming the responsibility. With nothing to use as a winding sheet, he had stripped his wife of her blood-soaked chemise and dressed her in her only gown before carrying her off into the forest where no one would look for them.

As he gazed down at her now, Heath had a fleeting notion he should simply leave her there for the animals. Evelyn had forsaken her way with God. With her eternal soul was now lost to Him, of what good were her earthly remains?

"No," Heath croaked aloud as he hovered over her body in the gathering gloom. After all the suffering his poor wife had been subjected to in her lifetime, she was at least owed a decent burial. Heath wouldn't let the scavengers ravage her remains, nor would he let Father Carnes burn her body as if she were some heathen.

"*Cuiridh mi clach air do charn*," he whispered in ancient Gaelic. *I will put a stone on your cairn.*

Heath sank to his knees and clawed at the forest floor with his hands. At first, the soggy earth came away in clumps, but he was soon obliged to use his axe to hack through the dense tangle of tree roots beneath the surface. It was hard work and Heath had plenty of time to contemplate what had happened since dawn. His mind kept returning to the same thought: the witch.

Heath would never fathom Father Carnes' decision to tolerate the Jacobs woman's presence in the village. It seemed unthinkable. *She isn't a threat to us*, Carnes had argued just that afternoon—only hours before Heath had come to claim Evelyn's corpse. *The only magic she wields is that of science. She is here to help us; she can be trusted.*

Heath knew better.

As long as sinners walked among them in Tahawus, God would punish them all. Gamblers like Hawes and Gill; drinkers like Prue; heretics like Beaulieu and even Heath's own dear Evelyn—all had fallen under the Almighty's wrathful eye and had been cleansed of their sins by blood or fire.

And now there was this Jacobs woman. It was bad enough that the villagers were forced to endure that heathen savage, Josiah Benedict. Now a *witch* walked among them, fouling them all by her very presence. *She* was the reason Evelyn was dead. Heath's wife had shown the witch kindness and had been damned for it.

An hour passed and nightfall was close at hand by the time Heath hit the solid mountain bedrock and was forced to stop digging. In that time, he had gotten no further than a knee-deep depression in the earth the length of Evelyn's body. It wasn't much, but it would do.

Heath moved to the thicket and gathered his dead wife in his arms. Her limbs fell aside and dangled listlessly as he raised her up and lowered her into the shallow grave.

Heath lit his lantern. His hands trembled as he removed a heavy stone from the waist-high pile and placed it over Evelyn's feet. The cold and heavy sensation of the rock in his palms transported him back to the day he had entombed his father beneath a cairn just like this one. There, on the desolate seacoast of Caithness, Evelyn had stood by Heath's side, even in her grief over the indignities she had suffered at the hands of that hateful man, Patrick Sellar. She had held Heath's hand as the piper played the *coronach* dirge. She had wept as Father Magraith delivered the liturgy. She had helped build the cairn for the Rite of Committal.

One after another, Heath now piled more stones upon Evelyn's body. From time to time, a sharp *clack* would ring through the forest as a wet stone slipped across the heap. The memory of Father Magraith stirred something in Heath. The old Highland priest had been wise and pious—nothing like this foolish whelp, Carnes. Magraith had known what the Bible said about witchcraft. He had cautioned his flock to be wary of the devil's snares. Even in this godless land of America, Heath had not forgotten those admonitions. He could still hear the echoes of Magraith's gravelly baritone as he preached the words of Deuteronomy: *Who practices divination or sorcery, interprets omens, engages in witchcraft, casts spells, or who consults the dead is detestable to God.*

If sorcery was an abomination to the Lord, then so was Abigail Jacobs.

Evelyn was all but buried now. Only her blank and ashen face remained. Her skin was almost opalescent in the lambent glow of the lantern. Heath allowed himself one last look, one last hope that those beautiful green eyes might somehow flutter open.

Then he put the final stones into their places and his wife was gone.

The sounds of the night creatures had arisen around him. Their haunting, lonely song brought on a vague recollection of the dreadful rumors sweeping through the village. *Something evil dwells in the forest, something that drives people to kill themselves...*

Heath knew he had nothing to fear. Whatever was in these woods wasn't evil. It was a thing of glory.

It was God's fury incarnate.

Heath was a righteous man. He remained faithful despite all he had endured—the loss of home, family, wife, and child. Even in the face of such afflictions, he would prove he was still God's devoted servant. If the Lord was angry with the people of Tahawus, then Heath would be the one to make atonement for them all. He alone would put on the armor of God to stand against the devil's schemes and rid the village of the Lord's enemies.

And he would begin with Abigail Jacobs.

Chapter 20

The door to Josiah Benedict's cabin creaked inward and his slender silhouette appeared in the frame.

"Good evening, Mr. Benedict." Abigail stood in the rain, illuminated by the orange glow that spilled out from the open door. "May I enter?"

The precipitation had intensified since nightfall and the inky blackness of the forest was alive with the trickle and patter of water penetrating the boughs. Distant peals of thunder reverberated across the high peaks. Another hour and the worst of the storm would roll over the sleeping village.

Shadows obscured Josiah's face, but Abigail could see glints of candlelight glittering off his black eyes as he studied her in silence. He was barefoot and dressed in a flannel undershirt and buckskin breeches. He remained there a moment with his hand resting on the latch. Then his shape receded and the door swung shut in her face.

"Mr. Benedict, I will not leave your doorstep until I have spoken to you!" Abigail rapped her knuckles against the hard wood. The other side was silent. She was about to knock even more forcibly when there came the hushed sounds of footfalls. The door swung open.

"It is not right for a woman to be here," Josiah muttered. These were the first words Abigail had ever heard the man speak. He uttered them with the gruff and halting inflection of his native tongue. His voice was deep and held the slightest hint of a rasp. "You must go now."

Abigail's hand shot out and caught the door as it came swinging toward her. "Mr. Benedict, I appreciate your apprehension at my presence here in the middle of the night, but you have my word that no one else need know about my visit."

"Your word." Josiah humphed.

"Mr. Benedict, by now you have no doubt heard what I am capable of?"

Josiah nodded once, his long topknot swaying like a horsetail. "You are Medicine Lady."

Abigail gave a thin smile. "That is a very kind way of saying it. Tell me, do you know why I have come to Tahawus?"

Josiah's eyes narrowed to black points. "You are here to stop the dying."

"Precisely. And I will need your help to do it."

Even through the shadows and rain, Abigail saw the intrigue gathering on Josiah's leathery face. He hesitated a moment longer, eyeing her before stepping aside to let her enter.

The interior of the cabin was nearly as spartan as Abigail's own. A beeswax candle burned on the nightstand. Next to it sat a clay tobacco pipe, a pair of cheap glass tumblers, and half a bottle of what looked to be whiskey. There were two mismatched chairs in the room. Abigail presumed the second was reserved for Josiah's only known associate, Glenn Colvin.

Josiah's red soldier's jacket hung from a peg, as did his leather satchel and the blue sash he always wore. His Baker rifle was propped next to the door. The rest of his weapons—his knives and tomahawk—were arranged on a crude birch-wood shelf, along with his iron jewelry and eagle feathers. A small fire burned in the woodstove and the sweet smell of tobacco smoke hung thick in the air.

Abigail shrugged out of her wet cloak, draped it over a seatback, and sat, her gaze gravitating to the whiskey bottle on the nightstand. "May I help myself, Mr. Benedict? I find myself with a chill in my bones."

Bewilderment bloomed on Josiah's face as Abigail uncorked the bottle and poured two fingers of whiskey into each tumbler. She took a gulp, the burn of the liquor feeling good as it spread within her.

"As you can see, I've no use for trivial notions of decorum," she said. "And you've no reason to be ill at ease in my presence. Please..." She motioned to the other chair. "Make yourself comfortable. We have many things to discuss, and our conversation may take some time."

Josiah remained standing, scrutinizing her as if sniffing out a trap. A deep rumbling of thunder sent a vibration through the cabin while Abigail waited for his curiosity to get the best of him. At last, he relented and sat, his bowlegs slightly apart and his spine straight and rigid. Abigail offered him the second tumbler, and he took it with a circumspect frown.

"Josiah Benedict is your Christian name, is it not?" Abigail asked between sips of her drink.

Josiah nodded. The whiskey sat untasted in his hand.

"May I ask what your name is in your own language?"

There was a flicker of amusement in Josiah's otherwise stoic expression. "I fear you would not pronounce it correctly."

"Surely there is an English translation?"

Josiah went quiet for a moment, then said, "River Stone."

"River Stone. A very beautiful name. May I ask how you earned it?"

"My village stood on the shores of Penobscot, a great river in the land you now call Maine. I spent many hours standing in the water, hunting fish. I could not move for fear of scaring my catch. I stood like a stone in the river. And so, that is what my people called me."

"May I call you that?"

Josiah shifted in his seat and inclined his head slightly.

"Splendid. River Stone, I want to ask you some questions about the mountains to the north." Abigail noticed Josiah still had not tasted his whiskey. His eyes remained unreadable as he gazed at her. "Duncan Emmons has told me you call those lands *empty*. Why is that?"

"Because nothing lives there."

"Nothing at all?"

"So says Mohawk legend," Josiah replied.

"Is that the reason you use the Mohawk word?"

He nodded. "*Anachaju.*"

"Were there any Mohawk settlements in this area before the white people came?"

"Never. For a time, Mohawk from the eastern valleys came to these lands for hunting grounds, but they soon believed Tawiskaron ruled the land and never returned."

"Who is Tawiskaron?"

"The Dark Twin Spirit who delights in destroying the creations of his brother, Tharonhiawakon."

Abigail felt a thrill of promise. "Tell me more about this dark spirit."

Josiah gave her a mistrustful look.

"Please, River Stone. You do want to help me end the suicides, don't you?"

After another moment's hesitation, Josiah said, "It is an ancient Mohawk story. When Tharonhiawakon, the Light Twin, created gentle animals like deer, his evil brother, Tawiskaron, created the wolf to devour it. When Tharonhiawakon created the rose, Tawiskaron gave it thorns. When Tharonhiawakon created fields that were wide and flat and easy to sow, Tawiskaron brought tall mountains to stand among them. When Tharonhiawakon created rivers that were long and calm and easy to paddle, Tawiskaron gave them turns and rapids to make them treacherous. And when Tharonhiawakon created man… Tawiskaron created monsters to walk among him."

Abigail's chair creaked as she leaned back and murmured, "For every good, there is an equivalent evil."

Josiah nodded. "As you say. What one brother creates, the other seeks to undo."

There was a brief pause as Abigail drained her glass. A sudden, booming crack of thunder rattled the room as she reached for the bottle and poured herself another. "What can you tell me about these monsters that Tawiskaron created?"

The sound of the rain drumming on the roof filled the silence until Josiah spoke again. "They are to man as wolf is to deer: they hunt and they feed."

"Are they still among us?"

Josiah shrugged. "When Tharonhiawakon saw what his evil brother had done, he swept Tawiskaron's monsters up into Sky World where they could do no more harm. But whenever Tharonhiawakon is not looking, Tawiskaron tries to steal back his evil beasts, to turn them loose on his most beloved lands where they feast on mortals, away from the eyes of his brother."

"How exactly do these creatures feast?"

"Tawiskaron's monsters began as man and it is through man that they feed. When they hunt, it is as men... and when they feast, it is from within."

Abigail took a moment to consider his words. "River Stone, what you are describing very much resembles what I call possession. Once brought into this world, the monster inhabits the body of a man and compels him to destruction, feasting on him from the inside."

Josiah shrugged. "As you say."

"Can they be killed? These monsters?"

This time, Josiah shook his head. "No. But they can be banished back to Sky World."

"How?"

"By killing the man who is hosting it."

The room went quiet as Abigail contemplated Josiah's story, looking for connections to the suicides. With the steady sound of the rain filling the silence, she felt a growing impatience, like the constant ticking of a clock in her ear. How much longer did she have before another villager committed suicide? And what if Father Carnes failed to persuade his followers to accept her help? How long did she have before they turned on her? How long until she found herself hanged by the very people she was trying to save?

The clock in Abigail's head ticked ever louder, faster. Josiah's tale of an eternal war between light and dark twins brought to mind the tragic story of the Legendre brothers. Was there some sort of link? Could the monsters of Native legend have driven Sebastian Legendre to murder his elder brother before taking his own life decades ago? It seemed impossible; if such mythical beings were real, they would be like nothing any witch had ever encountered in over five centuries of recorded lore. And even if they existed, how did any of this relate to the current streak of suicides?

And then it came to her.

The realization struck her with the force of a cannonball. There was one way of discovering what had motivated the victims to take their own lives. It was dangerous—perhaps even reckless—but if she was successful, it could yield all the answers she needed.

Abigail leaned forward, her whiskey now forgotten in her hand. "These lands where Tawiskaron's monsters dwelt. Do they encompass the lake where you and Mr. Colvin discovered Jed Hawes' body?"

Josiah nodded.

"Does this lake have a name?"

"Lake Tear of the Clouds." Josiah raised his tumbler to his lips and drained it off in one gulp before leveling his black, impenetrable eyes on Abigail. "Medicine Lady, I have answered many questions. Now please, tell me how I can help stop the dying."

"You have already helped me, River Stone." Abigail's eyes gleamed in the firelight as she finished the last of her own whiskey. "You have told me all I needed to know."

Chapter 21

The campfire spit and crackled in the gray morning quietude outside Glenn Colvin's cabin. The rain had ended before dawn, leaving behind a sky as ashen as the smoke spiraling from the campfire flames.

"Evil ghosts?" Colvin leveled a skeptical eye on Abigail. He sat on an upturned log, the heel of his big boot propped on one of the stones encircling the firepit. Abigail occupied another log to his right. Timber gazed mistrustfully at her from where he lay curled by Colvin's side. Duncan was there as well. Across the fire, Josiah stood with the butt of his rifle planted between his moccasins and his fingers interlaced around its long barrel.

Abigail nodded. "Ghosts, ghouls, lycanthropes, nosferatu—every creature from every corner of your imagination."

"And you kill them?"

Abigail returned Colvin's unflinching gaze. "All of them."

Colvin gave her another long and cagey look before pivoting to Duncan. "You truly believe this? You honestly think she can stop the suicides?"

"I've seen her defeat the most unimaginable horrors with my own eyes," Duncan replied. "She wouldn't have come all the way out here if she wasn't what she claims to be."

Colvin looked across the fire to Josiah and said something in the Native's own hard and clipped language. The strange speech came to the lumberjack naturally, with no hint of an accent. There was a brief exchange between the two men, Josiah's expression remaining somber throughout.

"You're certain?" Colvin asked in English.

Josiah nodded once.

"Why didn't you mention any of this before?"

"It was not important then," Josiah replied bluntly.

"But now it is?"

Josiah shrugged. "Who can say?"

Colvin frowned and scratched at his beard. Fishing a boiled egg from his shirt pocket, he cracked it and began peeling. Timber nosed at the shell fragments where they fell on the ground. "How do we know this isn't just another tall tale told by the Mohawk?" he asked.

"That is precisely why I must speak to Jed Hawes," Abigail replied.

"But Jed Hawes is dead!"

A knot of wood exploded in the fire and sent a shower of glowing embers across the ground at Colvin's feet. Timber sprang up as Colvin crushed the brands into the dirt with his boot and popped the egg into his mouth. "If I understand correctly, you expect us to escort you to North Camp so that you might have a conversation with a dead man?" Colvin didn't try to hide his incredulity as he gazed at Abigail and chewed.

"That is precisely what I am suggesting. Here are the facts as we know them, Mr. Colvin: Jed Hawes was the first man to commit suicide. He did so in a most hideous manner near Lake Tear of the Clouds—which, as it happens, is believed to be favored by Tawiskaron, the Dark Twin Spirit of Indian lore. Fifty years ago—on the shore of this same lake—a young missionary bludgeoned his elder brother to death before taking his own life. 'Tis not unreasonable to surmise that there may be some link between Tawiskaron's creatures and our most recent tragedies. However, there is only one means of being certain. We must visit Jed Hawes' grave and summon his spirit."

"This makes little sense." Colvin scoffed.

"On the contrary," Abigail returned. "If you want to know why your people are killing themselves, we need to ask one of them. For that, we will need a body… and Hawes' is the only one to which we still have access."

Colvin shook his head. "This is your strategy?"

"'Tis the only one we have."

"That's not very encouraging."

"Neither is the prospect of another suicide."

Colvin went quiet. His expression was hard and pensive as he stared into the fire and smoothed his dark beard absently. "Suppose you're right. Suppose these creatures are somehow driving my people to take their own lives. How exactly do you expect to stop them?"

"I am not entirely certain," Abigail replied. "But given recent events, I would say our present situation requires, shall we say, a much more aggressive intervention than has yet been attempted."

"You understand what you're asking will require an overnight journey through some of the toughest wilderness you'll ever encounter?"

"Mr. Emmons has apprised me of the difficulties involved. Nevertheless, I see no other alternative."

Duncan leaned forward. "Glenn, if we leave this afternoon, we could reach North Camp by tomorrow evening."

"You will not be accompanying us," Abigail stated.

Duncan froze and stared at her. "I beg your pardon?"

"You are to remain here."

"Absolutely not. Abby, if—"

"Do not pretend to have a say in this matter, Duncan. You almost had me leave Hannah Gill to die because you refuse to let me have anything to do with witchcraft."

"Abby, I didn't—"

"We'll bring Keenan and O'Brennan," Colvin declared with a cool finality that indicated the debate was over. "Emmons, you'll remain here."

Duncan swiveled and gaped at Colvin in disbelief.

Abigail interjected before Duncan could protest. "I'm afraid I must object to being accompanied by anyone other than yourself and Mr. Benedict."

"And why is that?" Colvin asked.

"The conjuring ritual is not without its risks. In fact, it can be quite deadly. In my experience, men without the proper mettle to withstand such an ordeal tend to get themselves killed."

Colvin smiled. "Well, in my experience, the people of this town can be a zealous lot—and they're already suspicious of you. We'll need trustworthy witnesses to assure them that our journey to North Camp consisted of nothing more than, let us say, interviews with the men who live up there."

"You mean to say you need witnesses who will lie," Duncan remarked.

A twinkle came to Colvin's dark eyes. "*Precisely*, as Ms. Jacobs is so fond of saying."

Abigail remained silent for a moment as she considered her options. "Very well. You'll apprise your men of the risks?"

"I will." Colvin returned his attention to Duncan, whose expression resembled that of a boy who hadn't been invited to play in a game of jackstraws. "There's a good reason I want you to remain here, Emmons. Five of our people have now died by their own hands and the village is wild with rumors. No one has seen Heath MacIntyre since yesterday, and despite Father Carnes' best efforts, there is a fair number who remain fearful that a woman suspected of witchcraft now resides among them. I need someone with a level head to be the voice of reason while I'm gone. You're the only man for it."

"Glenn, I—"

"Don't worry yourself, Emmons," Colvin smirked. "If your old friend Ms. Jacobs is half as formidable as you say she is, I've no doubt I'll be kept safe."

Duncan was about to protest again, but something told him there was no use; Colvin had already made the decision.

"When will we depart?" Abigail asked with some impatience.

Colvin gathered the fragments of his eggshell, stood from the log, and stretched his back. Timber sprang to all fours. "As soon as I can round up the men and you can change from that gown into something more fit for our journey. I'd encourage you to pack light, Ms. Jacobs. You're in for a helluva hike."

Chapter 22

They made their camp that night on the bank of the wandering river. For three hundred miles downstream, the steady current would wind and curl its way south through the Champlain Valley, growing steadily in size and might as it flowed south through the Catskill Mountains until it finally split against the ramparts of New York City and found release in the Atlantic. But up here in the Adirondack—just miles from its headwater somewhere to the north—the rush of what would become the mighty Hudson was now gentle and serene.

Abigail reclined on the blanket she had spread next to the fire and listened to the whispering babble of the water tumbling down the mountainside. It was twilight and a forbidding duskiness was gathering among the trees. The cool evening air was damp and thick with the pungent scent of autumn rot. Abigail pulled her heavy cloak tighter around her shoulders and found herself thankful for the wool breeches and layers of mackinaw shirts Colvin had brought her before their departure. The clothes were intended for a man of small stature and they were only slightly too large for her. It had taken some time for her to get accustomed to the unfamiliar cut, but she had come to embrace the practicality of men's clothing.

As Colvin had promised, the hike had been long and arduous. The trail they followed was little more than a narrow herd path hugging the river as it climbed relentlessly toward North Camp. Timber led the way, trotting up the trail. Nose down and ears perked, the dog stopped at regular intervals to allow his two-legged followers to catch up. Josiah followed close behind, keeping a brisk pace as he moved effortlessly through the woods.

The two lumberjacks, Keenan and O'Brennan, had gone next. Less than an hour into their trek, Abigail had understood why Colvin had recruited them. Both were young, unmarried, and carried conversations easily, although they seemed quiet by nature. They were Irishmen who had come to America together from Derry by way of Boston. The two friends couldn't have appeared less similar. Keenan was stocky, round-faced, and fair-haired, with a sprinkling of freckles. O'Brennan was taller with chestnut curls, heavy brows, and deep brown eyes. Both men lugged their heavy packs with ease and were surefooted while navigating the trail.

Abigail and Colvin had come last, traveling single-file with Colvin bringing up the rear. They said little as they went, Abigail finding it necessary to focus on the gnarled roots and muddy holes that threatened to snare her ankles. The trail was steep and slippery from the constant rains. Water ran freely over the exposed bedrock, submerging her leather boots to her ankles as if she were wading up a stream. There were times when she regretted the weight of the large canvas pack slung around her shoulders, but its contents were vital for what she intended once they reached their destination.

It was early evening when Colvin called the group to a halt. Dinner consisted of salted deer meat and potatoes boiled over the campfire. Abigail ate heartily and without complaint. After rinsing their pans in the river, O'Brennan produced a tin whistle and Keenan lent the lilting charm of his voice to a few *caoineadh* laments for their Irish homeland. The music helped to ward off the pall settling over the woods as twilight fell.

Abigail could now hear the sounds of the men readying to bed down for the night. O'Brennan was somewhere further in the forest, hanging their provisions high in the trees away from their camp. Abigail had offered to do her part to help, but Colvin wouldn't hear it, insisting instead that she rest and gather her strength for the day ahead. By nightfall tomorrow, they would arrive at North Camp.

By midnight, Abigail would be talking to a dead man.

Abigail wasn't sure what to expect once they arrived there. Upon first hearing Duncan's story of the tragic fates of the Legendre brothers, she had been filled with a mingled sense of excitement and relief. At last, she had found an explanation for the deaths in the village. But now that she'd had the long hike to think about it, there were some nagging details that troubled her. Were the ghosts of *both* brothers haunting the village? If not, which one was it and why? And perhaps most important of all: how were they compelling the villagers to commit suicide? Abigail had still not forgotten that she hadn't detected a single trace of possession among the victims. But if it wasn't a haunting, then what else could it be? Could the monsters of Josiah's Native legend be real?

A rustle of canvas caught Abigail's attention. She looked over to see Josiah disappearing into his tent without a further word. O'Brennan returned and, after wishing her a goodnight, he and Keenan also crawled into the tent they shared.

"Josiah and the boys are gonna turn in early," Colvin said as he ambled toward her with Timber loping at his side. "I'll be taking first watch."

Colvin flopped down on the ground next to Abigail, crossed his legs at the ankles, and reclined on his elbows. Timber curled close by and nestled his furry chin on his big front paws while keeping an eye on Abigail. Colvin shifted his weight to one side and reached into his shirt pocket. Abigail was sure he was going to produce a boiled egg. Instead, he withdrew a small tin flask. With a wink, he uncorked it, waved it under his nose to smell the aroma of the whiskey, and took a swig.

"Josiah tells me you've a taste for the finer things." Colvin grinned as he offered the flask. "Quite the gossip he is. Can't seem to shut him up. Go on… if you're gonna dress like a man, you might as well drink like one too."

A grudging smile came to Abigail as she took the flask and drank. The whiskey did wonders to dispel the chill sinking into her flesh. She returned the flask and it disappeared back into Colvin's pocket. They sat gazing into the fire with the darkness closing around them like a blanket. An eerie chorus of crickets and tree frogs was now coming to life.

It was Colvin who broke the silence. "Bringing you out here was as much for your own safety as it was to stop the ghosts."

Abigail nodded. "I assumed as much."

Colvin sighed as he shifted his weight on his elbows. "For my part, I've seen too much ugliness in God's name to call myself a believer anymore. Still, even if I don't throw in with 'em, I don't begrudge those church folks their beliefs. If it keeps my village calm and my men working hard, then to each his own, I say. Father Carnes seems to want to help you, but he's young and his views don't always sit well with the others. I figured it'd be safer if you left town for a couple of days to let the worst of the storm blow itself out."

"I appreciate your concern, Mr. Colvin."

"Call me Glenn. And considering as how I'm supposed to be the boss around here, I'm not gonna ask your permission to call you Abigail." He grinned again, his teeth gleaming from within his beard as he gazed at her in the firelight.

Despite the miserable conditions they had endured on the long trek, Abigail had never complained and had never fallen behind. Her dogged determination was enough to earn a measure of Colvin's grudging respect. She might even make a good traveling companion if she weren't so withdrawn and distant. There remained a coldness to her throughout the long journey. When she looked at him, Colvin saw no compassion in the fathomless blue of her eyes. There was only the cool intensity of a woman driven by obsession. And yet, there was something inexplicably alluring about her. It wasn't only her beauty—which was undeniable. Was it the mystery she represented? The supreme confidence she radiated? Colvin found the latter to be both irritating and engaging at once. He didn't know what to make of it.

"Tell me, what exactly makes you a witch, anyway?" Colvin asked after a moment.

The light in Abigail's blue eyes leaped and danced in time with the flickering of the fire. "I have mastered certain ancient occult arts that allow me to harness the power of the paranatural."

"Such as?"

"Spellcasting; conjuring; necromancy."

Colvin cocked an eyebrow. "Necromancy?"

"Communion with the dead, yes."

"These spells. Can you cast them on command? Light a candle with a word? Turn a man into a frog?"

"No. That kind of magic only exists in fairy tales. My power derives from my ability to interact with those who dwell beyond the Veil."

"You mean spirits."

Abigail nodded.

"These spirits—can you compel them to hurt people?"

"When necessary."

Colvin gave her a sideways look.

"If it will put your mind at ease, I vowed long ago that I would only use my craft to help others."

"How do you do that?"

"By hunting down the evils that haunt them."

Colvin ran his hand over Timber's thick, black coat and the dog made a contented rumbling noise deep in his throat. "How do you put an end to such hauntings?"

"Most involve the use of banishing rituals."

"Most? What do the rest involve?"

"Courage and violence."

Colvin heaved a deep breath and shook his head. "'Tis an interesting choice of profession for a woman. I take it this is the reason you're not married?"

"'Tis one of many reasons," Abigail replied a little more tightly than she intended. She went quiet for a moment, then said, "I want to thank you for trusting me, Mr. Colv— Glenn." She didn't know why she had said it, only that it seemed like the right thing to say.

"Oh, I wouldn't go so far as to say that I trust you." Colvin chuckled. "At least not with my life—not yet. I'm the sort of man who needs to see things for himself before he believes them. So far, all I have is the word of your friend Emmons that you are capable of the things you say you are."

Abigail's golden hair spilled across her shoulder as she sat up and brought her knees to her chest, wrapping her arms around her shins. "What can I do to convince you?"

Colvin smoothed his thick, black beard as he thought it over. "I suppose you'd have to show me some proof of this craft of yours."

"What did you have in mind? Shall I conjure a spirit for the two of us to share a drink with?"

Colvin gave a low chuckle. "Perhaps. Surprise me."

Abigail's eyes narrowed and glittered like blue stars in the firelight. "Alright. Gaze into the fire."

Colvin did what she asked, sitting up and crossing his legs Native-style. Abigail took his coarse hand into her own and he seemed to stiffen at her touch. She turned her attention to the fire and focused on the flames, clearing her mind of all conscious thought. The sounds of the night creatures; the trickling of the river; the scent of the rotting forest deadfall; the feel of the hard ground beneath her—all of it drained away, leaving nothing but a sublime clarity of mind. Only then did Abigail begin her spell.

It started with a chant: low and sibilant, with the haunting beauty of a strange and forgotten language. Abigail's pulse quickened and a rising tingle of power rushed from her veins to her muscles. She welcomed the sensation as if she were being swept into the arms of a lover. The chant went on and she became dimly aware of Colvin's hand closing tighter around her own as he stared into the small blaze.

Part of Abigail remained conscious of the effect her incantation was having on the man. He was witnessing the flames growing in intensity, going from orange to white, rising higher and higher until they filled his vision with an all-encompassing light. His pulse slowed, the intervals between his heartbeats growing longer and more pronounced as if time itself were slowing down and somehow breaking the thread that kept the beats together. A window opened in the brilliance, small at first but growing larger as Abigail continued her chant. Soon, it was the size of a door, a stark black rectangle cut from the dazzling glare.

Colvin saw himself drawn toward it.

He stepped through.

With a sudden gasp, he snatched his hand from Abigail's as if a viper had bitten it.

"What did you do?" he demanded breathlessly. His eyes were wide and his heart raced as he looked at her with mingled shock and horror.

Abigail gazed at him intently. "The flickering of the fire acted as a type of psychomanteum such as those used by the ancient Greeks for scrying. When combined with the hypnotic potency of my incantation, I opened a window into your memories."

Colvin's easy self-assurance seemed to desert him. His face paled and filled with something like fear. "You saw all that?"

Abigail nodded. "Is that truly how you met Josiah?"

Colvin fixed her with a scathing glare. For a moment, Abigail was certain he was about to storm away. Instead, he lowered his head and stared at the dirt between his feet.

"I was a trapper then," he said in a low voice, "trading with the Penobscot up and down their river. I was there the day the soldiers came and burned Josiah's village to the ground. The land was to be sold to white settlers. I was there—a white man—and I was powerless to stop it. I suppose I'll carry the weight of my shame until the day I go knocking on hell's black gates."

Colvin paused and raised his gaze to the fire. "When it was over, I stayed with the Penobscot to help them relocate to the new land that had been reserved for them. It was then that I met Josiah. He had a wife and newborn son to provide for, so we began trapping together. Somehow or other, we ended up as lumberjacks out here."

"Josiah has a family?"

"Aye. And it pains him every day that they're apart. There's a good enough reason he's out here, though. He might be an Indian, but the company pays him a decent salary to serve as our guide. Eventually, he'll put enough away to buy his family a portion of company land out here, far from their miserable reservation." Colvin sighed heavily and shrugged. "I expect he may one day put his tomahawk in my back for not defending his people that day when the soldiers came. If you ask me, he'd have every right to."

For a long moment, Colvin remained quiet and brooding. His deep amber eyes were molten with firelight as he gazed into the flames. When he spoke again, his voice was thick and husky. "Why would you do that? Why would you trespass on my memories like that?"

"Because I wanted to determine what kind of man you are. You desired to know if you could trust me; I felt I was entitled to the same."

"And? Are you satisfied with what you discovered?"

"Quite."

Without another word, Colvin stood and stalked away with Timber trailing at his heels. Abigail heard rustling in the darkness as he crawled into his tent and left her with the fire and the first watch.

Chapter 23

It was after midnight and Abigail had long been relieved of her watch when she heard the noise from beyond her tent. The forest had gone deathly quiet, and the sound was so distinct it woke her to instant alertness.

Something was moving out in the woods.

Abigail stayed very still in her bedroll, listening for the rustling of the underbrush to come again.

Nothing.

Whatever it was had gone silent.

She *had* heard it, though. Of that, she was certain. Who was on watch? Josiah? Keenan? Was either of them moving around out there? No. Whatever it was had been slow and deliberate. It had moved and prowled like a predator lurking in the night.

Abigail's blood quickened as she slid soundlessly from her bedroll and fumbled in the darkness for the flint to light her lantern. The blackness in the tent was absolute. Abigail couldn't see her hand groping around in front of her.

She heard it again: a twig snapping under a heavy weight;

the sharp *clack* of a shifting rock; a brief swishing of fallen leaves across the forest floor.

And then silence.

Abigail's heart fired up. Her muscles tensed as her body readied itself for a fight. The sounds had come from somewhere maybe thirty yards from their camp. Had anyone else heard it? Who was on watch? Abigail's hands located her leather boots, and she slipped them on.

A heart-stopping outburst shattered the silence.

Timber was barking furiously.

Abigail cast the canvas flap aside and hurried out into the cold. By the dying glow of the campfire embers, she made out the shadowy forms of the other men emerging from their own tents. Colvin had his pistol drawn. His other hand was clamped on the scruff of Timber's neck, holding the dog back as he barked madly into the darkness. Timber's hackles were raised high and his ears were flattened against his skull. His tail was pointed straight and his lips curled back over his fangs. Whatever was lurking in the forest had driven the dog into a vicious fury.

Keenan and Josiah stood on either side of Colvin. The Irishman had his timber axe gripped with both hands. Even in the dim light, Abigail could see his face was hard with tension. Josiah had the butt of his rifle locked into his shoulder, the long barrel aimed straight ahead into the blackness. One eye was closed, the other squinted down the sight.

O'Brennan was nowhere to be seen.

"What is happening?" Abigail whispered, loud enough to be heard over the sharp staccato of Timber's relentless barking.

Colvin held a hand up to silence her. His breathing appeared as furtive puffs of white in the cold air as he remained immobile, straining to see into the black void of the forest. His reply was low and tense. "Bear."

A nervous tension settled into Abigail's gut.

"We think it's a female," Keenan whispered. "O'Brennan was on watch when he heard her. He went out there to check on the food."

"What should we do?"

"We wait," came Colvin's curt reply. "She may have cubs. If we scare her any more than we already have, she'll take our noise as a threat and try to defend them. If we're lucky, she'll just move on."

"What if the dog's already frightened her?"

Colvin frowned. "Then we may have a bear to kill."

Abigail fell quiet. Her heartbeat counted the seconds in silence as they waited anxiously.

Nothing.

Minutes passed until Keenan leaned over to Colvin and whispered, "He's been gone too long. Do you think we—"

All at once, there came a deafening explosion and a brilliant blast of sparks from deep in the forest. For a split second, the bright muzzle-flash of O'Brennan's sudden pistol shot chased away the blackness. Abigail glimpsed something black and massive moving among the trees before the darkness rushed back in and devoured everything. She blinked away her blindness after the dazzling flare of gunfire and heard something enormous crash through the underbrush.

It was close—very close.

There was a terrible, bestial roar; a cry of panic; O'Brennan's footsteps running frantically, not making it far. Another cry—this one of pain and terror. It rose to a shrill scream before it withered abruptly into a horrible liquid gurgling.

"O'Brennan!" Colvin's bellow broke the awful spell of the moment. He released Timber and the dog shot forward, snarling and yapping as he vanished into the darkness. Colvin charged after him without a second thought, brandishing his pistol.

Keenan hefted his axe and made a move to follow, but Josiah shoved him back. "Stay with her," he grunted before whirling and barreling after Colvin.

Abigail was on the move before Keenan knew it. She dove into her tent and snatched her lantern. A frenzy of snarls and roars erupted from the forest as Timber collided with the bear. Abigail could hear Colvin shouting above the pandemonium as she dashed to the smoldering remnants of the campfire. She raised the lantern over her head and brought it crashing down, shattering the glass chimney and spilling whale oil across the coals. Flames shot up with a tremendous whoosh of igniting air.

The scene illuminated by the orange blaze was enough to make her freeze where she stood.

Timber and the black bear were locked in deadly combat less than thirty yards away. The raging beast was enormous, rising at least seven feet tall as it reared up to swat at the dog with its long, sharp claws. Its muzzle was peeled back, revealing the gaping pink and yellow of its fanged maw.

Timber dodged and skirted the bear's vicious blows and snapping jaws. Spit flew from the dog's snarling mouth as he attacked the giant beast from behind, where it was most vulnerable. The enraged bear whirled with a ferocious roar and caught the dog with a powerful swipe of its massive paw. Timber gave a sharp yelp as he went slewing through the underbrush. He recovered and rolled back to all fours, crouched low and ready to leap.

The brief window was all Colvin needed. He pulled the trigger and his pistol erupted. The shot caught the bear above the left shoulder and sent a spray of blood into the air. The giant animal staggered and slumped, but it didn't go down. The wound only further infuriated it. Its brown eyes blazed as it reared up and let out a thundering roar.

It charged with astonishing speed.

Timber leaped for the beast, but fell short and rolled to the side. The bear was almost upon Colvin before the dog could recover. There was no time to react. Colvin knew there was no sense in running and his spent pistol was useless. All he had to defend himself were his knife and his fists. Keenan charged at the animal, axe raised, but he would never get to it in time. Colvin had only seconds to brace himself for the bear's assault. His breath caught in his throat as the beast bared its monstrous fangs and went in for the kill.

An ear-splitting blast split the night and the side of the bear's head exploded. A shower of blood and brains went flying, as if a charge of gunpowder had detonated inside the animal's skull. Thrown sideways by the blast, the bear's wild rush came to a skidding halt. Momentum carried it another two staggering steps to the side before it teetered and collapsed in a dead heap.

The echo of the thundering gunshot still rebounded off the trees. From her place near the fire, Abigail let the air out of her lungs and looked to where Josiah was lowering his rifle. A tendril of acrid smoke rose from its muzzle as he gazed at the dead bear with his inscrutable black eyes.

"O'Brennan!" Colvin was rushing headlong through the woods now, combing the area for the missing lumberjack. Abigail seized a burning limb from the fire and darted after him, with Keenan following close behind.

O'Brennan's body lay sprawled across a trampled thicket. His neck was broken and his head was twisted at a grotesque angle. His jaw had been torn loose by a swipe of the bear's powerful claw and now hung low, like a ghastly necklace around his throat.

Keenan let out a devastated wail and crumpled to his knees next to his dead friend. Abigail stood in shocked silence as Colvin went to him. The light cast by her torch made her feel as if she was intruding on the moment like some ghoulish voyeur. This heart-wrenching display of raw emotion wasn't meant for her. She suddenly wished she could douse her flame and vanish. She walked away, leaving the men to grieve in the dark.

She found Josiah down on one knee next to the bear's lifeless bulk. She hung back as he placed a reverent hand on the shattered remnants of the animal's sleek black head and murmured something into the bear's unhearing ear. The gesture resembled an act of contrition, as if he were asking the animal for forgiveness.

Only then did the reality of what had just happened settle

in for Abigail: O'Brennan was dead. It didn't seem possible; the bear's attack had been too sudden, too savagely violent to be real. She had a flash of O'Brennan's mauled face. Had he looked surprised? Abigail knew he couldn't have—the facial muscles would have relaxed in death—but that was how she now remembered him: surprised.

Josiah was looking up at her from the bear's side. His expression had lost some of its usual passivity and was now dark and brooding. "*Sanoba*," he grunted in his own language, motioning to the black carcass. "Male."

"Why does that trouble you, River Stone?"

Josiah rose to his feet. "Bear like this do not hunt man."

"This one certainly did," Abigail remarked. "You saw how it went after O'Brennan, stalking him in the darkness."

Josiah gave a sober nod. "Yes. This *sanoba* had no fear of man. This bear wanted to *feed*." His expression became dour. Behind him, the fire was dwindling again. The shadows were already reclaiming their kingdom. "Something has gone wrong with nature, Medicine Lady."

Chapter 24

They buried O'Brennan in a shallow grave at first light. Keenan stood weeping in stony silence with tears running down his ruddy face while Colvin muddled his way through a eulogy. The sun never really rose that morning; the sky just went from black to gray. More rain was on its way. No one had slept after the bear attack and their gear was packed and ready. Timber lay curled by the fire, licking dried blood from his black fur while the others paid their respects to O'Brennan.

Josiah smoked his tobacco pipe and waited until the meager funeral was over. He then took Keenan's axe, went to the bear's carcass and, with one mighty swing, chopped off the animal's right front paw. He slipped the huge, clawed limb into a burlap sack, cinched the drawstring tight over his animal fetish and led the way into the forest.

They arrived at North Camp by mid-afternoon. It was a dismal site made even more unwelcoming by a chilly breeze sweeping off the mountains to the north. The tiny outpost consisted of four timber shacks clustered within a small, flat glade. It was the perfect image of what Abigail had imagined a logging camp to be: primitive, joyless, and uninviting.

Colvin drew to an abrupt halt as they emerged from the path. His eyes narrowed as he gazed across the clearing at the ramshackle buildings. "Something's wrong."

"What is it?" Abigail asked.

"Listen."

Abigail went silent and strained her ears. "I hear nothing."

Colvin nodded slowly. "Over a dozen men should be felling trees less than a quarter mile upriver. We should hear the echoes of their axes as clear as our own voices. And yet…" He pointed a finger into the air.

There was only the soft swish of the trees in the breeze and the running trickle of the nearby river. From time to time, a loose piece of stovepipe chimney would get caught by the wind and let out a rusty wail. Otherwise, the camp was imbued with the eerie stillness of a place abandoned.

Colvin stood listening a moment longer, his face growing stormier. "Come on."

He started toward one of the larger shacks and threw the door open to the camp's mess hall. It was dingy and dank, lit only by single windows at each end. Long, crude tables stood to either side, accompanied by timber benches. Each tabletop bore a haphazard stack of tin plates and utensils. The rear of the building was dedicated to the pitiful kitchen. A sad, coal-fired stove; a rusty washbasin; a crooked larder. Nothing more. The walls were bare timber and there was a stale scent of mildew in the air.

Colvin swept past the dining tables and went to the kitchen. He tested the heat of the air above the stove before placing his palm flat on the iron plate. His apprehension deepened as he looked across the room at Josiah. "It's cold."

Josiah wheeled to Keenan. "Check the doghouse."

The Irishman left at once.

Colvin turned to Abigail. "Bart Dalrumple is the cook up here. He'd never let his stove go cold. The boys would mutiny if they didn't get their breakfast this morning, but by the feel of it, I'd say they haven't used this stove in days."

"You believe the men have abandoned the camp?"

Colvin pursed his lips and kept his thoughts to himself.

A silhouette filled the door as Keenan returned. "It's locked."

"I beg your pardon?" Colvin arched a dark eyebrow.

"The doghouse is locked. I couldn't get in."

Colvin exchanged another uneasy glance with Josiah.

"What's wrong?" asked Abigail.

"There are no locks up here." Colvin brushed past Abigail, marched across the creaking floor, and left the mess hall.

Timber loped at Colvin's side, his tail swaying as they went, and the others fell in behind them as they crossed the distance to the lumberjacks' bunkhouse. The *doghouse*, as it was known, was a squat structure about fifty feet long and twenty feet wide.

Colvin lifted the latch and pushed on the door. It didn't move. He tried again, putting his weight into his shoulder. The door trembled, but still wouldn't budge. Colvin stepped back. "Something's blocking it from the inside." He paused a moment longer, eyeing the door before turning to Keenan. "Give me your axe."

Keenan unslung the axe from his pack and handed it over.

Colvin hefted it with both hands and brought it smashing into the door. It shuddered on its hinges and sent splintered chips flying. Again and again, Colvin brought the sharp blade crashing into the wooden planks.

An uneasy feeling took root in Abigail's gut as she watched him hack at the door. Something awful awaited them on the other side… and they were about to let it out. Her pulse quickened, and she had a sudden impulse to stop Colvin before he broke through the door.

It was already too late.

Colvin's blows came to an abrupt stop. He covered his nose with his forearm and gagged as he fell back. His face had gone a sickly shade of green.

A terrible reek came pouring from the ragged gap in the door. The cloying stink filled the air like a noxious cloud. Abigail recognized it at once. She hoped against hope that she was wrong, but she knew with dreadful certainty she wasn't.

Colvin held his breath and gave the door one final blow. The top half fell from its hinges and collapsed inward like a broken Dutch door. The rancid stench was suffocating in its intensity as Colvin peered into the ragged opening.

Beyond the slant of cold daylight streaming through the gap, the bunkhouse was drowning in darkness. Curiously, a waist-high load of firewood was piled against the inner side of the door.

"Why would they barricade it?" Keenan wondered aloud. A hint of nervousness had crept into the young man's Irish accent. "What were they afraid of?"

Colvin said nothing. His face was dark and brooding as he unfastened his lantern from his pack, lit the wick, and adjusted the flame. He raised the light high and pulled his neckerchief up around his nose. Then he climbed through the hole in the door and negotiated his way over the pile of firewood on the other side. Josiah went next, followed by Abigail. Keenan came last, leaving Timber outside as a light rain began to fall.

The gloom inside the bunkhouse was smothering. Somewhere in the darkness, Abigail could hear the frenzied scurrying of vermin fleeing Colvin's light. The patter of the rain on the tin roof resounded off the walls. A quiet wind breathed through invisible gaps in the timber as if the shelter itself was moaning.

Colvin moved forward, playing the lantern around him as he went. Clouds of dust rose and drifted through its dim glow. Abigail could make out rows of wooden bunks lining the room to either side. Most were heaped with piles of straw and woolen blankets. Here and there, Abigail saw some of the lumberjacks' scant possessions: a tin of tobacco; an extra pair of socks; a handful of candy.

The space had the empty feel of desertion.

Except Abigail knew they weren't alone. Something was in there with them. She could sense it lurking in the darkest reaches of the cavernous room. Her hand went to the iron talisman slung around her neck and held it tight.

Just then, another sound rose above that of the rain. Outside, beyond the smashed door, Timber was growling a loud, gravelly threat that rumbled from deep in his chest.

Abigail glimpsed Keenan to her right and saw his eyes were wide with fear. His bottom lip nearly quivered and a large vein in his throat throbbed furiously in time with his heartbeat. The Irishman sensed it too: something terrible was about to happen. He was frightened and Abigail knew he shouldn't be there with them. She wanted to send him back, but they were almost to the rear now.

Timber's growls turned to barking.

Loud. Scared.

Just a few more feet remained...

Abigail readied herself.

Colvin stopped short.

A dead man hung by his neck from a rafter.

The lantern light found the corpse. It was mottled with decay, the eyes a bluish white and turned back in the head. The gray gob of the dead man's tongue protruded from his slack mouth. A rat dangled from his lifeless hand, glutting itself on the rotting flesh of his forearm.

More bodies came into view—over a dozen—all strung by their necks from the rafters like forgotten carcasses in a butcher's shop.

"Oh dear God!" Keenan screamed and staggered back. "Oh God! All of them! Oh God, no! Dear God..." His hysterical cries climbed to a shrill pitch as the rat dropped from the dead man's hand to the floor. It glared at Keenan with eyes like ruby shards before scuttling away into the shadows.

"Get him out of here!" Abigail shouted.

Keenan kept screaming even as Josiah grabbed him and hustled him forcibly back toward the door.

Colvin stood gazing at the gruesome tableau, illuminated by the garish glow of his lantern. Dumbstruck with horror, words seemed to desert him. The gentle rhythm of the rain filled the silence. From somewhere outside, Keenan's panic-stricken moans could be heard as if from a great distance.

Without taking his eyes from the bodies, Colvin mustered his voice. "What on earth could have driven these men to do this to themselves?"

Abigail waited a moment before laying a hand on his shoulder. She had seen all she needed. "Come," she said quietly. "Bring me to Jed Hawes' grave. Tonight, we will have our answers."

Chapter 25

Abigail sat on a boulder in the woods not far from North Camp. Her cloaked back was to the wind, and she had a small pumpkin wedged between her thighs. It was dusk, and the landscape was a murky monochrome of bluish green. A veil of fog drifted like phantoms wandering among the trees.

A blond strand of hair escaped Abigail's hood and twirled in the breeze as she carved the pumpkin. Her breath bloomed white in the evening cold. The lambent light of a lantern at her feet glowed like a lonesome orange sphere adrift on a shadowy sea. She could feel the wet tingle of the air landing on her hands as she held her creation up and gazed at the jack-o'-lantern grinning back at her. She had stashed the pumpkin in her canvas pack before leaving Tahawus and was glad to discover it had survived the arduous trek up the mountainside. Soon, it might mean the difference between life and death.

Abigail could hear the hushed sounds of the men deeper in the forest as they prepared the site for the conjuring ritual. She rose from the rock, tucked the jack-o'-lantern in her arm, and went to join them.

Colvin was digging the ground at the center of a small hollow. A knee-high mound of soil and rock stood next to the shallow pit that was Jed Hawes' grave. Keenan had nearly finished hacking away the shrubbery in a wide circle around the open ditch. The Irishman's vacant expression didn't change at Abigail's approach, but he stirred enough to straighten his spine. Abigail suspected his thoughts were somewhere else, a dark and reeking place where dead men hung by their necks and stared at him with empty eyes. Regardless of his mental turmoil, he had done a good job of following her instructions. The space he had cleared was almost twenty feet in diameter and the ground was almost entirely bare, with the earth plainly visible.

Timber scouted the perimeter of the clearing, nosing the underbrush and stopping occasionally to paw at the ground. Nearby, Josiah was crouched before a smoky fire of wet wood. His face was as impassive as ever as he smoked his tobacco pipe and attended to the sickly flames.

Colvin stood up and stretched his aching back as Abigail approached. "Is that good enough for you?"

Sprawled in the muddy pit at his feet lay the exposed corpse of Jed Hawes. Despite having been interred for over a month, the primitive grave had slowed the process of decomposition. Still, the sour odor of putrefaction made Colvin grimace and lean away.

"Quite well done," Abigail replied, unperturbed. She crouched and placed her jack-o'-lantern at the head of the grave before producing her knife from the pocket of her cloak.

"What do you think you're doing?" Colvin demanded.

"The conjuring ritual requires both the blood of the conjuror and the remains of the ghost."

Colvin's face filled with revulsion. "No. I'll not let you defile this poor man's body."

"'Tis an abhorrent thought, to be sure," Abigail conceded. "But if I am going to end this haunting, I'm afraid it cannot be helped."

Colvin swallowed his disgust and stood by while Abigail cut through the filthy wool of Hawes' shirt and waistband. She then went to work at the mottled flesh, slicing strips from the dead man's gut and depositing what was necessary into a small tin pot.

Once the grisly chore was done, Abigail brought the pot to Josiah's fire and nestled it among the coals. A sickening smell of rancid meat soon drifted from within as she went about rendering the fat from Hawes' flesh. Next, she retrieved a scorched stick from Josiah's fire and used the blackened end to draw a ring in the dirt around the perimeter of the clearing. She did this three times, murmuring an incantation to herself as she went, circling from east to west in the trajectory of the sun moving from day to night.

Next, she drew a large pentacle in the ring. Hawes' grave lay at its center. She then added arcane sigils to the empty triangles of the pentacle's five points, each representing one of the elements. At the tip of the first point—that of the earth— Abigail laid a handful of dirt she took from Hawes' grave. She moved clockwise, lighting a small brass censer at the tip of the element of air. The heartening scent of wormwood incense coiled up to meet her. A red candle was placed at the third point for the element of fire, followed by a vial of water Abigail had taken from the stream.

Only the fifth and final element remained—that of the spirit. It was at the western point of the pentacle, in the direction of darkness and night.

Abigail moved to Keenan's pack and unstrapped his timber axe.

The young lumberjack eyed her uneasily. "What is that for?" It was the first words he had spoken since Abigail had set him to his task.

Abigail didn't reply. Instead, she positioned herself over Hawes' grave and raised the heavy axe high over her head. Before anyone could protest, she brought the blade swinging down and severed the dead man's head from his corpse in one swift strike.

Keenan couldn't stifle his exclamation as Abigail brought the decapitated head to the remaining point of the pentacle. With a small handsaw she produced from her pack, she proceeded to saw through the dead man's cranium above the empty eye sockets, separating the rounded top of the skull from the rest of the head. She then flipped the domed piece of bone over and returned it upside-down so that it lay like a bowl cradled in the open hole of the skull.

The men watched in horrified wonder as Abigail sliced through the flesh of her left wrist with the same knife she had used to carve the jack-o'-lantern. The instant flash of pain was both stinging and exhilarating at once. Blood poured from the wound and she let it drip freely into the waiting skull-bowl, filling it with crimson. Twilight was failing faster now, and the darkness was growing impatient. Very soon, it would paint the world in black.

Abigail savored the thrill of anticipation. She had been prepared for this moment since they discovered the dead men in the bunkhouse. Before this night was over, she would end this haunting.

Heedless of her bleeding wrist, Abigail retrieved the tin pot from Josiah and poured the dead man's fat across a flat piece of slate. She then let her wound bleed into the congealing mixture of fat and gave it a couple of minutes to cool before shaping the waxy substance into something resembling a candle.

"It is time," she said at last. "Join me in the circle."

As if waiting to see what Abigail would do with the silence it left behind, the wind seemed to settle as they came together at the center of the pentacle.

Abigail placed the tallow candle in the hollow jack-o'-lantern, sparked a flame, and imbued the grinning pumpkin with life. "In ancient times, jack-o'-lanterns were lit to illuminate the path for the dead to return to their graves." Her voice sounded strong and out of place in the lifeless silence of the hollow. "Jedediah Hawes' ghost will feel drawn to this place, but he will not come willingly. I must invoke the aid of Familiars from beyond the Veil—powerful spirits bound to my service—who will drag Hawes before us. But first, one thing more must be done."

She withdrew the iron talisman from around her neck and stooped to dangle the charm through the open hole at the top of the jack-o'-lantern. The candle's flame licked at the iron rune.

"As with many who dwell beyond the Veil, the Familiars I

am about to summon harbor an intense desire to live again. They will seek out any weakness you may unwittingly reveal."

"What kind of weaknesses?" Colvin asked.

"Fear; despair; mourning." Abigail gave Keenan a meaningful look. "If my Familiars find you sheltering such sentiments, they may very well use them to possess your body as their own."

Colvin's face grew grim. "How can we protect ourselves?"

"With this." Abigail held up the talisman. The iron now glowed a dull orange from the heat of the candle's flame. "It is a charmed ward against evil and instills courage in the face of death."

Colvin eyed the charm suspiciously. "How is it supposed to help all of us?"

The heated charm dangled from Abigail's hand as her eyes met his. "Open your shirt."

Chapter 26

The smell of sizzling skin and burning hair filled Colvin's nostrils until the blistering pain came to an abrupt end. When he opened his eyes and looked down, he saw the rune branded on his flesh above his left nipple. It was perhaps the length of his little finger and shaped like the letter "Y", except for a third line extending straight up between the two upraised arms.

Colvin waited, the fresh brand on his chest still throbbing as Abigail moved on to Keenan. Colvin half expected the young man to refuse, but the Irishman bared his chest and withstood the pain without question. When it was Josiah's turn, the Native pulled his red coat open and stood firm as the heated rune seared his bare skin.

Once it was done, Abigail let the talisman cool before returning it around her neck. "Join hands."

They did as she instructed, joining hands around the open grave at the center of the protective circle. Abigail positioned herself on the eastern side of the pentacle, above the glowing jack-o'-lantern and opposite the decapitated head of Jed

Hawes. Keenan stood to her right while Josiah took the place across from her. Colvin completed the circle to Abigail's left and took her palm into his right hand. Her fingers were sticky with her own blood, but she didn't seem to care. There was something different about her now, an excited flush to her face and an intense brilliance in her eyes that was fearsome to witness. A strange current passed through Colvin at her touch, as if she were radiating some strange power.

"Hawes' head will serve as a scrying mirror, a window to the realm beyond the Veil. It is the portal through which my Familiars must travel to bring Hawes' ghost before us." Abigail glanced around at the circle of men. "You may find the experience... *unsettling*. The charm I have given you will protect you from spirit possession, but we must not let go of each other. No matter what may happen or what you may witness, you must remember that we are safe only so long as our circle of the living remains unbroken."

Abigail paused a moment to make sure they understood. Only when she was satisfied did she close her eyes, drew a deep breath, and chanted. Her voice rang out from the center of the pentacle, invoking the names of her Familiars and commanding them to her service. The glow of the jack-o'-lantern caught her from below and cast her face in an eerie orange light. Over and over she recited the incantation, gaining volume with each repetition. Her voice seemed too loud in the breathless silence and made Colvin feel like a trespasser begging to be caught.

And then, something seemed to change.

There was a stirring in the air, as if some unseen power was awakening.

A shiver ran across Colvin's skin.

Something was coming.

An icy breeze brushed against Colvin's face, fluttering his hair and beard. He looked across the open grave and found Keenan staring at him, eyes wide and fearful. He became aware of Timber shivering and whimpering pitifully against his leg. At the same time, Josiah's hand clenched around his own. His old friend sensed it too. They all did.

There was a new presence among them, something invisible that hadn't been there moments ago. The air hummed and crackled with its energy.

The wind gathered in intensity, coming from everywhere and nowhere, whipping at them and howling in their ears. Timber let out a low whine from where he cowered by Colvin's side. Colvin felt the hairs on his own neck rising. Something told him he had made a terrible mistake; he should never have set foot in this foul and dreadful place. What they were doing was foolish! He should turn away; abandon this place; stop Abigail before it was too late!

That was when Hawes' head came to life.

Chapter 27

Keenan had never been so afraid in his life. He held fast to Abigail's hand, his blood thundering in his ears as Jed Hawes' gruesome head took on a life of its own.

It began with a flicker of light somewhere within the bloody bowl of Hawes' skull, like lightning seen through a porthole on a dark sea. Keenan thought it had been his imagination until, ever so slowly, the blood began to move. A ghostly mist appeared, swirling below the crimson surface. It filled the shallow bowl as if trapped behind a thin plate of glass, churning and coiling with a life of its own.

And then Keenan's very soul shriveled in terror as the mist rose up and came *through* the blood.

Too spellbound to move, Keenan trembled as Abigail's Familiars spewed from the portal like smoke billowing through a hole in the roof of a burning house. His mind became a chaotic riot of terror. One thought rose above the others, insisting itself over and over: *This isn't right! This isn't right! This isn't right!*

Abigail stood like a rock cleaving through a rushing stream

as the unnatural mist flowed past her to the outskirts of the protective circle. Her Familiars remained there, encircling the large pentacle. They defied the howling wind, slithering with a life of their own, a sinister white mass blanketing the darkened woods.

Keenan went cold all over as a chilling sense of evil rolled over him like a dark wave. An instinctive, panic-stricken impulse to break away and flee overcame him. He tried to swallow, but his mouth had gone dry. He wished Father Carnes were there to reassure him of the righteousness of their actions.

As if reading his thoughts, Abigail tightened her grip on his palm and held firm as her incantation climbed toward a frightening pitch.

Keenan's heart raced and slammed against his ribs.

This isn't right! This isn't right! This isn't right!

Just then, Keenan heard a voice whisper into his ear.

She wants you dead...

He froze, muscles going taut, ears pricked. He glanced around at the others. Their shadowy faces appeared disembodied in the dim light of the jack-o'-lantern. Abigail was lost in her chant. Her eyes were closed and her face had taken a feverish shine. Colvin and Josiah were both mesmerized by the sinister mist slithering around the outskirts of Abigail's protective ring.

Who had spoken?

Keenan was certain he heard a voice. Even through the pandemonium raging around him, it had been clear and crisp and strangely familiar. He tried to place it but found he couldn't. Had it been a man? A woman? Keenan's breaths came fast and heavy and his gaze remained riveted by the white mass crawling around the perimeter of the protective circle. There were shapes in there, the vaporous forms of Abigail's Familiars undulating within the murky depths. They rose and receded like figures made of nothing more than smoke.

Abigail's chant came to an abrupt end. Her chest heaved and there was something frightening about her face as she spoke. "Bring me Jedediah Hawes."

A heartbeat passed as Keenan's flesh tingled with the otherworldly electricity in the air. The mist came alive again, swirling and coiling as the Familiars circled the ring like a hunter stalking prey. They accelerated, gaining force with each revolution. Keenan felt small and powerless, like a sailor trapped in the eye of a maelstrom.

She's going to kill you and leave you to rot...

Keenan jumped as if something had stung him. A bone-tingling spark of panic went off in his mind. He *did* know that voice.

Keenan's wide eyes found Colvin's, but the lumberjack's grim expression gave no indication of having heard anything. A chill shot up Keenan's spine as a dreadful realization came to him: the voice was speaking to *him...* and *only* to him.

Keenan felt a strange vibration in his head and realized his teeth were chattering. He thought of what had brought him here to this godforsaken place.

Suicides.

An evil spirit driving people to take their own lives.

Did it whisper to them with a voice just like this one?

With a voice just like O'Brennan's?

Keenan was trembling all over now. It wasn't possible! O'Brennan's ruined body lay in a muddy hole miles down the river! And yet, Keenan couldn't deny he heard his old friend's voice.

Save yourself, my friend. Let go of her before she drags you down too...

"I mustn't," Keenan murmured aloud. "I must not break the circle..."

She's a witch, Keenan. She's going to use you and kill you just like she killed me...

Keenan's mind resisted the idea. Why was he listening? A bear had killed O'Brennan, not Abigail. She was there to save them, to put an end to the suicides.

Or was she?

It occurred to Keenan that he knew nothing about this mysterious stranger, this cool and calculating woman who seemed willing to risk all of their lives to satisfy her own designs. Abigail had barely batted an eyelash at O'Brennan's death. Keenan knew his most trusted friend wouldn't lie. O'Brennan had come to warn him, to save him. From what?

From Abigail.

A bestial snarl suddenly erupted from within the crimson void of Hawes' skull. It was deep and malevolent and charged with the promise of violence. Keenan's blood turned to ice. Nothing living could have made that sound. Abigail's Familiars were dragging something awful before them, something that wanted their blood.

Another snarl, this one of boundless rage. It was followed by a shriek that was shrill and piercing and terrible to hear.

Keenan cringed and shrank as another bloodcurdling

scream rose from the skull, evolving into words, a howling rush of menace and threats.

…tear you to pieces bathe in your blood strip your flesh smash your bones tear you to pieces…

Keenan shook all over as he opened his mouth. His throat had gone dry, but he mustered enough voice to pray. And yet, even as the prayer escaped his lips, O'Brennan's voice closed its embrace around his mind once more.

If you don't let go of her hand, you're gonna die horribly, just like those men in the bunkhouse…

Keenan slipped under the voice's spell like a drowning man pulled ever deeper by an undertow. Conscious thought deserted him and his jaw hung aghast at the image coalescing on the bloody surface of Hawes' skull.

A pale face appeared, the ethereal likeness of a bearded man made of mist. Like some ghastly cameo framed in crimson, the image became more distinct until the spirit finally pushed through the portal. The ghostly figure floated into the air. Even the shifting, colorless smoke of the apparition's eyes couldn't diminish their piercing intensity as Jed Hawes' spectral shape hung suspended above his own rotting head.

Keenan trembled at the soulless malevolence of the dead man's unearthly shrieks. He looked at Abigail, hoping for reassurance. What he saw in her face filled him with dread.

Save yourself, Keenan…

Keenan's head swiveled toward O'Brennan's voice. It was coming from the forest.

Yes. It's safe out here…

The howl of the wind became distant and the raging snarls receded. Keenan didn't feel the pressure of the hands clasped around his own. There was only his old friend urging him on, calling him away from the circle, beckoning him toward the dark safety of the trees.

They're gonna tear you to bloody shreds, Keenan. And when they're done, they're gonna drag you down, down, down to their cold black hell...

Keenan knew in his heart that O'Brennan spoke the truth. No one could master such infernal forces. And when Abigail lost control, her Familiars would tear him to pieces—tear them *all* to pieces. Himself, Colvin, Josiah, even Abigail herself; all would fall victim to the spirits' terrible thirst for warm blood.

Leave them, Keenan. Come to me. Let me protect you...

He no longer needed convincing; he had to flee before it was too late. If he didn't, he would die. Keenan knew this with an awful certainty. O'Brennan wouldn't lie. O'Brennan cared for him, loved him like a brother. Keenan couldn't resist; he had to follow his friend's warm, comforting voice away from this terrible place.

Keenan's gaze returned to the black void of the forest. Out there among the trees, he would find O'Brennan. He would find safety.

His grip on Abigail's hand relaxed ever so slightly.

Yes. That's it. Let go, Keenan. Save yourself...

Chapter 28

Something was wrong. Abigail knew it the instant the dead man appeared on the bloody surface of the scrying bowl. Never had she encountered a spirit so powerful.

Hawes' shrieks pierced her mind like an arrowhead, threatening the immense concentration required to maintain her mastery over his spirit. A frozen block hardened in the pit of her belly. She had a terrifying vision of losing control of the deadly Familiars that bound Hawes. The dead man was going to break loose and unleashed his terrible wrath upon them all. Abigail knew she had made an awful mistake, one that might cost all of them their lives. She hadn't been prepared for such otherworldly power, such unrestrained fury.

With rising panic, Abigail's instincts took over. She lifted her boot, intent on crushing the jack-o'-lantern and banishing Hawes' spirit back from where it had come. It was the only way they could leave the circle alive. She had to do it now, now, now—before it was too late...

No! she commanded herself. *You must maintain control! You must have answers!*

Even as the thought asserted itself in her mind, Abigail felt herself withering under the shocking force of Hawes' dark energy. The sensation filled her with horror. The ghost had her, and he was dragging her down into his dark realm of rage and despair. Abigail's throat tightened. She was losing consciousness, plunging toward a black void. A terrible chill crawled into her skin, biting like teeth into her very bones. It was the dreadful cold of Hawes' grave. His fearsome energy was pulling her inexorably down toward it. A sliver of terror pierced her heart. She was lost if she didn't find a way to resist. The men around her would be slaughtered and the village would be doomed. She had to fight back, to assert her dominance, to find some way to repel and subdue the dead man.

Remember who you are! A voice in her head screamed. *Remember your fearsome lineage! Remember what you have done! You are strong! You fear neither the living nor the dead! The dead flee before you and bow at your command! You will defeat this loathsome abomination! You will not fail!*

Abigail grit her teeth and summoned her courage. The world vanished around her. There was no forest, no jack-o'-lantern, no hands clutching at her own. There was only her and this terrible apparition, locked in a deadly struggle of wills.

Drawing upon all of her strength—all of her indomitable resolve—Abigail began to push against the excruciating shrieks assailing her mind. There was a terrible stalemate as two unstoppable forces collided. Abigail was staggered by Hawes' seething rage, his burning desire to split her open and empty her veins of her warm, living blood. She fought the agony exploding in her brain and pressed her thoughts to overcoming and dominating the horrifying spirit. She grimaced and gasped with the exertion.

Blood pounded in her ears.

Her muscles quivered and ached under the intense strain.

And then—very slowly—she felt Hawes' strength falter under the force of her own. A euphoric rush of ecstasy surged from Abigail's core, spreading through all parts of her being. She was vaguely conscious of Colvin's frightened eyes on her as she gradually brought Hawes' spirit under her control.

The terrifying moments of weakness had passed. She was shaken, but she was now certain she could maintain her dominance over the dead man—but only if she sustained her concentration. The danger was great. Even now, she could feel the ghost gathering his strength once again, testing her defenses, looking to exploit some unguarded hole that would crack her open.

If she made one mistake, she would doom them all.

Abigail didn't hesitate. She would have her answers from this hateful spirit, even if it meant gambling with all of their lives. "I am the necromancer who commands you by a bond of blood." She leveled her defiant gaze at the dreadful apparition. "I seek answers to questions you have left unresolved."

"I am beholden to none." The dead man's hollow voice rose from a realm of eternal darkness and his eyes were windows into nothingness.

"You will answer!" Abigail's tone rose with her confidence. "Or I will leave you bound to this earthly place for eternity! Here you will find no rest, no escape from the memory of your own shameful end! There will be no forgiving oblivion beyond the Veil! Each day of your unending existence, you will bear the pain of of that memory. Here, you will *become* Hell!"

The heat of the dead man's simmering anger radiated against Abigail's skin. An enraged roar burst from his vaporous maw like that of a wild beast awakening to find itself in a cage.

Abigail braced herself, ready to trample the jack-o'-lantern under foot. An eternity passed until the roar subsided. A tense, smoldering silence was left in its wake.

"Ask what you will." The dead man seethed.

In the hush that followed, Abigail noticed Keenan breathing a prayer over and over. She stole a glance and saw that he was terrified, coming apart, his eyes too wide for his face.

There wasn't time to worry about him. Abigail had to act quickly. Every moment Hawes' spirit remained before them was tempting their destruction. Her thoughts strayed back to those terrifying moments when she had felt the dead man dragging her down, down, down. She shuddered as she remembered the sensation of the bitter cold crawling through her flesh...

Keenan would have to fend for himself.

Abigail gathered her own courage, drew a breath into her lungs, and braced herself for what would come next. "Why did you take your own life?"

The dead man erupted with another shrill and tormented shriek, as if he were mortally wounded. The smoky figure writhed violently against his invisible shackles, his nebulous shape warping and distending like a serpent trying to escape its own skin.

"I ask you again, Jedediah Hawes!" Abigail shouted over his infuriated wail. "What happened on the shore of Lake Tear of the Clouds? Why did you take your own life?"

The dead man flailed in the air, struggling against the bonds that held him.

"I was deceived!" His hollow wail was now tortured with despair.

Abigail's pulse quickened and thudded in her throat. It was working! "By whom? Who deceived you?"

"The unlord!"

"Who is the unlord?"

The ghost thrashed, choking on the answer like a man who has been poisoned.

"Who is the unlord?" Abigail insisted again. "Name him!"

"The king of the wicked! The venom of God!"

Just then, Keenan's palm slipped from Abigail's.

Her weightless hand dropped unexpectedly through the empty air and landed against her hip. She shot Keenan a horrified look. He was backing away, staring at her, his lip quivering.

He had broken the circle.

"Keenan! No!" Abigail cried.

It was too late.

Keenan hesitated for only a heartbeat before dashing from the protective ring.

In a flash, Hawes' spectral shape burst into tendrils of billowing mist. Abigail's bloodthirsty Familiars released their hold on the dead man and streaked through the air after

Keenan.

Freed of his captors, Hawes' ghost came together once more and hung suspended above his own bloody head. He rose higher, arching his back like a viper ready to strike. The baleful hollows of his eyes smoldered with triumph as he glared down at the woman who had summoned him, this mortal witch who had held him captive and forced him to relive such awful memories.

He flew at her without warning.

Abigail had enough time to snatch the talisman from her neck before he lifted her from her feet and sent flying. She crashed to the ground on the edge of the clearing, landing hard on her chest and gasping as the air exploded from her lungs. Her hand scrabbled in the dirt for the talisman when she felt the spirit's claws tear through her cloak and rake across her back. A sudden gush of warmth washed over her skin as blood poured from the wounds. The dead man struck again and again, clawing at her flesh.

Abigail tried to scream, but her cry was cut short as the spirit hauled her up and flipped her onto her back. It all happened with the speed of a lightning strike, a dizzying blur of blood and pain. She glimpsed Hawes' vaporous form towering over her before he slashed his claws across her face, barely missing her eye. She could taste the hot copper of her blood streaming over her lips. Another strike tore through her cloak from her shoulder to her breast. The savage fury of the dead man's assault was overwhelming. He would flay her alive if she didn't find some way to defend herself.

At last, her palm found the talisman. She fumbled for it, closed around it, shot it up in desperation.

The spirit recoiled with a furious roar.

"Destroy the candle!" Abigail screamed.

Her cry jolted Colvin from his momentary shock. He leaped into action, raising his heavy leather boot and stomping down on the jack-o'-lantern. It exploded outward under the impact, shards of pumpkin flying from under his heel. The light of the enchanted candle was snuffed instantly.

Abigail scrambled back on her elbows as the spectral figure towering over her suddenly came apart. The dead man's ghostly figure lost its shape and dissolved into coils of black mist. The reaction spread upward, as if Hawes were being consumed by an invisible flame and transformed into a roiling cloud of black smoke. Hawes' spirit let out one last, furious howl before his spectral face disintegrated. The black cloud then seemed to ignite from within, breaking into thousands of swirling particles that glowed a hellish orange in the darkness. The fragments soared into the air like smoldering sparks blown from a fire, swirling in a dazzling vortex of twinkling light before vanishing into the night.

Abigail staggered to her feet. Colvin was at her side, shouting something she was too dazed to comprehend. Through the crimson haze of blood and pain, she heard Keenan's shrieks coming from somewhere amid the slithering cloud of mist.

Her Familiars were killing him.

Abigail shoved Colvin aside and lurched toward Hawes' rotting head. "By the blood of your conjurer and master! I banish you back beyond the Veil!"

There was an unearthly roar as the mist broke into four separate tendrils that shot toward her in a fury. Abigail fell to one knee and held her breath as, one by one, each coiling spear of mist dove into the bloody skull. When the last of the Familiars had vanished through the portal, Abigail kicked the head over and spilled the blood, sealing the gate.

It was over.

There was no time for relief. Josiah was already dashing to where Keenan lay sprawled in the underbrush. Colvin caught Abigail in his arms and steadied her as they went after him.

Keenan's ruined body was a nightmarish patchwork of lacerated gore. His torso was asunder, the flesh ripped away to reveal living organs. Four jagged slashes were flayed deep into his face from the right side of his hairline to his mouth. Portions of white bone were visible through the gouts of blood welling to the surface. The pulpy bulb of his right eye bulged from its ruined socket. His left eye was wide and blank, as if already given over to death. His jaw moved, but no sound came from his mouth. He was still alive but fading fast, his breath becoming more faint and shallow with every passing second.

Josiah was kneeling beside the dying man when Abigail shoved past him and dropped to her knees. "Why did you do it, Keenan?" she hissed, heedless of the severity of her own wounds. Blood dripped from her face and mingled with Keenan's as she peered into his vacant eye. "Tell me!"

"Leave him be!" Colvin laid a firm hand on her shoulder.

Abigail ignored him, brushing away his hand and shoving him back when he tried to return it. Some *thing* had driven Keenan to break the circle. She had seen it in his eyes before he had turned and fled. She had to get him to talk before it was too late.

"Keenan!" Abigail's blood-rimmed eyes blazed. "You looked at me for help! Why did you break the circle? What drove you to run for the forest?"

A sickening gurgle rolled up from Keenan's throat as blood invaded his windpipe. His jaw worked, again and again, mouthing words no one could hear. He swallowed, choked, found enough air to fill a whisper. Abigail pressed her ear to his lips.

"O'Brennan... said... save yourself..."

A bubble of blood welled from his mouth and slid back down across his cheek. His hand found Abigail's and crushed it in a death-grip while his left eye flew to an impossible size, straining from his skull. The dreadful moment lasted only seconds before his last breath went out of him with a wet rattle.

Abigail let Keenan's limp hand fall from her own and she dragged herself to her feet. Her head swam and the ground seemed to tilt beneath her. There was a buoyancy in her legs, as if her knees were about to buckle.

Colvin lent her his arm. She clutched at him for a moment before drawing away, ashamed of her momentary weakness. A dreadful numbness crawled into her chest, threatening to paralyze her. She fought to keep it down. Colvin was saying something about her wounds, but his voice didn't seem real. *None* of this seemed real. How could Keenan have been made to break the circle? He was warded against possession, protected by the charm she had given him. No spirit had ever overcome it. He couldn't have been possessed. Unless...

Unless it wasn't a spirit.

Abigail staggered as an awful realization fell upon her.

Whatever evil was plaguing the village wasn't a ghost. It was something much, much worse.

Chapter 29

They were waiting for her when she returned to the village. Heath MacIntyre was in the lead, marching at the forefront of a half-dozen men to intercept Abigail as she and her two companions emerged from the forest onto Main Street.

Colvin knew they meant trouble the instant he laid eyes on them.

"Where are the others?" Heath drew to a halt near the chapel, deliberately blocking Colvin's way. "O'Brennan and Keenan?"

Colvin gave him an irritated frown. "Mind who you're talking to, MacIntyre. You're in no position to be making demands of me."

"I asked ye' a question, Colvin," Heath insisted. "Where are the others?"

"*Mister* Colvin." Colvin's dark eyes narrowed to a hard point. "I'm still in charge around here and I can still send you packing should you happen to forget it." He glared at Heath, all the while wondering if he had just made an empty threat. What would he do if the big man refused to leave?

Something had changed in Heath. Colvin didn't like the look in his eyes. There was something dangerous there, something new and troublesome. Colvin took stock of the men who stood with the big man. They had it too: a hard and angry fervor. How many others in town now had that same look? It was exactly as Colvin had feared. Instead of blowing over, the storm of superstition and mistrust had only intensified while he and Abigail were gone. Where was Duncan Emmons? Father Carnes? What had they been doing in his absence?

Colvin knew he had better tread lightly. He ran a hand over his beard, swallowed, and chose his next words carefully. "O'Brennan was mauled by a bear our first night out. We buried him before we reached North Camp."

The revelation drew angry murmurs from Heath's followers.

Heath scowled and shook his shaggy head, fixing Colvin with a stern glare. "And Keenan?"

"Wounded, trying to save O'Brennan. He succumbed to his injuries and died at North Camp." The lie rolled easily from Colvin's tongue. He had been rehearsing it for hours.

The descent from the mountain had been swift at Abigail's insistence. They decided not to speak of what had happened at North Camp. The villagers were already frightened enough. The surviving trio had lingered at the camp only long enough for Abigail to clean her wounds and dress them with a poultice of dried flowers and herbs she had produced from her pack. Its effectiveness was nothing short of miraculous.

In the time that had passed since they had left the terrible scene of the ritual behind, they hadn't rested and hardly ate, stopping only so that Abigail could brew a foul-smelling tea that she sipped from a tin cup as they traveled. She remained withdrawn and said very little, insisting only that she meet with Father Carnes without delay, but refusing to elaborate when pressed for an explanation.

"Two more of our men dead," Heath grumbled.

Colvin exhaled wearily. "Move aside, Heath. We've traveled long and without rest and we've still much to attend to."

Heath didn't budge. Instead, he stabbed a finger at Abigail. "This is *her* doing."

The other men grumbled their approval. Colvin heard the danger in their tone. His veins flooded with adrenaline as he put himself between them and Abigail. "Walk away, Heath."

"We've come to do what should've been done the moment she arrived here," Heath growled. "The woman's a witch. Where she goes, damnation follows."

"I said walk away," Colvin insisted. "I'm warning you."

"Warning me?" Heath sneered. "The only warning I'll heed is the Lord's own. He's angry at this town, at this cradle of sin that *you've* been responsible for!"

Colvin's hand curled into a fist as Heath made a move to push past him. Timber let out a menacing growl and crouched low, his ears flat back against his head. The other men crowded closer to see what would happen next. Colvin put himself in Heath's way but kept his fist from swinging. If he struck first, he would provoke the other men as well. His one hope of maintaining leadership over the village was to remain calm and in control. Let Heath be the irrational one.

"Get outta me way!" Heath's face was going red around his thick goatee and a vein bulged and pumped like a cord in his neck. He rammed a shoulder into Colvin's.

Timber's growls turned into a loud, angry bark, but Colvin grabbed the scruff of the dog's neck and clamped down hard.

Heath's eyes burned as he rose up and drew back a fist.

There was a loud click and the big man froze. Heath's eyes whipped around to the pistol Josiah had pressed to the side of his skull.

"You godless bastard!" Heath snarled. "Get that iron off me!"

Josiah kept the pistol aimed and ready. His black eyes were hard, his face an unreadable mask.

The other men let out outraged exclamations, but they remained where they stood. All knew better than to challenge the inscrutable Native. Colvin could almost hear the pulsing tattoo of their collective heartbeats.

The standoff seemed to stretch on forever, everyone holding their breaths, waiting for the hammer to fall, the pistol to go off...

"Heath MacIntyre!" Father Carnes bellowed as he stormed from the chapel. "You men! All of you! That's enough, I say!"

No one moved.

As if looking for a signal, all eyes remained on Heath. Colvin prayed he would back off. A long, bated moment passed until the big man yielded. Colvin tried not to let his relief show as Heath threw Carnes a scathing glance and eased back, quivering with rage.

Josiah kept the pistol level with Heath's head as the lumberjack turned to the men gathered behind him. Heath's gray eyes swept over each of them, his face red and twisted in disgust. "The Almighty demands expiation! We must make atonement! We must rid ourselves of this witch!"

"Who are you to presume to know the will of God, Heath MacIntyre?" Carnes thundered. "Who are *you* to pretend to His divine wisdom? 'Tis not for a mere wretch such as you to decree who shall live and who shall die! None but the Lord himself shall be our judge!"

The hush that followed was the sort that follows on the heels of a thunderclap. Colvin had never witnessed such a forcible display of authority from the young priest. Carnes' chest was swollen underneath his cassock. His right hand clenched and released unconsciously, the knuckles going white. His pale green eyes blazed and the furious indignation in his voice imbued him with an impressive sense of power.

Even Heath seemed taken aback. He glared at Carnes, momentarily confounded, before turning away. "You'll rot in Hell, witch." He sneered over his shoulder at Abigail. "And I'll be the one to see ye' on yer way."

The other men fell in behind him as he stalked off, muttering and casting sidelong glances at Abigail as they went.

Colvin gave Carnes an uneasy nod and watched them go. An icy dread had settled into his gut. The situation in the village was much more severe than he had thought. Heath's menacing provocations weren't over; they were only beginning. Banishing him from the village now would do no good; MacIntyre already had too many followers. Carnes might have bought Abigail some time before the men came back for her, but the unrest would only escalate with every moment she remained among them.

Colvin realized he now had another problem to contend

with as well. What would happen once the rest of the villagers discovered what had become of the men at North Camp? It wouldn't be long before someone noticed that the timber had stopped coming downstream. They would think there was a logjam and Colvin would be forced to send someone to investigate. He guessed it would only be another day or two until it happened, maybe less. What would he tell them then?

And what would happen if yet another villager was to commit suicide?

Colvin tried to push the thoughts from his mind. He stole a glance at Abigail. She was a frightful sight. The slashes across her face were red and swollen and one eye was entirely bloodshot. Her bright blond hair was dull and matted and the clothes he had lent her were tattered and bloodstained. Colvin marveled at the strength that had allowed her to persevere this far.

And yet, throughout the altercation with Heath's small mob, Abigail had remained as cool and silent as a winter wood. Her scarred face was gray and drawn with exhaustion, but her cold, blue eyes gleamed dangerously. The look on her face gave Colvin a chill. He decided he didn't want to know how she intended to defend herself if Heath tried to make good on his threats. When the time came, better that he be the one to do it for her.

Chapter 30

"What do you know about demons?" Abigail asked from her chair at the vesting table of the chapel's vestry. A tin cup of black coffee resting on the bare desk before her steamed its bitter aroma into the dampness of the small room.

Father Carnes stood peering at her with his arms folded across his chest and his shoulder leaning against the pine cabinet he stored his vestments. He looked almost as exhausted as Abigail. His bearded face was haggard and dark rings confined his eyes, divesting them of what little color they held. Abigail could only wonder at the battles he had recently fought on her behalf. Why was he doing it? Why did he trust her?

Carnes had barely spoken as Abigail related the events of her journey to North Camp. His stony silence only seemed to deepen when she told him of her ill-fated conjuring of Jed Hawes' spirit and of Keenan's death. His face had gone dark then, but he had kept his reproaches to himself. Abigail didn't need to be reminded of her broken promise to refrain from what the priest had called sorcery. She had never intended to honor it, anyway.

"Demons?" Carnes repeated, arching an eyebrow. "I'm afraid I don't follow you, Ms. Jacobs."

Abigail took a long sip of her coffee. She was glad for its heat but longed for a good helping of whiskey. Every mile of her trek down the mountain and every sleepless moment weighed on her like heavy chains. Her potions had done wonders to help speed her recovery, but her wounds still stung and throbbed whenever she moved. She wanted nothing more than a hot bath and a strong drink, but both would have to wait. If her suspicions were correct, there wasn't a moment to lose. The entire village was in danger—and if her earlier encounter with Heath MacIntyre was any indication, it was only a matter of time before they ran her out of town. Or worse.

"Keenan was driven to break the circle against his will," Abigail said. "I am certain of it. I saw it in his face before he was drawn to the forest. He was possessed."

"But not by a spirit," Carnes interjected.

Abigail sipped her coffee again and shook her head.

"How can you be so sure?"

"I imparted him with a charm of warding. No spirit can take possession of one who bears it." Abigail paused for a moment, as if unsure of how to proceed. "But there are *other* beings with the ability to possess a man, ones upon which such a charm would have no effect."

Carnes gave her a dubious look. "Demons? You now believe a demon possessed Keenan and drove him to suicide?"

"I know how this must sound to you, Mr. Carnes, but please hear me out." Abigail shifted in her chair. "I have exhausted every other plausible explanation for what is happening here in Tahawus. I had hoped against hope to find answers at North Camp, but I have returned empty-handed. And yet, *something* drove Keenan to take his own life. If we rule out the possibility of a spirit, there remains only one other explanation that I can think of."

"The devil." Carnes lowered his arms and moved to take the seat across the table from her. "Ms. Jacobs, such notions may well have been fashionable in the Middle Ages, but this is the nineteenth century. There are now some among the clergy—myself included—who believe that biblical demons are actually metaphors for the personal failings that keep us from embracing the loving glory of God. Despite what devotees such as Heath MacIntyre may hold true, there is a growing belief that Hell is not a physical place of fire and damnation, but a *spiritual* one. It is a personal state of being where man endures the spiritual torment of his separation from God. To think that Keenan was possessed by some demon and driven to take his own life... well, it just doesn't seem rational."

"How very enlightened of you," Abigail remarked with a hint of sarcasm. She nodded to where Carnes' Bible lay on the corner of the table. "Unfortunately, there are some things in your Good Book that are actually true."

A silence fell between them and Abigail lowered her gaze to stare into her coffee. Its black surface conjured images of the bloody bowl of Hawes' skull. She looked away and said, "Perhaps if I were permitted to examine my Book of Shadows, I could—"

"That is out of the question, Ms. Jacobs. You have already

proven by your actions that I cannot trust you to refrain from sorcery. As long as you are a guest in this village, your infernal book will remain safely in my possession." Carnes indicated a cabinet set against the far wall of the room. Rows of worn books stood arranged behind its locked glass doors.

It heartened Abigail to see her Book of Shadows safe among them.

"You have my assurance that I will return it to you on the day that you put your back to this village and leave it behind," Carnes concluded.

Abigail glared at him before rising from her chair and crossing the room to stand by the only window. Beyond the pane, the sky was a dirty white shroud drawn over the village. It was now mid-October, and the colors were gone from the oaks and elms. The few remaining leaves were brown and shriveled, like bits of desiccated skin clinging to skeletal fingers.

"Do the words *the venom of God* mean anything to you, Mr. Carnes?" Abigail asked.

Carnes' beard drew together as his lips tightened. "Where did you hear that?"

The sharpness of his tone caught Abigail's attention. She turned from the window. "The spirit of Jed Hawes said he killed himself in order to find release from what he called *the venom of God.*"

Carnes frowned. "By your own admission, Hawes' spirit was murderous and mad. We cannot trust anything you might have gleaned from him."

"Perhaps. But what do the words signify?"

Carnes drew a breath and let it out. "'Tis an old term—

very old—appearing not in the Bible, but only in ancient texts of the Apocrypha. In the *Book of Enoch*, the venom of God is used as a reference to Samael."

"Who is Samael?"

"A fallen angel cast out of heaven for fathering children with human women."

Abigail's tired eyes came to life. "A demon?"

Carnes nodded but gave her a look that seemed to dismiss whatever significance she had inferred. "Ms. Jacobs, the *Church* doesn't formally recognize the Book of Enoch. I don't believe—"

"Please, indulge me. What else can you tell me about this Samael?"

Carnes shrugged and shook his head as he crossed the room to the book cabinet, produced a ring of keys from his pocket to unlock the doors, and plucked a volume from the rows. "Unfortunately, my knowledge of demonology is rather lacking." He handed Abigail the book. "Perhaps you can find your answers for yourself."

Abigail went quiet as she cracked open Carnes' copy of the *Book of Enoch* and perused the pages. Outside, a sudden gust sent a whirlwind of dead leaves brushing against the window. It was an eerie, lonesome sound.

Suddenly, Abigail shot to her feet and snapped the book shut. The abrupt movement made her light-headed, and she swayed for an instant. She closed her eyes, her hands going back to the table for support as she waited for the dizzying sensation to pass.

"Where are you going?" Carnes asked, grasping her elbow to steady her.

"To find Duncan." Abigail pulled her cloak over her shoulders and went for the door with the *Book of Enoch* clutched under one arm. Her other hand fished deep into her pocket and fell upon the object she was looking for. "There is something I must show him."

Chapter 31

Duncan Emmons squinted through his magnifying glass and examined the bright yellow stone he held pinched between his thumb and forefinger. "Where did you find this?"

He sat at the large worktable at the center of the company office. Abigail stood opposite, silhouetted by the cold light of the only window. The afternoon was growing late and the shadow she cast fell long and straight across the small room.

Glenn Colvin reclined in a creaky chair in the corner, his attention divided between their conversation and the peeling of a boiled egg. Timber lay curled on the floorboards at his feet. His deep, amber eyes were fixed on Abigail as he panted softly.

"Do you recognize it?" Abigail asked.

"I... well, yes." Duncan lowered the magnifying glass and adjusted his spectacles.

"What is it?"

"It's sulfur."

A dark look came over Abigail as she stepped from the window into the light. Once again, Duncan was shocked at the battered sight of her. When word of her return had spread throughout the village that morning, he had hurried to find her before Heath MacIntyre did. By the time he had arrived, it was too late; Abigail had already sequestered herself in the chapel with Father Carnes. When Duncan had returned to the office, he'd found Colvin waiting for him and they had spent the afternoon catching up on recent events.

"Sulfur," Abigail repeated, as if confirming something she had known all along. "Otherwise known as brimstone, correct?"

Duncan nodded.

"Brimstone?" Colvin sat up in his seat. "As in hellfire and damnation? *That* brimstone?"

"Well, perhaps not in so many words, but yes," Duncan said. "The term brimstone literally means *burn stone* or *the stone that burns*." Duncan held the stone up into the sunlight. "You see, if put to fire, this stone would catch and melt into a molten, burning mass—the fumes of which can be most foul and irritating, I might add. 'Tis because of these properties that sulfur accompanies most traditional depictions of Hell, a place of eternal fire where even the rock itself burns." He swiveled to Abigail. "Where did you find this?"

"There were fragments of it in Chester Prue's mouth."

"I beg your pardon?" Colvin blurted.

"I didn't recognize them for what they were when I examined his remains," Abigail explained. "In my haste, I mistook them for broken bits of Prue's teeth. In retrospect, I am convinced that had we the opportunity to examine the other bodies, we would have discovered traces of sulfur among them as well."

Duncan ran a hand through his straw-like hair. "What does that mean?"

"Perhaps 'tis a sign of demon possession, some remnant left behind by Samael."

"I don't understand." Colvin interrupted, the half-peeled egg now forgotten in his hand as he peered at Abigail. "What has any of this to do with this demon you've been speaking of?"

Abigail took a chair from the table and turned it backward to prevent the seatback from pressing against her wounded back while she sat.

"Apocryphal texts tell us that when God hurled the rebel angels from heaven, they fell through the earth on their way to Hell. If we take these stories to be true, is it not possible that such lands could have remained forever cursed? According to Mohawk legend, Lake Tear of the Clouds is favored by the Dark Twin Spirit, Tawiskaron. The monsters he let loose there are believed to feast on men from *the inside*. What if these creatures are simply another interpretation of the evil beings we call demons? What if Lake Tear of the Clouds is one of those cursed spots where the rebel angels fell? Could it not then have become some sort of gateway to Hell? A portal through which a demon such as Samael could arise and lead human souls to destruction?"

Colvin's brow furrowed as he gazed at her, unconvinced.

"Don't you see?" Abigail persisted. "How else can we explain the fact that in every instance of suicide, there has been absolutely no evidence of the influence of the paranatural? 'Tis because what is happening in Tahawus is not paranatural but *demonic*."

Colvin shook his head as he finished peeling his egg. "The last time we pursued one of your theories, I lost two of my men."

Abigail's face flushed and she shot him a scathing look. But there was nothing reproachful in Colvin's expression. Instead, she saw a heavy sorrow haunting his usually cool and confident face. For the first time, she considered the toll the suicides were taking on the man. Justified or not, he felt responsible for each of them and bore the weight of his failures wherever he went.

"We've another problem to contend with." Duncan broke the brooding silence that had settled on the room.

"What would that be?" Colvin sighed.

"Heath MacIntyre. He's gained power in your absence, Glenn. Carnes and I have done our best to defend Abby, but Heath's been relentless in his efforts to turn the townsfolk against her. He blames her for his wife's death."

"That's absurd." Colvin sniffed dismissively.

"Perhaps. But everyone saw what Abby did to heal Hannah Gill. Instead of being grateful, Hannah's own mother brought the girl to Carnes to seek absolution for witchcraft. The villagers are frightened and Heath's using their fear to turn them against the stranger in town. Carnes has opposed him at every turn, denouncing Heath's tirades and trying his best to assure the people that the days of superstition are a thing of the past. Still, Heath's influence is growing daily. At first, no one paid him any attention. Most just pitied him for what had happened to Evelyn. Maybe it was because he's got a wife of his own that Owen Delaney was the first to listen to what Heath had to say. It was only a day or two before other men fell in with him. It happened quickly and it's gaining momentum. They've stopped working, refusing to return to their logging until something is done about Abby."

Duncan sighed as he turned to Abigail. "For the moment, I believe Carnes still wields enough clout to keep you safe, but I'm not sure how much longer that will last, especially if there's another suicide. Whatever you're planning to do, you had better do it soon, before Heath scares enough people into believing his insane notions about you. I don't know how far they'll go to act on them, but you don't want to still be here when they do."

"I appreciate your concern," Abigail said. "I will deal with Mr. MacIntyre if and when the need arises."

"Deal with?" Duncan gave her a wary look. "What do you intend to do?"

Abigail left the question unanswered, but her blue eyes seemed to flush and deepen. It was as if she almost welcomed the promise of violence. The look lasted only an instant before it vanished.

"So how do we stop it?" Colvin asked, leaning forward in his seat. "How do we defeat this demon?"

Abigail's answer was swift and decisive. "We don't."

"What?" Duncan's hopeful expression fell as he gazed at her. "Then how—"

Abigail cut him off with a raised a hand. "I have never before encountered an evil such as this. 'Tis far beyond our power to overcome. At this point, we've only one recourse if we are going to survive." She turned to Colvin. "You must call a town meeting without delay—tonight even. Every man and woman in Tahawus is to attend."

Colvin's face filled with confusion as he swallowed his egg. "What? Why?"

"We must evacuate the village."

Chapter 32

Glenn Colvin leaned against a dining table at the head of the mess hall as the villagers arrived. He projected the calm confidence that made him a leader of men. But apprehension knotted his insides tighter than the ropes binding the stacks of timber down by the lake.

This is a mistake, he thought. *It's too risky. I should never have let her convince me otherwise.*

It was nearing seven o'clock, and the sun had set about an hour ago. It was a chilly night, the coldest yet. A frosty wind swept through the darkened paths as if winter had extended its long finger and drawn it across the village.

The dining tables had all been cleared inside the huge mess hall. Oil lamps filled the makeshift meetinghouse was with a warm, orange glow that fell away to shadows in the corners.

As the cavernous space filled with people, Colvin's mind ran through everything that could go wrong. What if the villagers didn't believe him? What if they refused to leave? If Abigail was right, there was no telling how many more would fall victim to this bloodthirsty demon.

And then there was Heath MacIntyre.

What would the bereaved widower do when he arrived for the meeting? How loudly would Heath speak out against Abigail and how many more would he convince of her guilt? Colvin knew he was taking a dangerous gamble. The townsfolk would be frightened by what he was going to say. He wondered how many more would believe Heath's way of thinking might make it all better? He remembered the dangerous look he'd seen in Heath's eyes when the big man had confronted Abigail that morning. Heath's words echoed in his mind. *You'll rot in Hell, witch. And I'll be the one to see ye' on yer way...*

An unpleasant chill crawled up Colvin's spine as he heaved a deep breath and stole a glance over his shoulder. Abigail sat between Duncan and Father Carnes at the table behind him. She had undergone a remarkable transformation since Colvin had parted ways with her that afternoon. The ruined, bloodstained clothes were gone, and she was now dressed in her comfortable linsey-woolsey dress. Her golden hair was washed and elegantly braided, and her skin was clean and white. The jagged wounds across her face were the only reminders of the terrible incident at North Camp. And yet, even those seemed to have healed over the past few hours. They were now little more than four long, pink scratches.

Colvin marveled at how quickly she had recovered from the spirit's vicious attack. The unwelcome memory of those terrible moments only filled Colvin with more doubts. What if Abigail was wrong again? What if there was no demon? What if he was abandoning the village for nothing?

Colvin pushed those thoughts from his mind. All

afternoon and well into the evening, he had thought long and hard about his decision to evacuate the town. He could hardly believe he was even considering the possibility. It seemed rash and absurd; there had to be another way.

But the only thing to do was to evacuate. At North Camp, Abigail had opened Colvin's eyes to an entirely new world, a dreadful realm of darkness and creatures who lived beyond the grave. Colvin could no longer deny the possibility that something evil was at work in his village. He had buried too many bodies and seen too many horrors to doubt it. Somehow, he knew with awful certainty that even more would die if he refused to act. He wasn't about to second-guess his decisions now.

Too much is riding on what happens here tonight, he brooded. *Too many lives hang in the balance. I mustn't fail to convince them.*

The hall was brimming with people now. Men and women crammed together on the benches. Others leaned against the timber columns or stood shoulder to shoulder around the room. Word of the meeting had spread quickly. The entire village had come to hear what Colvin had to say. Never had so many gathered together under one roof. Only the children were absent, having already been tucked into bed by their mothers.

There was a nervous tension in the air. Colvin felt it in the stares that fell upon him and heard it in the hushed murmurs and whispers that drifted to his ears. The dangerous contest of wills between Heath MacIntyre and Father Carnes was taking its toll. As the villagers took sides, the mood of the community became one of division and mistrust. They were turning against each other, casting sidelong glances at their neighbors and sticking with those they trusted. Battle lines had been drawn in Colvin's absence, and he understood why Carnes had refused to address the audience himself. The embattled priest didn't oppose the idea of an evacuation, but he couldn't bring himself to lend the weight of his church to Abigail's theory about demon possession. Instead, Carnes was convinced most of the villagers still trusted Colvin and looked to him for leadership.

How much longer will that last? Colvin wondered bitterly.

As his eyes wandered over the crowd, Colvin caught a glimpse of Sally Gill, mother to little Hannah and widow of the unfortunate Cyrus. The petite woman was sandwiched between two other matrons on a bench near the back of the room. Her strawberry-blond hair was tucked beneath her cap and her hands were folded on the white apron across her lap. Colvin felt a swift prickle of guilt at the sight of her. After her husband had doused himself with oil and set himself ablaze, Sally had remained in the village simply because she had nowhere else to go; Tahawus was her only home. What would she do now that Colvin was forcing her to leave? What would become of her and her young daughter?

Sally looked up. Her eyes met Colvin's from across the room and he looked away. The gesture made him feel cowardly, but he couldn't bear to have the woman's eyes on him. Not now, not with what he was about to do to her.

Unconsciously avoiding eye contact with anyone else, it occurred to Colvin that Heath MacIntyre hadn't yet arrived. For a brief instant, he entertained the idea that Abigail's nemesis had boycotted the meeting altogether. But Colvin's hopes fell when the doors to the mess hall swung open at the last minute.

Heath lingered there a moment, his wild mane of hair buffeted by the wind. His cold, gray eyes wandered over the room, scouring the crowd before settling on Abigail. Owen Delaney and the rest of Heath's followers strode in from the night after him. They had grown from half a dozen to ten men in a single day.

At this rate, he'll have an entire congregation by morning, Colvin thought ruefully. *Damn him!*

Colvin kept an eye on Heath and his men as they settled into place at the rear of the hall. They fanned out with barely a word to anyone and stood in the shadows on either side of the door. Their faces were hard; their arms crossed over their chests as if taking up positions to stand guard. Colvin had a sinking suspicion he knew exactly who they intended to prevent from leaving: Abigail.

Colvin's eyes sought Josiah lingering in the shadows to his left. The Native had also taken notice of Heath's entrance. With a silent look, Colvin told him to be ready for trouble. Josiah understood and nodded once, his face a wooden mask.

Butterflies swarmed in Colvin's stomach and he realized he was stalling. Everyone was waiting, looking at him expectantly. The time had come; it couldn't be put off anymore. He raised a hand and brought the meeting to order.

"I've called you all here this evening to get some things out in the open." Colvin's strong voice carried across the room. "Things I know many of you have been thinking but haven't been talking about… the suicides."

Suicides.

The word seemed to hang in the air, drifting like a dark specter through the hush in the hall, brushing everyone with its chilling touch as it went.

"It's no secret that something strange has been going on here in Tahawus," Colvin continued. "You've all felt it, I know. Too many people have died for no reason. Too many good people." He paused, thinking of all the bodies he had buried in the past couple of months. Without thinking, his eyes fell on Sally Gill again and he quickly looked away. "It's also no secret that myself and Emmons have been working with Ms. Jacobs here to see if we can't get to the bottom of what's been going on. By now, you've all heard the rumors about our journey to North Camp. I figure it's time you all knew the truth about what we found there."

Colvin's next sentence caught in his throat and a moment passed before he could finally get it out. "Everyone at North Camp is dead."

A shocked uproar simmered up from the crowd like a pot boiling over. Colvin's gaze went to the back of the hall and saw Heath glowering back at him. His face was dark, his arms folded over his barrel chest. For the moment, the big man seemed content to remain silent.

What's he waiting for? Colvin wondered uneasily. *What's his game?*

"What happened to 'em, Colvin?" A voice shouted. "How'd they die? Indians?"

Colvin wrenched his gaze away from Heath and brought his attention back to the audience. He swallowed. His mouth had gone dry, and he wished he had poured himself a glass of water. "They killed themselves. Every one of them. Barricaded themselves in the bunkhouse and hanged themselves."

There was a great collective intake of air from the crowd that almost made the lamps flicker. Several of the women were weeping now, their quiet sobs rising and falling beneath the swelling tide of outrage.

"Why? Why'd they do it?" Another voice cried.

"Some *thing* made them do it," Colvin said. "The same thing that drove the others to take their own lives over these past few months. I know we're all thinking it, so I might as well come out and say it… something evil is at work here in Tahawus, something old and terrible and bent on our destruction. I'm not entirely certain what it is, but there's one thing I am certain of: we're no longer safe here." He paused, giving his words a moment to sink in. "That's why I'm proposing that we evacuate the village as soon as possible."

There were gasps and exclamations as the significance of what Colvin was suggesting took hold. He held a hand in the air, calling for order.

"The way I see it, we've no other choice," he said, once the commotion had settled. "Whatever this evil is, I don't believe it will stop. I've seen what it can do with my own eyes at North Camp. The same fate could be our own if we don't leave."

"And go where?" Heath's deep voice rang out as he unfolded his arms and strode to the aisle between the rows of tables. "We've nowhere else to go!"

"He's right!" Delaney joined Heath at the center of the room. Young and hearty with a granite chin and thick, auburn hair, Delaney was a fitting complement to Heath's harsh and grizzled demeanor. "I've a wife to care for. If we abandon the town, the company will fire us all! And good luck finding work someplace else, what with a war being waged all around us. We'll all be left homeless and penniless!"

"At least you'll have your lives," Colvin argued.

"I've a better solution." Heath sneered at Colvin before sweeping around to the crowd. "Tahawus is our home. Why should *we* all be the ones to leave it when it's clear that *she's* the only one who must go!" His finger shot through the air at Abigail.

Abigail stared back at him, her blue eyes never wavering, just gleaming defiantly in the lamplight.

Colvin heard a few murmurs of agreement rise from the audience. He didn't like where this was going, but it was already too late; Heath was already warming to the moment.

"'Tis true what Colvin says," the big man went on. "Evil walks among us. But 'tis *her*! She's the one who's brought the Lord's wrath down upon this town! He has sent His vengeful angel to punish the sinful with blood and fire. By our own hands, we will die as long as we permit this witch of the black arts to remain among us! There are none here that are safe. None!"

From the corner of his eye, Colvin saw Josiah step from the shadows, his black eyes fixed on Heath. Colvin shot him a look and shook his head. The last thing he wanted was a fight. There had to be a way of settling this peacefully and maintaining lawfulness.

A woman's voice rose from somewhere near the side of the room. It was shrill and quaking. "What do you suggest we do, MacIntyre?"

Heath turned, his tone going low and somber.

"Atonement."

"How?"

"Show the Lord you repent of your wickedness." A frightful look came over Heath's face, icy and cruel and dangerous. "Offer Him a sacrifice."

"That's enough, MacIntyre!" Father Carnes boomed. His chair skittered across the floor behind him as he shot to his feet. "We'll have none of that sort of talk here!"

But Heath wouldn't be stopped. "The Lord commands that we will not suffer a witch to live, and yet even now this hellion sits before you! Welcomed by Father Carnes himself! She tells us we must leave our homes to face death in the wilderness! I say 'tis her that must die! Not us!"

The crowd erupted into another uproar, opposing voices clamoring to be heard over each other.

Colvin had heard enough. He started down the aisle, but another man stepped in his way. It was Ned Fitch, the wiry physician.

Fitch rose from his bench, fist balled, and swung it at Heath, catching him squarely to the side of his scruffy goatee. "You shut up that talk, MacIntyre!" Fitch's voice quivered. "You shut it up right now! No one here's killin' anyone! So you just shut the hell up!"

Fitch's punch did little more than split Heath's lip. Heath spit a gob of blood on the floor and wheeled on the physician, his eyes smoldering with anger. One blow from his massive fist sent the smaller man sprawling across the floor.

Fitch rolled to his knees. Blood poured from his nose in a stream, pooling on the floorboards. He let out a shuddering groan, then went flat on his stomach in a pitiful heap, groggy and clinging to consciousness.

A woman screamed. Chaos descended into the hall.

Heath's followers rushed from where they stood as a handful of outraged men bolted to their feet and came to Fitch's defense. There were shouts, shoves, fists.

In a heartbeat, Colvin saw his worst fears realized. His village was degenerating into hysteria. He and Josiah both dove into the scuffle, yanking men from both sides apart. Something hard caught Colvin on the bone below his eye and he staggered around, dazed.

Heath was there. He tossed a man aside as if he were a child and dragged himself free of the fray. He spun around, fists up, daring someone to challenge him.

"Which of ye' will be the next to strike me? Who will it be?" Heath's hair was wild and his face was an ugly shade of red. Blood dribbled through his goatee. His booming voice echoing through the hall brought an instant end to the tumult. "You go ahead and wait! Wait until it's yer turn! Wait until ye' wake in the night and slip a rope around your neck! Wait until ye' take a blade and run yerself through, just like my poor Evelyn! The angel of vengeance will come for ye' soon enough! Perhaps even tonight! The Lord demands expiation for our sins and He will have it, be it her blood or yours!"

Heath's eyes blazed as he cast one last baleful look around at his audience. Chest heaving, he stormed from the hall, slamming the door behind him and leaving a nervous quiet in his wake.

With the echoes of the skirmish still lingering in the hall, Colvin called for order and managed to bring the meeting back to the subject of the evacuation.

Owen Delaney remained behind to observe the proceedings, along with a couple more of Heath's men. As the arguments for and against abandoning the town went on, Colvin wondered how many had been swayed by Heath's dire warnings. How long would it be before someone came for Abigail? Would it be in the morning? Sooner? In the dead of night?

Half an hour later, they took a vote. Delaney insisted on joining Colvin in counting the raised hands of those assembled. The matter was settled.

The villagers chose to leave.

Those who wanted to stay were free to do so, but as Colvin watched the men and women file from the hall, he knew most would decide to abandon the village. With what had happened to the men at North Camp, they had experienced enough death to remain any longer.

Father Carnes was already on his way toward the door when Colvin turned to Abigail and Duncan at their table. The priest and Colvin exchanged sober glances from across the room before he slipped out into the windy night.

"When can we expect the evacuation to begin?" Abigail asked.

"If all goes well, we could be on our way by tomorrow afternoon," Colvin replied. "We'll need some time to pack and prepare the wagons. We've only a few horses up here, so the men will have to hike out on foot."

"You do realize we now have yet another problem to contend with," Duncan interjected.

"What would that be?" Colvin asked wearily.

"The war. By sending these people down into the valley, we're delivering them right into the middle of it."

"Out of the fire and into the frying pan," Colvin murmured.

"Tell them to head for North Hudson," Abigail said. "It remains a safe haven. My coachman awaits me there. When you arrive, kindly tell him to delay his return for me by five days."

Duncan's eyes snapped toward her. "When *we* arrive? What are you talking about?"

"I intend to remain here to fight Samael."

"What?" Colvin exclaimed. "But you said evacuation was our only recourse! You said the demon was too powerful, that you couldn't—"

"Mr. Colvin, I never walk away from a fight and I never leave a monster unvanquished," Abigail said. "I told you what you needed to hear in order to convince your people to get themselves to safety. Make no mistake, the danger here is great. I may risk my own life, but I have no desire to watch more innocents die."

"I'm staying with you," Duncan insisted.

"No," said Abigail. "You will return home to your family."

"And then what? What if you die up here, Abby? Would you have me live with the knowledge that I should have been here to help you? Would you curse me with the same guilt you've been living with these past twenty years?"

Abigail glared at him. "Very well." Her voice was as icy as a winter river. "If your wish is to join me on this path, I'll no longer stand in your way. But be aware that you may only be exchanging one curse for another. For once you have stared into the Abyss, you will forever feel it staring back at you."

Chapter 33

Hannah Gill lay curled in her bed and wondered when her mother would return from the town meeting. The hour was growing late and Hannah had to use the outhouse. But the young girl didn't dare venture outside alone. It was cold and dark outside.

And the witch might get her.

Hannah shuddered at the thought and pulled the wool blanket up under chin. Five days had passed since that awful Jacobs woman had bedeviled her with her sorcery. *Nothing good can come from witchcraft*, Hannah's mother had admonished.

At first, Hannah was confused when Mother brought to the chapel to seek absolution from Father Carnes. Hadn't Ms. Jacobs saved her life? And besides, Hannah herself had done nothing wrong. Why should *she* be blamed for anything? Why should *she* be forced to go to confession?

But in the days that followed, Hannah understood. *She's cursed you, Hannah*, her playmates had taunted. *She's put a mark on you so the devil can find you and drag you down to*

Hell....

Hannah shrinking from the image and rolled over in her bed. She forced her thoughts back to her mother. What was taking her so long? If she didn't return soon, Hannah feared she would wet the bed.

Minutes crawled by. The only sounds were the dwindling crackles of the dying fire and the whine of the wind as it clawed and beat at the window. To Hannah, it sounded as if it was trying desperately to get in at her. As the time wore on, another terrible thought crept up on her, unbidden. What if her mother never came home? What if she died, just like Hannah's father? Who would care for her then?

She'd be alone. An orphan.

No! Hannah reprimanded herself. Her mother *would* come home. Whatever they were discussing at the meeting was terribly important. Hannah had caught murmurs throughout the village all afternoon. She wondered what could possibly have the adults looking so distressed. Even as a child, Hannah had her suspicions.

It was the witch.

Hannah wrapped herself tighter beneath her blanket and drew her knees up into her small chest. Her mother had left her bedroom door open to let the heat in from the woodstove. But the fire was burning low now, and it was growing cold in Hannah's tiny room. Mother had warned her against stoking the fire when no one else was around. That was when her father had been around to take care of it; before she was left with no one but Mother; before she was forced to spend hours alone in the cold, dark cabin.

All of a sudden, Hannah froze.

Was that a sound?

Hannah went very still in her bed and listened intently. Had Mother returned? She waited for the sound of the latch at the front door; the familiar rustle of her mother's cloak as she hung it on its peg; the squeak of her mother's tread across the floorboards as she came to see if Hannah was asleep…

Nothing. Only the eerie howl of the wind.

Hannah opened her mouth to call out, but a sudden, fearful thought stole her voice away.

What if it wasn't her mother?

The idea sent a chill through Hannah's bones. Alone in her bed, an unwanted image took shape in her mind. She imagined the Jacobs woman riding the howling winds, withering all she looked upon, stopping at nothing until she had snatched Hannah from her bed and spirited her away into her realm of unending night…

Hannah fought to keep from trembling as she waited, listening for the sound to come again. Her heartbeat throbbed in her ears and a cold sweat covered her skin, soaking her cotton nightgown. If only her mother were here; if only she had never left!

And then it came again.

It was a sound so clear and jarring in the silence; it sent a jolt through the whole of Hannah's little body.

Her bedroom door was moving.

Hannah's eyes snapped shut, but still that dreadful sound persisted: the creak and groan of rusty hinges as her door slowly, slowly swung shut.

The flickering rectangle of light from the stove in the next room grew more and more narrow. It kept reducing to nothing more than an orange sliver until the glow was gone and there was only darkness.

Hannah trembled uncontrollably and tried to convince herself it had been the wind. Yes! The wind was able to find its way through a crack in the window! Mother would be home soon to open the door and let the light in again. Hannah would tell her about the window and a man would come to fix it. Perhaps that nice Mr. Delaney? Yes! Mr. Delaney would make sure her door never swung shut by itself ever again.

Hannah's breath suddenly caught in her throat and she went cold all over.

Something was in the room with her.

It made no sound. No footfalls. No breaths. But Hannah could sense its presence lurking there in the darkness. She could feel the weight of its eyes on her from across the room.

It was waiting there, watching her…

And then—with a sickening rush of horror—it was creeping toward her as she lay trembling and helpless in her bed.

Paralyzed with fright, Hannah remained there, her woolen blanket cinched over her head and her eyes squeezed tight. The sound of her heart pounding in her ears was deafening, and she wished she could somehow silence it.

But it didn't matter. There was no way she could hide from the silent horror stealing toward her. It knew she was there, trapped and defenseless in her bed. She could feel its sinister presence beside her now, looming over her in the darkness. Its malevolent heat radiated against her back and she knew the horror was real. This was no dream; no nightmare she could wake from. An overwhelming wave of panic washed over her and she could no longer hold her bladder. A warm, wet sensation spread out under her as she held her breath and tried to remain motionless, praying that this unseen apparition would go away, that it would spare her.

Don't be afraid, Hannah…

That voice! That kind, familiar voice! Hannah recognized it at once. She heard it every night in her dreams, chasing away the nightmares. It was one of the first voices she had ever heard…

Her father. Her *dead* father.

Hannah…

No! It couldn't be! It had to be a trick. It was the work of the witch! The witch had done something to Hannah when she had healed the bee sting. It was all true; everything they said about the Jacobs woman was true. Father Carnes had made a terrible, terrible mistake. He had been wrong to say the woman meant well. She was evil and black-hearted, just as the village boys had said. The witch had done something awful to Hannah that day when she had lain helpless in the street. The witch had cursed her and put her black mark upon her.

And now the witch had sent an abomination to claim her.

Look at me, Hannah. Let me see your dear, dear face…

Hannah didn't dare roll over, didn't dare open her eyes, didn't dare face the unholy terror at her bedside.

There is nothing to fear, Hannah. Look at me…

Hannah hoped and prayed that her mother would come home, that anyone would come to save her.

But no one did.

She was alone, unprotected.

Hannah wondered if she would feel the pain before she died; if she would have a chance to scream before she felt the claws tearing at her skin and the fangs ripping at her flesh.

Long, unending moments passed in silence as Hannah remained there, cowering in fear, awaiting the inevitable. There was no escape. At last, her nerves could take no more. She would die of fright if she didn't do something.

She slowly opened her eyes.

There was nothing there.

Hannah gasped and let out the breath she had been holding. She sat up in bed and scanned the darkness.

The room was empty.

Come to me, my daughter…

Hannah jumped with fright. The voice—her father's voice —came to her again. It was clear and vivid, but it hadn't come from inside the room.

It came from somewhere outside.

"Father?" Hannah whispered. Her tiny voice quivered in the dark.

The witch is coming for you, Hannah. Come to me. Let me protect you…

Hannah wavered, her mind thrown into confusion. Could it be possible? What if it wasn't a trick? What if it *was* her father?

She'll come for you tonight, Hannah. She'll get you unless you come to me…

Hannah brushed aside her blanket and let her feet drop to the floor. The planks were cold beneath her toes as she snuck to the bedroom door, heedless of her soiled nightgown. She lingered there for a moment, hand on the latch, ear pressed to the door, listening for sounds in the next room.

Silence.

With a deep breath, Hannah released the latch and pushed on the door.

The room beyond was painted with heavy shadows. Only embers remained in the stove, glowing like red eyes in the gloom. The cold brought goosebumps to Hannah's flesh as she emerged from her bedroom. A gust of wind rattled the window and rooted her in place. Her eyes searched the shadows.

There was nothing there. The room was empty.

Hannah steeled her nerves and crept to the front door. She hesitated there for a heartbeat. What if it was a trap? What if something awful awaited her on the other side of the door? Something with sharp claws and long, long fangs?

Don't be afraid, Hannah. I will protect you...

Hannah swung the door open.

The forest stood vast and sprawling before her. The wind was whipping itself into a fury, but deep in the shelter of the woods, a mist was forming in the crisp night air. It drifted between the trees, dancing green in the shards of moonlight that knifed through the skeletal boughs.

"Father?" Hannah's whisper was snatched away by a chilly gust of wind. "Father!" Her voice echoed eerily through the trees and vanished into nothingness.

Hannah stood in the doorway, shivering in the silvery moonlight and waiting for a response. When she lowered her eyes, what she saw there turned her blood to ice.

She was casting two shadows.

She saw her own, framed by the dim light spilling from the cabin. The black silhouette of her nightgown rippled in the wind. But there was another shadow by her side: tall and slender and unmistakable.

A chill crawled up Hannah's spine like frost creeping up a windowpane. "Father? Is that you? Are you truly here with me?"

I'm here, Hannah...

Hannah felt the hairs rise on the back of her neck. "Why can't I see you?"

You must come to me...

"Where, Father? Where can I find you?"

The forest. You'll find me there...

Hannah raised her eyes and gazed deep into the forbidding expanse of shadows and moonlit mist. She hesitated a moment longer, fighting back the fear that threatened to consume her. Then, shivering all over, she clutched her nightgown around her throat and stepped from the cabin.

The forest closed in around her, the tall pines enfolding her in their darkness. Hannah's bare feet stumbled over roots and stones as she made her way, one fearful step after another, drawn ever deeper into the forest by her father's kind and gentle voice.

That's it, my daughter. Don't be afraid...

The mist swirled and wrapped around her like a shroud. Sounds came to her from all directions, an ominous chorus of night creatures excited by her presence. More than once, Hannah thought she felt a hand brush against her bare flesh and a terrible chill shot up her spine. She whirled around. There was nothing there but endless mist. Tears sprung to her eyes. It was too awful, too frightening. She would die out here in these black and terrible woods. She would die here and no one would hear her frantic screams. And when it was all over, no one would ever find her.

"I'm frightened, Father," she whimpered, fearful of what horrors the sound of her voice might attract.

Don't be afraid, my brave little girl. Come to me. I'll protect you...

Hannah fought back her tears and ran deeper into the forest, tripping through the underbrush, mindless of the sticks and thorns that tore and lacerated her feet and legs. Dark shapes lurked in the mist on all sides of her, but if they were trees, Hannah couldn't tell. She closed her eyes to them and ran, wanting only to find her father, to seek protection in his arms...

Suddenly, she stopped.

The forest had ended.

Hannah panted breathlessly at the top of a tall bluff overlooking the lake. Moonlight spilled down around her. Far below, the surface of the water shimmered like a galaxy of twinkling stars. The wind was merciless here, howling and lashing at her as it swept over the bluff into the empty void beyond.

A spark of recognition flared in Hannah's mind. She knew this place; she had been here before. She looked up into the bare boughs of a giant oak.

There—looming in the darkness high above the ground— was the watchtower.

Hannah gazed up at it, her heaving breaths streaming white in the night air. The children called it the *treehouse*.

Built around the oak's massive trunk, the decrepit shack was perched dozens of feet above the ground like a tiny house clutched in the palm of a skeletal hand. Its walls sagged at awkward angles, their planks green with moss and rot. Gaping holes were visible in a slanted roof that was blanketed with dead leaves and pine needles. An empty window looked out over the valley and the lake, guarding against a Native attack that would never come. A crumbling series of crisscrossing ladders climbed up to the shack from the ground. Even as Hannah watched, the ruined structure shuddered under a powerful blast of wind.

Go to it, Hannah. I've left something in there for you...

Mindless of the numbness in her cold and bleeding feet, Hannah went to the first ladder and climbed. The rungs beneath her were slick and treacherous with moss and mildew. They creaked and sighed beneath her as she ascended, moving carefully from one ladder to the next. Higher and higher she went, her nightgown whipping and flapping in the wind. Below her, the autumn leaves swirled and skittered in small twisters across the dirt.

Hannah didn't look down. The boys had teased her when she had first come here with them. *You'll be too scared to climb*, they had said. *You'll fall and break your neck.*

Hannah had shown them that day. She made it to the top and she could do it again now—as long as she didn't look down.

My brave, brave little girl...

Hannah heard her father's voice coming from above as she ascended the final ladder. She clung to the highest rung with one hand, reached up with the other, and nudged open the rotting plank of the trapdoor.

There was nothing but yawning blackness beyond the square hole.

Hannah remained there, dozens of feet above the ground, clinging to the ladder and peering into the inky darkness. None of the children had ever ventured inside the watchtower. They had climbed the ladders, daring each other to see who could climb the highest. One courageous boy had even stolen a peek through the trapdoor.

But none had dared to enter.

It's haunted, the boys had said. *You'll die if you go in there. The ghosts will get you and no one will find you again.*

For a moment, Hannah's courage failed her. She wanted nothing more than to retreat, to climb back down from this terrible place and race home to her mother.

Her father's voice urged her on, dispelling her fears.

Hannah moved slowly, cautiously. She pushed her way up through the trapdoor and crawled into the watchtower.

The stench of vermin and feces greeted her. Hannah covered her nose to keep from gagging and inched toward the fresh air of the open window. Moonlight streamed through the crooked rectangle. Hannah saw the shadowy giants of the mountains rising in a panorama around the valley. Their massive black shapes blotted out the stars along the horizon. Far below her, the lake was a great, glittering void. The vista was staggering and dizziness suddenly overcame Hannah. She turned away from the window.

A large timber axe leaned against the wall.

Hannah's eyes fell upon it. Like the rest of the shack, it was old and rotting. But somehow, its sharp blade still shone brightly in the moonlight.

It's mine, Hannah. Go to it. Take it into your hands…

Hannah hesitated. She didn't dare move.

Take it, Hannah. It will protect you from the witch…

Hannah took a tentative step forward, like a marionette dangling from its strings. The decaying floorboards creaked and flexed beneath what little weight she carried. The walls groaned and shuddered around her.

Another step.

And another.

She reached for the axe.

That's it, Hannah. Feel it in your hands, my brave little girl…

Chapter 34

There were empty seats in the pews at Mass. Row after row of sturdy pine benches sat vacant as Carnes delivered his sermon. The few parishioners in attendance were women who prayed for Hannah Gill's soul. The other villagers were searching for the missing girl.

Carnes' voice sounded strange and hollow as it reverberated off the walls of the nearly empty chapel. As he brought his lackluster sermon to a merciful end, he blessed the handful of matrons and allowed them time to rise before escorting them to the door. He lingered there at the threshold with them, giving them his dutiful assurances that Hannah would be found. Then he opened the door and ushered them out into the street.

Left alone in the quiet solace of his chapel, Carnes swiveled on his heels and made his way up the aisle to the altar. His tread was weary and sluggish. He, too, had been up all night searching for something.

But not for Hannah Gill.

Carnes rubbed his bleary eyes and attempted to rouse

himself as he went to the vestry and divested himself of his vestments. A glance at the brass clock on the shelf told him he had a little less than fifteen minutes before he was supposed to meet Abigail Jacobs by the lake. He splashed a handful of cool water on his face from the washbasin and let it drip from his cheeks and nose. Moments later, he left the chapel.

A dense fog had descended in the early morning. The deserted expanse of Main Street was now a dreary sea of gray and white. Carnes headed south and could barely distinguish the bulky silhouettes of the buildings to his left and right. Ahead, the muddy lane was visible for only a few yards before it vanished into nothingness. It was like the village had been snatched away overnight, leaving nothing behind but a vast, white wasteland.

With the fog had come an eerie silence as the townsfolk emptied the village in search of Hannah Gill. Carnes could now hear the occasional distant echo of a voice calling the missing girl's name. The searchers had spread deep into the woods, having scoured the village and found nothing. There were miles of forest to cover and the girl could be anywhere.

Carnes' thoughts were dark and brooding as he crossed the outskirts of the village and made his way through the forest toward the lake. The fog was so thick here it was almost suffocating. For a brief instant, Carnes became disoriented in the white void, unable to distinguish the direction from which he had come. He came to a halt and turned in a slow circle until he caught the sound of the water lapping somewhere to his left. He went toward it.

Two shadowy figures materialized from the gloom, and

Abigail and Duncan turned at Carnes' approach. Abigail held his copy of the *Book of Enoch* tucked under one arm. Only a few feet of shallow ripples were visible behind where they stood at the water's edge. The thick veil of fog cloaked the rest of the lake.

Carnes returned Abigail's greeting and said, "You have heard about Hannah Gill?"

Abigail nodded. Her face was drawn and somber. She had offered to assist Colvin and Josiah in their search for the missing girl, but Colvin had thought it wiser that she continue her research on the demon, Samael. There were few who would welcome the help of the witch.

"Has there been any news?" Abigail asked.

Carnes smoothed his beard and shook his head. "None. The last time anyone saw Hannah was when Sally Gill put her to bed before last night's meeting. When she returned, Hannah was gone."

Abigail shuddered. The girl's disappearance was too eerily similar to her own childhood abduction. A mother put her child to sleep, only to return to an empty bed. It brought back too many painful memories of that fateful All Hallows' Eve, memories that Abigail had fought long and hard to keep buried.

Once again, she wished she had been permitted to help in the search. It had even occurred to her that a divination spell might help to reveal Hannah's whereabouts. But that sort of witchcraft would require the participation of the girl's mother in a blood sacrifice the likes of which Abigail doubted Sarah Gill would find palatable. Besides, Abigail was also bitterly aware that the precise incantation required for such a spell was contained within the Book of Shadows that Carnes kept under his own lock and key.

"And the evacuation?" Abigail asked, although she already suspected the answer.

"Postponed," Carnes replied. "No one is leaving until we discover what happened to Hannah."

Abigail frowned. Was the girl's disappearance just a coincidence? Or was it part of some greater and more sinister plan to keep the villagers from abandoning the town?

"You don't think that Hannah could have…" Duncan let the rest of his thought trail away. His voice was weary and his eyes were thin and bloodshot from the sleepless hours he had spent searching for the girl. He had stolen away under the pretense of retrieving some maps, but he would soon be obliged to rejoin the search to avoid Heath MacIntyre's suspicion.

No one answered Duncan's question. As disturbing as the idea was, they were all wondering the same thing. Was Hannah Gill already dead?

"Did you find what you were looking for?" Carnes asked with a nod at the *Book of Enoch* clutched under Abigail's arm.

"I did," she replied. She was glad for the change of subject as she returned the volume to him. "Before he was cast down from heaven, Samael was known as the Angel of Death, a fearsome and loyal archangel who slayed men with poison at God's behest. He was tasked by God to tempt and seduce humanity and to execute His wrath upon those who were found sinful and unrepentant. Many early Christians believed it was actually Samael who planted the Tree of Knowledge in Eden and seduced Eve into partaking of the forbidden fruit.

Others think it was Samael who deceived Sarah of the Old Testament into believing Abraham had sacrificed their son, leading the poor woman to die of grief. However, modern pathology has taught us it is impossible for someone to *die* of actual grief. I propose that Sarah's grief at the loss of her son led her to *suicide*."

Carnes' pale eyes widened. "That is quite a leap in assumptions."

"Perhaps. But considering the deaths here in Tahawus, is it only coincidence that Jed Hawes should invoke the name of a demon known to deceive and tempt innocents? Or could there be some truth to his words? Consider the possibilities. According to the *Book of Enoch*, Samael slays men with poison. Perhaps this is not to be taken literally. Perhaps the demon poisons the man's *thoughts* and turns him against himself. Before Keenan died, he told me he heard O'Brennan telling him to save himself. That is why he broke the circle and ran; he thought he was saving himself from the Familiars I had summoned. What if the voice Keenan heard was that of Samael, luring him to his own destruction?"

"Just as Samael is said to have done to Sarah in the story of Abraham and Isaac?" Duncan suggested.

"My thoughts exactly." Abigail's eyes were lit with excitement now. "As an archangel, it was Samael's duty to test humanity on God's behalf and to bring death to those that failed. Now that he has become a demon cast down from heaven, perhaps he continues in his grim duty not out of loyalty to God, but out of spite."

Carnes stroked his beard as he peered at her. For a moment, there was only the eerie silence of the fog and the gentle lapping of the water against the rocks. "Very well, Ms. Jacobs," he said at last. "I concede what you are proposing is a possibility. But there remains one other problem with your theory."

"What is it?"

"According to what I learned last night from my study of apocryphal demonology, a demon cannot simply enter our world of its own volition. Even if you are correct about Lake Tear of the Clouds—that it is some sort of gateway to Hell— God will see those gates locked until the end times of the Apocalypse come upon us."

"When the gates shall open and Hell shall spew forth its abominations and the dead shall walk the Earth?" Abigail interjected with a hint of sarcasm. "I'm sorry, Mr. Carnes, but that is one part of the Bible that remains a myth. I have already seen the dead walk the earth with my own eyes."

"Regardless." Carnes persisted, undaunted. "If we accept the writings of the Apocrypha as truth, demons such as Samael cannot slip free of their fiery prison. There is only one way such a demon could be present among us here." Carnes paused and swallowed. "Someone must have summoned it."

"Summoned?" Duncan repeated, as if he hadn't heard correctly.

Carnes gave a grim nod. "When God created the Earth, He gave dominion over it to His most beloved creation: Man. According to ancient legend, a demon can only enter our world if it is first welcomed by Man himself."

A look of astonishment came over Duncan. "Are you saying that someone here in Tahawus invoked this demon? That there is a person here who is responsible for all this death?"

"If Ms. Jacobs is correct, then yes. It is the only way Samael could walk among us."

"Who would do such a thing?"

"Therein lies our problem." Carnes sighed and gazed into the endless depths of the fog. "It could have been any of us."

An uneasy silence settled over them.

"Well then," Abigail said at last. "We finally have a reason to take heart."

"What?" Duncan sputtered. "Why?"

"Because we now know that someone of flesh and blood holds the secret to defeating this demon... and people with flesh and blood can always be made to talk."

Duncan stared at her for a moment, unsettled by the eager gleam he had seen flash across her eyes. "We must keep this information to ourselves. If Heath MacIntyre were to find out, he would accuse you of—"

"Shhh!" Abigail's hand suddenly shot up. "Listen..."

They quieted, listening for whatever it was she had heard. There was nothing but the ebb and trickle of the water at their feet. Then, a single dull and hollow thud echoed through the fog.

"It sounded like an axe blow," Duncan murmured.

"Today is Sunday," Carnes remarked. "'Tis the Sabbath. No one is logging." He waited a moment, listening for the sound to come again. There was only silence. "Do you suppose the men looking for—"

"Listen!" Abigail hushed them again. She cocked her head, ears pricked, straining to hear.

A voice came floating from somewhere deep in the fog. It was so soft and faint, it would have been imperceptible if it weren't for the deathly silence that hung over the lake.

But once the voice was perceived, it was unmistakable.

Somewhere out in the murky white depths, a young girl was singing a haunting lullaby.

"Hannah!" Abigail cried.

Chapter 35

"Hannah!" Abigail cried again. Her voice echoed across the lonely silence of the lake as she dashed through the fog, skirting the rocky shoreline between the woods and the water. "Is that you, Hannah?"

There was no response, only the eerie melody of the girl's lullaby drifting like a lost soul through the endless mist.

Abigail rushed toward the sound, letting the soft voice guide her like a beacon in the heavy gloom. Ahead, there was nothing but an impenetrable expanse of gray. And yet, the girl's song grew ever louder as Abigail drew closer. Drawn forward by the voice, she plunged ahead, determined to discover its source. She was certain it was Hannah; it *had* to be.

Another sound came resounding through the fog: the same loud and hollow *thud* that had attracted Abigail's attention. Duncan was right: it sounded like an axe blade striking wood. Its echo reverberated in the stillness as Abigail raced toward it. She was close now, so close she could make out the words to the girl's eerie lullaby.

"Oh, don't you remember, how a long time ago; two little babies whose names I don't know; were stolen away on a bright summer's day; and left in the woods, I've heard people say..."

Shadows coalesced ahead. They were solid and massive, like the silhouettes of monoliths looming in the fog. Abigail judged them to be buildings, but in the same instant realized that wasn't possible; there weren't any structures of that size built this close to the lake. The hulking shapes grew more distinct, and Abigail slid to a halt with the mists swirling around her. She was at the stacking ramp. What she had mistaken for buildings were the enormous piles of timber logs lashed together and stacked dozens of feet high at the water's edge.

Abigail looked up.

A small figure stood veiled in mist, high atop a mountain of logs.

"Hannah!" Abigail shouted.

No response. Abigail's cry failed to even interrupt the girl's haunting song.

"Babes in the woods, babes in the woods. Oh, don't you remember, those babes in the woods..."

The mists parted. For one fleeting instant, Abigail glimpsed the girl's face from where she stood far below. It was Hannah Gill. But there was something wrong. There was something strange about the girl's face. Was it her eyes? Was something wrong with her eyes? Abigail strained to see, but the fog closed around the girl again, reducing Hannah to nothing more than a ghostly silhouette.

Another shout rose in Abigail's throat, but it retreated when she saw the dark shape of the timber axe in Hannah's hands. A sickening dread gripped her.

Hannah was chopping through the thick ropes that kept the enormous stack of logs lashed together beneath her.

"Hannah! Don't!" Abigail cried. "Come down from there!"

The girl wasn't listening. As if in a trance, she raised the axe high above her head and brought it crashing down on another rope, severing it cleanly. The stack of logs shuddered and groaned beneath her, but Hannah didn't seem to notice. Oblivious to Abigail's presence, the girl struggled to free the axe blade from where it had bitten into the solid piece of timber. She then inched across the log and found the next rope stretched tight at her feet. She raised the axe over her head, never wavering in her eerie lullaby.

"*And when it was night, so sad was their plight; the sun went down, and the moon gave no light. They sobbed and they sighed, and they bitterly cried; then the poor little babies, they laid down and died...*"

Without thinking, Abigail started up the steep slope of logs. The timber was sodden from the steady autumn rains and slippery beneath her. She was forced to crawl upward on her hands and knees. The rough bark skinned her palms and bloodied her shins, but she felt none of it. Her only thought was getting to Hannah. The mountain of timber was already shifting alarmingly beneath her. She had to stop the girl before it was too late.

Whack! Hannah brought the axe slicing through another rope.

An ominous rumble reverberated through the pile as the giant logs suddenly lurched beneath Abigail. She froze and went flat, clinging to the timber and digging her nails into the wet bark. Her breath caught in her throat and her heart nearly stopped. This was it! The giant stack was going to collapse beneath her! She braced herself…

But the logs held together.

Behind Abigail, the braces that kept the enormous stack of timber from spilling into the lake creaked and groaned ominously. How many more severed ropes could those braces endure? How many more swings of Hannah's axe before the entire weight of the pile released and the logs came crashing apart beneath her?

With her heart hammering at her chest, Abigail looked up. She was halfway up the slope; only about twenty more feet stood between her and Hannah. She could see the girl more clearly now: the dingy white of her soiled nightgown; the dirt and blood caking her legs and feet; the sharp blade of the axe clutched in her hands. Only Hannah's face remained obscured behind tendrils of dampened hair.

Duncan and Carnes had arrived. Abigail was vaguely aware of their shouts and cries coming from below. There was nothing they could do. There was no one around to help them.

And there wasn't time. It was up to Abigail. She had to get to Hannah before the girl severed the last rope.

Abigail gathered her courage and resumed her climb, scrambling up over the giant logs. Above, Hannah staggered across the pile like a sleepwalker. Only a few more feet and Abigail would reach her. She saw the axe rise into the air, heard the chilling sound of Hannah's voice, singing.

"*And when they were dead, the robins so red; brought strawberry leaves and over them spread. And all the night long, the branches among; they mourned as they whistled, and this was their song...."*

Propelled by fear, Abigail scrabbled upward.

She stretched out her hand for Hannah.

Another foot...

A few more inches...

"Hannah! No!" Abigail lunged for the girl.

The axe fell.

Chapter 36

A hideous rumble shook the mountain of timber. Abigail lunged and scooped Hannah into her arms as a piercing series of *cracks!* split the air like rifle shots. With a fearful glance over her shoulder, she saw the thick wooden braces splitting and giving way. One by one, they splintered and snapped like dry twigs.

Abigail clutched at Hannah and tried to scramble up and over the shifting, lurching logs. She clawed her way up like a sailor staggering across the deck of a listing ship, desperate to crest the top of the stack and start down the other side before the logs dragged backward.

It was too late. There was a nightmarish, thundering roar…

And then she was falling.

Hannah was ripped from Abigail's arms as they tumbled downward like rag dolls caught in a landslide. Without the braces to keep it in place, the massive stack was now releasing itself and spilling giant logs into the lake. Abigail had enough presence of mind to cover her head with her arms as she was carried along with the logs rolling and bucking beneath her.

The terrifying moment lasted the length of a heartbeat. In that time, she was gripped by the horrifying certainty that she would be crushed beneath the cascading avalanche of timber.

She hit the lake with a great splash and spray of water. The impact came so suddenly that she had no time to hold her breath. Water filled her mouth as she was instantly submerged and dragged downward by the weight of her sodden clothes. The cold was paralyzing, pricking at her flesh like thousands of sharp needles as her chest constricted. She heard the steady barrage of the logs as they splashed into the lake over her head, one after another after another. Their long, bulky shapes came together like a puzzle on the surface of the water, obliterating the gray light and sealing her beneath like she was being entombed.

A hot bolt of panic shot through Abigail's gut. She was trapped underwater. If she tried to surface, she would be crushed. Her only hope was to remain deep enough to avoid being struck by a falling log. Her cloak had become twisted around her during her tumble and her lungs ached as she struggled to free herself. It was too long, too tangled, too heavy to manipulate.

She tore at the buttons. One came off in her hand. Then another. Where was the third? Her hand scrabbled for it as she sank ever lower into the freezing blackness. The pressure of the depths pressed at her ears. Her fingers brushed across the last pewter button and she yanked at it to rip it off. The cloak fell away from her shoulders, but its hem remained twisted and snared around her waist. She strained to wriggle out of it, releasing one leg, then the other.

Suddenly free, Abigail kicked and swam desperately. Her

lungs were blazing now, screaming in agony for air. But she couldn't surface, not yet. She had to get away, to swim clear of the giant logs crashing into the water overhead. How long had she been submerged? Seconds? Minutes?

Abigail felt herself becoming lightheaded as she moved through the turbid water. A strange and terrible darkness was creeping into the corners of her sight and she knew she would lose consciousness if she stayed down any longer. She had to reach the surface, had to breathe. She couldn't wait. If she didn't do it right now, she would drown.

Wild with panic and certain that her lungs would soon burst under the torture, Abigail changed direction and propelled herself upward. Above, the spaces between the floating logs were only wide enough to admit thin slivers of dancing light. She didn't know if she had come far enough or if she was about to be crushed beneath the enormous weight of a tumbling log. Her only thought as she clung to consciousness was *air, air, air!*

She broke the surface with a tremendous gasp, sputtering and gulping air into her lungs at the same time. There was a moment of sublime relief, but the reprieve lasted only an instant.

Something huge was coming at her. Abigail glimpsed it through her lightheaded daze and spun in the water as the blunt end of a massive log floated toward her head. Caught between it and another log, she dove back underwater and ducked beneath with barely a breath to spare. If she had waited a second longer, the drifting length of timber would have crushed her skull.

Abigail tried to ignore her cramped and aching muscles as

she stayed submerged and swam further away. She came to a place where the spaces between the logs seemed wider and safer. Here she surfaced again. The intense cold was sapping her strength. She couldn't tread water much longer. She felt herself fading as she swam for the nearest piece of timber and wrapped her arms around it.

The giant log rolled beneath her and plunged her back underwater.

Abigail called on all that she had as she kicked and launched herself upward. She landed on the log on her stomach and the wind went out of her. With her weight now distributed evenly across both sides, the timber teetered but remained stable. Abigail clung to it like the survivor of a shipwreck hanging on a broken mast and caught her breath before raising her head and looking around.

Countless logs now floated across the rippling lake. The heavy fog had swallowed the stacking ramp and the shoreline, but the sounds of timber splashing into the water had ended. There were only the trickling ripples of the giant lengths of timber drifting through the water punctuated by heavy *thuds* as they collided with each other.

No—there were other sounds as well.

Abigail became aware of frantic cries from somewhere in the fog.

It was Duncan and Carnes. They were shouting for her, calling her name. She opened her mouth, but she was too frozen to speak. Her teeth were chattering and she couldn't hear anything. She closed her eyes to fight off an alarming rush of dizziness and opened them again, concentrating on the voices. The cries seemed ghostly, echoing to her from all directions. Where were they coming from? Which way was the shore?

Adrift in the endless fog, Abigail knew she had to act quickly. She couldn't wait for rescue; the frigid cold would strip her of consciousness before anyone found her. Her body trembled as she tried to remember the layout of the lake, but couldn't. It was long and narrow, stretching lengthwise from north to south. But in this fog, she had no way of orienting herself. If she could determine in which direction lay east or west, she might have enough strength to swim to the nearest shore.

But if she swam further out into the lake by mistake...

Abigail strained her eyes and peered deep into the impenetrable fog, searching for any clue that would reveal some direction. Her gaze fell upon something floating in the water. She couldn't tell what it was. It was too obscured by the mist, too small as it bobbed up and down in the water among the logs. Abigail waited for it to drift closer.

Her shivering breath froze in her throat.

It was Hannah Gill.

The girl was motionless, floating facedown in the water with her arms splayed.

Abigail tried to assess the distance that lay between her and Hannah's lifeless body. It was hard to tell on the water, but she guessed it was about thirty yards. Strewn across that watery span was an ever-shifting maze of drifting logs. Abigail wasn't sure she would have enough strength to swim the distance, but if she clung to the logs—using them for support and ducking beneath them when necessary—there was a chance she could make it to Hannah.

Abigail drew a deep breath into her sore lungs and let herself slip back into the water. The shock of the cold gripped her with crushing force. She shivered uncontrollably as she kept one hand on the log, careful not to roll it while pushing herself along its length. When she came to the end, she let go and kicked twice across the open water until she came to the next log. Again and again she repeated this process, moving from one log to the next, conserving her strength as she negotiated her way through the treacherous labyrinth. She trembled all over now and she knew she would no longer have the reflexes to react if another errant log forced her to duck underwater to avoid being struck.

Ahead, Hannah's body drifted motionless in the water, bouncing off one log to another. She was much closer now, only fifteen or twenty feet away. A clear path of open water lay between her and Abigail.

Pushing clear of the log on which she hung, Abigail swam toward the girl. She glanced around as she went, ever fearful of the massive pieces of timber threatening to crash into her at any moment. When she finally reached Hannah, Abigail gripped her by her sodden nightgown and flipped her over in the water. The girl's eyes were closed and her blue veins were visible beneath her pale skin. One of the girl's cheekbones was swollen with a terrible welt. Blood oozed and dribbled from between lips that were purple and cut.

She didn't seem to be breathing.

Abigail struggled to tread water while she smoothed Hannah's hair away from her ashen face and did her best to search the rest of the girl's body for injuries. Hannah's left forearm appeared to be broken. It dangled in the water at a grotesque angle. The girl's legs hung too low for Abigail to examine. She strained to look deeper into the depths.

Hannah's eyes flew open.

Abigail gasped and went rigid with a sudden, all-encompassing terror.

The girl's pupils were gone. Her eyes were rolled back in her head so far, only the whites were visible—whites and a red spiderweb of bloodshot veins rimming her eyelids as the connective tissue behind her eyeballs strained at their sockets.

Hannah's mouth fell open with an animalistic snarl. Her lips curled back to her gums and blood came pouring down her chin into the water. Her teeth were chipped and broken in countless places, leaving her with a hideous mouthful of jagged fangs.

Horrified, Abigail let go of the girl and reeled away, kicking and swimming backward as fast as she could. But the ghastly thing that was Hannah Gill came at her, hissing and snarling and churning in the water. She was fast and Abigail was weakening by the minute.

Abigail flailed and kicked, propelled by sheer panic, until her shoulders came up against a log caught in a jam. It didn't float away or budge under the impact; it just remained there, solid and immobile. Trapped, Abigail could only watch in wide-eyed terror as the demonic creature flew at her. She saw the girl's broken teeth gnashing in her mouth; the terrible whites of her pupil-less, bloodshot eyes.

The girl shrieked as she stretched out a claw-like hand, aiming for Abigail's throat.

Without warning, an enormous piece of drifting timber struck the shrieking thing to the side of her head. There was a sickening crunch of bone as the impact knocked Hannah sideways and out of reach. For a moment, she bobbed motionless in the water like a buoy. Blood streamed down her pale face as she stared at Abigail with her empty, hideous eyes. There was too much blood; her skull had to have been fractured. Abigail had heard it, but she didn't make a move.

Whatever was inside Hannah wasn't dead—not yet.

And then—very suddenly—Hannah threw back her head and let out an ear-splitting wail as a bolt of crimson burst forth from the crack in her skull. At first, Abigail thought it was blood spurting like a fountain into the air. But that wasn't it. Whatever it was streaked high above them and vanished into the fog.

It didn't come back down.

For a moment, Abigail was overcome by a sense of evil so powerful, she felt her insides shriveling under its malevolent force. Darkness enveloped her, and she went hollow. Despair rushed in to fill the empty void. She cringed and shrank back, cowering against the log pressing at her shoulders.

Hannah's horrific wail came to an instant, abrupt stop. Her mouth snapped shut and her head fell forward, splashing face-first into the water—but not before Abigail glimpsed the girl's eyes. She dove forward and caught Hannah's limp form in her arms to raise her bleeding head above the water. The girl's eyes were no longer rolled back in her head. They were human again, but so terribly, terribly vacant. Abigail pressed her fingers to Hannah's throat, searching for a pulse. Her hand trembled too much to detect anything. She lowered an ear to Hannah's mouth. Was that a breath she heard escape the girl's blue lips?

With one arm wrapped beneath Hannah's armpits, Abigail spun in the water, searching desperately for the shore. It was hopeless. She was lost in a floating maze. There was only fog and the great, hulking shapes of the logs in every direction.

Abigail struggled to keep her head above water as she strained to catch the cries of the men coming to her from out in the fog. Her vision dimmed, and the world seemed to blink out of existence. She was losing consciousness. She clung to the lifeless girl and struggled to focus, to keep from sinking down, down, down…

A sudden, furious splashing brought her back to her senses.

Abigail's eyes snapped open.

Timber was there, splashing through the water.

Abigail hovered on the edge of consciousness. It took her a moment to recognize the dog as he navigated his way through the labyrinth of logs. Once she realized what was happening, she gathered all of her remaining strength and swam toward him, hauling Hannah's dead weight along with her.

Timber had something clenched in his teeth. As he drew nearer, Abigail saw it was the end of a length of rope. She lunged for it, grasping it as the last of her strength gave out and the cold claimed her.

The last thing Abigail remembered before darkness closed around her was the rope going taut in her hand. She was vaguely aware of being dragged through the water, of having Hannah Gill wrapped in one arm, of bouncing and ricocheting off the logs as she went. It should have been painful, but she was too numb to feel anything. A voice in her head kept repeating, *Don't let go, don't let go, don't let go…*

No. The voice wasn't in her head. It was a man's voice,

Glenn Colvin's voice. It was growing louder…
And then the voice went quiet and there was nothing.

Chapter 37

Heath MacIntyre sat hunkered on a log on the edge of a desolate tract of cleared forest. A cheerless fire burned in a pit at his feet. Behind him, the pines of the forest towered above like the seatback of a monstrous throne. Some distance to Heath's left, a lone crow danced across the bloodstained ground where Chester Prue had died. Its shrill cry rose from the clearing and vanished into the dusky evening sky.

"Even here, in Tahawus, the works of the flesh are evident," Heath scowled, his voice low and gravelly. He let his gaze roam around the loose, half-circle of men gathered with him around the fire. "Each of ye' knows of what I speak. Sexual immorality, impurity, greed, lechery, drunkenness. Which of ye' haven't seen it for yerselves? Ye' hide from it; try as ye' might to blind yer eyes to it. But oh… the Almighty sees it! The Almighty sees it all! There are none here who can hide from His wrath."

The men sat and listened intently, eyes transfixed by the big man before them. There was a vacancy to their faces, the yielding blankness of those who have given their minds over to another.

"'Tis His will that we should die by our own hands," Heath continued. "Hawes, Gill, Beaulieu, Prue: all were but warnings of the fate that awaits the shameful and immoral. But now has come another, sent by the devil himself to tempt us, to lead us all to destruction… Abigail Jacobs!" Heath spit the name through his lips. "Carnes would have us believe we should accept this witch. He'd have us welcome her into our fold, into our town. A heretic is what Carnes is! *The only magic she wields is that of science*, he says. Bah! Science? Idolatry is what it is! What is science but a blasphemy against the Almighty? Who but a charlatan would have the arrogance to presume to explain the awesome mysteries of the Lord's creation? The Bible is all the explanation ye' need!" Heath's eyes narrowed, his voice dropping low once more. "What does the Bible tell us about witchcraft?"

He paused, waiting for a response, knowing none would come. None of the men gathered here could read the Bible for themselves. Heath himself could barely put his own name to paper. But he had heard enough sermons from old Father Magraith to have committed the passages to memory.

"Ye' shall not permit a sorceress to live!" Heath hissed. "For anyone who practices in the black arts is an abomination to the Lord!" His eyes raked across the men. "And what is the punishment for disobedience? Who here can tell me?"

Another pause. No one spoke. The men sat mute, captivated, hanging on Heath's every word.

Heath glimpsed an image of himself, imagining what the men perceived as they gazed at him. What he saw was every bit as righteous and mighty as Father Magraith had been in the pulpit of his old stone chapel. Heath heard his own words and felt something rising within him. He was flush with the power of his virtue. It energized him, galvanized him, gave him the only spark of life he had known since that dreadful morning he had discovered Evelyn in the woods, butchered by her own hands.

"The Lord will set His face against any man who whores after mediums and necromancers," Heath said sourly. "Any such man will be cut off from his people. *Cut off from his people!* Such will be yer own fates if ye' fail to drive this witch out before ye'! One by one, each of ye' cut down by your own hands in the black of night. Such was the reward for the kindness my poor Evelyn showed the witch!"

Heath let his voice go low once more. "Now there is poor, poor Hannah Gill... 'Tis the witch that holds the poor child in thrall. Carnes may well tell us it was the Jacobs woman who saved the girl when she lay dying in the street. He may try to convince us all that she risked her own life to save poor Hannah again today. But we all know better, don't we? We all know even Satan may disguise himself as an angel of light to lead the Lord's people astray."

Heath's eyes hardened to cold, sharp points. "Now... which of ye' will be the next to suffer the Almighty's wrath? Will it be ye', Tibbetts?" Heath's intense gaze fell upon a stout, thick-jowled man and remained there, as if burning a hole right through the man. "Will ye' be the next to take a blade to yer own throat?"

Tibbetts seemed to shrink, stammering something, but Heath had already moved on to Owen Delaney. "How about ye', Delaney? Will ye' be the one to make a widow of yer young wife? Or will ye' show the Lord ye' repent of yer sinful ways?"

Heath saw the man flinch. He kept his eyes on Delaney a moment longer before swinging them back around to the others. "Suicide! 'Tis the punishment we must suffer unless we show Him we are repentant! Death by blood or fire! There is but one way to save yerselves. Expiation! For as it is written, everything is purified with blood! Look to the Book of Hebrews!" Heath didn't need a Bible to quote from. The words of Father Macgraith flew into his mind. "*Without the shedding of blood, there is no forgiveness of sin!* The Almighty demands atonement and ye' must give it to Him or face His wrath! Atonement!"

"Atonement," Delaney repeated to himself. He said it again and again like a chant. "Atonement, atonement, atonement..."

The crow let out a sudden screech as it took flight, soaring from the clearing with a flutter of black wings. A strange sense of elation came over Heath as he watched it go into the twilight sky. *Yes. The foul ones will flee before us*, he thought. He knew then that he would be successful; he would save the wayward villagers from themselves. He would succeed where Father Carnes had failed. And he would begin with the Jacobs woman. Then they would punish Carnes himself for his heresy. Colvin and the heathen Josiah would be next. Heath wouldn't rest until he had purged the village of *all* its sinners. He alone would redeem his people in the eyes of their God.

This was his purpose. This was *his* atonement.

Heath reached down and plucked a large stone from a pile at his feet—stones he had brought from the dark and secret place he had buried his wife. One by one, he passed them around to his circle of followers. The men took the stones with eager hands, their eyes shining like penitents accepting the body of Christ.

"As it says in Leviticus," Heath intoned. "*She shall be stoned. Her blood will be upon them.*" He paused, his steely eyes traveling from one man to another, leaving none untouched. "Which of ye' will have the courage to cast the first stone?"

Chapter 38

Abigail was bruised and scraped in dozens of places. With a forgotten glass of whiskey in her hand, she lay propped on her bed in the warmth of her cabin. Her eyes stared at the wall, but she didn't see it. Her thoughts were far away as she pondered what linked all the possessed victims. She was certain she was overlooking something, but she couldn't put her finger on what it was. It was a nagging sensation, like an itch that can't be reached. If she could just determine the connection between them all, it might give her some clue to who had summoned the demon.

Why Hannah Gill? a voice in her head insisted. *Is she the key? First her father was possessed, then the girl herself. Why Hannah Gill...*

Abigail's mood darkened the longer she thought about it. Night had fallen and there was still no word on Hannah's condition. The last Abigail had seen of the girl was when she woke up on the shore of the lake. Colvin had been there with Duncan and Carnes and Josiah and some other men Abigail didn't recognize. Someone had gathered the lifeless girl up in a blanket and whisked her away, shouting for Ned Fitch, the physician.

Abigail had spent the following hours recovering her strength and fending off Duncan's irritating concern for her wellbeing. The wasted time grated on her nerves. Every minute that passed was one she could have spent hunting the demon.

But Abigail knew she had pushed herself too far in the lake. She had been in the icy water too long and no amount of whiskey seemed to warm her. She needed rest if she was going to be of any use. After stoking the fire in the stove, she had wrapped herself in her thick flannel nightgown and contemplated why Samael had targeted Hannah Gill. Was it the young girl's corruptible innocence? Or was there even more to it? A pattern or link that connected all the suicides? And perhaps most troubling of all: was it merely a coincidence that Abigail herself had been in direct contact with the last three victims?

It was this possibility that she pondered the longest as she downed her whiskey. *Evelyn. Keenan. Hannah.* The only thing that seemed to connect them all was Abigail herself. Had she somehow been implicated in Samael's murderous designs? If so, what role was she intended to play?

A knock at her front door jolted her from her thoughts.

Abigail set her empty glass on the nightstand and rose. She tried to ignore her aching muscles as she drew her nightgown tighter around her shoulders and crossed the room. The orange glow of her bedside lamp spilled out into the darkness as she pulled the door open.

Glenn Colvin was there. His face was drawn and grave.

"How is she?" Abigail asked eagerly.

"Unconscious, but alive. Ned's done all he can to stop the bleeding, but her skull's been cracked. She needs a surgeon and a proper hospital if she has any chance of surviving. Ned and a couple of my men left with her by wagon an hour ago. With any luck, they'll have the girl down the valley before sunrise."

Abigail allowed herself a momentary relief at the possibility that Hannah might live after all. What kind of life the girl would be left with if she survived was another matter.

"The rest of the townsfolk are getting ready to leave even as we speak," Colvin added. "It'll be a hard go down the mountain in the dark and most will be forced to travel by foot, but there's not a soul that wants to stay here any longer than necessary, not after what happened today. By morning, this whole place will be a ghost town."

Abigail took heart at the news that the evacuation was finally underway. No more innocents would fall prey to the evil that was afflicting the village.

Why Hannah Gill? the nagging voice echoed in her head. Abigail tried to ignore it and said, "I appreciate you keeping me apprised of the situation."

They stood there for a moment at the open door to Abigail's cabin. The late autumn nights were growing ever colder, and this one was no different. The crickets and cicadas had all but vanished in advance of the coming winter. Only a few hearty tree frogs remained to fill the silent void with their lonesome song. A breeze stirred the fallen leaves, and the air whispered the promise of another storm.

"Will you come in for one last drink?" Abigail offered

unexpectedly, stepping back and pulling the door open wider.

Colvin hesitated and glanced around self-consciously.

"I'm sure the presence of a man in my cabin cannot possibly lower my standing in the eyes of the townsfolk, if that is what's troubling you." Abigail smirked. "They already know I'm an immoral witch."

Colvin shared her wry smile as he entered. Abigail closed the door behind him and went to the large chest beneath the window, where she produced her bottle of whiskey. She pulled the cork, took a swig, and savored the warm burn before offering the bottle to Colvin.

Colvin sat on the edge of the bed as he raised the bottle to his lips. Abigail had exquisite taste; the whiskey was just the way he liked it: strong and fiery.

Much like Abigail herself.

After a moment, Colvin said, "Listen, Abigail. You aren't likely to hear this from anyone else in town, but I… I wanted to thank you for what you did, for saving Hannah's life, that is."

"She hasn't been saved yet," Abigail remarked bitterly as she took a seat on the lid of her trunk.

"All the same." Colvin passed her the bottle. "You risked your life going after Hannah like that. From what Emmons tells me, you didn't think or hesitate. You reacted without a care for your own safety. What you did gave Hannah a chance to live and I… well, we *all* owe you our gratitude, even if there's no one but me to admit it."

"You may well consider your debt paid." Abigail took another gulp. "Seeing as how I find myself owing *you* my gratitude for coming to my rescue."

Something about her tone told Colvin she bore some resentment at having needed his help. He understood; she was proud and independent and he respected her for it. "Think nothing of it," he said, flashing her an easy grin. "The rope was Timber's idea."

A smile came to Abigail's lips. "And here I was under the impression your dog didn't like me."

"On the contrary. I don't see how he could help himself."

The two of them went quiet for a moment as Abigail gazed at him from across the room. Illuminated in the warm lamplight, his eyes were deep and captivating. All at once, she had a flash of those amber eyes looking down on her as Colvin had hauled her from the lake. She remembered the sensation of his muscular arms around her, his warm hands on her frozen cheeks as he struggled to revive her. Not since her father had died had any man showed such sincere care for her. She had known many men over the intervening years, but she had never wanted such attention from them—never *allowed* it.

But now, she found herself wondering what it would be like to have those same amber eyes gazing down on her once more as she lay beneath him. To have those tattooed arms wrapped around her not on the rocky shoreline of the lake, but somewhere much more soft and warm. To have those hands gliding down from her cheeks to somewhere more intimate, more delicate…

Colvin's voice broke the silence. "Was Hannah—"

"Possessed? Most certainly," Abigail finished for him, recovering from the startling fantasy. What had come over her? Where had those sudden thoughts for him come from?

Abigail banished any lingering visions of Colvin from her mind as she described the hideous look in Hannah's eyes; the shocking viciousness by which the injured girl had attacked her in the water; the bolt of crimson that had shot into the air from the wound in Hannah's head. "I have witnessed nothing like it. More than ever, I am convinced 'tis the work of Samael."

"Then why did this demon release his hold on the girl so suddenly?" Colvin asked.

"I have been pondering that very same question. And I believe I may have an explanation. Are you familiar with the procedure of *trepanning*?"

Colvin gave her a look that told her she should have known better than to ask.

"'Tis an ancient practice," Abigail explained. "A hole is drilled into the individual's skull—often when fully conscious —thereby releasing the unclean spirit residing within. It was especially common in the Middle Ages as a popular method of liberating the possessed from demons."

Colvin's brows furrowed. "You believe this happened to Hannah? That the demon was released from her when the log fractured her skull?"

"Think back to the story of the Jesuit brothers who were left to die on the shore of Lake Tear of the Clouds," Abigail said. "Once he had slipped his own bonds, what did the younger of the Legendre brothers do instead of seizing the opportunity for escape?"

"He murdered his elder brother."

"Precisely. And how exactly did he do it?"

"He did it by—" Colvin realized what he was about to say.

"He did it by crushing his brother's skull."

Abigail's eyes gleamed as she gazed at him. "A coincidence?"

From somewhere outside came the first rumbling boom of thunder as the storm rolled toward them over the mountains.

"Terrific," Colvin sighed. "The only way to prevent Samael's victims from killing themselves is to split their heads open."

"No. There is one other way... Exorcism."

Colvin's eyes widened. "Are you serious?"

"Quite." Abigail rose to her feet. "I must speak to Mr. Carnes before he leaves the village. I must retrieve my Book of Shadows and—"

"There's no rush for that. Carnes won't be leaving with the others."

"I beg your pardon?"

"After what happened today, he's decided to remain here with you and Emmons. As he puts it, you may need his *spiritual assistance* when fighting Samael."

Under any other circumstances, Abigail would have rejected the idea. But in the time she had spent alone with her thoughts, one idea had stuck with her: whoever had summoned Samael wouldn't just abandon the town. If the demon was at all bound to the cursed land through which it had entered—the gate at Lake Tear of the Clouds—then whoever had summoned it would want to remain here as well. Until now, the only candidates had included herself and Duncan. Abigail had a hard time imagining what could have motivated her childhood friend and former lover to undertake something so unspeakably abhorrent.

And yet, she knew she must remain suspicious of everyone.

Now, Carnes had elected to remain as well. Abigail was curious to see who else would find some excuse to stay behind by the time the sun rose.

"It's getting late," Colvin said, handing her the bottle. "There's still much to do before dawn. I'll be among the last to leave, but I'll be sure to say farewell before I go."

He stood and walked to the door, resting his hand on the latch. "Why don't you come with us, Abigail? Why stay here and fight? After tonight, there will be no one left here for Samael to harm. Why risk your life needlessly? Leave this place. Come with us."

Abigail gave him a wistful smile as she went to him. "And what of the unsuspecting people who come here after us? Tahawus is worth a fortune to Witherbee & Rand. Do you think they will accept your explanation that their most profitable logging camp was founded on a gateway to Hell? That it is haunted by some demon? Do you truly believe they won't send anyone up here after us to salvage what's left?" Abigail shook her head. "No, Glenn. One does not simply lock a rabid dog in the pantry and leave the key on the kitchen table for someone else to find. One puts a bullet in the dog's head before it can cause any harm."

Colvin's face was dark and somber as he gazed at her. Abigail could see the thoughts playing out behind his penetrating eyes. For a moment, she thought he would object. Instead, a melancholy smile came to his lips. "You're an interesting one, Abigail Jacobs. I knew it the moment I laid eyes on you that night in the shed with poor Chester Prue."

His words stunned Abigail. "That was you? Why didn't you say anything? Why didn't you—"

"Reveal you to the others?" Colvin finished for her. "Because I dare say there are few things more interesting—and attractive—than a woman with a secret."

He remained there a moment, his roguish smile twinkling in his eyes. Abigail felt the heat of his body against hers. "You need to be with your people. You should go now. Farewell, Glenn."

"Goodnight, Abigail," said Colvin.

He slipped out into the night.

Left alone, Abigail uncorked the bottle in her hand and took another swig of the fiery whiskey. What was wrong with her? What was it about Colvin that had inspired that swift and unexpected longing she'd had for him? It wasn't like her—at least, not during an investigation.

And yet, she couldn't keep her thoughts from straying back to those eyes, arms, hands. She couldn't forget the way he had made her feel when she lay vulnerable and helpless by the lake. That strange and enchanting sensation of being cared for, of being protected…

There was a knock at the door.

Colvin, Abigail thought with a sudden, uncontrollable thrill. *He's forgotten to tell me something. Or maybe—just maybe—he came back to…*

Abigail forced herself to abandon the idea as she went to the door and swung it open. The bottle was in her hand, ready to be offered.

Only it wasn't Colvin.

Chapter 39

A hand clamped tight on Abigail's mouth before she could scream. "Quiet, bitch," Heath MacIntyre growled. "Can't have ye' hexin' us with that dirty mouth of yers, can we?"

Heath shoved her back into the cabin and barged his way through the door. Owen Delaney and the others stormed in after him. How many men? Five? Ten? Abigail couldn't tell; it all happened too fast. Heath's massive hand was smothering her, cutting the air from her mouth and nose. Stars exploded in her vision. She had to get loose before she fainted. A terrifying vision of being alone and defenseless in the cabin with these men sprang into her mind. What would they do to her? How far would they go?

She couldn't let it happen. Somehow, she had to get away.

The bottle! She still held the whiskey bottle in her hand!

Twisting and struggling under Heath's iron grip, Abigail brought it up, swung it hard at his shaggy head...

Someone's hand shot out and knocked it from her grasp. The bottle hit the floor and shattered into pieces.

"Get her arms!" Heath hissed.

Abigail fought and thrashed as they yanked her hands behind her back. She tried to sink her teeth into Heath's palm, but he pressed it too tightly over her mouth. A rope was looped around her wrists. She felt it snap tight, digging painfully into her flesh and cutting off the circulation. Her fingertips went tingling and numb.

"Her mouth too!"

Heath snatched his hand away and a gag was shoved between Abigail's teeth. The same rope that bound her wrists was wrapped around her neck and mouth to keep the filthy rag in place.

Abigail whirled on them, her eyes blazing furiously.

"Oh..." Heath taunted, his gaze cold and narrow. "If only yer looks could kill as well as yer curses. Eh, bitch?" He balled his fist and gave Abigail a vicious punch in the stomach. The wind exploded from her lungs and her mind went out like a snuffed candle. She doubled over and staggered before falling to the floor among the shattered glass and spilled whiskey. Her head struck the floorboard and rebounded. Through the blurry haze clouding her mind, her only thought was that they had her now. They were free to do whatever they wanted to her...

Abigail had the sudden sensation of being dragged—across the floorboards, across the room, out the door. She didn't feel the impact as her body bounced down the steps from the cabin. She was too stunned, too disoriented. Trees and underbrush went by in a blur. She had a dreamlike awareness that she was in the forest. The crunch of footsteps on twigs came to her as if she were underwater, as if she was once again somewhere deep in the lake. There was darkness and torchlights and lightning and thunder. She was being dragged and dragged and dragged. Where were they taking her? How far would they go?

They stopped.

Someone hauled her to her feet and shoved her forward. She stumbled and fell sprawling in the dirt again. A voice swore and they yanked her up. A hand gripped her shoulder, kept her upright, led her forward and spun her around. The hand pushed her backward and her shoulders came up against the rough and unyielding trunk of a tree. A rope encircled her body, tightening around her chest, waist, legs. Someone yanked the rag from her mouth. The sudden intake of air cleared her head, and she struggled and squirmed.

Her efforts were useless.

She was lashed to a bare elm at the edge of a small hollow. Something about her surroundings seemed familiar. A sudden revulsion swept through her gut as she realized where she was.

This was the place where they had found Evelyn MacIntyre's mutilated corpse.

Eight men surrounded her. Some of them bore torches. The bright flames danced in the gathering wind of the approaching storm. The flickering light cast heavy shadows among the trees and made the leering faces of the men ghoulish to look upon. A purple blast of lightning forked across the sky as Abigail's eyes darted around, searching for something—anything—that she could use to her advantage.

There was nothing. It was hopeless.

Abigail's wild panic gave way to a terrible despair. Even if she could somehow free herself, there were too many men. She couldn't fight them off. She was helpless and at their mercy.

And now they would do whatever they wanted to her.

"Four things there are that make a witch," Heath intoned from the center of the ring of men. He had a large stone in his hand that he tossed into the air and caught absently as he glowered at her.

Abigail's gaze fell upon the stone and a sickening dread flooded through her. She had faced many horrors over the years, abominations and monstrosities the likes of which would snap the sanity of most men. She had faced them all with steadfast courage, never wavering, never shrinking. But now, she faced a different monster, one with flesh and blood the same as her own.

For the first time, she felt real terror.

"Four unholy sacraments for which the devil grants a witch her power," Heath continued, snatching the stone from the air. "Name them."

Abigail remained silent. Even as she trembled with fear under the rope that bound her, she wouldn't submit herself to the deranged commands of these fanatics.

"Name them!" Heath cried. "Name the sins of which you are about to be purged!"

Again, Abigail said nothing.

A blast of thunder exploded overhead and raindrops began to fall.

With a vicious snarl, Heath drew back the heavy stone and hurled it at Abigail. It struck her on the collarbone with such force that she was certain a rifle had shot her. A white bolt of agony went off in her brain.

"Contempt of Christ!" Heath exclaimed as the rain came

down and made the torches hiss. "A witch forsakes the blessed faith at the behest of her master, the devil!"

Another stone came streaking at Abigail and caught her in the ribs. She jerked and writhed in pain and this time she did scream, a pitiful cry that went nowhere in the wind.

"Homage to the devil and devotion to his service!" Heath shouted again.

Another man stepped forward with a stone in his hand. He was short and stout, with thick, unshaven jowls. Water dripped from strings of hair plastered to his balding pate. Tibbetts was his name.

Abigail's eyes widened with panic as he raised the stone and let it fly at her face. Thrown off target by the wind and rain, it glanced off her cheek and tore a gash.

The floodgates opened.

More and more stones came shooting through the rain as the other men unleashed their arsenal, hammering her from all directions. Abigail moaned in agony and felt the world going dim around her. They would not stop. She knew it now.

They were going to kill her.

"Sacrifice of babes in the name of Satan!" Heath's face was twisted and frenzied in the fading torchlights and the hellish lightning exploding above. "Feasting on their flesh! Drinking of their blood!"

Through the foggy haze of pain, Abigail saw another man stepping forward. It was Owen Delaney. Lightning crashed overhead as he stood there for a moment, studying the look of suffering etched on her face as if he were committing it to memory. *He is the one*, Abigail thought with a strange sense of certainty. *His stone will be the one that will finish me.*

"Fornication with the devil!" Heath shrieked. Spittle flew from his mouth, and his eyes were wild and fervent.

Delaney drew back the stone, ready to hurl it at her head.

Abigail closed her eyes. *Just end it. Just please make it end...*

And then—all at once—Delaney's hand exploded in a spray of blood as a tomahawk sailed through the air.

Chapter 40

Delaney screamed and fell to his knees, clutching at the bloody pulp of his ruined hand. Josiah was on him in an instant. He charged from the darkness of the rain-drenched forest and rammed the butt of his heavy rifle into the base of Delaney's skull. The blow knocked Delaney senseless and sent him crashing forward into the muck.

In a flash, Josiah swung his rifle around and aimed it at Heath. He didn't speak or hesitate, he just pulled the trigger. The rifle erupted with a blast of smoke and a spray of sparks. Heath's eyes went wide and stupid with surprise. He blinked and looked down, expecting to see his chest blown wide open.

The rifle had misfired.

With a guttural roar, Heath lowered his head and charged at Josiah. With lightning reflexes, Josiah swung his rifle at the big man's head like a club. Heath ducked beneath the swing and caught Josiah in the ribs, tackling him into the mud.

Through the sheets of rain, Abigail saw them both go down in a heap. Heath's fist came up and shot down again. The other men crowded around, shouting, piling on like a pack of wolves.

Colvin flew from the darkness with a furious cry and hurled himself, kicking and swinging, onto Josiah's attackers. Cries of pain erupted as Timber joined the fight, snapping and snarling viciously.

All of a sudden, Duncan was at Abigail's side. There wasn't time to speak. He cut through the rope that bound her, eased her to the ground, and left her with a knife before turning and diving into the melee.

Abigail cast off the remains of the severed ropes and lay there a moment, gathering her wits as the rain came down upon her. She could hear the grunts and cries of the men as they clashed. She was beaten and shaken and cold to the very bone.

But something about the feel of the knife in her hand electrified her. The cold and hurt vanished and there was nothing but black and irresistible rage. Staggering to her feet, Abigail turned and looked for Heath, ready to bury the blade deep into his throat.

Something big and heavy tackled her and sent her crashing back to the ground. Abigail rolled onto her back and lashed out with the knife, slicing through Tibbetts' fleshy cheek. A thrill of exhilaration shot through her. At last, here was something she could *kill*.

Tibbetts let out a cry but didn't relent. Lightning flashed on his ruddy face, and his eyes were wild and rabid. He caught Abigail by the legs and heaved, hauling her backward through the mud before she could scramble away. She twisted and brought the knife swinging through the air, slashing through his other cheek. At the same time, her free hand raked at his face. She had the satisfaction of feeling something squish and pop as she gouged her thumb into his eye.

Tibbetts howled in agony and swung blindly with his fist. The surprise blow caught Abigail in the jaw and knocked her flat. Tibbetts pounced on her.

"You'll kill us all!" he shrieked into her face. Blood streamed from his mangled cheeks. His ruined eye was a pulpy mess, and a string of drool hung from his split lips. "You'll kill us all, you wicked bitch!"

Abigail struggled and thrashed beneath Tibbetts's weight as he clamped his meaty hands around her throat and squeezed. She swung the knife in a wide arc and plunged the blade deep between his shoulder blades. Tibbetts screamed, but the hands wrapped around her throat only seemed to clutch harder. He wasn't just going to strangle her; he was going to crush her throat completely.

Again and again, Abigail stabbed with the knife, even as she began to lose consciousness. She felt her blade slip between Tibbetts's ribs and knew with certainty that she had killed him. The wound would bleed him out and there would be no sewing him back together.

But he could still live long enough to wring the life from her.

Abigail felt the man weakening as she gasped and choked for air. In vain, she tried to struggle out from under him, but he was too heavy and pinned flat. Rain splashed and pattered on her face as a horrible darkness rushed into her vision. She felt herself falling into nothing, hurtling toward a black and empty void...

A thundering blast tore away the crown of Tibbetts's head.

Abigail's eyes flew open as the hands around her throat went limp. There was an instant of confusion as she wondered why the rain had suddenly become red and warm. Then she saw the blood spilling over her from the massive hole in Tibbetts's skull. A tendril of smoke rose from the gaping wound as he teetered and collapsed on top of her.

Abigail squirmed out from underneath the limp body and found Colvin standing there. Drops of rain fell from the barrel of the big pistol he held in his outstretched hand. Helping Abigail to her feet, he swung the pistol around toward the scuffling men. The deafening roar of his shot had brought the fighting to an abrupt halt. No one moved. The men stared at the pistol in mute silence as the rain came down upon them.

"This didn't need to happen," Colvin growled through clenched teeth. "No one had to die... but more will if any of you so much as flinches."

Colvin kept the pistol leveled on them as Josiah dragged himself from the mud and went to stand by Duncan. Both men were bloodied and bruised from the fight.

Just then, Abigail noticed something wasn't right.

Heath was missing.

Colvin realized it too. "Where's MacIntyre?" There was an edge of worry in his voice. His eyes darted around the hollow and found a trace of trampled underbrush. He whirled to Josiah. "Find him! Don't let him get away!"

With a firm nod, Josiah recovered his tomahawk from the muck and disappeared into the forest.

Colvin returned his attention to Abigail's attackers. Owen

Delaney still lay sprawled and motionless in the mud. Colvin wondered if Josiah's blow to the head had killed him. Five more men remained standing. Without Heath around to whip up their courage, their fervor seemed to have fled. Now, they just looked scared and pathetic as they stood with their hands raised in the rain.

Colvin kept his pistol trained on them as he sidestepped to Duncan. "Emmons, I'm going to see Ms. Jacobs safely to her cabin. Please escort these men to the village limits." He handed over the pistol. "See that they leave this town at once. They are not to stop to gather possessions and they are not to speak to anyone. If anyone should ask what happened to Delaney and Tibbetts, please tell them what these cowards tried to do to Ms. Jacobs."

Duncan's gaze strayed to where Tibbetts's corpse lay in the mud. "What will we do with him?"

"We'll return for him later, if there's time. If there isn't, we'll let the scavengers pick him clean." Colvin paused and returned his attention to the men cowering before him. His gaze was every bit as hard and intimidating as the pistol in Duncan's hand. "You've heard what I said. If any of you should fail to cooperate in any way, I will find you and I will shoot you on the spot. I will do it in front of your wives and children if I have to. For their sakes, I suggest you be thankful for the mercy I'm showing you here and that you leave this place with as much haste as your miserable asses can muster." He glared at them a moment longer. "Get moving, you sons of bitches."

Duncan kept the pistol aimed as two of the men picked Delaney from the mud and hauled him away. An instant later, they were all gone, swallowed by the forest.

Colvin turned to Abigail. Her nightgown was soaked and torn and she shivered uncontrollably as the rain washed the blood from her skin. And yet, there was a strange shine in her eyes as she gazed at him through the downpour. It was as if there was some part of her that had actually thrived on the pain and violence.

"Come with me," Colvin said, lending her his arm. "Let's get you inside."

Chapter 41

Abigail's fury simmered like molten lead destined to become bullets. She hadn't said a word since leaving the hollow. Even as she flung open the door to her cabin and marched in from the rain, she seemed to have forgotten Colvin was there with her. Too many images consumed her mind, too many emotions: the humiliation of being taken by surprise; the violation of being battered with stones; the shameful panic at having Tibbetts's hands wrapped around her neck.

And the embarrassment of needing Colvin to rescue her yet again.

Shards of the shattered whiskey bottle were still strewn across the floor as Abigail went to the tin kettle, filled it, and left it to boil on the woodstove. She was shivering all over from the rain and the flood of adrenaline was now draining from her body. She had to get warm, had to get out of her soaked and tattered nightgown.

Colvin stood by the door and watched as she went to her clothes' chest for something dry to put on. "Abigail, say something. Tell me what I can do."

Abigail threw the gown in her hand back into the chest and whirled on him. "Let me make something clear," she said icily. "Never have I required assistance in my work. I operate alone, in secret. 'Tis the only way to keep others from being killed. Keenan and O'Brennan are proof of that. For twenty years, I have taken care of myself. I have survived countless encounters with unspeakable creatures thanks only to my own skills and abilities. I didn't require your help today at the lake and I didn't require it back there in the hollow. I could have taken care of Tibbetts on my own."

Colvin's face darkened. "Is that a fact? What about Heath and the others? What exactly was your plan for freeing yourself from that tree? What magic of yours would have made those stones drop out of the air before they killed you?"

Abigail's eyes flashed as she fought to keep from striking him. Her fist trembled with fury. Something angry and hurtful sprang to her lips and begged to be released. But she knew he was right. As much as it galled her to admit it, she knew she owed her life to this man. And after all, it wasn't Colvin she was truly angry with… it was herself.

For years, she had thrived on her own independence, reveling in her own strength. She had gratified herself whenever and however she pleased, spurning the undesired tenderness of lover after lover. She didn't need a man to protect her, didn't need a man for anything other than the occasional wanton encounter. Colvin had now taken part of that away from her… and she didn't know if she loved him or hated him for it.

The kettle was boiling on the stove. Abigail turned her back on Colvin and emptied the hot water into the washbasin.

Steam spiraled into the air as she stripped off her nightgown and let it fall to the floor around her ankles, heedless of Colvin's presence in the room. She was too cold, too tired, and too frustrated to care about modesty. She soaked the cotton cloth in the washbasin and pressed it to her frozen skin. The water was nearly scalding, but she didn't care. She needed its heat, needed to feel it washing over her, cleansing her of her shame and humiliation.

Colvin spun around and looked away—but not before he glimpsed the patchwork of bruises and scars that marred the flawless white of Abigail's lithe and slender body. Most were fresh and new; others were very old. Colvin was careful to keep his eyes averted as he crouched and busied himself with sweeping the shards of broken glass from the floor while Abigail continued to bathe herself behind him.

"I'll be alright now," she murmured after a moment. She pressed both hands to the table before her and leaned over the washbasin, breathing in the warm steam. "You must go. The evacuation must be—"

"I'm not going," Colvin said. He kept his back to her as he brushed the broken shards toward a corner.

"I beg your pardon?"

"I'm not leaving you here alone, not while Heath's still out there. If you prefer, I'll wait outside. But I won't be leaving here until I'm certain you'll be safe."

Something went off inside of Abigail, a spark of something thrilling that she couldn't name or place but quickened her heart and spread throughout her. She drew herself up and turned to him. Water ran in rivulets down her body and glistened in the lamplight as it dripped to the floor.

"Look at me," she said huskily.

Colvin slowly stood, but kept his back to her naked body.

"Glenn… look at me."

He turned around and she saw those eyes again. Those deep, amber eyes gazing at her, penetrating her defenses, seeing a part of her she kept hidden and locked away.

Such worry, such care…

This time, she didn't stop herself.

Abigail reached for his head with both hands and kissed him. She felt him go tense with surprise before his body relaxed and yielded to her embrace. Her tongue found his as she fell back on the bed and pulled him down on top of her. She clutched at his body, pressed it down hard against her own. Her hands dove into his hair, ran down his back, pulled at his shirt. She felt his skin, flesh, muscle; his lips tasting her own, his mouth covering hers as he kissed her. Her hand sought his and she brought it up to her chest, sighing with pleasure as he cupped the supple flesh of her breast in his palm. There was a sudden flash of pain when he brushed his other hand over a raw bruise. She flinched and felt him relent, his caresses becoming gentler, more tender.

But she didn't want him to be gentle. She wanted him to take her. She wanted to yield control to him. She wanted to release the darkness and rage inside of her and feel him there instead. Her hand slid down beneath his belt and found him hard and ready for her. She opened her legs and pressed him closer, leading him to her, showing him what she wanted. It was the last willful thing she did before she gave herself over to him. She gasped and moaned and shuddered beneath him, feeling the sweet oblivion of his embrace as the rain came down on the window and the thundering tempest shook the walls around them.

Chapter 42

Josiah stood as still as the trees in the forest's darkness. Rain came down in sheets around him, but he didn't make a move to shelter himself. If he felt the cold, he gave no outward appearance of it. He remained there, silent and motionless, waiting for the next blast of lightning to reveal the clue he desired.

Long ago—when he was known as River Stone and his village still stood on the banks of the great Penobscot— Josiah's father had taught him how to *see in the dark*, as his ancestors had called it. *Every creature leaves a sign of its passage*, his father had explained. *Only the dead leave no trace.* In the dense and virgin forests of his homeland, young River Stone had learned that even the smallest animal could be followed if the hunter knew what to look for.

Years had passed since those early adventures and Josiah had now become a master in the art of tracking his prey through any terrain. It was a skill that had proven useful when he and Colvin had spent those lean years as trappers before finding themselves in Tahawus. In time, Josiah hoped to pass his knowledge on to his own son when they were reunited at long last. He dreamed that someday they would hunt together as the men of his tribe had done for generations before them.

Now, every bit of Josiah's deadly prowess focused on finding his enemy. He had already failed to kill Heath MacIntyre once this night. He wouldn't fail again.

The lightning came; a forking blast of white that streaked across the night sky in long, claw-like fingers. Before the thunder had time to follow, Josiah had seen all he needed. A single spruce sapling stood bent at a peculiar angle to his left. For Josiah, it revealed an entire story. Spruce grew straight as an arrow pointed toward the sun, never at such an angle.

His enemy had come this way.

Josiah moved with the slow and silent grace of a predator as he followed the faint trace of Heath's trail deeper into the woods. He was bare-chested now, having cast off his red coat some time ago. Josiah would give his enemy no opportunity to see him coming. Rain streamed across his dark and hairless skin as he moved like a phantom through the forest. He breathed through his nose, exhaling long and slow to keep his breath from being visible in the cold. The black length of his topknot clung to his bald scalp and snaked down the back of his neck. One hand gripped his tomahawk while the other carried his big hunting knife. He had smeared sticky pinesap on both palms to ensure he wouldn't lose his grip on the weapons in the rain. When the fight finally came, he would be ready.

More signs of Heath's passage came into view: a trampled fern; a scuff across a bed of pine needles. And then, a very obvious footprint left in a long patch of mud.

Josiah paused and crouched low to study it as best he could, glimpsing it in flickering blasts of lightning. His eyes scanned the ground a few feet ahead. There was another track. This one was much less distinct, but noticeable, nonetheless. From the distance between the footprints, Josiah could discern that Heath was no longer running; the tracks were too close together. Heath was walking now, probably at a brisk pace.

Josiah rose and digested this new information. Had Heath come to believe he wasn't being followed? Or was the big man tiring?

A booming peal of thunder exploded overhead as Josiah remained there, trying to envision his enemy. As when hunting any animal, the key was to put himself in the mind of his prey and anticipate its behavior. *Do not waste daylight letting the deer lead you through the trees*, his father had instructed long ago. *Find where it eats and wait for it there.*

Josiah used that same philosophy now as he resumed his stealthy pursuit through the forest. What was Heath thinking? Where was he going? Josiah knew the big man wasn't fleeing the village for good. He was heading north, in the wrong direction. Would Heath try to double back once he had put enough distance between himself and any pursuers that had come after him? Josiah doubted it. What would Heath gain by returning to the village? Colvin and the others would be there waiting for him. No; Heath must know that he had been defeated now that his murderous plan had failed. He must have understood it back there in the hollow. It was why he had fled into the woods and deserted his followers.

Where, then, would he go?

Josiah's palm clenched tighter around his tomahawk as he crept his way through the darkness and contemplated Heath's motivations. He was certain the man wouldn't abandon his desire to see Abigail dead. Heath was too fanatical, too convinced of his own righteousness. Josiah had known such men before. They had been among the first to come to his village: servants of the white God who demanded red blood as the price of disobedience. Heath was like them. His zealousness had already carried him too far to surrender now. He would return for Abigail at the first opportunity. Until then, he would hide and wait.

Josiah froze where he stood.

Hide and wait…

Yes, *that* was what Heath was thinking. He wasn't scared. He wasn't wandering the woods aimlessly, hoping to outrun his pursuers. In fact, he wouldn't have ventured too far from the village at all. If he were being followed, he would lead his pursuers on, luring them in, letting them come to him to be ambushed. Only when the evacuation was complete and the village was deserted, would he seek to finish what he had started with Abigail.

Josiah's heart quickened as he squinted into the heavy rain and revolved in a long, slow circle. Was Heath watching him even now? Was he hidden somewhere in the darkness?

With his vision now unreliable, Josiah fell back on his hearing. Nature had remarkable ways of defending itself. When danger was around, smaller creatures like tree frogs would go silent as a warning to others. But now, even Josiah's acute ears failed him. The rain was too heavy. All he could hear was the steady patter of water filtering through the heavy boughs.

A brilliant crash of lightning went off and revealed a fresh depression in the underbrush ahead. Heath had gone through there.

Josiah's senses remained sharp and vigilant as he pushed onward. He pricked his ears for even the slightest disturbance in the forest. Heath would make his move very soon now. The big man wouldn't have wasted too much energy trudging through the rain. Perhaps he would have passed over the first few opportunities for an ambush to fool his pursuers into believing he was on the run. But Josiah knew he had now come far enough. By now, Heath would have started to search for the perfect place to bide his time until his unsuspecting pursuers fell into his trap.

Josiah inched forward—step after wary step—and conjured an image of Heath as he had been back in the hollow. Had the big man been armed? Of course, there had been the stones he had hurled at Abigail. But had Heath carried a firearm or blade of any sort? No; as far as Josiah could remember, Heath was unarmed. If he had a weapon, there had been enough opportunities to draw it during the scuffle.

Still, out here in the forest, there were plenty of heavy tree limbs with which to—

Suddenly, there it was.

Ahead, the pines of the forest stood crowded closer together like giant soldiers standing shoulder to shoulder. Josiah crept closer and saw their needles were saturated and dripping with rain. Millions of tiny beads of water glistened in the pink and purple glare of the lightning. Except for one place. It was a shadowy area where the heavy boughs of two pines met. Something large had brushed the dew from the limbs. The spot stood directly in Josiah's path.

Somewhere in that dense foliage, Heath waited for him.

Minutes went by as Josiah assessed the situation. The stand of pines was the perfect place for an ambush. Heath was on the other side of the boughs, hidden, waiting for his pursuers to squeeze their way through. It was where Josiah himself would have set his own trap.

This was the place. He was certain of it.

An idea came to him. Instead of following Heath into his ambush, Josiah slowly and cautiously sidestepped his way laterally to his right. Now that he had identified the trap, he would circle around behind the dense copse of pines and take Heath by surprise. His enemy wouldn't see him coming. An eager thrill came over Josiah. He hadn't taken a scalp in many, many years. Now he would make an exception.

After he had traversed about forty yards, Josiah decided he had gone far enough. He changed direction again and pushed his way forward once more through the brush. The footfalls of his leather moccasins were slow and soundless as he stole ever deeper into the woods. The relentless patter of the downpour swallowed what little noise he made. Josiah's veins quivered with adrenaline in anticipation of the fight. The sensation warmed him in the cold, driving rain.

Soon Heath would lie dead at his feet. It wouldn't be long now.

Before long, Josiah came to a rocky brook that had become swollen with the heavy rain.

Something sent a prickle of fear racing into his heart.

There was a single footprint imprinted in the muddy bank. It was so deep and distinct, it had begun to collect rainwater.

And it had come from the brook.

Josiah's gaze fell upon it, and he knew he had made a fatal mistake. There would be no fight. There would be no scalping. Heath wasn't waiting for him back there on the other side of those pines. He had kept going until he had come to this stream. He had waded up it, using the rocks and the rushing current to hide his tracks until he had exited it here. Then he had doubled back, circled around... and gotten behind his pursuer.

All of this, Josiah realized too late.

From behind came a tremendous crashing of underbrush. Josiah whirled around in time to see something big and heavy hurtling at his face. Something crunched in his head and he saw his own blood spraying out before his eyes.

And then he saw nothing at all.

Chapter 43

Abigail left Colvin sleeping in her bed and slipped from the cabin. As she eased the door closed behind her, Timber raised his furry head and peered at her sleepily from where he lay on the doorstep. True to his word, Colvin hadn't left her side all night. Their lovemaking seemed to have lasted hours, repeating itself over and over until they had both lain spent and exhausted.

In all that time, Josiah had not returned.

The thought haunted Abigail as she made her way through the eerie morning stillness of the deserted village. Josiah was a cunning warrior, but the longer he was gone, the more Abigail suspected she hadn't seen the last of Heath MacIntyre. Was he still out there somewhere, lurking in the shadows of the misty forest? Did he have his eyes on her even now, watching her as she moved along the silent paths?

Having lost her own cloak while saving Hannah Gill in the lake, Abigail had pulled Colvin's wool coat over her dress before leaving the cabin. She had also helped herself to his leather belt and the knife and pistol he kept fastened to it.

Her hands now fell to her waist and she felt the grips of the weapons. The next time MacIntyre crossed her path, he wouldn't catch her unprepared. Let him show himself. Let him come to her.

Main Street was a muddy mess as Abigail made her way toward the chapel. The previous night's fearsome thunderstorm had ended shortly before dawn. Now, the sky was leaden and the cool air pregnant with moisture. Ominous gray shadows lurked like specters among the clouds. The heavy autumn rains weren't done with the village yet and Abigail suspected the worst was yet to come. Within hours, the heavens would pour down their wrath once more.

As Colvin had predicted, Tahawus had become a ghost town. Even amid last night's raging storm, the villagers had fled, taking with them only what they could carry. All around her, Abigail saw nothing but darkened windows and empty cabins. There were no sounds of lumberjacks readying themselves for work; no smells of breakfast being prepared in the mess hall; no wood smoke wafting from the chimney pipes. There were no signs of life. There was only the strange and foreboding silence.

Something about the quiet stillness comforted Abigail. No matter what happened in her clash with Samael, the rest of the villagers would now be safe. Later, she would rouse Duncan and have him search the village to be sure no one else had stayed behind. But she already suspected he wouldn't find anyone. Only six people now remained in Tahawus: herself, Duncan, Carnes, Colvin, Josiah, and Heath MacIntyre.

In all likelihood, one of them had summoned Samael.

As she thought about it now, a glimmer of doubt took root

in Abigail's thoughts. Could she have been mistaken? She had a hard time accepting that any of the five men could have summoned the demon. One man she had known since childhood. Another was a man of God. A third she trusted enough to have taken into her bed. Even Heath—who had tried to murder her just hours ago—seemed too devout to be capable of such a blasphemy.

But what about Josiah? He alone had known of the ancient Mohawk legends that spoke of Lake Tear of the Clouds as a place of evil. He had known what fates had befallen the Legendre brothers up there in the high peaks. Could Josiah be the one who had summoned Samael? Of the five suspects, he was the only one who might have had a motive. White men had destroyed his village. They had cast his people from their ancestral lands, condemned his family to live on a wretched reservation, forced him to leave his wife and son.

Was summoning the demon Josiah's way of exacting revenge?

Abigail's gut instinct told her the loyal Native she had come to know and trust wasn't capable of such horrors. Once again, she wondered at her own assumptions. Perhaps the culprit wasn't one of the men who had stayed behind. Perhaps whoever had summoned the demon had used the cover of the evacuation to steal away undiscovered.

And yet, something instinctive told Abigail she was right. Whoever had summoned Samael had done so for a reason. She didn't yet know what that reason was, but she was certain the malefactor wouldn't have fled the village with the other evacuees. He would have remained to see his diabolical intentions through to the very end. Again and again, Abigail's thoughts circled back to the same conclusion: Duncan, Carnes, Colvin, Josiah, or Heath.

Which one was it?

Abigail's mood was gray and troubled as she reached the chapel and mounted the steps. She pushed on the door and found it unlocked. "Mr. Carnes?" Her voice rolled over the pews and reverberated through the hollow space of the empty sanctuary.

Carnes appeared from the vestry. He was missing his cassock and his shirt was rolled to the elbows. "Ms. Jacobs! I've only now learned what happened last night. I meant to come to you as soon as—"

"Thank you for your concern, but I assure you I am quite alright. My injuries will heal. At the moment, we have more pressing issues to discuss."

"Of course," Carnes said with a curious look. Abigail's forehead and cheek were bruised and torn from the stoning and her throat still bore livid bruises from where Tibbetts had tried to choke the life from her. But the firm set of her jaw as she gazed at the priest revealed she clearly didn't want to discuss the previous night's events.

Carnes ushered Abigail through the sanctuary to the vestry, where he offered her a chair at the desk and closed the door behind them. He had been reading from a small Bible when he heard her call and the book still lay open on the desk. He marked his place with a strip of felt and set it aside. "How can I be of help?"

"I've an idea about how to banish the demon," Abigail replied, waving off his offer of coffee. "If Lake Tear of the Clouds is the gate through which Samael entered our world, what would happen if you were to bless it in the same manner as you would bless holy water?"

Carnes' expression became thoughtful as he drew back a chair and sat with her at the desk. "You mean, could blessing the lake somehow cleanse it of the evil within and force Samael back to Hell?"

Abigail nodded. "Is it possible?"

Carnes pressed a finger to his lips and thought it over. "I suppose so. Whenever a new place of worship is established, it is consecrated or solemnly blessed in order to ward it from demons and remove it from the influence of Satan. I don't see why the same logic couldn't apply to Lake Tear of the Clouds. Holy water itself has long been believed to be one of the most powerful weapons we have against the afflictions of the devil. At the very least, if blessing the lake doesn't actually banish Samael, it may seal the gate and prevent any more such beings from passing through."

An eager shine came into Abigail's eyes. "Will you then accompany us to the lake and perform the ritual?"

"If you believe it will rid the world of this evil abomination, then yes. Absolutely."

"I am glad to hear it," said Abigail with visible relief. "And now, there is one more thing, Mr. Carnes."

"What is it?"

"You must teach me how to perform an exorcism."

Carnes raised his eyebrows. "I beg your pardon?"

"We still do not know how Samael is able to manipulate his victims' thoughts. Until we do, every one of us is vulnerable—including yourself. If you should fall under the demon's influence before you can perform the ritual and seal the gate, then I must bear a means by which to liberate you."

Carnes stared at her as though reading something in her face. Abigail could tell by his sober eyes and the deep creases in his forehead that his mind was wrestling with its own conflicting thoughts and emotions. Part of her feared he would resist, that he would dismiss the idea of exorcism altogether.

But then, with his mind seemingly made up, Carnes rose and moved to the cabinet of books against the wall. Abigail's gaze went immediately to her Book of Shadows, still locked away with the other volumes behind the cabinet's glass doors. Carnes released the lock and selected a slim, leather-bound volume from the top row. He handed it to Abigail.

"The holy Roman Rite of Exorcism," he said gravely. "I suspect you will have time enough to study it as we make our journey to Lake Tear of the Clouds. You will find the necessary holy water in the font on your way from the sanctuary." He paused and studied her a moment longer. "But there is more to the ritual than the mere recitation of words and the sprinkling of water."

"What more is required?"

"All Christians have the power to perform an exorcism as children of God. But the exorcist must have a clean and unburdened soul." Carnes paused. "You must confess, Ms. Jacobs."

Abigail stared at him. "Confess? I fear that will prove quite useless, Mr. Carnes. I don't believe in your God."

"Fortunately, his existence does not require your belief," Carnes quipped, his words echoing her own on the day of their first encounter. "You say you don't believe in God, and yet you willingly accept the existence of His adversaries. Why is that, Ms. Jacobs?"

"Perhaps because I have seen the work of the devil with my own eyes."

"And what of the splendor that surrounds you every day? The beauty of nature? The love of family and friends? What are these but the work of God?"

"My eyes do not see such things, Mr. Carnes," Abigail replied with a note of bitterness. "Mine is a world of pain and fear and loss."

A look of sincere sadness crept into Carnes' pale green eyes. "Ah, you see Ms. Jacobs... I believe you have just made your first confession. I'm afraid only one who is distinguished for his piety and purity of life can drive the devil out before him. Pardon me for saying so, but I suspect yours has been a life of wickedness. If you are to perform an exorcism successfully, you've no choice but to show contrition for your sins and be absolved. Otherwise, you might as well be reciting your favorite sonnet while Samael tricks me into slitting my own throat."

A swift and nearly irresistible impulse to get up and storm from the room overcame Abigail. One of the other men could learn how to perform the exorcism. Duncan could do it. She wouldn't submit herself to this sort of violation. The thought of revealing her darkest secrets to this man—this *stranger*—filled her with revulsion. Who was he to promise her forgiveness? Who was he to think he could absolve her of years and years of guilt? If it weren't for her, both of her parents would still be alive. What words of his could make the ever-present pain of that knowledge go away?

And there was more—much more. For all her talk of saving others from evil, there remained part of Abigail that was honest enough to admit that she was driven only by her own selfish desire for revenge. Revenge on the spirits that had taken her parents from her; revenge for the childhood she never had; revenge for the life and family she never *would* have. In her heart, Abigail knew her crusade to rid the world of its monsters was centered squarely on herself, on satisfying her own bloody lust for vengeance. Whatever lives she saved along the way were convenient excuses to justify her own vengeful acts. She never truly grieved the loss of others. She simply used them to gratify her own cravings, to ease the rage that threatened to consume her always. She knew this admission should sadden her, but it didn't. She had come to accept it, even embrace it.

How could Carnes possibly absolve her of that?

And yet, something kept Abigail rooted where she sat. Every fiber of her being told her to get up and leave, but she found herself unable to move. If only it were so simple! If only she could find redemption by unburdening herself to this man! And what if this was the only way to save them all from Samael? Was she willing to risk all of their lives simply because she was too fearful of confronting her own *personal* demons?

Abigail's heart quickened and a strange and nervous sensation settled in her stomach. "Very well," she murmured. She felt like a child who has just realized she has become lost and separated from safety. She hesitated a moment longer, still wrestling with her decision. "I... I don't know how to begin."

Carnes gave her a warm smile. "I will lead you. Do you open your heart to me and welcome me into your soul as your confessor that I may give you absolution?"

"I…" Abigail faltered and struggled to overcome her unease. What secrets was she about to reveal? What words would come out once she started her confession? "I—"

She stopped, her words hanging on the tip of her tongue.

All at once, it came to her.

The terrible realization exploded with the force and brilliance of a cannon blast. Every part of her seemed to go cold at once.

She knew who had summoned the demon.

"I—I'm sorry, Mr. Carnes," she stammered, rising from the desk. "I can't do this now. There are too many emotions, too many memories of sins long forgotten. I need some time to contemplate and come to terms with my guilt. There will be time enough for this during our journey to the lake. In the meantime, I will gather the others. You should prepare to depart within the hour."

Abigail didn't hear Carnes' confused objections as she left the vestry and hurried through the sanctuary. Only one thought held her mind.

She had to find Colvin as soon as possible.

Chapter 44

Timber leapt to all fours and let out a throaty growl as Abigail appeared from the path. She had come upon the dog by surprise, but once he recognized her, he settled back into his bed of pine needles and eyed her suspiciously as she hurried to her cabin door.

"Glenn!" she called.

Colvin appeared in the doorframe. He was shirtless, dressed only in breeches that hung low around his trim waist. His hair and beard were wet. "What is it?" he asked, alarmed by the tension in Abigail's voice. "What's going on?"

"It's Carnes." Abigail panted between heaving breaths.

Colvin's brows came together in confusion as he stepped from the cabin and went to her. "What? How do you know —"

"The confessions!" said Abigail. "The confessions link all the victims together! All the victims visited Carnes to seek absolution—even Hannah Gill. *He* is the connection we've been looking for!"

"Connection? What connection?"

Abigail was too excited to hear him. "There had to be something all the victims had in common, something that made them vulnerable to the demon's deceptions. Don't you see? Carnes didn't just summon Samael; he *is* Samael! He has been possessed! And every time a confessor opens their heart to him to seek absolution, they are revealing their darkest secrets to the demon within him. *That* is how Samael poisons his victims' minds and tricks them into killing themselves."

Colvin shook his head. It was all coming at him too fast. "But why would Carnes have done such a thing? What would he have to gain?"

Timber slunk to Colvin's side and let out a low, menacing growl as he gazed into the woods. Something out there had caught his keen eye. Colvin's hand fell absently to the dog's head and gave him a reassuring pat.

"I don't know," Abigail admitted. "But we must act quickly. If Carnes suspects that I—"

Just then, Timber's fur sprang up and he barked furiously.

Abigail whirled.

The roar of the gunshot came without warning.

All at once, Colvin's eyes flew wide and he pitched forward. Abigail felt the sharp sting of something slicing through the flesh of her bicep. A red hole had blossomed in the middle of Colvin's bare chest. Blood welled and poured from it as he staggered and fell to his knees.

Behind him—emerging from a cloud of gun smoke among the trees—was Heath MacIntyre. Josiah's rifle was in his hands.

Abigail couldn't tear her eyes from the blood seeping from between Colvin's fingers. Heath had shot him in the back.

The bullet had passed through him and exited his chest, grazing her arm. Blood was pumping steadily from his wound —too much blood.

There wasn't time to go to him. Heath was already advancing, his gray eyes filled with murderous intent.

Abigail didn't hesitate. Her hand dropped to the leather belt she wore—Colvin's belt—and drew the pistol from its holster. Her gaze was fierce and unflinching as she leveled it on the big man barreling toward her.

The sudden appearance of the firearm in her hand took Heath by surprise and he faltered in his charge.

The pistol went off.

Abigail's shot caught Heath in the right shoulder and sent him reeling. He staggered, his right arm hanging uselessly from its shattered socket like a rag doll with ripped seams. Blood soaked the filthy linen of his shirt. He had enough time to raise his head, to see the merciless look in Abigail's eyes.

And then Timber had him.

The dog snarled viciously as he surged forward and leaped at Heath, catching him in the chest. The impact propelled them both backward and they went toppling to the ground. Sprawled in the underbrush, Heath cried out and raised his good arm to protect his face while Timber snapped at him in a bloodthirsty frenzy. Spittle flew from the dog's jaws as he bared his fangs and lashed out at Heath's throat, intent on tearing it to shreds. The snapping jaws found the exposed meat of Heath's raised forearm. With a loud and horrible crunch, the bone snapped under the incredible pressure of the big dog's bite.

Heath screamed as Timber sank his teeth deep and whipped his head savagely from side to side, ripping away skin and flesh and veins and tendons. Blood sprayed from the ruptured arteries, soaking the dog's snarling muzzle and thick, black hide. Again and again Timber struck, biting and ripping and tearing at Heath's arms, chest, and face.

Heath shrieked and writhed in agony as the enraged dog ravaged him. In vain, he flailed and beat at Timber with his fist. With one last desperate effort, his left hand fell upon the rifle where it had fallen and he swung it hard, bringing the heavy butt crashing into the dog's skull. Timber let out a startled yelp and went limp before slumping to the side.

Heath rolled in the dirt, dazed and weakened from the blood loss. The world wobbled and spun beneath him as he tried to sit up.

A shadow fell upon him.

Heath looked up and found Abigail standing over him as he lay sprawled on his back. She held something in her fist, something long and sharp and gleaming. Heath's hand fumbled for the rifle, but she kicked it away and stepped on his wounded forearm, pinning the mangled mess to the ground beneath her boot.

Heath howled in pain, but Abigail paid him no attention. She dropped to one knee over his heaving chest and pressed the tip of Colvin's knife up into Heath's chin, piercing the skin behind the blood-drenched tangle of his goatee. She looked into his eyes to be sure he understood what she was going to do. Fear dawned in those gray eyes, and she felt a fleeting glimmer of satisfaction.

And then she rammed the blade up through his jaw and

into his skull.

Abigail left the knife embedded where it was as she rose and turned her attention to Timber. Heath's blow to the head had stunned the dog, but he was shaking it off and recovering. His long, pink tongue was stained red as he licked the blood from around his teeth and lips. Abigail saw him gazing hungrily at Heath's torn and lifeless corpse.

"Have at him, boy," she murmured into the dog's ear.

Abigail left Timber to his feast and went to Colvin's side. There was no need to hurry. There was too much blood; it was already too late. Colvin was on the verge of losing consciousness as Abigail knelt next to him and took his head in her lap. There was nothing she could do for him now but be with him while he died. In her experience, it was all anyone could ever really ask for: to not die alone.

Colvin's face was still and ashen as he stared up at the sky. His amber eyes became vacant and sightless. Death came upon him swiftly.

When the moment passed, there were no tears and no goodbyes. There was only a hollow feeling in Abigail's heart that hurt her more than anything she had endured in a very long time. Unable to bear the awful stillness of Colvin's lifeless gaze, she slid his eyes closed and remained there in the blood-soaked dirt, cradling his head in her lap.

Everyone dies, she reminded herself over and over, letting the familiar refrain comfort her and numb her pain. *Everyone dies. Your parents, your family, your friends, your lovers. Everyone dies, everyone dies. And one day, you will die too...*

Chapter 45

Abigail was leaving Colvin's cabin behind when Duncan found her trudging up the path. "Abby! I heard gunshots! What—"

"Glenn's dead," she said. Her voice was blunt and detached. "MacIntyre shot him. The bullet was meant for me."

"Oh, God…" Duncan's face lost its color.

"We haven't time to mourn," said Abigail.

Something about her tone gave Duncan a chill. She might say the same thing about him soon.

"We must go to the chapel," she continued. "We must retrieve my Book of Shadows… and we must finally put an end to this evil."

Duncan knew better than to ask many questions.

The town was a body without a spirit as they stole through the lanes, the empty husk of something left behind. A cold breeze had arisen, stirring leaves and whistling a ghostly song as it breathed through the desolate cabins. It was early afternoon, but the sky was growing ever darker. Soon the rain would come.

When Abigail eventually did speak, it was to brief Duncan about what she had pieced together about Father Carnes. She would say no more about Colvin. Duncan suspected she would never speak of him again.

The white steeple of the chapel loomed over them as they drew near. Abigail pushed at the unlocked door and it creaked open.

There was nothing but silence within.

Carnes was nowhere to be found.

"Be vigilant," Abigail warned as Duncan slipped across the threshold and closed the door behind them. "A powerful demon lives within Carnes... and he could be waiting for us anywhere."

"Do you think he suspects you?" Duncan whispered.

"He would be a fool not to."

An icy prickle of dread ran up Duncan's spine as they crept up the aisle toward the altar. Forward and to their left stood the closed door of the vestry. What would they find within? Was Carnes in there, waiting for them? Worse yet, what if the priest was no longer himself? What if the demon had overtaken completely?

The floorboards creaked unnervingly beneath even their lightest tread, announcing their presence to anyone who was listening. The tall windows shuddered under the force of a strong wind as the storm outside gathered strength. Duncan steeled his nerves and focused his attention on the closed door, now only a few feet away. Part of him expected it to fly open at any moment. He envisioned some nightmarish creature hurtling toward him from the vestry. His heart quickened in his chest as they drew to a halt.

Abigail quietly leaned forward and pressed an ear to the door. A long moment passed in silence as she remained there, listening for movement on the other side.

A gust of wind whistled a mournful tune through the bell tower high above them.

Abigail gave Duncan an apprehensive look as she withdrew from the door and shrugged silently. She had heard nothing from inside the vestry.

But that didn't mean it was empty.

Abigail reached for the door handle and let her palm rest on it for a moment, bracing herself for whatever was going to happen next.

Sweat sprang to Duncan's palms as he watched her release the latch.

The door cracked inward.

Nothing happened.

With a gentle push, Abigail eased the door wider.

The vestry beyond was silent and deserted.

"He's gone," said Abigail as they stepped inside.

Duncan was unsure if he should be relieved or dismayed. "Gone where?"

Abigail left his question unanswered as she moved swiftly across the room to the book cabinet. Relief washed over her at the sight of her Book of Shadows still tucked behind the glass doors. She had feared what Carnes might do with it once she had given him reason to suspect her. She had been a fool to trust him with her most valuable possession. It would never happen again.

Abigail didn't bother examining the lock on the cabinet. Instead, she reached for Carnes' washbasin, shielded her eyes with her forearm, and smashed the glass doors. Broken shards fell noisily to the floor and crunched under Abigail's boot as she stepped forward and took her grimoire into her hands. The crimson leather seemed to radiate a strange heat of its own as she sprung the iron clasps and cracked the volume open. Her gaze moved like a loving caress across the yellow parchment as she inspected the ancient tome for damage.

Satisfied that all was in order, Abigail laid the book on the vestry desk and returned her attention to the books arrayed in Carnes' cabinet. Some volumes were familiar, but most were obscure religious treatises she didn't recognize. Abigail drew a finger across the worn spines as she scanned the titles.

She stopped abruptly.

"What is it?" Duncan asked, moving to her side.

Abigail didn't answer. Instead, she curled her fingers into a fist and wrapped her knuckles against the lowest row of books.

The sound she produced was strangely hollow.

"A false front," Abigail murmured. Her eyes lit with fascination as she leaned closer to examine the volumes. What she discovered was a flat piece of wood expertly carved and painted to resemble leather book spines. A small space was visible where one fake book was made to seem shorter than its neighbors. Abigail probed the narrow opening with her finger and slipped it through to the other side of the wooden front. She pulled at it. Four of the false book spines came away as one and revealed a concealed drawer. Abigail's heart danced with excitement as she drew it open.

Inside was a small, leather-bound book.

Abigail plucked it from its hiding spot, flipped it open, and studied the pages of neat, flowing script. "Impossible..." she murmured.

The look on her face alarmed Duncan. "What? What is it?"

"Carnes' diary. He's been documenting everything..." Abigail skipped forward through the pages, scanning the entries. "It's all here, an entire account of the ritual he used to summon Samael. And there is more, much more. Spells and rituals such as I have never seen. It's his own Book of Shadows!"

Abigail handed the journal to Duncan to examine for himself. Her eyes fell upon the Bible Carnes had left on the desk. What had Carnes been reading when she had interrupted him that morning? Abigail seized the Bible from where it sat and cracked it open at the page the priest had left marked. Her eyes flicked back and forth as she scanned the passages, searching for clues.

"No," she said abruptly. "It can't be..."

An anxious look bloomed on Duncan's face. "What is it? What have you found?"

"Look here." Abigail swung the Bible around and slid her finger down the page. "It concerns the Fall of Adam and Eve in the Book of Genesis. In tempting Eve to eat the fruit of the forbidden tree of knowledge, the serpent says, *then your eyes shall be opened, and ye shall be as gods, knowing good and evil.*"

"Yes, but everyone knows the devil is a liar," Duncan remarked. "He would have said anything to persuade Eve to transgress."

"Perhaps, but many believe the serpent in the garden was actually *Samael.*" Abigail's finger slid to another passage further down the page. "Look here. Once Adam and Eve have eaten the fruit of knowledge, God Himself says, *Behold, the Man is become as one of us, to know good and evil.*"

Duncan stared at her, trying to put it all together in his mind.

"This passage is the key," Abigail persisted. "To be a god is to have knowledge of both good *and* evil. That is why Carnes summoned Samael."

"So that he might somehow attain godlike wisdom?"

"Precisely. Carnes had already known good—he was a man of faith, a pious messenger of the word of God. But in order to be graced with true enlightenment, he had to commit an act of ultimate *evil*. And according to Scripture, what is the greatest sin against God?"

Duncan gave it a moment's thought. "Murder?"

"No. It's *rebellion*. Lucifer and his followers were cast into Hell because they rebelled against God. Evil as we know it began with Lucifer's rebellion. In Carnes' mind, the only way to know ultimate evil is to commit a similar act of treason."

Duncan's face lit up as it all became very clear to him. "And what could be more treasonous than for a man of faith to embrace one of God's most rebellious adversaries: the same demon that tempted Adam and Eve to sin?"

Abigail's blue eyes twinkled with excitement as the pieces all came together. "By aiding Samael to harvest the lost souls of the suicidal, Carnes aims to attain a level of enlightenment forbidden to all but God Himself."

Duncan ran a hand through his coarse hair and shook his head in disbelief. "'Tis an insane idea. Carnes would have to be a madman."

"Most certainly," Abigail agreed. "Who else but a lunatic

would volunteer to live out here in this godforsaken wilderness?"

Duncan gave her a look that told her he wasn't amused. "But if Carnes has been possessed by Samael, then why has he been defending you? Why has he been helping us?"

"Has he? It seems to me that he's done only enough to avoid our suspicion. In fact, he's denied the possibility of demonic possession at every turn, hasn't he? Not to mention the fact that he tried to coax me into revealing my darkest secrets to him. What do you suppose Samael would have done with that knowledge? What better way of riding himself of me than by leading me to death by my own hand?"

Abigail went quiet for a moment before continuing. "There is another question that troubles me. How did Carnes happen to come across the portal at Lake Tear of the Clouds? It can't be a simple coincidence that Witherbee & Rand sent him of all people to this remote part of the country where there just happens to be a gateway to Hell."

Duncan looked like he'd been struck by lightning. "Carnes wasn't sent here by Witherbee & Rand."

"I beg your pardon?"

"Carnes doesn't work for the company. He arrived here as a roaming missionary years ago and never left."

"A missionary?" Abigail's eyes widened as another realization came to her. "Did Carnes ever study with the Jesuits?"

"I seem to remember him speaking of having spent some time among the French to the north. I suppose it's possible that he interacted with the Jesuits."

"Then he could have heard the tale of the Legendre

brothers! The Jesuits knew about this place; they knew it was a portal to—"

A door slammed shut in the sanctuary.

Abigail went rigid and exchanged a fearful glance with Duncan.

They were no longer alone.

Chapter 46

Footsteps echoed from beyond the closed door of the vestry. They were slow and shambling, as if someone was plodding through the chapel on unsteady legs. There was no mistaking their intent: they were heading directly for the door.

Carnes had returned.

Step... Step... Step...

Abigail retreated across the small room. Her eyes darted left and right, searching for a way out. Her gaze fell upon the window. It was too small for an escape.

They were trapped.

Step... Step... Step...

The footsteps grew ever louder.

Just by listening, Abigail could trace Carnes' path through the sanctuary. He was nearing the head of the aisle. Soon, he would reach the chancel in front of the altar. From there, it was only a few more steps across the transept to the door of the vestry.

Abigail's hands shot to the belt slung around her waist. She had left Colvin's knife embedded in Heath MacIntyre's head but she still had his pistol. Her palm closed around the worn grip even as a sinking realization came to her.

She hadn't reloaded after firing at Heath.

Step... Step... Step...

Abigail rummaged through the pockets of Colvin's coat. She found his powder kit and bit the stopper from the pouch. Willing herself to keep her hand steady, she poured the gunpowder and primed the pistol's flashpan. She felt Duncan's fearful eyes on her, silently pleading with her to hurry.

Step... Step... Step...

The footsteps halted just beyond the door.

Abigail's heart pounded furiously as she dropped the lead ball into the pistol's barrel. Her hand fumbled with the ramrod, almost dropping it in her haste as she packed the ball.

From outside, she heard a hand settle on the door handle.

The latch moved.

Abigail swung the pistol up and cocked the hammer.

The door creaked open.

Abigail's finger tightened around the trigger.

She didn't fire.

"Josiah!" she exclaimed at the sight of the battered and bare-chested Native standing in the open doorway.

Josiah's face was a hideous sight. His nose was bent sideways at an ugly angle across his face. Both eye sockets were nearly swollen shut, his black pupils almost completely hidden beneath bruised flesh. One cheek was a strange color and appeared oddly flat, as if the bone beneath had been crushed. Blood streaked his lips and chin and there were gaping holes in his gums where teeth had been knocked from his mouth.

Abigail and Duncan both rushed to him and eased him into a chair at the table.

"What happened to you?" Duncan asked.

When Josiah spoke, his broken nose and swollen mouth turned his voice muffled and strangely nasal. "Heath," he rasped with obvious effort. "Ambushed."

"MacIntyre's dead," said Abigail. "I killed him."

Josiah's head turned. His swollen eyes found Abigail and he bowed his head once at her in silent approval. His gaze swept over the room as if he were looking for something.

Duncan read his mind. "Glenn's dead too. Heath shot him."

A look of profound sadness came over Josiah's battered face. He lowered his head and his topknot fell forward as he gazed at the floor between his feet.

Duncan gave him a moment before continuing. "Father Carnes is the one who summoned Samael. We've no idea where he is."

"Yes, we do," Abigail said. She retrieved Carnes' journal from where Duncan had laid it on the desk and flipped it open. Josiah's ragged breathing filled the silence of the long moments that passed as Abigail scanned page after page of the priest's notes. "He's going to Lake Tear of the Clouds." She spun the open journal in her hands and showed a passage. "Carnes' covenant with Samael demands one last soul as a sacrifice... his own. And he must do it at the very place from which the demon arose. Until their pact is complete, the demon is bound to an earthly vessel. It *needs* a human body to possess like a parasite requires a host. But if we allow Carnes to drown in those waters, he will exchange his place on Earth for Samael's place in Hell and release the demon upon our world with all of its unholy strength. It will be free to take innocent victims at will and what has happened here in Tahawus will be repeated again and again to no end."

Duncan heaved a heavy breath as the gravity of her words fell upon him. "If we go after him, what will we do when we get to the lake? Only a priest can bless the waters of the lake and seal the gate."

"We will have to think of something." Abigail she tucked the pistol back into her pocket. "Regardless, there isn't a moment to lose. We must go after Carnes immediately."

Duncan shook his head. "Abby, Lake Tear of the Clouds sits miles past even North Camp, high on the shoulder of the Cloudsplitter. The journey is too long; we can't possibly—"

"There is a faster way to *anachaju*," Josiah murmured. "Very dangerous."

Duncan swiveled. "How dangerous?"

"It doesn't matter," Abigail said "We're leaving. Now."

And then it had struck him like an epiphany. Only in knowing true evil would he be granted such a revelation. And only one sin could unlock such godlike wisdom. It was the original sin, that of Adam and Eve. The sin of rebellion.

Since that fateful realization, Carnes had spent almost a decade pouring over heretical books and writings that had long ago seen their authors burned at the stake for blasphemy. When he had finally come across an arcane ritual to summon a demon, he had discovered that it required two things: a cursed place where the boundary between Hell and Earth was at its thinnest, and a mortal soul willing to exchange his place on Earth for the demon's place in Hell.

The irony wasn't lost on Carnes that only in death would he be granted the answers to his life's most burning questions. But oh, what a small price to pay for such enlightenment! To have the wisdom—even for a fleeting instant—to understand the wondrous and terrible ways of God! As he cast himself into the lake and sank into its freezing depths, there would be a moment of glorious revelation in the instant before his death when no secret would be kept from him. When the universe unlocked its mysteries to him, the question that haunted him day and night would finally be put to rest. In that one sublime instant, Carnes' eyes would be opened to the divine purpose behind all the suffering and horror he had witnessed throughout his life. At the moment of his death, his own tortured existence would be granted meaning.

The first time Carnes had stood by the waters of Lake Tear of the Clouds, he could sense the evil in the air like smoke perceived through a keyhole. This is where Samael—God's Angel of Death—had fallen through the Earth on his way to

Hell. As he began the ritual of summoning, Carnes felt no remorse for the evil he was about to unleash upon the world. Humanity had long ago given itself over to the devil. He had seen it with his own eyes. The kingdom of Mankind was one of wickedness and hate; it was only fitting that it should be tested and punished by the venom of God. The demon would bring death and despair to all it came across, while God gathered the faithful and pious to His loving embrace.

The rest would be left to burn.

But what Carnes hadn't foreseen was that Samael wouldn't be satisfied with the sacrifice of his own soul. He hadn't anticipated that the demon would possess him, that it would have the power to push his conscious mind aside at will and use him to lead innocents like Evelyn McIntyre and Hannah Gill to their own destruction. Carnes had never intended for harm to come to a child like Hannah. God was supposed to lend His strength to the innocent so that they might withstand the temptations of the wicked. It was only then that Carnes understood the true depths of the evil he had awakened.

Samael murdered innocents for nothing more than the love of destruction.

With the dreadful magnitude of his folly laid bare, shame had kept Carnes from admitting what he had done—shame and fear of what the villagers would do to him once they discovered he was responsible for the deaths of their loved ones.

When Abigail had arrived in his village, Carnes had prayed that her Book of Shadows might reveal some secret spell to sever his bond with Samael and rid himself of the demon's influence. But he hadn't been able to overcome the grimoire's powerful warding. Still, he had helped Abigail as much as he dared and had done his best to forestall the moment of his own sacrifice for as long as possible. But when Samael had pushed Carnes' mind aside to lure Abigail into a confession, Carnes had known all was lost.

Now, with the town abandoned and no souls left for Samael to ruin, the demon had finally turned on the priest. There was a searing heat simmering in Carnes' blood as he ascended the miles toward Lake Tear of the Clouds. He tasted something acrid and sulfurous seeping from his throat into his mouth. A terrible pressure was building behind his eyes, as if the demon he carried inside was trying to claw its way out through the sockets.

Carnes knew Samael was transforming him into something monstrous, but he was helpless against it. The demon had stripped him of every shred of free will. Carnes' only hope was for Abigail to find him and stop him before he reached the lake and the demon within him was unleashed.

A vicious thunderclap exploded in the roiling clouds above. Lightning forked across the sky and the rain began to fall in fat droplets. Carnes didn't cringe or waver as he pressed on. Somewhere inside his head, an irresistible voice urged him ever onward.

The storm is a sign… The very heavens are opening themselves to you…

Carnes couldn't resist the demon's fearsome call.

Yes… Find me at the lake… Give yourself to me… Set me free…

They were the last words Carnes heard before his own

consciousness was devoured and he was lost forever.

Chapter 48

"We can't go up there," Duncan said. "Small wonder no one has dared come this way before. It's impossible. Only certain death lies that way."

A narrow canyon split the face of the mountain as if some titanic axe had cleaved it in two. Sheer granite walls soared a hundred feet into the air on either side of the deep cleft. In between the two cliffs, the giant fissure was strewn with enormous boulders, massive heaps of rubble, and towering rock buttresses that stretched upward at sharp angles. Water cascaded in a rushing stream through the yawning chasm. Green patches of moss mottled the gray slabs. Flash floods had washed the giant remnants of fallen trees into the gorge and they now protruded like massive stakes between the boulders. High above, the upper reaches of the canyon disappeared into the murky gray of the storm clouds.

Rain beat down heavily upon the trio as they gazed up at the imposing route ahead. It was nearly dusk. The sun seemed to have never risen and the stormy sky was already surrendering what little light it held.

"We've no choice," Abigail said. "It's the only way of reaching Lake Tear of the Clouds before Carnes does." She looked at Josiah. "Are you certain this route will lead us straight to the lake?"

Josiah nodded. The long trek through the forest had taken a toll on his injuries and he now said little. The swollen and bruised flesh of his face had gone a bluish-gray and he swayed on his feet as if lightheaded.

"But look at it, Abby!" Duncan had to shout over a sudden eruption of thunder. "Just look at it! We can't climb up through that. That canyon's a deathtrap! It will be flooded within an hour if this rain gets any worse. It'll sweep us right off those rocks and send us crashing back down through the gorge. Not to mention some of those rock ladders look to be nearly vertical. Look at them! They rise dozens of feet high!" He frowned and shook his head. "No. There has to be some other way."

"There is no other way, Duncan," Abigail insisted. "This is it. If we don't stop Carnes before he drowns himself in the lake, who knows how many innocents will die at the hands of Samael? Dangerous or not, I'm going to find Carnes before he damns us all. If you wish to remain here with Josiah, then I welcome you to do so."

"I will lead," Josiah mumbled through his swollen mouth. His speech came out slow and slurred, as if he were teetering on the verge of a great, deep sleep.

Abigail gave him a concerned look. "No, River Stone. You have done enough for us already. I will go alone. You are exhausted and hurting."

"I am dying," Josiah said.

Abigail knew he was right. Heath's vicious blow to Josiah's head had done more damage than was visible. Heath himself must have believed he had killed the Native. As it was, Josiah's skull was likely bleeding from within. The pressure of the blood on his brain was the reason for his deteriorating speech. Soon, he would fall unconscious. Not long after, his brain would drown and go dark.

"I will lead," Josiah repeated. Lost within his swollen eye sockets, his black eyes still peered at Abigail with resolute determination. There would be no convincing him otherwise; he would die proudly and on his own terms.

Abigail's grateful smile hid her sadness. "Thank you, River Stone."

"Count me in too," Duncan said sullenly.

Abigail looked at him. "Duncan, you—"

"I'm going. Your plan won't work without me."

Abigail gave him a moment to change his mind. When he didn't, she didn't challenge him further.

No one spoke as they approached the mouth of the monstrous canyon. They moved in a line, with Josiah leading the way, followed by Abigail and Duncan. The rock columns looming ahead seemed to grow ever taller as the trio drew closer. A nervous lump grew in Abigail's stomach as her eyes traced their way far, far up the gorge.

Josiah chose a line to the right of the rushing stream, brought them to the base of the enormous rockslide, and climbed.

The giant boulders were slick and treacherous beneath Abigail's hands as she followed his lead, scrambling upward through the rain. To her left, the whitewater roared in her ear as it crashed and sprayed over the bedrock. The flood had already swollen and intensified since their arrival. Duncan was right: they could very well drown in this deep chasm if the downpour got any worse.

But it was already too late to turn back. The gray light of day was failing and their lanterns would be useless in this rain. They were trapped between towering cliffs on either side, and if they didn't climb their way out of the canyon before darkness fell, they weren't likely to survive the night.

Abigail caught her breath and glanced over her shoulder. Duncan was picking his way over the wet boulders, perhaps ten yards below her. Far beneath him was the rock-strewn base of the canyon. She looked skyward into the rain. Josiah was there, finding hand and footholds and climbing steadily up the steep pitches. After all he had endured, Abigail didn't know how he had the strength to carry on. She admired his courage and felt an ache in her heart to know it would soon be extinguished.

Up beyond Josiah's dark figure, the top of the gorge was lost in the gray fury of the clouds. It felt as if they had already been climbing for hours—and they still had far, far to go.

Abigail bowed her head and kept her eyes on the slippery rocks beneath her as she resumed her climb. Before long, they came to a small waterfall plummeting over a cliff to their left. Josiah paused a moment to re-evaluate the route ahead. Satisfied, he continued to the right of the stream. Again, Abigail noticed the rush of the water becoming more powerful. If the immense walls of the canyon constricted the chasm any further, there would be no way around the cascading torrent.

An ear-splitting blast of thunder erupted in the clouds. It was followed by a bolt of lightning that licked the sky and touched down somewhere high up the canyon.

Abigail flinched at the explosion and lost her footing. She slipped on a boulder and stumbled to the side, breaking her fall with her hand. Her breath trembled as she regained her balance and fought to clear her thoughts before resuming her climb. In the moments that followed, she was so focused on her steps she didn't notice the roar of a second waterfall. She looked up.

Josiah had halted on a tiny ledge at the base of a sheer rock face. Just a few yards to his left, a powerful waterfall gushed over a cliff. Torrents of water crashed to the rocks sixty feet below. To Josiah's right, the vertical wall of the canyon towered high overhead, boxing him in. Caught between the wall and the waterfall, there was nowhere to go but up.

Abigail remained perched on a ledge almost thirty feet below and waited as Josiah studied the imposing rock face. He twisted at the waist and raised his index finger into the air as if giving a sign for the number one. Then he pointed his finger at himself, followed by Abigail and then Duncan. Abigail understood his meaning: they would go one at a time, ascending to each other's ledges and waiting there until the way ahead was clear. Abigail looked down at Duncan to be sure he understood. He nodded and they all began to climb.

When Abigail reached the spot where Josiah had started his difficult ascent, she stopped to study his progress. He was now just below the halfway mark of the steep pitch. He moved slowly and gingerly, the sinewy muscles of his forearms quivering with the strain as he probed the smooth face for holds. Abigail did her best to study his movements, trying to memorize the handholds he used.

As he neared the top of the precipice, a lack of decent holds forced Josiah to move laterally to his left. The pounding rush of the waterfall surged just a few feet from his shoulder. Water crashed over the rock and sprayed into his face. The icy wind flowing from the frigid current lashed at him mercilessly. He balanced on a ledge barely the width of a coin and pressed himself flat against the rock. He searched the wet surface with his palms, probing for anything that would provide him with a grip.

There was very little.

Josiah looked up. He was almost there; only a few more feet and he could haul himself over the ledge at the top of the face. But the cold and exertion were sapping his strength and he was fading rapidly. If he didn't find some way to climb out of his exposed position, he would die where he stood.

Far below him, Abigail was gripped with tension as she watched Josiah's slow and careful explorations. He hadn't moved in minutes. She wondered what they would do if the steep pitch revealed itself to be insurmountable. Even if Josiah found a way to scale the rest of the dangerous crux, would she be able to follow in his footsteps? Would Duncan?

Abigail glanced down and saw her old friend balancing on a ledge twenty feet below. He was looking up past her, towards Josiah's dusky silhouette. She followed his gaze skyward again. Josiah had his right arm stretched high over his head. There was a crack in the rock up there. It was long and paper-thin. His fingers fumbled for it and could barely squeeze inside. In another moment, his left hand found an eroded ridge in the bedrock beneath the surging whitewater. He hesitated a moment, gathering his strength. Then he crimped tight with his fingers and hauled himself upward.

The leather soles of his moccasins scrabbled against the sheer face as he scaled higher, higher, moving inch by agonizing inch.

Without warning, his right hand slipped from the crack.

Abigail's heart lurched and jumped into her throat as Josiah swung away from the face. She saw his left hand clinging desperately to its precarious hold as he twisted around. With his back now to the steep wall, the momentum of his spin sent him directly beneath the punishing force of the waterfall.

Abigail witnessed the terrible sequence of events unfolding before her as if in a dream—everything moving slowly but with a dreadful inevitability that she was powerless to stop. She saw Josiah dangling high above her, hanging on with one hand with his back to the rock wall. The weight of the waterfall crashed down on his shoulders as he flailed beneath it.

"Josiah!" she cried. "I'm coming up! I can save you!"

Without thinking, Abigail started to climb. She followed the dangerous line Josiah had taken up the face. Her blood surged. Her fingertips were cut and bleeding from the tiny handholds, but she ignored it all. She wouldn't let her fear get the best of her.

A glance upward revealed Josiah didn't have the strength to hold on much longer. She saw him dangling there and knew his end was near. The trek from the village had been too much for him. His conscious mind was failing him fast.

But she was getting closer with each passing second! She

was a mere few yards beneath him now! If only he could hold on just a few minutes longer…

From far below, she heard Duncan shout something loud and panicked.

And then Josiah was falling.

Chapter 49

Abigail had enough time to hug the wall and brace herself as Josiah lost his grip and came hurtling toward her. Her hand shot out in a foolish effort to seize him and somehow pluck him from the air as he flew by.

It was no use.

Abigail's head swiveled around in time to glimpse Josiah plummeting through space before he vanished into the billowing mist far below. She heard Duncan's anguished scream and then her mind went strangely quiet as it recoiled from what she had just witnessed.

A long moment passed as Abigail remained breathless, clinging to the steep face just below the spot where Josiah had fallen. He hadn't made a sound as he hurtled toward his doom. Part of her wondered if he had already lost consciousness before he had tumbled headlong from the high precipice. She hoped for his sake that he had.

With the rain beating down and the waterfall gaining strength with each passing moment, Abigail peered up at the way ahead.

The deadly crux had already claimed one life. Now it was her turn to attempt it.

Abigail's heartbeat pounded in her ears as she inched upward and eased into position on the razor-thin ledge that marked the limit of Josiah's ascent. She shifted her weight and leaned into the wall, pressing herself flat against the slippery rock face. She extended her right hand high over her head and found the long and treacherous crack. With that one hand, she would have to pull herself high enough to wedge the edge of her boot into the same crevice. Only then could she pause for a moment's rest before sliding her hand up the crack and repeating the movement to continue upward.

Abigail squeezed her fingers in as deep as they would go into the fissure and crimped her fingertips against the rock to increase the friction of her grip. She wouldn't be able to hold on long. The small muscles of her hand were already threatening to cramp.

Abigail shot a glance down at Duncan.

He waited below, staring up at her fearfully as she readied herself.

Abigail returned her attention to the wall and thrust her left hand into the rushing water. Her fingers probed the smooth bedrock below the surface until she located the thin lip that had been Josiah's last hold. She had to remind herself to breathe as she gazed up at the imposing wall. It was perhaps ten feet until the next safe ledge... but it seemed to stretch for eternity.

She could wait no longer; the waterfall was swelling too rapidly next to her. If she didn't get moving, Duncan would be cut off completely. She tensed her muscles and heaved with her arm, pulling herself upward.

Inch by inch, the tiny ledge fell away beneath her feet. Abigail's forearms trembled and burned from the strain. She grit her teeth, hauling herself upward with her right hand while pushing down against the rock with her left. Her boots scrabbled against the wall, searching desperately for the edge of the tight crack. Over and over, her soles scraped across the exposed lip but could find no purchase.

Abigail grimaced, her face flushed a deep red from the strain. The muscles of her arm shook with spasms.

She couldn't hold on.

She was going to fall.

If only her boot would catch...

Just then, her fingers began to slip from the tiny crevice.

Abigail shifted all her weight to her left palm and tried cramming the fingers of her right hand deeper into the crack. The rain penetrated the fissure and made her palm too wet to create any friction. Her heart raced as she flexed and wiggled her fingers, scrabbling for even the smallest nub of a hold. Centuries of erosion had worn the inside of the crack smooth.

A surge of panic swept over Abigail as she realized she was going to lose her grip. "Duncan! I can't hold on!"

Slowly, inexorably, her fingers continued to slide free of the crevice, slipping a fraction of an inch at a time. Abigail grit her teeth and dug her fingernails into the rock. A white-hot surge of pain shot up her arm as one was torn from her flesh.

Duncan shouted something, but whatever it was got lost in a booming blast of thunder.

Cramped and numb from the exertion, Abigail's fingers were ablaze with agony. Despite her frantic efforts, her hand continued its relentless slide from the crack. Her palm was completely visible now. Only her fingertips kept her from tumbling backward. It was only a matter of seconds before their strength gave out.

Abigail knew she only had moments to live.

And then it happened.

The edge of her boot found the crack and caught it just in time to keep her from plummeting to her death.

In the same instant, Abigail's right hand popped loose. She was sent twisting around, her right arm and shoulder swinging out dangerously over the empty void.

Below, Duncan was scrambling up toward her. Abigail heard his frantic cries as she hung, balanced between the rock pressed beneath her left hand and the crevice into which she had wedged her right boot. The frigid spray of the waterfall splashed on her face as she fought to maintain her footing. She gasped and choked, her mind going blank with fear.

It was impossible. She couldn't sustain this position much longer.

With one last, daring effort, Abigail windmilled her right arm, using the momentum to swing herself forward into the rock wall. In the same motion, she lunged upward with her hand, aiming for the pencil-thin crevice.

This was it. If she missed, the weight of her body as she fell back would rip her from the cliff face.

Her palm slammed into the slippery rock, slapped against it, slid downward…

…and found a hold inside the crack.

Slowly—very slowly—Abigail hauled herself upward, inching higher up the crack until, at last, her palm stretched up and found a flat, wet surface. She hoisted her legs and swung them up, heaving with all of her strength until she rolled onto the safety of a narrow shelf.

She had done it. She had crested the crux that had claimed Josiah's life.

But there was no time for rest.

Abigail staggered and peered back over the ledge. Duncan was already following her route up the terrifying pitch. From her vantage point above, she was able to guide his ascent, pointing out holds that were invisible from below.

When he was within reach, she lay flat on the ledge and stretched out her arms. "Take my hands!"

Duncan found them and held tight as Abigail hauled him up next to her on the shelf.

Exhausted, both collapsed onto their backs and remained there, shivering with cold and shock as the rain splashed down upon their faces.

Abigail was the first to drag herself to her feet. Duncan followed, joining her at the head of the waterfall. They stood there in silence, staring sightlessly down into the swirling mists where Josiah had vanished. Long moments passed until the time came to resume the treacherous climb.

Foot by foot, they ascended ever higher into the clouds, scrambling over slick rocks and scaling steep pitches. Hours seemed to pass until the walls of the canyon fell away. They found themselves at the base of a gigantic slab of bedrock rising hundreds of feet before them. Pressed flat and crawling upward on all fours like spiders, they moved up the slope with painstaking slowness. Lightning crashed in streaks all around them. The constant awareness that the slightest slip could send them rocketing hundreds of feet down the solid sheet of rock frayed their nerves to the point of snapping.

And then there was nothing more to climb. They could go no higher.

Abigail rose to her feet at the rocky pinnacle of the steep rise and gazed at the bleak panorama laid out before her. Wind rocked her with tremendous force. Lightning raged and blasted the desolate expanse of the rocky landscape.

At the center of it all, Lake Tear of the Clouds lay churning and cold like a black teardrop.

Abigail surveyed the landscape. It was a grim, unforgiving place where all life seemed to have fled the purging wrath of the high alpine elements. At this altitude, what few trees remained gasped for air and grew stunted. They crowded around the rocky shore of the lake like misshapen gargoyles. Further up the shoulder of the mountain, their meager ranks dwindled and gave way to nothing but rock.

Abigail and Duncan lingered there a moment longer, buffeted by the windy gusts as they took in their surroundings. There was a frosty chill in the air and Abigail could almost smell the presence of snow. Up here, thousands of feet above sea level, winter would come much earlier than in the valley.

A momentary window in the shifting storm clouds revealed a glimpse of the mountain known as the Cloudsplitter. It towered a thousand feet over the rain-swept lake. For one brief instant, Abigail caught a full view of the peak's snowy summit dominating the northern sky like an angry behemoth. Having spent her whole life on the shores of the eastern coast, she had beheld nothing like it. It was majestic and sublime and fearsome all at once. She felt small and humbled by the sense of her own insignificance, of nature's absolute indifference to her presence.

Then—as quickly as they had parted—the clouds came together again. The awe-inspiring summit cone vanished behind a heavy gray curtain.

"*Anachaju*," Duncan murmured, his gaze settling on the lake.

Its black waters stared back at them like a window into nothingness as twilight gave way to night and the last of the light drained from the sky.

Abigail gave a slow nod. "Empty."

Chapter 50

Carnes was drawing nearer. Abigail sensed a powerful malevolence in the night air, as if something dark and monstrous was sweeping up the mountainside toward her. She didn't know from which direction he would come, but she knew he would soon arrive at the lake.

She looked at Duncan. "Be ready."

They stood on the craggy shore of Lake Tear of the Clouds. The torrential rain had subsided to a drizzle, but the night sky was still torn asunder by lightning and thunder. Jagged bolts of electricity split the darkness and came down all around them, illuminating the land with a frenetic and hellish glow. A fearsome wind swept down from the Cloudsplitter and scoured the blasted landscape. Behind where Abigail stood, the black waters of the lake rippled and churned as if they had been brought to a boil.

"Are you certain this will work?" Duncan asked. He swallowed as he peered across the windswept terrain in the valley's direction.

Abigail hesitated for a fraction of a second. "It must. It's the only plan we have."

As if searching for reassurance, her hands went into the pockets of her coat and closed around two iron spikes she had taken from a storage shed before leaving the village. Both were about six inches and pointed at one end, with a rounded head at the other.

When the time came, she hoped they would be enough for what she had in mind.

Suddenly, a fork of pink lightning split the sky and struck a lone pine less than half a mile away. The tree burst into flames and the force of the thunderclap that followed shook the ground beneath their feet. They both cringed under the deafening force of the concussive blast. With her ears still ringing, Abigail looked into the distance where the orange glow of the smoldering tree lit the horizon. Carnes wasn't the only threat they faced out here. Exposed as they were on the shoulder of the highest mountain in the region, lightning could kill either of them at any moment.

A sudden movement in the distance drew Abigail's attention, and her blood quickened.

A shadowy figure was coming into view. Limned against the blackness, the silhouette was tall and slender and bore the severe profile of a man cloaked in a long cassock. He loomed like a wraith in the night,

"Here he comes," Abigail warned. Her eyes remained fixed on the spot from where the forbidding figure was advancing. "Whatever happens, we must prevent Carnes from entering the lake. If I should fall, you must not come to my aid. You must not stop until we have completed the ritual." She peered at Duncan. "Do you understand?"

He didn't respond.

"Duncan? Do you understand me? My life is not worth more than those who will die if Samael is unleashed upon the world."

Duncan looked at her and gave a solemn nod. Together, they waited as the sinister figure drew closer. It stalked slowly and confidently through the gnarled and twisted shrubs guarding the lake. Abigail's heart drummed furiously in her chest and her muscles went tense in anticipation of the battle.

The figure drew nearer, nearer, closing the distance...

What emerged from the gloom was no longer human.

Bathed in lightning, Carnes was a thing of nightmares to behold. His pale skin was scorched and blistered, as if scalded with boiling oil. Blood oozed from open sores across his cheeks and forehead. The flesh of his face was shrunken and cadaverous above his thick beard and a glistening string of drool hung from lips that were cracked and split. Most hideous of all were the priest's eyes. Like Hannah Gill's, they had rolled back to their bloody roots in his head. None of their pale green color remained; all that was visible were the whites and the fleshy red eye-muscles straining in their sockets.

Abigail's blood turned to ice as Carnes strode closer. There was nothing left of the priest she had known. The demonic presence inside him had corrupted him absolutely and turned him into an infernal abomination. Against all hope, Abigail had thought she might save him, but Carnes was beyond salvation. He was already dead and in his place stood Samael, the venom of God.

Without warning, Abigail dipped her shoulder and

charged.

She launched herself bodily at the hideous monstrosity that used to be Carnes and caught it by surprise. They both went crashing to the ground, where they struggled among the rocks. The demon's teeth clicked and snapped in its head as it tried to bite Abigail's face. She broke free of the powerful hands that beat and clawed at her savagely and sprang to her feet.

Samael's hand whipped out and grabbed for her, but Abigail dodged and stepped on the exposed forearm, pinning it to the ground beneath her boot. In one motion, she seized an iron spike from her pocket, aimed it at the center of Samael's trapped palm, and stomped hard on its head with her other foot.

The demon howled with rage as the six-inch spike pierced flesh and bone and impaled its hand deep into the gritty earth of the lakeshore. It thrashed on the ground and reached for the spike with its free hand, intent on ripping it loose. Abigail anticipated the move and kicked the scrabbling hand aside, crushing it beneath her boot. With the same fluid quickness, she produced the second spike and skewered Samael's other fist into the ground.

"Do it now!" she cried over the demon's furious roar.

Duncan rushed forward with the Rite of Exorcism splayed in his trembling palms. He traced the sign of the cross over himself and did the same for Abigail before moving on to Samael. Crucified in the dirt, the demon hissed contemptuously and spit blood at him. Undaunted, Duncan began the litany.

Abigail took the silver flask he produced from his coat and

sprinkled holy water over Samael's writhing body. The demon flailed in agony as tendrils of red steam rose into the air wherever the drops touched its flesh. It arched its back off the ground and strained against the iron spikes that riveted its claws into the rocky earth.

Duncan's eyes grew wide and frightened as he progressed through the rite. "Save your servant, who trusts in you, my Lord! Let him find in you a fortified tower in the face of the enemy. Let the enemy have no power over him!"

The demon spread its drooling mouth and laughter came out in a voice that wasn't of this world. It was deep and soulless and conjured images of innocents being burned alive. Peals of thunder exploded in the night. Lightning came down all around them. Still, Duncan's voice swelled in intensity. "I command you, unclean spirit! Along with all your minions now attacking this servant of God, that you tell me by some sign your name!"

Something happened.

Samael's mocking laughter died away. In its place came an anguished, bloodcurdling wail.

Abigail's confidence soared. It was working! The exorcism was working!

"I command you to name yourself!" Duncan shouted again over Samael's infuriated shrieks.

Then—very suddenly—the demon squeezed its right palm around the head of the spike and pulled against it with inhuman strength. The hand came free with a gruesome sound of ripping flesh as the spike tore through the demon's fist and remained embedded in the earth.

"It's breaking loose!" A sickening wave of panic overcame

Abigail.

Within seconds, Samael had pried the other spike from the ground and was free.

Duncan staggered back, the words of the exorcism now forgotten as the thing that used to be Carnes rose to its feet. The demon's blood-rimmed eyes glared balefully at him as it surged forward. Samael's bloody, claw-like hands seized Duncan by the throat and lifted him from the ground, squeezing hard on his windpipe. Duncan's eyes bulged in their sockets. His face went a horrific shade of purple as he gasped for air.

Abigail knew then that all was nearly lost. No exorcism would work; only one option remained. She still had Colvin's pistol holstered on the belt she wore around her waist. It was loaded and ready to fire. A bullet to Carnes' skull would expel the demon. Without an earthly mind to possess, she would banish it back to Hell. But if she missed, she would have squandered her only remaining chance.

"Samael!" Abigail's voice rang out.

Lightning exploded overhead, drenching the demon in a frenzy of white and purple. Its head revolved around and its hideous eyes seemed intent on setting Abigail ablaze.

With a squeeze of the trigger, she sent a lead ball roaring straight through Carnes' skull.

The demon released its grip on Duncan and he fell to the ground, gasping for air. Blood poured from the gaping hole in Carnes' forehead. With a horrific shriek, the demon threw back its head and a billowing stream of crimson smoke burst forth from the bloody hole in its skull. The cloud hung in the air for a moment, coiling and swirling like a thing alive while the remnants of Carnes' tortured body fell to the side in a lifeless heap.

Abigail shrank back and stared up at the swirling mass. It had worked! She'd done it!

Then the crimson smoke shot straight at her.

Chapter 51

The impact picked Abigail from the ground and hurled her backward. All at once, she felt the demon's presence inside her, boring into her thoughts, unearthing her most hidden fears. A terrifying blackness descended on her mind and an awful wave of despair washed over her from within. Darkness pervaded her thoughts, urging her to surrender her will as she withered under Samael's crippling influence.

Abigail summoned all of her resolve and fought against the malevolent presence poisoning her mind. Somewhere in the recesses of her consciousness, she knew that if she didn't act immediately, she would succumb to the all-consuming sense of hopelessness. She couldn't resist much longer; she had to do it *now*. She couldn't let Samael overcome her, couldn't allow him to lead her into drowning herself in the lake.

Even as the demon filled her thoughts with despair, Abigail's hands fumbled to reload the pistol. Somehow, she had always known her life would end like this. She would sacrifice herself so that others may live, just as her mother had done long ago. Without warning, a long-forgotten memory flew into her mind. She saw her mother beneath the gallows tree in the haunted Northern Woods of Salem. She heard the echoes of her mother's desperate cries as she begged for Abigail's life...

Abigail raised the pistol up, pressed the muzzle to her head, cocked the hammer. It was the only way to stop herself from freeing the demon.

Her mother's voice stopped her.

Come to me, Abigail...

Abigail heard the plaintive call in her head as clearly as if her mother were standing by her side.

I am lost, Abigail... It is dark, and I am so very, very cold...

Abigail's gaze went to the black waters of the lake.

Her mother was there, somewhere far beneath the icy surface.

I gave my life for you, my daughter... Now you must rescue me...

No! Abigail felt the irresistible pull of the cold, black waters and knew it was the work of Samael. The demon was deceiving her, calling her to her own doom. And yet, she was powerless to resist! Samael's influence on her mind was too powerful, her thoughts too poisoned by the overwhelming sense of hopelessness. All she wanted was release, to find comfort in her mother's embrace the way she had as a child before that terrible night when her mother had been taken from her. Dread filled Abigail's soul at the awful inevitability of what was to come. She knew she would follow her mother into the lake and release the demon from its prison of flesh.

Unless...

Abigail's trembling finger tightened on the trigger.

A simple squeeze would end it all.

No, my daughter! Your fate lies here with me, down in the dark, dark depths…

Abigail closed her eyes and curled her finger.

Just then, the pistol was knocked from her grip.

Abigail's last conscious image was of Duncan standing over her, silhouetted against the frenzied spectacle of the lightning. Then her thoughts succumbed completely to the will of the demon inside her. Trapped in her own mind, she saw herself seize Duncan and hurl him away, sending him crumbling to the rocky ground.

Her mother's pleas came to her again.

Come to me! Find me below the surface!

Abigail turned toward the lake.

Its terrible pull was magnetic, overpowering.

She gave in to it.

Yes! Come to me!

Abigail saw herself stalking across the rocky shore. She felt the frigid bite of the water as she waded deeper and deeper.

Up to her ankles…

Knees…

Waist…

Come! Come to me, daughter!

The lake bed fell away beneath Abigail's feet. Endless darkness engulfed her as she sank below the surface. Icy water filled her lungs and a terrible numbness constricted her chest. There was a moment of serene and transcendent oblivion.

And then there were strong hands upon her.

Abigail felt herself shoot upward with a spray of water as Duncan caught her and dragged her kicking and shrieking back onto the rocks. Enraged, her hands flew at him as she thrashed on the shore. She raked his face with her nails, drawing blood and tearing away skin. Duncan weathered the savagery of her assault as he fought to bind her ankles with the purple stole he had retrieved from Carnes' corpse.

But the demon within her was too strong.

With a bloodcurdling shriek, Abigail aimed a powerful kick at Duncan's chest and sent him splashing backward into the lake. She lurched to her feet with her mother's furious cries roaring in her head.

Kill him, my daughter! Kill him before he kills you!

From the prison of her own mind, Abigail witnessed herself advancing. Her hand stretched out and wrapped around the sharp surface of a heavy stone. She drew to a halt, towering over Duncan as he lay sprawled and sputtering in the water. Her old friend's eyes filled with fright at the sight of her. Unable to stop herself, Abigail let loose a silent, heartbroken scream even as her hand rose into the air, raising the stone high over her head.

Do it, my daughter! Crush his skull! Do it now, now, now!

Abigail was helpless to resist.

Do it! Kill him! Kill him for me!

With a great and terrible blast, a jagged shard of lightning spiked from the sky and struck Abigail's upraised fist. The searing blast of the current coursed through her body. Her muscles seized, constricted, spasmed with convulsions. Her veins simmered as a white-hot agony lanced through her mind, obliterating her thoughts. The moment of weakness lasted a fraction of a second.

It was all Duncan needed.

He launched himself at Abigail, tackling her to the ground and flipping her onto her stomach so that he could press the weight of one knee into the small of her back. Abigail writhed and thrashed violently beneath him as he looped the length of Carnes' purple stole around her ankles and cinched it tight.

Duncan stood, leaving Abigail bound and shrieking by the water's edge. Her skin blazed in scorching agony as he doused her with holy water. Over the ear-piercing fury of her enraged screams, Duncan's voice rose strong and clear, reciting the words of the exorcism. "Almighty God, I beg you to keep the evil spirit from further afflicting this servant of yours, and to keep it far away, never to return!"

Abigail felt the infuriated presence of Samael raging within her as Duncan went on. His voice thundered at a fever pitch, commanding the demon to surrender and leave her body. She flailed madly, kicking her legs and clawing at the ground to drag herself across the rocks to the lake. A voice that wasn't her own spilled a torrent of tortured wails from her gaping mouth. Every command that Duncan pronounced seemed to scald her with the searing intensity of molten iron.

The demon was weakening, losing its hold on her mind.

Without warning, a scorching rush surged up Abigail's throat like bile.

Her head fell back and she opened her mouth to let it out.

A churning cloud of crimson smoke shot into the air.

Light spilled across Abigail's mind as if through an open door. She was in control of herself again. She rolled onto her back and looked skyward.

The crimson cloud whirled like a vortex above the turbulent waters of the lake. Thunder crashed and lightning shot through the swirling, blood-red mass. Faster and faster it accelerated, picking up speed, intensifying until it could no longer keep itself together. With a thunderous roar and an explosion of water that sprayed a geyser high into the air, the dreadful shadow of Samael plummeted into the lake and vanished beneath its roiling surface.

Exhausted, Duncan dropped to his knees and collapsed by Abigail's side. The pages of the Rite of Exorcism fell from his fingers and splashed into the water. As the ripples moving across the lake subsided and became no more, Abigail took her trembling friend into her arms. Time became meaningless as they lay together on the rocky shore, too weak and wasted to move. They remained there until dawn, sharing each other's comforting warmth as the violence left the heavens and the sun rose like a torch over the mountains.

Epilogue

The heavenly aroma of roasted turkey filled the humble country cottage. Beeswax candles and oil lamps illuminated the rooms with a lively orange glow. A cheerful fire burned on the hearth. Beyond the walls and windows, the late November chill swept over the darkened fields and promised frost in the morning. But inside the old home, it was delightfully warm and comfortable.

From his seat at the head of the dinner table, Jonas Hobbes let his hungry eyes wander over the Thanksgiving feast spread out before him. The turkey glistened a golden brown and overflowed with rosemary stuffing as it sat, ready to be carved, on a platter at the center of the table. Steam rose from bowls heaped with delicious sweet potatoes, cranberries, and roasted parsnips. A basket of cornbread, fresh from the oven, lay covered beneath a towel. On the sideboard, the spicy scent of a warm pumpkin pie heralded a sweet and tantalizing dessert.

A sense of serenity came over Jonas as his gaze traveled from the food to those who had gathered around the table. His entire family was there. Emily and Duncan sat to his right. To his left, his two grandsons were eyeing the food hungrily. His new dog, Timber, was curled contentedly in a corner.

And at the opposite end of the table sat Abigail.

Jonas' gaze lingered on his adopted daughter for a long while. As was her way, Abigail appeared distant, smiling mildly at the conversations happening around her but sharing little of the family's merriment. Jonas had long ago grown accustomed to her demeanor and had learned to accept it for the sake of their relationship. He was just relieved to have her safe and seated at his table.

Three days had passed since Abigail and Duncan had returned to Salem. The sight of Emily's tearful reunion with her husband would bring a smile to Jonas for a long, long time. In the days that followed, Duncan had taken his time describing the dreadful events that had taken place at Tahawus. After defeating Samael at Lake Tear of the Clouds, he and Abigail had made the long trek down from the mountains and rejoined the villagers at the tiny outpost of North Hudson. There, they had received the news that Hannah Gill had survived her injuries and was slowly recovering. Her encounter with the demon had left her with a terrible legacy. The damage to her eyes was irreparable, and she had been stricken blind.

With the help of Ned Fitch and a few of the other men, Duncan had made arrangements for the refugees from Tahawus to travel to Fort Ticonderoga, where they would be sheltered from the war. Owen Delaney and the other men who had stoned Abigail were not among them. Shunned by their former neighbors, they had scattered to the winds after arriving in North Hudson. No one had seen them since. Duncan had been glad to hear it. He had no desire to see what Abigail would have done had her path crossed theirs again.

The way home had been long and grueling. Chauncey Beck had done a formidable job navigating his coach over the rough backcountry trails, but early snows made the journey even slower and more exhausting. At last, they had arrived in Salem.

As they all now joined hands around the dinner table for the blessing, Jonas gave thanks to the Lord for their safe return. "Our Father in heaven, we give thanks for the pleasure of gathering together for this occasion…" He kept his head bowed and his eyes closed as he continued with the prayer. When he was done, he reached for the butcher's knife and began carving the turkey. Warm juices flowed from the tender white meat as he piled slices onto the waiting plates.

"We've plenty to be grateful for this year," Jonas said while the others helped themselves to the contents of the steaming bowls. "But the thing that I am most thankful for is having this family together again under my roof."

The sentiment brought smiles to those seated around him and inspired Emily to offer her own gratitude. "I am thankful that my husband has been returned to us." Her hand sought Duncan's and gave it a loving squeeze. Then her gaze went to Abigail and their eyes met. "And for the brave kindness of my sister."

A warm feeling blossomed in Jonas as he watched the silent exchange between the two women he had once called his *girls*. He smiled and moved on. "Duncan?"

Duncan didn't need to think about it. He swallowed a mouthful of stuffing and looked across the table at his two young boys. "I am thankful to have such strong and courageous sons to have kept their mother safe and protected while I was gone. I pity the unwitting creature that would dare cross the path of these two terrors!"

Duncan hunched his back and bared his fingers like claws, snarling like an attacking bear. The boys broke into delighted giggles and started firing at him with invisible rifles from across the table. Duncan let out a gasp, clutched at his chest as if wounded, and played dead.

The laughter subsided and the attention now turned to Abigail. She kept her head bowed and said nothing as she picked at the food on her plate.

Jonas peered at her from across the length of the table. "Abigail?"

Another moment passed.

With a deep breath, Abigail looked up, and they were all startled to see tears welling in her clear blue eyes.

"I…" she began but faltered.

The jovial smile faded from Jonas' face. "What is it, Abby?" Never had he seen her so emotional. It worried him. "What's wrong?"

"I…" Abigail's voice quaked and she went quiet again. An instant passed as she struggled with her emotions. "I… I never thought it would happen. I never thought I would be telling you this…"

Jonas' concern for her swelled. A nervous knot tightened in his gut. "Telling us what, Abby?"

A slow and wistful smile came to Abigail's lips, despite the tears rolling across her cheeks. "I am thankful for the baby growing in my belly."

Author's Note

Thank you, dear reader, for the generous gift of your time and attention. If you enjoyed this book and would like to see more, please consider taking a moment to leave a quick review on Amazon and/or Goodreads. A kind word from a reader like you is one of the best ways you can support independent authors and is very much appreciated.

Until next time, look under the bed, close the closet door, and whatever you do, don't turn around...

The *BOOK OF SHADOWS* series continues in *THE WOLF SOCIETY*

<u>Chapter 1</u>

Anna Jacobs was going to kill the man she was dancing with. She wouldn't do it here, not under the brilliant glow of the reception room chandeliers. And she wouldn't do it now, surrounded as she was by the cream of Vermont's genteel society. But within the hour, the beguiling young Southerner with the chestnut curls and whiskey eyes would lie headless at Anna's feet.

"You truly are an elegant dancer," the gentleman said. He pressed his palm lightly into the small of Anna's back and kept her at a decent arm's length as he led her through the intricate steps of the English country dance. If his hand slipped lower, his wrist would brush against the six-inch blade strapped to Anna's slender thigh beneath the folds of her silk ball gown.

"How kind of you to say," Anna replied demurely. "I was raised to be prepared for any situation, including the occasion when a handsome gentleman might ask for the pleasure of a dance."

"Have there been many such occasions?" The man's sly grin revealed two rows of pearly teeth.

"Would it pain you to know there have?"

"Not in the least."

Anna indulged the gentleman's smug confidence with a smile and glanced around the room. The governor's wife had spared no expense on her party in honor of Burlington's celebrated architect and surveyor, John Johnson. Over fifty guests had been invited to the governor's mansion to celebrate the inauguration of Johnson's latest accomplishment, the university's new Middle College building. While the mansion had no formal ballroom, the spacious second-floor reception room had been cleared of furniture to allow space for dancing. A quartet tucked into a corner kept time and tune with a lively medley. Three other couples now shared the floor with Anna and her partner while an assembly of guests in fashionable ball gowns and fine tailcoats stood admiring them from the periphery. The bright lights of the chandeliers glittered off an abundance of fine jewels and gold buttons. To ensure the women wouldn't slip while dancing, the First Lady of Vermont had hired an artist to chalk the polished pine floor with an assortment of fanciful floral patterns, arabesques, and nymphs.

The song drew to a close and the dancing came to an end as the quartet went quiet. The bystanders applauded politely as the couples bowed to each other and began leaving the floor. Soon the guests would be invited to sit to dine and the dancing wouldn't resume until after dinner.

Anna wouldn't get another chance to end the man's life. She had to act now.

"I would enjoy some fresh air before dinner," she said. "Would you be kind enough to accompany me?"

"I know just the place for it." The Southerner flashed a grin and offered her his arm.

Anna swept the room with another glance as he led her toward the door. To avoid attracting unwanted attention, she had chosen an unassuming lilac gown with a fashionable natural waist and a modest neckline that only hinted at the swell of her bosom. But she had still needed to catch the Southerner's eye. For that, she had relied on her own natural beauty. At seventeen, she was in the prime of her womanhood. Her thick, coal-black hair was twisted into a bun and tied with a simple ribbon. Delicate ringlets framed her fine features and angular jaw. Her large blue eyes sparkled like shards of sapphire and her soft lips were rosebuds blossoming from her snowy skin.

Intent as they were on their own conversations, none of the guests seemed to be taking notice of Anna's departure—except for one woman. She was elegantly dressed and strikingly beautiful, with honey-blonde hair and eyes like a winter sky.

Anna's heart lurched at the sight of her. What was *she* doing here?

There wasn't time to give the woman any more thought; Anna and her companion were already leaving the room behind. Instead of making their way down the curving staircase from the mezzanine floor to the entrance hall, the young man led her down a candlelit corridor that ended at the landing of another set of stairs. Anna quickly understood that it ascended to the squat cupola atop the mansion's roof. The bold Southerner intended to take advantage of the intimate privacy of the rooftop where they would be alone, three floors above where the other guests would soon be gathering to dine.

It was the perfect place for a trap.

Anna marveled at her luck and chided herself for not having thought of luring her prey to the quiet spot herself. Her heart quickened in her chest as she climbed the steep and narrow staircase. She had waited weeks for this moment and her veins now thrummed with the promise of violence.

"What has brought you this far north?" she asked cordially.

"My family has profited considerably from the cotton trade in Charleston, but I myself have no taste for slavery," the young man drawled. "Timber is where I'll forge my own fortune—and of that, Vermont is plentiful."

Anna knew it was all a lie. This man was not who he claimed to be.

But neither was Anna.

The cupola at the top of the stairs was a small observation room surrounded on all sides by arched windows. Anna went to the nearest one and casually scanned the rooftop, making quick mental notes of anything she could use to her advantage. Three storeys up from the estate's sprawling hilltop grounds, the roof was flat and open with nowhere to hide. A waist-high balustrade ran around its perimeter and the cupola's door was the only way on or off. Days might even go by before anyone discovered the Southerner's corpse. There would be no better place for Anna's bloody task.

The Southerner went to the door and cast it open. In the darkness far below the rooftop, a trail of torches snaked their way up the hill from the burgeoning village of Burlington, lighting the way for the party's guests. A hint of fresh pine from the surrounding forests mingled with the earthy scent of fallen leaves. To the west, the black void of Lake Champlain lay shimmering under the pale light of a moon that was only a sliver shy of full. It was an unseasonably warm night for mid-October, but perched high atop the roof, a stiff breeze still fluttered Anna's dress and twirled the ringlets of her hair. She wasn't surprised when her companion removed his wool tailcoat and wrapped it around her shoulders.

"Where I come from, we'd call this weather positively frigid," he said with a wink. He gestured for her to lead the way out to the roof.

Anna realized too late that she had made a mistake in turning her back on the Southerner.

As soon as the door closed behind them, he lunged for her.

The gentleman's grin vanished and his lips peeled back. His teeth gleamed like ivory saw-blades as they snapped and gnashed, intent on ripping Anna's flesh from her bones...

READ THE WOLF SOCIETY

**She was innocent of witchcraft when they arrested her.
She was guilty when they hanged her.**

A Firebrand of Hell, a short story prequel to the best-selling
Book of Shadows series, is now available absolutely free!

Set one hundred years before the events of *All Hallows Eve*,
find out what drove Rebecca Hale to sell her soul to the devil
on the eve of her hanging.

Visit www.michaelpenning.com to download your free copy!

Books by Michael Penning

Book of Shadows Series
Novels:
All Hallows Eve
The Suicide Lake
The Wolf Society

Companion Stories:
The Damnation Chronicles

Standalone Novels
Solitude

Michael Penning is a bestselling author and award-winning screenwriter of horror and dark fiction. He has been obsessed with all things dark and spooky since before he could finish his own sack of trick-or-treat candy. When he's not coming up with creative ways to scare the hell out of people, he enjoys traveling, photography, and brewing beer. He lives in Montreal with his wife and daughter. For updates and free giveaways, visit www.michaelpenning.com and follow Michael on social media @michaelpenningauthor.

Made in United States
North Haven, CT
10 September 2023

41379058R00232